MW00476499

CATCH HER DEATH

BOOKS BY WENDY DRANFIELD

CATCH HER DEATH

WENDY DRANFIELD

bookouture

Published by Bookouture in 2022

An imprint of Storyfire Ltd.
Carmelite House
50 Victoria Embankment
London EC4Y 0DZ

www.bookouture.com

Copyright © Wendy Dranfield, 2022

Wendy Dranfield has asserted her right to be identified as the author of this work.

All rights reserved. No part of this publication may be reproduced, stored in any retrieval system, or transmitted, in any form or by any means, electronic, mechanical, photocopying, recording or otherwise, without the prior written permission of the publishers.

ISBN: 978-1-80314-655-3
eBook ISBN: 978-1-80314-654-6

This book is a work of fiction. Names, characters, businesses, organizations, places and events other than those clearly in the public domain, are either the product of the author's imagination or are used fictitiously. Any resemblance to actual persons, living or dead, events or locales is entirely coincidental.

For Kevin. Enjoy the trains.

PROLOGUE

THEN

With his mother's melodic voice singing along to Christmas carols in the kitchen, the young boy glances up to peer outside his cozy living room window. The snow that has been falling for days is almost fully obscuring the glass, with the white peak of Grave Mountain just a blur in the distance. He smiles, because he wants it to keep snowing for as long as possible.

The boy turns, ignoring the cartoon on the TV to return to the sparkling Christmas tree. Sitting cross-legged, he concentrates on the amazing train set he unwrapped this morning. It was a gift from Santa, supposedly, but he knows it's more likely from his daddy, who has had to leave them temporarily to rescue a car. His daddy has a tow truck that will help free it from the snow. It's not the first time the police have asked for his daddy's help in this kind of weather, and he promised he wouldn't be gone long.

The toy train's passenger cars hook together and glide smoothly along the wooden tracks as the family's black cat sits watching from her seat on a piece of discarded gift wrap. The look on her face tells him she's not as impressed with the train set as he is.

A scream, loud and shrill, bursts from his mother in the

kitchen. The boy jumps and watches as the cat vanishes, leaving the piece of gift wrap floating back down from the air. The sound is shocking. He's never heard his mother scream before. Looking up, he watches his mommy tear into the living room, followed by a man with a black ski mask pulled over his face. Her apron is smeared with food stains, protecting the pretty red dress beneath.

"No! Please don't!" she yells.

She's silenced with a hard crack to her head from what looks like a hammer from their garage. The boy has his own set of tools, but they mustn't be very good because his daddy never wants to use them for fixing things in his auto repair shop.

His mommy drops onto the floor next to him, blood leaking from her head. He knows it's blood because he scraped his knee real bad one time at the playground near their house and his mom said he shouldn't worry because he has enough blood in his body to be able to lose a little every now and then. Her eyes are wide open and staring straight at him, and she's making funny gurgling noises. Her teeth are red now, and she's lost one of her snowman earrings. She slowly reaches for his hand. "Not my baby. Please."

He's confused. He's not a baby anymore; he's *four years old*! Her eyes squeeze shut just as the man strikes her head again and the boy feels a warm spray on his face. His mother doesn't open her eyes this time, and after a gentle squeeze, her hand goes limp on top of his.

The boy looks up at the stranger just as he turns and walks away. Without saying a word, the man leaves through the kitchen, slamming the back door shut behind him. He's gone.

Using his sweater, the boy wipes the blood off the passenger car he's holding before placing it back on the tracks so that he can shake his mother's shoulder. She makes a slight groaning sound, but she doesn't wake up. She must be tired. He knows she'll be okay, though, because he was when he scraped his knee. His throat is dry, so he goes to the dinner table to find his juice carton. With shaky hands he takes a sip before returning to his mother. While she sleeps, he goes back to pushing his new train along the tracks, gently moving her hand out of the way to avoid a crash.

The blood from her head is spreading closer to his train set, so he fetches a blanket from the couch and places it on top of the warm, sticky liquid to act as a barrier. He doesn't want Daddy to think he doesn't care about his new gift. Because this is the best Christmas present he's ever been given, and he can't wait until Daddy gets home to play with him.

CHAPTER ONE

NOW

Julie Reid needs to finish her gift shopping, and fast, because it's the night before Christmas Eve and the mall closes at eight. But with the baby screaming and her legs aching from having already spent three hours browsing the stores, she can't muster enough enthusiasm to go into any more after this one.

The bright, twinkling fairy lights reflect off the many mirrors in the jewelry store, giving her a headache. And the same old festive songs playing on repeat for what seems like her entire life make her want to sit in a silent padded room by herself. She could do without the stares of the retail staff too, judging her harshly for letting her baby cry. But what can she do? Susie has been fed, she's been changed and she doesn't want to nap. Maybe she's as sick of shopping as Julie is.

That decides it for her. Her mother-in-law can do without a gift this year. If the woman were less critical, it would be worth the effort to find something special, but Julie refuses to spend one more minute in this place for someone who doesn't appreciate a goddam thing she does for her. "Come on, sweetie. Let's go home."

The decision to quit causes the tension in her shoulders to ease and her step to quicken. She pushes the baby's stroller, which is weighed down with bags and gift-wrapped boxes, through to the exit that will take her to the parking lot. The cold air slaps her in the face as the electronic doors open, but it's refreshing compared to the stuffiness inside.

There are at least three inches of snow already on the ground, and the soft white snowflakes appear to be falling faster and heavier as the evening advances. Julie doesn't stop to zip up her jacket; instead she heads straight to her car, which is parked over in the far corner. It was the only spot left when she arrived earlier. As she approaches it, she realizes the overhead security light in this corner of the lot has been smashed. Glass shards lie on top of the snow, and the few remaining cars sit in the shadow of darkness. Was it like that when she arrived? If it was, she didn't notice. Turning around, she sees that the parking lot is almost empty now. Only a few other people have stayed to shop this near to closing time.

She hurriedly opens her trunk and loads the gifts inside. Then, after another quick glance around, she lifts Susie out of the stroller and walks to the front passenger side to open the door. With no vehicle parked next to them on this side, she has room to open it wide. She has to lean in in order to place Susie into the car seat. A chill goes through her as she rushes to secure the clasps, because she's imagining someone creeping up behind her while she's distracted. Once her daughter is safely strapped in, Julie stands up straight and pulls her cell phone out of her purse. Using the flashlight, she waves it around to see if anyone is hiding in the bushes at the edge of the lot.

She can't see or hear anyone, but the feeling of unease won't leave her. She checks on Susie, who is smiling up at her, waving her arms excitedly. Finally she's stopped crying. She loves being in the car, and Julie and her husband have spent long nights driving around town in the dark to settle her. Julie can't help but smile back and lean in to rub her rosy cheek. "Let's get home to Daddy, shall we?"

After closing the passenger door, she wrestles with the clasps on the stroller, trying to get it to collapse flat. That's when she hears a strange muffled noise close by. Standing bolt upright, she looks around. There's just one other person in sight: a woman on the other side of the lot, who's getting into her car. Julie watches as she drives away, and finds herself overcome with envy that the woman is on her way home already. She's safe.

The sound repeats itself, and this time she can tell it's a child's cry.

She swallows as the hairs on her arms and neck stand up. Something's wrong. "Hello?" she says to the darkness. She really doesn't want a reply, and considers dumping the stroller on the ground, jumping into her car and getting the hell out of here as fast as possible. But the stroller was expensive, and before she can make a decision, she hears the child again.

"Momma?"

It's coming from the car on the other side of hers. It's in complete darkness, but she sees movement in the back seat. The first thought that runs through her is that this is some kind of trap. After all, using a child's cry to lure a lone woman to her death isn't unheard of. She isn't stupid, she watches the news. But what if she's being paranoid and this child is real and in need of her help?

Julie looks around her again. She can't see anyone else in the darkness, and the car is parked next to her driver's side, so she has to squeeze between the two vehicles anyway in order to get out of here. She drops the stroller and slides between the cars, keys in one hand, cell phone in the other. Leaning forward, she peers hesitantly through the back window. Her cell phone's flashlight illuminates a little boy strapped to a child seat, no more than three or four years old. He appears to be unharmed and is sucking his thumb, with big fat tears rolling down his cheeks. He winces at the bright light and says,

"Momma" again, but it's not a question this time. It's a statement.

Julie swallows hard as he points to the front seat. She slowly cranes her neck and moves the flashlight to peer in through the front passenger window. An involuntary scream bursts up through her throat and out of her mouth when her eyes lock onto those of a bloody and battered woman staring right back at her from the driver's side.

She knows immediately that there's no life in those eyes. Which means the poor little boy in the back seat has been sitting alone for Lord knows how long with the badly beaten body of his dead mother.

CHAPTER TWO

Detective Madison Harper shivers in the cold as she leaves the comforting warmth of her car to inspect the large downtown parking lot. Silent white snowflakes fall steadily, covering the patrol officers and their cruisers. The ground coverage is bright white, but the rest of the crime scene is otherwise shrouded in darkness. At almost nine o'clock, all the stores are closed, with just the Christmas lights in the shopping mall's windows for illumination.

Her footsteps crunch through the snow as she approaches the Lexus, which is screened from prying eyes. Today was Madison's last day working without a detective partner and she almost got off lightly, with no homicides or sexual assaults. That is, until this call-out on her way home. Her previous partner died last month, and rumor has it that his replacement starts tomorrow. Chief Mendes plays her cards close to her chest, so Madison doesn't know who the successful candidate is. She'll find out tomorrow morning, the same as everyone else.

She spots Officer Shelley Vickers nearby, wrestling with some portable lighting to help illuminate the crime scene. Shelley applied for the vacant detective role, but she's been sworn to secrecy about whether she got the job. She's in her early thirties and is a fine officer, but so is the other internal candidate, Sergeant Steve Tanner. Madison would be happy for either one of them to investigate alongside her, but she's heard there were some external candidates too, so nothing's guaranteed.

To her right, the ambulance crew is finishing up, but one of them—Jake Rubio—is hovering nearby. Shelley looks pissed and is avoiding eye contact with him, leaving Madison to wonder whether they finally went on a date and it didn't live up to her high expectations. Shelley was well aware of Jake's reputation as a womanizer, so she's always resisted his advances until now.

Madison turns her attention to the Lexus, snaps on some latex gloves and crouches in the snow. The passenger door is already wide open. Although the victim is seated in the driver's side, she's slouched this way, as if straining to get away from her attacker. It looks like she didn't even have time to put on her seatbelt or get her key into the ignition before she was ambushed. Her hands are bagged so that their forensic technician can take fingernail scrapings.

Madison would guess the victim is in her mid-late thirties. She's dressed casually, in jeans and a formerly white T-shirt under a thick winter coat. Her eyes are open and staring right through Madison, who doesn't recognize her, which isn't as unusual as you would think for a small town like Lost Creek, Colorado. There are lots of people Madison doesn't know, and some residents choose to work up in Prospect Springs, a large town north of here that has better job opportunities, so she'll probably never cross paths with them. Madison doesn't think she could do a two-hour commute every day, but that doesn't seem to bother others.

The victim's face and clothes are covered with blood from the injuries to her head. Her long brown hair is matted and a clump of skin hangs down to her right eyebrow. Thanks to the freezing temperatures—it's twenty-five degrees tonight, and only getting colder—and possibly due to the time of her attack, she doesn't smell of decay yet.

Madison sighs. This woman didn't stand a chance. She wonders who's waiting for her at home; who will be the one tasked with breaking the news to the rest of her friends and family. Looking around, she can see random blood spatter on the steering wheel, windshield and ceiling. The killer attacked the victim right here, out in the open, which means someone might have witnessed it. Madison turns her head as Shelley lights up the car from the outside. She notices a child's car seat behind the passenger seat, along with a few toys scattered around and a bag containing some gift-wrapped boxes, presumably purchased tonight in the mall. One of them has spilled onto the back seat. Her heart sinks. This woman was a mother. These gifts will likely never be opened by the intended recipients. Her family will never experience a joyful Christmas again without first thinking about the murder of their loved one.

She stands to survey the parking lot. It doesn't take long to notice the overhead light in this corner has been smashed. Shards of glass poke out from under fresh snow on the ground beneath. Hopefully whoever did it was caught on camera. A quick look around shows there are no surveillance cameras nearby, but she knows the mall must have at least one out front. Whether or not it would have caught anyone this far away remains to be seen.

A news truck pulls up beyond the yellow crime-scene tape, but it's not Kate Flynn, her friend and local TV reporter. Kate's been slow to react to breaking news stories these past few weeks. She's struggling right now, and Madison was planning to visit her for coffee tonight on her way home from work. A couple of camera operators exit the truck as another car arrives. Madison watches as Gary Pelosi, a reporter for the *Lost Creek Daily* newspaper, gets out. Word is spreading fast.

Alex Parker, Lost Creek Police Department's British forensic technician, approaches and says, "Evening, Detective. How are you?"

"I was doing good until I saw this."

He nods. "Horrible, isn't it? Would you like my preliminary findings?"

"Please. Do we know this woman's name?"

"Yes, her driver's license was in her bag, along with her phone and other belongings."

"That's something," says Madison. More often than not they're reliant on tracking down cell phone records because the attacker has taken the victim's phone to destroy any evidence on it.

"She's thirty-four-year-old Sarah Moss," Alex continues. "She was attacked *in situ* as she was about to drive home from her shopping trip. A toddler, presumably her son, was found strapped into his car seat but completely unharmed."

She runs a hand through her hair. "That poor child. Where is he now?"

"In the ambulance with a paramedic. He doesn't need to go to the hospital, but I'll want his clothes as evidence in case the killer touched him."

She nods. "Do we know what his mother was attacked with?"

Alex takes a deep breath. "It's difficult to say right now, as it appears the perpetrator took the weapon with them. Once she's at the morgue, Lena and I can have a proper look at her injuries." Dr. Lena Scott is the town's medical examiner.

"Is Lena on her way?"

"She is."

"Do we have any witnesses?"

He turns and nods to a woman sitting in the back of a cruiser, stroking a baby's head. "That's who found her."

Madison will speak to her in a second. She looks at the ground and notices that the snow around the car has been disturbed with various footprints, unfortunately too many to provide any clues as to what happened or who did this. "Have you found anything useful in the vehicle yet?"

"Not really. Although there is a perfectly round circle of clean glass on the rear passenger window, directly behind the driver's seat, that has me confused. It could be nothing—maybe where the victim once stuck a sticker or something."

"Strange place for a sticker," she says.

"That's what I thought. Anyway, I'm hopeful I'll find something more useful on closer inspection once the car is at the station. Here, you'll need this."

With a gloved hand, Alex passes her the victim's driver's license so she has her home address. Madison notices he keeps peering over at Shelley and Jake, who appear to be having a heated discussion behind them. "Everything okay with them?" she asks.

Alex reddens. "I wouldn't know. It's none of my business." He walks to the driver's side of the car and Madison gets the impression there's a messy love triangle going on there. The last she knew, Shelley and Alex were getting close, not Shelley and Jake. This is the problem with dating co-workers, and why Madison would never consider it.

"Detective Harper!" Gary Pelosi shouts behind her. "Can you give us the victim's name?"

Madison approaches the yellow tape that's keeping the crowd of onlookers at bay. She recognizes a few faces from the media, as well as some locals hanging around in the hope of catching a glimpse of the body. A bright light suddenly blinds her and she flinches. "Give me some warning before you switch that thing on, would you?"

"Sorry," says the other male reporter present. "He's new." He nods to the cameraman, who hides his face behind his equipment. "I'm Mark Lacey for Channel 8 news. This footage won't go out live, but what can you tell us?"

Gary gets his phone out and holds it out to her, mic end first, so he can record audio. Madison notices they're all bundled up against the cold, in thick jackets and snow boots. She wishes she'd dressed as warm. "Nothing until I've notified the victim's family."

"So someone was murdered?" asks Mark.

Madison gives him a stern look. "A woman and child were found in this location less than an hour ago. The child is unharmed. The woman is deceased. Until the medical examiner and our forensic tech have had time to process the scene, I can't tell you any more than that." She pauses. "When's your footage going out?"

"It'll be on the ten o'clock bulletin."

That doesn't give her long to notify the victim's family before they see this on TV and realize it happened where their loved one was shopping. Hopefully the car is screened well enough from the cameras that they won't recognize it. She looks into the lens to make a direct plea to the public. "If anyone was here shopping or passing the area tonight between around five p.m. and eight thirty p.m., and you saw or heard anything unusual, such as a female screaming or arguing, please get in touch with Lost Creek PD immediately. I'm sure there will be a more detailed press conference held in the morning." She turns away and Mark doesn't ask any more questions. He immediately starts preparing a piece to camera, while Gary starts taking photos of the scene ready for tomorrow morning's paper.

Madison heads to the cruiser to speak to their main witness. She opens the back door and crouches down next to the woman and baby. Her hands are frozen, so she removes the latex gloves and swaps them for a woolen pair from her pocket. "Hi, I'm Detective Harper. I just have a few questions and then you can be on your way."

The woman nods, holding back tears. "I thought I was going to die. I thought…" She covers her mouth with her spare hand. The cute baby girl on her lap looks at her mother before starting to whimper.

"I'm sorry you were the one to find her," says Madison. "I imagine that was traumatic."

The woman nods.

"Can I get your name?"

"Julie Reid. I came here for some last-minute gifts, and when I returned to my car, I noticed the overhead light was smashed."

She's observant, that's good. "What time did you arrive and head into the mall?"

"I left home right around four fifteen and got here at about four thirty, I think."

"And what time did you find the woman in her car?"

"Around seven thirty," says Julie. "I think the mall closed at eight tonight, so it was quiet out here."

Madison's heart sinks. It's going to be difficult to find other witnesses. "Was there anyone else in the parking lot at the time you returned to your car?"

"Just a woman who drove away in a red Nissan. She was alone."

That's useful. Madison wonders whether a female could have done this, and that's why the child was left unharmed. Although that could just be because the perp didn't spot the child in the back seat during his fit of rage.

"Can I go home now?" asks Julie. "My baby's diaper needs changing, and I've already told that officer over there everything." She points to Shelley. "I'm sorry, it's not that I don't want to help, but I, I'm so..." She tears up again, and Madison notices she's shaking hard. It could be the freezing temperature, or it could be shock.

"Of course. Do you need any medical attention before you go?"

"No, I'll be fine if I can just go and see my husband. He's been calling to see where I am, but I didn't feel able to answer my phone. The baby was crying and the officer was trying to talk to me."

"I understand. We have your contact details if we need to speak to you again. I'll have an officer drive you home right away."

Julie frowns. "I can't take my car?"

Madison glances over at the two cars side by side, Julie's and the victim's. They're so close, the killer could have touched Julie's when getting away. "Not yet, no. We won't need it long, just twenty-four to forty-eight hours probably. It's due to the proximity to the crime scene. It might yield some evidence for us. I know it's inconvenient and I'm sorry about that, but it's important we find who did this."

Julie lowers her eyes and holds the baby a little closer to her chest. Madison stands to call Officer Luis Sanchez over. He's the youngest serving officer at LCPD at only twenty-five. "Would you give our witness a ride home? She's badly shaken and wants to get out of here."

"Sure thing." Officer Sanchez carefully closes the back door of the cruiser and gets in the front.

Madison watches him drive out of the parking lot before pulling Sarah Moss's driver's license from her pocket. Having grown up in Lost Creek, she's familiar with the victim's street. It's a nice area, and not far from Kate Flynn's home. Maybe she'll stop by and check in on Kate while she's there. But not before she delivers some devastating news.

CHAPTER THREE

Sarah Moss's single-story home looks pretty in the snow. The family's Christmas tree stands proudly in the living room window, the white lights twinkling prettily. Madison can imagine the family opening their presents together in front of the fireplace the day after tomorrow. Except now that won't happen. And she's the one who has to break it to them. Normally she would have Detective Don Douglas with her, but since he died and she's without a partner, Shelley volunteered to come. She has the victim's toddler with her.

Madison steps out of her car, pulling her coat tight, and waits as Shelley gets out of the cruiser behind her, carefully carrying the little boy in a car seat they keep on hand for emergencies. His own car seat is now considered evidence, along with the clothes he was wearing. He's wrapped in an oversized LCPD T-shirt and a thick blanket to keep him warm. "How's he doing?" she asks.

"He was silent the whole way," says Shelley. "I can't get a smile out of him and he won't even acknowledge me when I talk to him."

He's staring over Madison's shoulder toward the house, his eyes wide and teary. He witnessed something horrific tonight and will undoubtably require psychological help over the coming months to help him process whatever memories linger. It's a parent's worst nightmare, and Madison knows his mother would have been terrified that her attacker would harm her child too. She leans down and strokes his face, which is warm from being in the car. He grabs her hand tight, clearly seeking comfort.

Taking a deep breath, she leads Shelley past the blue Ford in the driveway, up to the front door. As she rings the bell, she has no idea who or what to expect.

"Mommy's home!" shouts an excited child from within.

She briefly closes her eyes. *Oh God.*

The door opens wide to a man a little older than her, maybe thirty-nine or forty, with dark hair and a neatly clipped beard. He has a young boy, about six or seven, enthusiastically hugging his leg. "Sorry," the man says, looking confused. "I was expecting my wife. She's late."

Madison steels herself. "My name's Detective Madison Harper, from Lost Creek PD, and this is Officer Shelley Vickers. Do you mind if we come in?"

Fear sweeps over his face as his eyes hover on Shelley's police uniform. It's then that he notices she's holding a car seat carrying his younger son. Madison watches his reaction closely for any telltale signs that he could have been involved in his wife's murder. Death notifications are hard, not just because of the devastation they bring to the victim's family, but because she has to read people's reactions and figure out whether the partner, friend or family members had anything to do with the crime she's there to report. She has to figure out whether they're acting, and it's not always as easy to tell as people might think.

Without a word, he steps aside. The older boy looks at his brother and asks, "Where's Mommy?"

No one answers him. He reminds Madison of her own son, Owen, at that age. They have similar blond hair and quick smiles. Owen is seventeen now, and she missed out on seven years of his life while she was incarcerated for a murder she didn't commit, but that's over now, and they're enjoying what little time they have together before he leaves for college next year. She's painfully aware that their reunion has been too short and she'll never get back those years they lost.

Sarah's husband looks down at his older son. "Scotty, why don't you go play in your room?"

"Shouldn't you be asleep?" asks Madison, kneeling down to his level. "It's almost ten o'clock!"

"But I don't want to," says the boy. He shows her a plastic trumpet. "Do you want to hear me play?"

She smiles widely. "Sure!"

He blasts it, spitting everywhere but inside the mouthpiece. The noise goes right through her, but she says, "Wow, I bet it won't be long before you start your own band!"

He grins at her, and then Shelley leans in. "Why don't you show me your bedroom? Would that be okay with Dad?"

His father nods, pale and afraid, and the boy runs off to his bedroom in excitement. As Madison watches them leave, she notices that Shelley doesn't disappear all the way into the room at the end of the hall. She's glancing back at them in case things take an unexpected turn.

The victim's husband switches off the loud cartoon playing on the TV before leaning forward to take his younger son out of the car seat. "You okay, Danny?"

The boy says one word. "Momma." Within seconds his bottom lip quivers and he starts crying.

His dad looks at Madison. "What's going on? Where are his clothes, and where is my wife?"

Madison pulls out her pocket notebook. "Would you confirm your name for me?"

Without missing a beat, he says, "David Moss."

"And you're Sarah Moss's husband?"

"Right. Why? Just tell me, please." If he's acting, he's good at it, because his eyes are wide with an uncertainty that's difficult to fake.

"I'm sorry to have to tell you that your wife was attacked tonight in a parking lot downtown. She had already succumbed to her injuries by the time she was found." She tries not to look at Danny as she speaks.

A look of horror washes over David's face and he takes a step back. He slowly lowers himself onto the couch, still holding his youngest son. His mouth opens wide as his eyes search Madison's face for signs that she's joking. "You're kidding, right?"

She shakes her head. "I'm so sorry. There was nothing the paramedics could do. Danny is completely unharmed, but we've taken his clothes and car seat for evidence. We'll need to keep your wife's car for now too."

His spare hand goes to his forehead. Madison walks toward him and takes the young boy from his arms, allowing David to collapse backward into the cushions. His hands are trembling. She sits next to him on the couch, giving him some time to absorb everything. Scotty is banging around in his room.

After some time, she says, "I appreciate this is a terrible time to ask questions, but I want to catch who attacked her as quickly as possible. Is there anyone you can think of who might have done this?"

He looks up at her. There are no tears, but his face is now flushed with anger. "How would I know who did it? Wait, how was she killed?"

"It looks like she was beaten with something as she has extensive head injuries, but we'll know more after the autopsy."

He runs a hand through his hair. "*Autopsy? Beaten?* I can't believe I'm hearing these words. It's Christmas! She went out to buy *gifts*. How could this happen? Are you sure it's even her?"

Although they brought his son home without his wife, shock is trying to trick David into believing they've made a mistake with the victim's identity. Madison's heart aches for him. "She was found in a black Lexus with your son in the back seat. The photograph on her driver's license confirms it's her. We'll still need someone to formally identify her, but that can wait for tomorrow." She rests a hand on his back. "I'm sorry. I know this is devastating for you, and we can provide support for you and your sons, but I need to ask again: Can you think of anyone she had any problems with? Any recent arguments or unwanted attention?"

He looks at her. "The only arguments I'm aware of were with me. We were talking about divorcing." He breaks eye contact. "She wanted to separate. I didn't. It's complicated."

Madison stands and takes a wander around the living room with Danny balancing on her hip. He's sucking his thumb and resting his head on her shoulder. It won't be long before he falls asleep, but she imagines he'll wake more than once tonight, from terrible nightmares. She peers into the kitchen. Nothing looks out of place; there are no signs of a struggle. The house is not especially clean or tidy, which is a good sign. Hopefully it means no one has tried to hide evidence of an altercation.

Although she's certain Sarah Moss was killed in her car, it doesn't mean there wasn't a domestic incident before she left to go shopping, one that resulted in her husband working himself into a rage. She could have left the house to give him time to cool down. Maybe it didn't work. Maybe instead he followed her to the mall, waiting for her to emerge alone. That could explain why Danny wasn't harmed; David could kill his wife, but he couldn't bring himself to kill his child. She'll see if she can get a child psychologist to speak to the boy tomorrow, because he's their best chance at finding out what went down in that car. "Were you home all night?" she asks David.

His head snaps up. "Yes. With Scotty. Sarah was shopping

with Danny because he cried when she tried to leave without him. He's clingy at the moment; he's only three. She didn't want to take both children with her, so Scotty stayed home with me."

She nods. He still hasn't shed a tear. That isn't completely unusual; everyone reacts differently to a death notification. "Is there anyone who can corroborate that? Did you receive or make any calls from your landline, or did any visitors stop by?"

"No, but that doesn't mean I'm lying."

Scotty runs back into the room with a crate full of toys. "I have more instruments to show you." Shelley follows him.

Madison smiles at him. "Scotty? Have you and your dad been home all evening waiting for your mom and Danny to return?" She feels David's eyes on her, but she has to ask. Children this age rarely lie when asked a direct question by a stranger.

Scotty appears to think about it. "We went out for breakfast."

"Was that this morning?" she asks gently.

"Uh-huh. I had pancakes and syrup. Mommy had toast. Daddy had bacon and eggs and Mommy told him he'll have a heart attack one of these days."

She feels goosebumps on her arms. Little did Sarah know she would die first, and so soon. "And what did you do after breakfast?"

"For God's sake," mutters David, clearly offended.

Scotty makes a thinking face. "Mommy went to work. Me and Danny watched cartoons and played all day until Mommy went to the mall. I colored my drawing book." He rummages through his crate of toys and pulls out the book. "Look! I can stay in the lines, but Danny can't. He's a poopy head." He laughs at his own joke.

"So you didn't go out to meet up with your mommy after she left to go shopping?"

He shakes his head. "Will you play with me?"

Madison returns her attention to David, who takes Danny off her before sitting on the couch again. He appears completely overwhelmed and his knees are visibly trembling. "Not now, Scotty. She's leaving. They both are."

He wants them gone, which is understandable. "Do you need me to contact anyone for you, or will you notify Sarah's family?" she asks.

"I'll call her parents." His expression finally cracks, and the tears he's been holding back suddenly fall as he realizes how difficult that will be.

Madison hates to leave him like this, but she knows most families can't begin to process what's happened until the police leave them alone to deal with the news. She pulls a card out of her pocket. "I'll put my contact details by your phone. You'll hear from me again soon, but if there's anything you can think of that will help my investigation, please call any time. And I'd like to offer my condolences. If there's anything I can do to help over the next few days, please get in touch. There are resources available to you and to the rest of Sarah's family."

He nods, but his wet eyes stay fixed on the carpet. Scotty squeezes into his father's lap next to his younger brother. "What's the matter, Daddy?"

Shelley opens the front door and Madison follows her out into the cold. At the bottom of the icy driveway, Shelley turns to her. "Think he's involved?"

Madison looks back at the house. "It's too soon to tell. But for the sake of those boys, I really hope not."

CHAPTER FOUR

Madison has left officers questioning employees from the mall to see if anyone noticed a suspicious person hanging around the parking lot where Sarah Moss's body was found. The whole area is cordoned off, with a search in progress for the murder weapon, and Chief Mendes is fully briefed on the case, which means Madison has time to get some sleep before returning to work early tomorrow morning. But not before she calls on her friend.

Her navy Honda, already well past its prime, makes some worrying noises as she pulls into Kate Flynn's driveway. The car has been plagued with faults for a while now and she doesn't think it will last the winter, but she can't afford to replace it yet. Kate, on the other hand, has a brand-new BMW sitting on her driveway. It's the only other car present, which means her husband, Patrick, isn't home yet. Madison checks her watch: it's 10.45 p.m. He works as a bank manager and the couple has two small children. He should be home by now. Madison knows the pair has had some problems lately, but she hopes he hasn't moved out.

She presses the doorbell, which is one of those smart security ones with a built-in camera. Kate's big on safety and security as a result of the crimes she reports on, and Madison was tempted to get one herself until she heard of cases where hackers managed to monitor the live footage over Wi-Fi and use it to their advantage, carrying out a spate of burglaries. It put her off. Although if anyone burglarized her place, all they'd find was a cat who would demand the intruders feed him before they leave with the TV. She smiles at the thought, because her son's cat is obsessed with food.

Kate opens the front door within seconds, and the sound of a little girl throwing a tantrum inside the house drowns out Madison's greeting. She follows Kate into the spacious living room. There are toys all over the floor, and the house smells of cinnamon and nutmeg, bringing back memories of childhood Christmases.

"Sally, you have to go to sleep now," says Kate. "It's Christmas Eve tomorrow; you don't want to sleep through that, do you?"

The little girl, who is the spitting image of her mother, with her blue eyes and dark brown hair, starts hiccuping as she reaches the end of her tantrum. "But I want to see Santy Claus," she gulps.

"And you will, honey," says Kate patiently. "I've told you already that he'll be here *tomorrow* night. But if you don't sleep now, you won't be able to stay awake tomorrow."

"But what if I go to sleep now and I don't wake up in time?" Sally gulps. "I'll miss Christmas!"

Madison smiles. She can't fault the child's logic. It's a perfectly valid concern for a five-year-old.

Kate closes her eyes and takes a deep breath. "I promise I will wake you when he gets here. Okay?"

The front door opens and Patrick appears. Sally runs to him and starts crying again. "Mommy won't let me see Santy Claus."

Patrick glances at Madison before picking Sally up. "Let's get you upstairs." He doesn't smile and he doesn't acknowledge his wife as he disappears. Madison realizes this is the second household she's been to tonight where the couple isn't happy. The holiday season can be tough on relationships.

"Thank God," Kate says with a sigh. "I was losing my mind. Coffee? Wine? A two-week vacation in the Bahamas without any kids, leaving right away?"

Madison smiles as she follows her into the kitchen and slips onto a stool at the breakfast bar. "Coffee, thanks." It's too late for coffee really, but she's too buzzed to sleep yet anyway. The TV on the wall in the adjoining dining room is switched to the news channel, on silent. Madison watches the officers from her department scour the crime scene at the mall. The victim's car is still hidden from sight and it looks as though the coroner's van has left, which means the body has been removed.

A sneeze behind her makes her turn. Kate's other child, four-year-old Ben, is seated at the dining table. Kate and Patrick adopted him when he was younger, not knowing anything about his life before them. Madison knows he struggles to sleep at night because of his fear of the dark, so he naps in the daytime and stays up as late as possible. Kate has sought advice from a variety of doctors about that, and about the more concerning condition of selective mutism he's currently experiencing. Despite being assessed for all manner of things, including autism, he hasn't been diagnosed with anything. The doctors have concluded he's just going through a phase and that he'll start talking again when he's ready. But she knows Kate isn't convinced. "Hi, Ben!" she says. "Are you excited it's almost Christmas?"

He nods and then starts recording them on his iPad, something he's obsessed with since he stopped talking.

She turns back to Kate. "Is he still carrying that thing everywhere he goes?"

Kate rubs her forehead. "He sure is."

Madison looks at her friend and notices, not for the first

time, that Kate's not herself right now. Normally impeccably dressed and made up in order to be on-air ready at a moment's notice, her hair is tied back in a messy ponytail and looking a little greasy, and she's only wearing mascara as far as Madison can tell. For anyone else, that would be normal, but Kate likes to look good on TV. She's also been slow arriving to crime scenes. It's as if she doesn't care about beating the other reporters to the latest news anymore. "How's Ben when it's just you and Patrick here?"

Kate takes a deep breath. "He hasn't said a word in three weeks. Not even yes or no. He'll nod or shake his head, but he won't form words anymore. A month or so ago it was just at preschool where he stopped talking, and in some social situations. He was still speaking to us. Then he stopped talking to Patrick completely, and now it's me too. The doctor seemed sure his selective mutism was just a phase, but I'm worried it's not. The problem is that Ben has got used to talking through the app on that thing." She nods to the iPad. "He prefers the automated voice to his own, and neither Patrick nor I can figure out why."

Madison feels for her. It doesn't make any sense, as Ben now has loving, attentive parents. But they don't know what life was like for him before he came to live with them. "How does Patrick feel about it?"

Kate rolls her eyes and then sips her coffee before replying. "We argue over it all the time because we both have a different approach. I spend hours googling the condition, whereas Patrick thinks he knows better than anyone else. He thinks we need to stop talking to Ben until he talks to us. But he's pushing Ben away because his frustration is coming across as anger." She pauses. "I have a feeling we're not going to make it. That we'll end up divorcing over this. And that could just make Ben worse."

Madison reaches out to rub Kate's arm as Ben loses interest in them and stops recording. "I couldn't take Patrick's approach," she says. "But I can understand why he'd want to try anything."

"Let's not talk about it, it's too depressing." Kate takes a deep breath and nods to the TV. "What have I missed?"

Madison fills her in on the basics around the crime scene, careful not to say too much. Not that she knows much herself right now. "It was brutal, from the looks of it. And to do it out in the open like that where he could've been caught suggests this guy is deranged."

"Maybe it's not the first time he's done it," suggests Kate.

Before Madison can respond, Sally comes flying down the stairs, screaming at the top of her lungs, "No! I don't want to go to sleep!"

Patrick follows her with an exasperated look on his face. He appears just as exhausted as his wife, and Madison doesn't envy them. He enters the kitchen and finds a clean mug before slamming the cabinet door closed. "Your turn," he says.

Kate looks at Madison with raised eyebrows before turning back to her husband. "So that's it? You've spent five minutes with her and now it's my turn again?"

Ben raises his iPad to resume recording. He likes to play these videos of his parents when they're not around. The doctor thinks it's a way to comfort himself, but no one knows why he needs comforting. Having felt the tension here tonight, though, Madison thinks it might be because of what he's witnessing.

"Here we go again," says Patrick with a loud sigh. "I can't have this argument again, Kate, I just can't. We do this every day and it's exhausting."

Madison slips off the stool and grabs her jacket. "Guys, I'm going to go. If there's anything I can do to help, just call me. I'm always happy to babysit. Just give me some notice first."

Kate hugs her, but not before Madison sees tears in her eyes. "Thanks. I'll call you."

"I'm sorry, Madison," says Patrick. "I don't want you to feel like you have to leave."

"What do you expect after your little outburst?" says Kate. "*I'd* leave if I could!"

Madison listens to them go at it in hushed tones as she slips out of the house. The cold darkness is a relief after the atmosphere inside. Sometimes she's glad to be single.

CHAPTER FIVE

Nate Monroe opens the back door of his car and watches as Brody, a German shepherd–Siberian husky mix, runs ahead of him and up the steps to Madison Harper's front door. It's a clear, crisp morning and Nate notices that the compacted snow has turned icy on the driveway. As he's brought breakfast from Ruby's Diner, he ascends the steps carefully, because if he drops the food, Brody will be all over it in seconds.

The front door opens before he knocks, and Owen appears. Madison's seventeen-year-old son lets Brody run inside. "What have you got there?" he asks.

Nate smiles. "It's for your mom. I hear she was up late working the homicide case and I thought she could do with something more substantial for breakfast than cereal."

Owen steps to one side as Nate walks in. He heads to the kitchen at the rear of the house, where Madison is sipping coffee. She looks like she hasn't fully woken up yet, but she's dressed and ready for work, with her gold shield and service weapon both positioned on her hip. With a smile she says, "Morning. Please tell me that bag contains waffles."

"Would I dare bring you anything healthy?" He places it in front of her along with a copy of the *Lost Creek Daily*, which has the images from last night's crime scene splashed across the front page.

Madison glances at it. "Damn that guy."

"Who?" he asks.

"Gary Pelosi, the reporter for this rag. He managed to get a photograph of the car while the victim was still in it. Look." She holds the paper up.

The photo was taken with a long lens pointing into the car's rear window. Nate can just about make out the back of a head slumped to one side. "Most people won't notice she's still inside."

"That's not the point. And it's not just Gary. I'm so sick of the press always trying to get the most shocking photo. These victims have families. How do you think Sarah Moss's husband will feel when he sees this?"

Nate knows it's a rhetorical question, so he doesn't respond. With a sigh, Madison opens the takeout bag, places the waffles on a plate and hunts for some maple syrup in the cabinet behind her. When she's poured more than Nate would have, she pulls out a fork and starts eating. He looks around the kitchen. "Where's your dad this morning?" Madison's father, a retired federal agent, has recently come back into her life after a long absence. He was based in Alaska, hunting serial killers, and was too busy to keep in touch with his two daughters.

"He found an apartment and moved out a few days ago," she says. "This place isn't big enough for three people, as you well know."

He smiles. He spent some time living in Madison's spare room before he got his own place. Unlike her, he isn't from Lost Creek, or even Colorado. They met in California this past summer, where they managed to find a missing child together. Madison was fresh out of prison and needed a job, so he let her tag along on his missing person case. He's an unlicensed PI and she had law enforcement experience. It wasn't plain sailing, but they worked together to get the job done. Afterward, she talked him into coming to Lost Creek with her, to find out who had framed her for murder. Since then, he's stuck around. Mainly because Madison and Owen are as close to family as he's ever likely to get.

"Hey, Mom, guess what?" says Owen as he wolfs down some toast. His three-month-old kitten, Bandit, is trying to climb inside the bread bag, while Brody sits on the floor waiting for the cat to drop him some scraps. The pair get along surprisingly well considering their contrasting sizes and species.

Madison licks syrup off her fingers. "What?"

"Guess who I saw downtown yesterday? He was in the diner ordering coffee."

Madison shrugs. "Who?"

"Richie Hope."

Nate smiles widely. "No way." Richie Hope is a charismatic lawyer based in Prospect Springs. He came to their rescue this past summer, when all three of them found themselves in trouble with the police. That was before Madison managed to get her job back at LCPD. "What's he doing in town?"

"Get this," says Owen excitedly. "His office up north was burned to the ground last month, so he's moved here to start fresh. He's got a new office downtown."

Madison stops eating. "Was the fire deliberate?" she asks.

That's exactly what Nate was thinking, because Richie has a way of upsetting bad guys. He's not afraid to stand up to anyone who tries to bully others, including law enforcement.

Owen shrugs. "I don't know. I asked, but he just laughed and said he never liked that office anyway. You know how he is, good at putting a positive spin on bad news."

Madison laughs. "Only *he* could put a positive spin on that!" She finishes the last bite of waffle and places the plate and fork into the sink.

"Anyway, he says he's going to need help around the place

and he might be able to offer me an internship until I go to college. I'm going there now to find out more."

Nate raises his eyebrows. "That's a great opportunity."

Madison doesn't seem as keen. "Wait a minute." She drops the takeout bag in the trash. "Richie Hope's old office got burned down by what I think we can safely assume is a disgruntled criminal, and you want to go work at his new office? What if that's attacked too?"

Owen swallows the last bite of his toast. "It'll be fine, Mom. They're not going to go after him twice. Whoever burned his office down has already chased him out of Prospect Springs."

Madison shakes her head but bites her tongue. Nate can understand why she'd be worried, but it would be great experience for Owen, considering he wants to be a lawyer. "Want a ride to his office? I wouldn't mind taking a look myself."

Owen grabs his backpack. "Sure." He kisses Bandit on the head and then gently places him on the tiled floor. "Catch you later, boy."

Nate turns to Madison as Owen heads out to the car. "Don't worry, I'll find out why Richie was targeted. But this is a good opportunity for Owen. Besides, he's almost an adult now. You have to let him make his own decisions sometime."

"I don't have to let him walk into a bad situation, though," she says with a sigh. "Let's see what you think after you've spoken to Richie. In the meantime, I have a killer to catch. Did you watch any of the news coverage about the homicide?"

He nods. "It sounded vicious."

"It was. At least he left the child unharmed, I guess. The victim's husband was distraught when I told him. Imagine waking up on Christmas Eve to be reminded that the woman you loved was savagely beaten to death the night before."

Nate doesn't have to imagine too hard. It may not have happened during the holidays but his fiancée was brutally murdered in the same way. He served seventeen years on death row in Texas for her murder before finally being exonerated just two years ago.

Madison touches his arm. "Sorry. That was a stupid thing to say."

He puts his hand on hers and smiles. "It's not about me. And I know you'll find the asshole who did this."

She looks thoughtful. "I wish you were working with me. Can't you become a cop? It would make my life a lot easier."

It's not the first time she's said that, but he scoffs at the idea. It was a dirty cop who helped land him on death row, so he doesn't have the same level of respect for law enforcement as Madison does. "Don't you get a new partner today?"

She moves her hand and takes a deep breath. "Sure do. Fingers crossed it's Shelley or Steve. But I can't help worrying about who would replace them."

She grabs her car keys and they both head outside, with Brody following them. The dog jumps into the back seat of Nate's Chevy Traverse when Owen opens the door for him.

To Madison, Nate says, "I'll let you know what Richie tells us. Good luck with your investigation."

"Thanks."

He watches as she backs her car out of the driveway first. He'd give anything to be working the homicide case with her, but he's only a PI. And since he helped solve the disappearance of Ruby and Oliver Rader last month, he's a PI without a client. Which means it's time to find another case to work on.

CHAPTER SIX

Madison enters the station and makes her way to the offices, expecting to see either Shelley or Steve preparing for their new role as detective. There's no sign of them. She approaches the dispatcher's cubicle, where Stella Myers is just finishing up a call. Stella's worked at the station for years and has just switched from the graveyard shift to days in preparation of eventually retiring. "Morning, Stella. Did any tips come in overnight about the Sarah Moss homicide?"

"Morning." Stella spins around in her seat and lowers her headset to her shoulders, careful not to pull off her short wig in the process. It's gray with blue tips that match her glasses. "Dina took a couple of calls overnight," she says, "but nothing promising. Sergeant Tanner has been following up." Dina Blake is the other dispatcher, who mostly works nights.

Madison nods. She peers over at Chief Carmen Mendes's office and does a double take when she sees a man in a navy suit sitting opposite the chief's desk. He looks like a Fed to her. Mendes notices her and motions for her to enter. Madison turns back to Stella. "Who's that guy?"

Stella slips her headset on as if she doesn't want to be the bearer of bad news. "I'll let the chief introduce you."

Madison has a bad feeling about this. She approaches the office and opens the door.

"Madison," says Chief Mendes. "This is Don Douglas's replacement, Marcus Adams."

Madison looks at the guy as he stands. He's about forty, with jet-black hair, a tanned complexion even though it's winter and a stiff posture that leads her to believe he's uptight. She shakes his outstretched hand before turning to Mendes. "Could I speak to you in private, Chief?"

Mendes crosses her arms and ignores Madison's question. "Detective Adams previously worked as a sergeant in Denver. He has excellent credentials and I think he'll be a good fit in the department."

Marcus Adams clears his throat. "I'm guessing you're disappointed one of your buddies didn't get the job?"

Madison doesn't want to make the guy feel bad, but it's a strange decision to employ an outsider who doesn't know the town or the locals. Detective Douglas was an outsider, and the locals never took to him. There's a small-town mentality that a city cop might not get. That's going to make both their jobs harder when it comes to getting witness testimony and the trust of the community. "I'm sure you're a great cop," she says, "but why in the world would you move to somewhere like Lost Creek from a big city? Were you fired or something? Got caught doing something you shouldn't?" She doesn't mean it as an insult; she's genuinely interested.

"Are you serious?" he says. His jaw tenses.

Chief Mendes looks at Adams. "Give us a minute, would you? Why not get someone to show you around the place. I'm sure you'll want to know where the facilities are."

Adams eyeballs Madison as he brushes past her. He's clearly the sensitive type, which is another reason he's wrong for the job. She closes the door behind him. "With all due respect, Chief, why would you hire him over Shelley or Steve? You're sending the message that the team here can't progress.

Shelley's a fine police officer and Steve's the best sergeant I've ever worked with. Don't they deserve a chance to do something else if they want to?"

Chief Mendes takes a seat behind her desk, which is finally starting to show some sign of her personality. Previously neat and tidy, like Mendes herself, it now has a small potted cactus in one corner and a stack of paperwork scattered on top. A spare suit jacket hangs from the coat rack, and the walls are starting to fill with certificates and accreditations. It's taken five months in the role, but Madison thinks Chief Mendes has finally decided to stay in town and make this job work. She's relieved, as the woman is better than the previous chief she worked under.

Mendes looks at her. "What does it say on that gold shield you wear on your hip, Madison?"

She sighs, anticipating a telling-off. "Detective."

"Exactly. You're in charge of investigating serious crimes. I'm in charge of running this department, and that includes hiring and firing. Detective Douglas's death hit us all hard, no matter what anyone thought of him, but we need the right person to replace him. A person with experience who can hit the ground running. It will make your job easier to have Marcus Adams investigating alongside you."

"I hear you," says Madison. "I know we're a department that will always be small and understaffed, but I would've taken the time to help train Shelley. And Steve's been a sergeant here for years and already has the instincts of a detective. Can't this Adams guy take Steve's job instead?"

Mendes shakes her head. "Adams didn't uproot his family and move down here to end up in the same role he was already in, and for what is probably less money. Besides, I value Sergeant Tanner in his current position, and I think it would be more difficult to replace him than to fill the detective role. In my experience, the position of sergeant is the most important in the whole department, and Steve did a fine job of supporting all of us after Douglas's death."

Madison is surprised she's given it that much thought. "Does Steve know you feel that way?"

"We've talked. I've explained my reasons for not moving him to the detective role. And because of that, I think he's happy to stay where he is for a little while longer. With regards to Officer Vickers, well, I've recommended she gives some thought as to whether she might be more suited to a sergeant position, in case Steve moves roles. I think she'd be good at it, and once she's a sergeant, she'd be better placed to eventually become a detective in the future, if that's what she wants." Mendes stands. "I'm trying to put in place a solid structure for this department, for both now and the future. I'm looking beyond people's knee-jerk reactions to unexpected vacancies and offering them a long-term plan for their careers."

Feeling awkward for trying to tell the chief how to do her job, Madison cautiously asks, "And what about me? You've never called me in to discuss my future here."

Normally serious, Mendes smiles. "You haven't been back on the payroll for long. I was giving you time to find your feet." Madison feels like she needs to point out everything she's achieved since leaving prison and returning to her role, but Mendes is ahead of her. "You've done a great job so far. In fact, I have bigger aspirations for you than I do for the others."

She frowns. "What do you mean?"

With a deep breath, Mendes elaborates. "I don't intend to stay in Lost Creek forever. In fact, I give it five years before I move on. I have no links here, and I guess I saw this position as a challenge, and a way to get out of a heavy situation at the Colorado Bureau of Investigation. So maybe one day in the not-too-distant future, my role will need to be filled, and I'd prefer it wasn't by some old guy who plays golf with the DA."

Madison's mouth drops open in surprise. That was the last thing she was expecting to hear. She's never considered a move upward, as she's been too focused on getting her job back after the wrongful conviction.

"However, in order to recommend you when the time comes," adds Mendes, "I'd like to see you work independently of your PI friend from now on."

"You mean Nate?"

The chief nods.

"But what's the difference between having his help and having this new guy's help?"

"Well, for one thing, Detective Adams has never been on death row with his personal life splashed across the internet for all to read about, and for another, Nate Monroe is not a police officer. He has no law enforcement background and he is not employed by this department in any capacity."

Madison resists the urge to explain how Nate has better instincts than some of the cops she's worked with over the years.

Mendes continues. "I realize you come as a pair because of your shared experience with wrongful convictions and prison time, but I think you rely too heavily on him sometimes. The media has noticed too. Some people are questioning why he's allowed at crime scenes, which technically he isn't."

Madison doesn't know what to say. She suspected it would come to this eventually, that she'd have to work independently of Nate, and she does mostly. But they work well together. He's supportive, and he forces her to consider alternative theories she might not have otherwise thought of. That's *because* he doesn't have a law enforcement background. He's less rigid in his thinking. He's also lived with some of the worst killers in the US while locked up in Texas. He's had a unique glimpse into the minds of those who commit depraved acts of violence.

A knock at the door makes them both turn. Detective Adams opens it. His look is serious. "Are we hunting a killer or not, partner?"

Madison wants to cringe at his enthusiasm, which seems

faked for the chief's benefit, but she knows she has to give him a chance. That doesn't mean she can't give him all the crap to deal with: the paperwork, taking witness statements and learning the hard way what life as a cop in a small town is like. That will give her time to focus on the leads.

She exits the office. "Follow me."

CHAPTER SEVEN

As it's Christmas Eve, downtown is already getting busy with last-minute shoppers, and for now, everyone appears to be in good spirits. The fast-food joints already have cars lining up at the drive-throughs, parking spaces outside the stores and strip malls are filling up, and traffic is heavy. Something about the holidays makes people want to spend money. Of course, come January, the majority of them will regret it.

The snow is holding off for now, but it's still as bitterly cold as it was last night, and Madison had trouble starting her car outside the station. It sparked into life eventually, and now she stands waiting for Detective Adams to pull into the parking lot outside the medical examiner's building. She told him to follow her, as he didn't appear to know where he was going. She only realized from seeing him in her rear-view mirror what kind of vehicle he drives. A sleek black Chevrolet Camaro sports car that she doesn't know how he afforded as a cop, or why he would need it. It made her roll her eyes. He'd clearly bought it in response to some kind of midlife crisis.

She checks her watch: 9.30 a.m., and no sign of Adams. If she had just moved to a new town and secured a job in law enforcement, you better believe she would have familiarized herself with the place before she started her first day at work. Maybe the fact he didn't is a sign that Adams sees this as a short-term position until he can find something better. Which further suggests he could've needed a new job at short notice, perhaps because of his involvement in some kind of scandal at his last PD. She sighs. Or maybe she's been a cop too long and he just wanted a change of scenery.

Once he finally arrives, she walks over to his car and peers inside. It's pristine, with no garbage anywhere. "Red leather seats? Wow." She straightens. "You must have that rare thing I've heard about."

He raises his eyebrows. "What's that?"

"Disposable income." He doesn't laugh, so she turns and leads him into the building. As they wait in the warm reception area for Dr. Scott to appear, Madison brings him up to speed on the Sarah Moss homicide, giving him the facts he wouldn't have heard by watching the overnight news. "What we need from Lena today is a confirmed cause of death and an idea of the instrument used. We don't have the murder weapon right now and we need to know what we're looking for."

"Got it. Did anyone hear our victim scream?" he asks. "Because I'm guessing she fought back, with her kid on the back seat and all."

"Our best witness so far is the woman who found her, Julie Reid. She had just returned to her car and saw another woman exiting the parking lot in a red Nissan." Adams pulls his cell phone out and starts taking notes as she talks. "I need you to trace that vehicle and driver using the CCTV footage from the mall and by speaking to any other shoppers from last night that you can track down."

He stops typing. "Can't patrol do all that?"

She looks at him, trying to figure out if he's going to be one of those detectives who expect other people to do their work for them. "No, they're busy, and we're a small team, so we all pull our weight. Besides, you need to get to know the locals. It will do you good to learn where everything is in town and who runs which business."

He sighs heavily. "You're not in charge of me, you know. I may be new here, but I won't be treated like your own personal intern. We're supposed to work together."

She scoffs. "Trust me, I don't have time to be in charge of you, but I do need you to know more about the community you work in. If you weren't around, I would be chasing the driver of the red Nissan myself, but I can't do everything. I don't expect patrol to do my job and they wouldn't expect me to do theirs. Maybe it's different where you come from, but you're not there anymore, so you better get used to how we work down here."

Lena Scott appears from behind the reception desk. "Hi."

Adams's eyes light up as he gives her an appreciative once-over. It's brief, but Madison knows Lena would have noticed it too. Women always do, especially when you look like Lena. She must get it all the time. A glance at his wedding finger confirms to Madison that he's married. She has to stop herself from rolling her eyes again. "Hey, Lena. This is Douglas's replacement, Marcus Adams. He's new in town."

He holds his hand out and Lena shakes it before leading them into the cool morgue, where she slips a white coat over her smart pants and pale blue shirt. Adams looks around the clinical room with interest and Madison wonders whether he spent much time in morgues in his last role as sergeant. You get used to the smell eventually. It's not half as bad as the aroma of a rotting corpse at a crime scene. But it's obviously cold in here, and the fluorescent lights make everyone appear tired and pale.

Sarah Moss is lying on a mortuary table with a sheet covering most of her body. Her long brown hair still shows signs of the care she took when styling it yesterday morning, when she was oblivious to how her day would end. Her makeup is all gone, and the blood around her injuries has also been carefully wiped away.

"Okay," says Lena, slipping on some latex gloves. "So, she has the obvious injuries to her head, as well as some minor injuries to her hands, specifically the fingernails, and also some significant bruising to her knees and shins." She pulls the sheet down to Sarah's ankles, exposing the autopsy incisions, now stitched closed, as well as a thin horizontal scar just below the bikini line.

"Is that from a C-section?" asks Madison.

"Right."

The bruising to her legs looks painful and stands out against her pale skin. Madison leans in to Sarah's left hand without touching it. "Ouch." She's missing a whole fingernail, presumably as a result of grabbing her killer. Her remaining nails are trimmed painfully short. Perhaps she had a bad habit of biting them and cut them short to avoid temptation, or perhaps her killer removed potential DNA evidence.

"She definitely tried to defend herself," says Lena. "I think the bruising to her legs is consistent with trying to kick her way out of the driver's side as she was being attacked. They would have made contact with the dashboard, glovebox and perhaps the car door; maybe even the attacker. The missing fingernails —one from each hand—suggest she managed to pull or push the guy at some point, so if we ever identify him and secure the clothing he wore, that could be invaluable for evidence. He could have scratches or marks on his arms, neck or face too, depending on how well wrapped up he was last night."

It had been freezing, and the assailant would have tried to hide his face from security cameras, so there's a good chance he was well covered, but Madison turns to Adams. "Something for us to be aware of when questioning witnesses."

He nods.

With a sigh, Lena says, "Her injuries tell me she fought tooth and nail to survive for her child."

"She has another boy at home, too," says Madison.

Lena shakes her head. "Those poor kids."

"Any sign of sexual assault?" asks Adams.

"None at all."

He walks to the end of the table. "What do you make of the injuries to her head?"

The scalp, having clearly been lifted away from the skull during the autopsy, now lies back in place, looser than before. It almost looks like her skin has melted. Now that they've been cleaned, the lacerations appear too small to have caused any serious damage, but the skull fractures don't.

"She had a massive internal bleed on the brain and lost a lot of blood as a result of the blows," says Lena. "It's difficult to pinpoint exactly what was used to do this, but I would classify it as blunt cranial trauma caused by some kind of metal tool. Something like a wrench or a hammer."

Adams nods along, like he's an expert himself.

"I'm sure Alex will be able to narrow it down if we find a potential weapon," says Madison, before turning to her new partner. "Alex Parker is our forensic tech."

His raises his eyebrows. "You only have one?"

"I told you we're a small PD. You didn't research us before you applied for the job?"

He turns away from her so she can't read his expression, but she senses he's annoyed at her comment. Lena pulls the sheet back over Sarah's body and says, "I'll wait for Alex to visit before I write up my report. He should be here shortly."

"Okay, thanks. Make sure he takes some fingernail scrapings, would you?"

"He already has, at the crime scene. I believe they're on their way to the crime lab for analysis."

Madison smiles. Of course they are. Alex is always one step ahead of her. "Do you have a time of death?"

"I would say she died soon after the attack, and that it

occurred within the hour before she was found, so between six thirty and seven thirty p.m." When the landline on the wall rings, Lena excuses herself. "Good to meet you, Detective Adams."

Adams nods at her and then follows Madison out of the morgue, through reception and outside. She decides to clear the air before they go their separate ways. "You seem uptight. What's wrong? Have I offended you?"

He shrugs. "Trying to embarrass me in front of the ME is about what I expected from someone like you."

She crosses her arms. "Someone like me? What are you implying?"

"I've read all about your conviction for manslaughter." He shakes his head as if he's disappointed in her. "I guess six years in prison will teach you to be underhand."

She blinks, unable to believe what she's hearing. "Are you for real? My conviction was overturned. I was *framed*. I caught the people behind Officer Levy's murder."

"Sure," he says, nodding in a patronizing manner. "I read all about that too. And I thought to myself: how does this woman who has links with a notorious criminal family manage to wear a police badge and be in the privileged position of protecting the public?"

Madison is stunned.

Adams leans in. "I don't know how you managed to get your job back, but you better be damn certain that I have no intention of taking lessons about how to be a good cop from the likes of *you*."

The urge to snap back is hard to resist. She can't believe he would use any of this against her. "So, you googled me. Well, two can play at that game. Maybe I'll find out why you really left your last police department and moved all the way down here."

"Whatever. You're crazy."

Madison is so angry she has to walk away. She was

prepared to give him the benefit of the doubt before he used her past against her.

He sighs, as if realizing he's been too harsh. Following her to her car, he says, "Listen, you pissed me off in there, so I retaliated. Of course I'm going to google my new partner. I never expected you to have such a shady history, that's all. It makes me wonder if you're trustworthy. Besides, if you back me into a corner, I'm going to react. I'm hotheaded, like most cops."

She doesn't trust herself to speak. She gets into her car, slams the door shut and speeds out of the parking lot.

CHAPTER EIGHT

Nate parks outside the old three-story brick building that houses Richie Hope's new law office. It's narrow, with a glass storefront window that offers a glimpse of the reception desk behind, and it looks like the other two floors would be good for storage or small apartments. Perhaps Richie bought the whole building with the intention of living here. It's sandwiched between a bookstore and a run-down sports bar.

Nate considers leaving Brody behind in the car, but he remembers that Richie took a shine to the dog when they first met, so he probably won't mind him coming inside. Owen enters the building first, and from the sawdust, ladders and contractors milling around, it becomes obvious the place is undergoing a renovation.

"Can I help you?" asks a petite middle-aged woman with bleached-blonde hair who appears from behind a stack of boxes. She's wearing a skintight leopard-print dress and she has two nicotine patches on one skinny, sun-damaged arm.

Owen approaches her. "I'm here to see Mr. Hope. I'm Owen Harper."

With no warning, the woman screams at the top of her lungs, "Richie! You've got a visitor."

Nate tries to contain a laugh as Owen turns to him with raised eyebrows. The woman pets Brody before putting her hands on her hips and giving Nate the once-over. "How about you, honey? Do you need any help?"

"I'm here to see Richie too, but not on business." He steps forward and holds out a hand. "Nate Monroe."

"Janine Blake, and believe me, the pleasure's all mine. I've seen you on the news several times over the last few months." She stands up a little straighter, pushing out her small breasts. "You have a steady lady friend, Mr. Monroe? Or are you on the market?"

Nate is saved by Richie arriving. "At ease, Janine," says the lawyer. "I've told you before: no dipping your pen in the company ink."

One of the contractors who is up a ladder behind them snickers to himself, and Nate wonders if he's also been on the receiving end of Janine's advances. She reluctantly returns to sorting through a box of paperwork. A look around shows there's a lot of construction work going on, which is a shame because the dark oak wood that runs through the office—around the doors and on the floors—looks like it could be a hundred years old.

"Impressive, isn't it?" Richie appears. "This used to be the town's jail in the eighteen hundreds. When I learned that, I just had to have it!"

Richie is shorter than both Nate and Owen, and he looks just the same as last time they saw him in the summer: dressed in a cheap suit, with reading glasses perched on the end of his nose and a glint in his eye. He looks at Owen. "Well, well, well. If it isn't my favorite client." He pulls him in for a hug. "How's your mom? I saw on the news that she not only had her conviction overturned, but she got her job back too. I yelled *good for her* at my TV so loud I almost gave my cat a heart attack." He chuckles.

"She's fine, I guess," says Owen. "Always busy. I have a cat now too, Bandit. What's your cat's name?"

"Justice."

Owen laughs, then it's Nate's turn for an embrace. He'd forgotten Richie was a hugger. He winces at the pain in his ribs as the lawyer squeezes him. Last month he was clipped by a speeding car, and although his other injuries have healed nicely, his ribs are still sore.

When Richie pulls away, he keeps hold of Nate's arms. "I saw they got the asshole who killed your fiancée all those years ago. I'll be watching that trial with interest when the time comes. If you need any coaching on how to act on the witness stand, you call me. You understand?"

Nate tenses, not at the embrace, but at the thought of the murder trial. Testifying in court against the man who ruined his life is not something he's mentally prepared for yet. The stress of attending his own murder trial almost killed him. It certainly shortened the life of his father, the only person from his family who bothered to show up every day and offer the support he so badly needed. Nate only wishes his dad had been alive to see him freed from death row. It just adds to the bitterness he feels for the killer, someone he had placed his trust in as a young man.

Brody barks in anticipation of his hug.

"Well, hello, my favorite shepsky," says Richie, bending down and rubbing the dog all over. "I hope you've been a good boy?"

Brody pants with delight as he laps up the attention, and Nate is reminded of how much the dog has changed over the last six months. Being a former cadaver dog who lost his police officer handler in the line of duty, Brody was stand-offish when he and Madison first stumbled across him. He preferred his own company and didn't act much like a pet other than his love of chasing tennis balls and squirrels. Once Nate unofficially adopted him, Brody joined them on the road to Colorado and has been an invaluable partner ever since.

Richie looks up at Owen. "I'm glad to see you've stayed out of trouble since we last spoke, but even more glad to see you brought your friend along. I have propositions for the both of you."

Nate raises his eyebrows. "Sounds... interesting."

"Come, follow me." Richie leads them out of the reception area and into an office behind. The wall that separates the two rooms has been knocked down. "This is going to be a glass panel, so I can keep an eye on who's coming and going. And I know what you're thinking: he's committing a crime ruining this old building! But aside from the glass and some much-needed repair work, I don't plan on changing anything else."

With the glass yet to be added, there's no privacy from Janine or reprieve from the banging and drilling of the contractors.

Richie pulls two wooden chairs over to his large oak desk and dusts them off with a handkerchief. "Take a seat." He looks over Nate's shoulder and shouts to his receptionist, "Three coffees, Janine!"

She lets out a long sigh. "Do you want coffees or do you want that case file for the Miller trial? I can't do both at once."

"Coffees first. Thank you." He chuckles. "Janine's worked for me since the very beginning, so we fight like an old married couple."

Owen sits down. "No coffee for me, thanks. I can't stand it. Prefer soda."

Richie appears genuinely shocked. "You better get a taste for it if you're to become a lawyer, son. It's the only thing that'll motivate you to see a case through. Well, that and a love of other people's money."

Nate laughs. At least the man is honest. "How are you keeping, Richie? I heard your last office was firebombed."

Richie waves a dismissive hand. "Oh please, they did me a

favor. The insurance covered it, and now I get to try out life in little old Lost Creek."

"Do you know who did it?" asks Owen.

"Of course I do. And don't worry, they'll pay. One way or another."

"Aren't you worried they'll come and do the same thing here?" asks Nate.

"No. They're stupid, but not *that* stupid."

Janine enters and places two coffees and a Mountain Dew on the desk. She winks at Nate on her way out.

"So, Owen," says Richie, sitting up straight. "As you can see, the new office is a mess and my receptionist has no respect for me, so I need an intern to do all the boring tasks: filing, typing, fetching things from clients and the court, et cetera. I don't expect you to work for free, but you might be disappointed by the hourly rate. However, I can promise you a lot of work *and* life experience while you're here. Dealing with some of my clients will teach you lessons in patience that will stand you in good stead when you become a lawyer yourself. How does that sound?"

Owen looks at Nate like he wants his opinion. Nate's flattered, considering he's not the boy's father. "It's not like you've got anything better to do until you head off to college," he says.

Owen nods. "Sounds good to me. I can start right away, but I'll have to fit it around school."

"Excellent," says Richie.

"Morning, boss." A male voice behind them makes Nate turn. A guy dressed in a blue denim shirt and black jeans, under a thick winter coat, fills the doorway. He reminds Nate of a middle-aged Kevin Costner, and he wouldn't look out of place as a cowboy in one of those old Western movies. Nate's willing to bet Janine loves him.

"Frank!" exclaims Richie. "Perfect timing. Frank Brookes, meet Nate Monroe and Owen Harper. Owen's our new intern."

"Pleasure." Frank nods at them both and remains standing where he is.

Janine appears with a coffee for him. "Here you go, sweetie. Two sugars, just how you like it." She receives a wink in return and hovers next to him.

Richie turns to Nate. "Right before my office in Prospect Springs was destroyed, I was forced to hire Frank as an investigator. My last one died unexpectedly." He must notice the surprise on their faces as he adds quickly, "Not as a result of working for me! He had a heart attack while sleeping with his wife's younger sister."

Janine nods. "Turns out he was banging her like a screen door in a hurricane."

"That'll be all, Janine." Richie watches her leave, then says, "It's a long story. Anyway, Frank now manages anything I need up north in Prospect Springs and the surrounding areas, but you weren't interested in moving down here, were you, Frank?"

He shrugs. "Lost Creek is the back end of hell as far as I'm concerned."

Richie laughs. "What can I say, he's dramatic! Anyway, since I'm sure to generate new business down here, I need someone else to handle any investigating I need doing in Lost Creek. How are you fixed, Nate?"

Nate raises his eyebrows. "You want to hire me as an investigator?"

"I do. I'm aware you were awarded a substantial sum after your exoneration and don't actually need to work another day in your life, but I'm also aware that investigating is something you can't seem to resist. After all, you've helped Detective Harper out on numerous occasions. And I'm guessing that now she's back on the force with her own team around her, you've had to take a back seat. Am I right?"

Nate takes a sip of his coffee. It's only lukewarm. Richie's hit a nerve there. Nate might not need to work for the money, but he needs it for peace of mind. If he didn't work, he'd have nothing to do but relive the torture of his time on death row. The busier he keeps, the longer his demons stay at bay. It's also true that Madison doesn't need his help anymore, and he needs something new to focus on. "What kind of investigating would I be doing?"

"Oh, just this and that. Documenting crime scenes, obtaining medical or legal records, interviewing witnesses. All the fun stuff!"

That would all involve stepping on Madison's toes if he's needed to investigate one of her open cases. He can't imagine she would be happy about that if he's trying to get one of her suspects off the hook.

Richie adds, "I'm a good employer, wouldn't you say, Frank?"

Frank says yes at the same time as Janine shouts no from behind a stack of boxes. "He pays me on time," says Frank. "That's the main thing. And I'm easy to get along with as long as you pull your weight. I don't mind visiting town occasionally, but as far as I'm concerned, I'm based in Prospect Springs."

Owen turns to Nate. "I think you should do it."

Nate's not sure how he feels about working for an employer. He likes to be able to move around at a moment's notice. *Escape* at a moment's notice. On the other hand, he has a home here now. It's only leased, but he doesn't have any immediate plans to go anywhere else. He doesn't have anyone chasing him anymore, so it's probably time he relaxed. He decides to go for it. "Sure, why not? I'll give it a try."

Richie beams at him. "Fantastic! The law firm of Hope & Associates just expanded to five employees. I told you being firebombed was a good thing."

Nate can't help but laugh. Richie's optimism is infectious.

CHAPTER NINE

Still annoyed with her new partner, Madison enters Ruby's Diner. She needs a caffeine boost before heading over to the health clinic where David Moss and his young son are shortly due to meet with a child therapist. She wants to know whether the doctor can coax from Danny anything useful about what he witnessed in the mall's parking lot last night. He's only three years old, so she's not expecting miracles, but anything is worth a try.

The diner is loud this morning. You'd think people would be spending Christmas Eve at home with their families, but it seems half the town has decided to treat themselves to a trip out for brunch. Festive tunes play low on the speakers, which means the TV above the counter is muted. As usual, it's switched to the news. The locals love obsessing over crime, and who can blame them when Lost Creek has so much of it.

"Maddie!"

She cringes. She always hated that abbreviation of her name, and the only person who gets away with it is her dad, Bill Harper. She turns and looks for him. He's seated at the other end of the counter talking to Vince Rader, the diner's owner, and is looking smart but casual in his crisp white shirt, open at the throat, and ironed pants. His black leather boots are newly shined but wet from the snow and ice outside. She approaches him, and he hugs her. She's careful not to touch his upper arm, where he took a bullet last month. As far as she knows, it's healing well. He never mentions it, anyway.

"You okay, sweetheart?" he asks.

He still treats her like a child, which is surprisingly nice in some ways. Maybe it's because she had no family around her for years until her return to Lost Creek. "I'm good." She looks at Vince, who is taller and skinnier than both of them and sporting a buzz cut from his time in the US Navy. "How's Oliver?" she asks. "I bet he's excited for tomorrow." Ten-year-old Oliver Rader is Vince's grandson.

"He sure is. He's busy decorating the tree in my apartment for the fifth time." He rolls his eyes, but Madison knows how much he loves the boy. "Anyway, what can I get you? I imagine you have to rush off pretty quick, what with last night's homicide."

"Just coffee, thanks." She hands over her travel mug. Then she remembers it's going to be a long day and she didn't make herself any lunch. It's only mid morning right now, but she'll be hungry again soon. The cold weather always increases her appetite. "And a ham salad sandwich to go."

Vince pours her coffee before heading to the kitchen.

"I watched you on the news last night," says her father. "What happened?"

Madison keeps her voice low. "A woman was beaten to death in her car after doing some last-minute gift shopping."

"Is the guy who did it in custody?"

She shakes her head. "Not yet."

"Was she married? Have you checked out her husband and any potential lover or sleazy co-workers?"

Madison tilts her head. "You know I can't give you any details. And of course I'll be checking out the husband. But I've got to tell you, he was devastated."

Bill appears unconvinced. "Don't mistake a good actor for a grieving husband. Some of the worst monsters I've caught deserve an Oscar."

Madison notices that the old guy seated next to her dad is listening in, so she changes the subject. "How's your new place? Have you met the neighbors yet?"

Her father nods. "I like the apartment, but the complex is full of old people waiting to die."

"You're not exactly young yourself, you know," she says with a smile.

"I'm only sixty! There's plenty of life in the old dog yet. Anyway, the guy in the apartment next door keeps inviting me to play bridge, so I try to avoid him. You know, tiptoe past his door. Luckily, he's mostly deaf."

Her father has only recently come back into her life. He divorced her mom when Madison was only fourteen. She's thirty-seven now, and it feels nice to have him around again. It was an amicable divorce, even though he'd left her mom for another woman and disappeared to Alaska to work for the FBI. He had been a detective at Lost Creek PD before that. Now that he's retired, he's decided to return home without the second wife. He never mentions the woman, so Madison has to assume they also divorced. He says he wants to be near his family again, which comprises Madison and Owen, and Madison's sister, Angie. But he'd have to schedule a prison visitation if he wants to reunite with Angie, and so far she's declined to see him.

"Vince has been quizzing me about my old cases," says Bill. "People just love hearing all the gory details about serial killers."

Madison's been meaning to ask him about his time in the FBI too, but it's difficult to catch him when Owen's not around. She doesn't want her son exposed to all that. He's already had a rough childhood, and if she can keep him from hearing the kinds of sordid details her dad knows about, then she will.

"Did I tell you I'm planning to write a book about my time at the FBI?" he adds.

With raised eyebrows she says, "Surely you can't talk about your investigations? Would the Bureau even allow you to publish it?"

"Oh please." He gives a derisive snort. "I don't see how they could stop me telling my life story. I own everything that happened to me." He smiles. "It'll be about my experiences as a special agent and the work that goes into hunting sadistic killers."

Vince listens in as he serves another customer. He approaches them with a wide smile. "Your dad's going to come on the podcast and read out excerpts when he's finished writing it."

Madison groans. Vince runs the *Crime and Dine* podcast —*get your crime while you dine!*—from his apartment upstairs. He started it as a way of coping with the disappearance of his wife, Ruby, six years ago. Madison hoped he might lay it to rest now he has the answers about what happened to Ruby—a case Madison and Nate got dragged into last month—but her dad is probably encouraging him to keep it going. She'll need to keep an eye on this pair. If they team up to become armchair sleuths, they could unintentionally get the public all riled up with misinformation about a case she's working on. "Do you really think that's a good idea, Dad? What about the victims' families? Will they want all the gory details of what happened to their loved ones out there for public consumption?"

"You worry too much, Maddie. I'm not a complete moron; I'd be sensitive about it." His face clouds over. "I carry their pain in my heart every day. What some of those families went through doesn't bear thinking about."

Vince nods thoughtfully.

"I'd never want to cause them extra suffering. But the fact

is that some cases were never solved, and if getting the details of those cases out to the public can assist with that, then I'd be helping them even in my retirement."

Madison realizes that writing a book would be her father's way of making sense of the horrors he experienced during his career. He would have attended countless bloody crime scenes, spoken to hundreds, if not thousands, of grieving loved ones. And she's willing to bet he never sought therapy for dealing with any of it. Maybe writing a book would be cathartic for him. Or maybe he'll give up halfway through. Either way, it's his decision.

He appears to reconsider. "Maybe I'll take up a different hobby." He looks up at Vince. "Do you play bridge?"

"Are you kidding me?" says Vince, handing over Madison's sandwich. "I'm not *that* old. Besides, I've got this place to take care of."

"Do you ever think about selling the diner now that you know Ruby's not coming home?" she asks gently.

He lowers his eyes and wipes the counter. "Sure. It's a lot of work. And as I've told you before, I kept it open in the hope she'd walk back through that door one day." He swallows. The grief is still evident. "But what's the alternative: playing bridge in my slippers with the likes of him?" He nods to Bill.

Bill winks. "Maybe we need some lady friends to help guide us into old age."

Madison rolls her eyes with mock exasperation. "I can't listen to this. I'm out of here." She hears them laughing as she exits the diner.

CHAPTER TEN
OCTOBER 1994

Detective Bill Harper slowly and cautiously approaches the small family home, which sits in darkness. The sleet that threatened snow has turned to rain, and his hands betray him by trembling slightly as they grip his Glock in front of him, aiming through the open front door. He's been a detective at LCPD for five years now, but you never get used to entering someone's home uninvited, oblivious to what lies in wait. Sometimes the patrol guys get there first and secure the scene, but in this instance, Bill is the first to respond. He's warned anyone inside to make themselves known, but his demand has gone unanswered.

The only sound from inside the house is a child's wailing. The neighbor called 911 after returning home from a long shift at the gas station. She could hear the boy crying non-stop through the wall that separates the two residences. It quickly drove her crazy, but when she knocked on the door, she got no answer. She waited almost an hour before calling the police, telling dispatch that it was unusual for the child to cry this long, as Michelle—his mother—was normally attentive. There's no father in the picture, and the neighbor couldn't see inside as there were no lights on downstairs and it was past eight on a wintry night. She said the situation left her feeling "creeped out."

Bill knows how she feels. A burning smell reaches him. Like something's been left in the oven too long. He rounds the corner into the small kitchen, the first room off the narrow hallway, and reaches for the light switch. Once his eyes adjust to the brightness, he finds the room empty, but the oven is humming as it burns the food inside. He'll need to switch it off, but not yet. The child's whimpers are louder now, and they're coming from upstairs. Bill peers up the staircase for movement, but it's too dark to see anything, so he advances cautiously, stopping regularly to listen for sounds other than the creaking of the stairs under his weight.

At the first doorway he comes to upstairs, he reaches for the light and is confronted by a carpet covered in blood. It's everywhere. All over the closet, the walls and the small child sitting on the floor next to the bed. The boy, who looks to be around three or four years old, has spatter on his face and hands. His shorts are soaked with blood.

"Jesus," says Bill. The strong coppery aroma floods his nostrils.

What strikes him next is that there's no body. The bloodstains on the carpet suggest it was dragged out of here, but it's too dark to tell where it ended up, and switching on all the lights would give away his position to the perp. He looks at the little boy. From this angle he appears to be unharmed, but some of the blood could be his for all Bill knows. He has a split second to decide whether to take the boy out of here and wait for backup to arrive, or to search the rest of the property for the body and the assailant.

The child's face is bright red with emotion. Big fat tears leak from his eyes and Bill knows he's suffered long enough. He tries to approach the child without disrupting the crime scene too badly. Tiptoeing through the blood, he picks the boy up with one arm, gun still poised in his other hand, and lets him scream into his ear as he carries him to safety. Once outside, after checking the assailant isn't hiding in the shadows, he finds some plastic evidence bags in his trunk and places them on his lap as he sits in the back seat of his car. He rests the boy on top of them, careful to preserve any evidence from the child's clothes and to minimize cross-contamination from his own.

Sirens wail in the distance as drapes and blinds twitch all over the street. They're being watched. "It's okay, little guy. You're safe with me," he says soothingly. "We'll get you a ride in a shiny big police car as soon as possible."

The boy's cries are dwindling as he runs out of energy. Who knows how long he's been screaming? Both of them are trembling from a mixture of shock, fear and the cold night. The weight of him against his chest reminds Bill of when his daughters were little. Angie, his oldest, hated being hugged, but Madison would sit on his lap for hours, falling asleep against his chest as he told her stories of bad guys getting caught by the good guys. If he ever tried alternating the ending over the years, with the bad guys getting away, she'd cry. He was trying to prepare her for reality, but she was having none of it.

She's twelve now and doesn't want to hear his stories anymore. That time has passed. He wonders if she'll look back on her childhood as fondly as he does. That remains to be seen. What he does know is that tonight, thanks to a homicidal maniac, the little boy on his lap has been denied any fond childhood memories of his own.

CHAPTER ELEVEN

Madison spots David Moss sitting in the waiting room at the health clinic. There is only one other person there, a teenage girl who isn't paying them any attention. David is busy messaging someone on his phone, but looks up as Madison approaches him. "Hi," she says. "How are you?"

He rubs the back of his neck and shrugs. "Not great. Scotty knows something's wrong. He won't stop asking for his mom. And Danny is much quieter than usual. He's done everything I've asked so far this morning, which for a three-year-old is highly unusual."

Madison feels for him. It's clear he had a sleepless night, as his skin is greasy and pale, with heavy bags under his eyes. He slips his phone away before standing to remove his thick winter coat. He's only wearing a T-shirt underneath, so she can see his arms and neck clearly. There are no visible scratch marks or bruises. She glances at his coat for any damage or bloodstains. Nothing. He notices her looking, so she says, "Who's taking care of Scotty?"

"My parents. They think bringing Danny here was a good idea, but to tell you the truth, I have my doubts."

"Trust me, it's good for him to see Dr. Chalmers," she says.

"He might be able to provide some comfort. It might benefit Scotty at some point too."

David scoffs. "They only person who could provide comfort to my children right now is Sarah." His eyes well up. "Her dad is identifying her body this morning. I couldn't bring myself to see her like that, so when he volunteered..."

"Of course. I understand."

"Have you caught the guy yet?"

She shakes her head. It's only been around sixteen hours since Sarah's body was discovered, but Madison's not surprised he wants the perpetrator caught already. "Not yet, but I'm working on it. We have surveillance footage to check and possible witnesses to question. Have you thought any more about who might have wanted to hurt her?"

He nods. "I don't have a single suspect for you. I'm not saying she was perfect and never argued with anyone, but we surround ourselves with good people, Detective. People like us with young kids. I don't believe any of our friends or co-workers would be capable of this."

"Did Sarah work?"

"She was an office manager, and because I work full-time too, her mom would babysit Danny during the day." He hesitates, before adding, "I don't even want to know the answer to this, but the press are speculating so it's driving me crazy. Was my wife raped before she was murdered?"

Madison is glad to be able to put his mind at ease on that one. "No. I've just come from the medical examiner's office, and she confirmed there was no evidence of sexual assault."

He lets out a long sigh of relief.

The door behind them opens and Dr. Phil Chalmers appears. Madison has spoken to him before. He was Nikki Jackson's therapist at the time of her murder at Fantasy World amusement park on Independence Day. Madison introduces him to David and the doctor invites them both into his office.

Danny is sitting at a child's table, leafing through a colorful picture book. He glances up at them, and then looks behind them as if waiting to see if anyone else will enter. "Momma?" he asks.

The hopeful expression on his face is gut-wrenching. Madison has to look away. David crouches next to his son. "Hey, buddy. What have you got there?"

Dr. Chalmers speaks to Madison in a low voice, so Danny can't hear. "He hasn't said anything about what happened to his mother. He's focused on Christmas instead and told me what he asked Santa to bring him. Like most kids his age, his favorite word appears to be 'toy.'"

David joins them. He and Madison sit on the leather couch while Dr. Chalmers sits opposite them. Danny goes back to leafing through his book. "Will he remember what happened for the rest of his life?" asks David, his expression intense. "Will it negatively affect him?"

Dr. Chalmers leans back in his seat. "I wish I could put your mind at ease, but I'm sorry, there's no way of knowing. He could have nightmares about it, or flashbacks when he thinks about his mother. I would suggest he comes to see me regularly for the next month at least, in order for me to assess his recovery. Do we know if he was actually awake during the crime?"

Madison shakes her head. "We don't know anything yet. It's possible he was placed in the car afterward and didn't see the attack occur, but that would've slowed the killer down, so I'd be surprised if that were the case."

David's face fills with hope. "So there's a chance Danny was still in his stroller while Sarah was attacked and didn't actually see it happen?"

It sounds far-fetched, but it's not impossible. They'll know more once they've checked Danny's clothes for DNA. If the killer touched him, and he wasn't wearing gloves, they should find something. If there's no DNA on his clothes other than his mother's blood, then it's likely he was already in his car seat before the attack. "It's possible. We need time to examine the evidence."

Dr. Chalmers says, "I recommend you keep your sons' routine as close to normal as possible. Don't cancel Christmas. I know how difficult it will be for you and your wife's family, but children are resilient, and the more you can keep a smile on your face, and leave the room whenever you need to compose yourself, the fewer negative memories they'll associate with their mom's death as they get older."

David's eyes are brimming with tears. "How do I even break it to them that she's gone?"

Madison lowers her eyes.

"Danny's three and Scotty's six, is that right?" asks the doctor.

He nods.

"Toddlers aren't mature enough developmentally to understand the concept of death, but Danny will still understand that one of his favorite people is missing. They'll both ask about her repeatedly, no doubt. What I would recommend is not ignoring their questions, and explaining in the simplest way possible that Mommy died but she loved them very much. They'll need reassurance that although their lives have changed, they're still going to be well cared for. You need to comfort them when they cry, listen to their questions and be a good substitute for their mom."

David weeps quietly.

Dr. Chalmers reaches out and pats his shoulder. "I can't pretend it's going to be easy for you, so call upon family and friends to help. If the boys have grandparents, use them. Keep them in their lives. I'm sure they will draw comfort from the children too. But most importantly, seek therapy for your own shock and grief, because you need to be well in order to raise happy, healthy children." He sits back. "You're at the start of a long and painful journey, David, but the light at the end of the tunnel will appear sooner than you think. You have your boys to get you through this, and I saw on the news how much good-will there is for you in the community."

Madison has seen the same reports. The media have been harassing friends and neighbors of the couple for quotes, and everyone has said the same thing: that Sarah and David were a well-liked couple who would help anyone in need. She hasn't heard any salacious rumors about David, which is a good sign. It doesn't mean they won't start if she doesn't find Sarah's killer soon, because it's normal to suspect the husband in a case like this. But her gut tells her that he wasn't involved, because his wife's death has clearly had a huge emotional impact on him. She just hopes her instinct is right.

Seeing his father cry makes Danny gets out of his seat and slip into David's lap. He sucks his thumb, and with his spare hand reaches for the tears running down David's face.

Madison has to swallow the lump in her throat.

CHAPTER TWELVE

It's early afternoon by the time Madison returns to the station. The heavy clouds overhead threaten more snow, with small random flakes darting to the ground in the brisk wind. A storm has been forecast for this evening, with up to ten inches of snowfall predicted. That will keep the patrol guys busy with traffic chaos. Lost Creek's roads have already been noticeably busier than usual lately, with out-of-towners visiting their loved ones and kids home from college for the holiday season.

The station is reassuringly warm as Madison makes her way to the offices behind the front desk. She throws the wrapper from her diner takeout sandwich into the trash. She ate it while driving, knowing that might be the last opportunity she gets to eat for the rest of her working day. She's never been one of those people who can skip meals and still function. She needs hearty food and at least six hours' sleep in order to get through the long days she works.

Approaching the dispatchers' cubicle, she says, "Hey, Stella. Got anything for me?"

There's a small musical Christmas tree slowly spinning on Stella's desk. She lowers her headset. "Nothing to do with your homicide, no, but it's busy. The phones haven't stopped ringing. I've had seven callers threatening suicide already, and the domestics are starting to ramp up." She shakes her head. "I hate the holidays."

Madison sympathizes. "It'll be worse tomorrow." Once the drinks start flowing and everyone receives their visitors—people they normally steer clear of the rest of the year—all the old family disputes will start up and it won't be long before the fighting begins. Madison's memories of being a patrol officer come back to her. Almost every house she attended on Christmas Day had children crying and at least one inebriated adult ruining things for everyone. Festive all-day drinking sends people crazy to the point where they want to kill either themselves or their family members. Then there's the drunk drivers who scream at you for pulling them over. "You're ruining my Christmas!" they yell. Better she ruin theirs by getting them off the roads than deliver a death notification to their victim's family.

"That's Dina's problem," says Stella. "She's working tomorrow. I'm going to be at home with the dog, watching Bing Crosby and stuffing my face."

Madison studies her closely. "You don't have any visitors coming?"

Stella shakes her head. "No. None of my kids invited me for dinner this year. Guess they're busy living their lives." Stella used to foster children when she was younger, but they all moved on and rarely visit her these days. "Although I did receive some beautiful Christmas cards."

Madison feels sorry for her. "You're welcome to come to my place tomorrow night. I'll be working all day, but I have a dinner planned. Nate and Owen will be there, and you can meet my dad at last." This will be Madison's first Christmas with her dad in twenty-four years, and the first Christmas with her son in eight years. She only wishes she could spend all day at home as planned, but this murder case means that's now impossible.

Stella's face lights up for a second, but then she shakes her head. "No, don't you worry about me. I like peace and quiet."

Sergeant Tanner approaches them. "Hey, Madison. Want to hold a briefing? Some of the officers are hanging around and I can fetch Alex."

"Sure."

Steve grabs the coffee on his desk before leaving to find Alex, whose office is located on the other side of the building. Madison turns back to Stella, but she already has her headset in place again, about to take a call. Chief Mendes is also busy on the phone, so Madison enters the briefing room without her. Officers Shelley Vickers and Gloria Williams are chatting inside, but Detective Adams isn't here. Their earlier argument is playing on her mind. She always thought that if she could work with the late Don Douglas, she could work with anyone, but now she's met Marcus Adams, she's not so sure. She checks her cell phone before realizing they didn't swap numbers so he has no way of contacting her. "Anyone know where the new guy is?" she asks the room.

Shelley nods behind her. "Here he comes."

Adams is removing his wet jacket, but he doesn't appear to know where to put it. Madison goes out and shows him to his desk. It's the one opposite hers, where Douglas used to sit. Nodding to the computer, she says, "I've emailed you a list of important names and numbers so you have them ready when you eventually need them. Places like the morgue, child services, the crime lab... Put them in your cell phone. It'll save you looking them up." She pulls her own phone out of her pocket and hands it to him. "Here. Put your number in mine. We need to be able to keep in touch."

Adams looks like he wants to say something sarcastic, but instead he swaps phones. He has a photograph of two newborn babies as his background, and his screen is full of all the popular social media apps, almost all of them showing red notifications. She wonders how he finds the time to use them. She's never been interested in social media. She's seen what a highly effective tool it can be for criminals, especially sexual predators. And the people in charge of the sites aren't interested in helping victims, if her last couple of investigations are anything to go by.

When she's added her number, she hands the phone back to Adams, takes hers from him, and leads him into the briefing room behind Steve and Alex. She walks to the front and turns to face everyone. "Okay, so here's where we're at so far: Lena's confident that Sarah Moss wasn't sexually assaulted, and her cause of death was a combination of blood loss and blunt cranial trauma." To Alex she says, "You've sent some evidence to the crime lab, is that right?"

Alex nods. "That's correct, Detective. The victim's clothes, the child's clothes and swabs from his car seat, some trace evidence, and the scrapings I took from under the victim's fingernails. Although I must warn you, the nails were cut extremely short so I had little soft tissue to work with. I'm not expecting what I did get to yield any useful results."

"Could you tell whether the killer deliberately cut them after the attack?" she asks. Criminals are wise to how forensics works these days.

"It's a possibility," he admits. "I found the victim's two missing fingernails on the floor of the car, so I've sent them off too. The results should come back in a couple of days, but Christmas may delay things. The crime lab is always busy, without the holidays adding pressure."

"Aren't we all." She pulls out her small notebook and pen and writes a reminder to ask David Moss whether his wife favored short nails. "Do you have a theory on what the murder weapon was? I know Lena thought it could be a hand tool of some kind."

He takes a deep breath. "Yes, we both believe it was some kind of blunt instrument, but that doesn't really narrow it down, because that could be a baseball bat, a heavy flashlight, a wrench and so on. However, given where our victim was found—in the front seat of her car—and assuming it was an average-sized male who attacked her, he wouldn't have had much room to swing the object in order to create enough force to cause the damage he did. My best guess at this stage is that he used a short-handled tool. I'll try recreating the scene with several potential murder weapons and get back to you."

He looks excited at the prospect and Madison wonders how many forensic technicians are tempted into a life of crime, knowing full well they have the knowledge needed to cover their tracks. "What if it was a woman?" she asks.

He raises his eyebrows. "It's a possibility, of course, although we know most crimes of this nature are perpetrated by males."

She looks at Shelley. "Have any possible murder weapons been found near the scene?"

Shelley glances at Gloria for confirmation before answering. "No. We've searched a wide radius from the parking lot, but there was nothing found that fits that description."

Madison bites her lip as she thinks of the next steps to take.

Detective Adams clears his throat. "I've spoken to some of the mall employees who were working yesterday afternoon and evening." He looks at everyone in turn as he talks. "A female employee from the ice cream parlor was taking a cigarette break outside the building when she thought she heard a muffled scream. She looked up from her cell phone, but it had all gone quiet. When she returned her attention to her phone, she thought she saw something in her peripheral vision: a dark figure darting across the parking lot."

"I can't believe only one person heard our victim scream," says Steve.

Shelley speaks up. "The stores are playing Christmas music, and Sarah Moss was parked at the far end of the lot. Our best witness to screams would be anyone driving by or returning to their car, but they might be too afraid to come forward."

Alex says, "It's possible she was silenced with the first blow to her head and therefore didn't get much opportunity to scream for help."

Madison thinks about the bruises on Sarah Moss's legs. They prove she was conscious long enough to fight for her life. "What time did the witness hear the scream and see the figure?"

Adams meets her gaze. "She thinks it was just after seven p.m., as that's usually when she takes her final break."

That would fit with Lena's suspected time of death—between 6.30 and 7.30 p.m. "And when she says she saw a dark figure, does she mean the person was dressed in black?"

He shakes his head. "She couldn't elaborate. It was too dark out and the snow was falling at that point. She could only say it was like a shadow figure and it moved fast."

"Have you checked the CCTV footage yet?" she asks.

He crosses his arms defensively. "No. I've been interviewing witnesses like you told me to."

Madison realizes she's bruised this guy's fragile ego. She's going to have to treat him with kid gloves until he settles in and drops his wall. "Watch the footage next. That's our best chance of catching this guy." Then she adds, "It's good that you managed to confirm a time for the attack. It matches what Lena suspected."

He nods. "I also have a name for the woman in the red Nissan. You know, the one who was seen driving away from the parking lot just before the victim was discovered. One of the employees at the discount store told me who she was."

"Great. What's her name?"

"Tracy Jones. Works at the hair salon on Delta Lane, but I don't have a phone number for her."

She writes it down. "That's okay, I can get it."

"I was going to call her next," he says.

Madison is aware that everyone is watching to see how she gets along with the new guy. "I'd like to speak to her myself, so I'll pay her a visit. You should concentrate on studying the CCTV." Before he can say anything else, she turns back to Alex. "Did you find anything on Sarah Moss's cell phone?"

Alex removes his glasses to wipe the lenses clean on his sweater. "I've been through all her messaging apps, her emails and her photographs. She wasn't a big user of social media and only had the Twitter app on her phone. No Instagram or Facebook. There's nothing of any concern. Nothing that would suggest she was having an affair or was in a disagreement with anyone. Well, apart from with her husband. Some of their messages were a little... heated."

Madison's heart sinks. David Moss was honest about Sarah wanting a divorce, but escalating arguments between them could be a sign he was feeling desperate. "What was the tone of the messages?"

"I would say the simmering tension was evident. She accuses him of working too much, leaving all the housework and childcare to her, and so on. He retaliates by accusing her of losing interest in him and not caring whether he comes home or not. There's one message from earlier this week where he asks her if she's seeing someone else."

"Does he name anyone?" If she had a love interest, it could be worth questioning them.

"No, and she denies it."

Madison takes a deep breath. "Any outright threats between the pair?"

"Not that I've found."

Madison nods as she thinks. "From what you've seen, does your gut tell you her husband might have wanted to harm her?"

Alex considers it before answering. "They were obviously experiencing marriage problems, but nothing that would cause me concern, or that could look incriminating in court."

Madison's not so sure about that. She knows from experience that a prosecutor can make anything look incriminating if they're hell-bent on getting a conviction.

"We've spoken to the victim's neighbors and co-workers," says Gloria, LCPD's longest-serving officer. "And what's unusual is that no one has pointed the finger at anyone. I mean, usually everyone blames the husband, right?"

It's true. "Despite their heated exchanges," says Madison, "I don't think David Moss was involved. He doesn't have any obvious injuries on his hands, arms or neck, and he appears genuinely cut up about losing his wife. But I can't rule him out completely, as he was home alone with the older son last night. I can't confirm that he never left the property."

"Have you asked the son whether his dad took him out?" asks Adams.

"Of course. Scotty said they were home all day after going out for breakfast that morning, but he's only six years old." She crosses her arms. "I think it's worth keeping an open mind about whether this murder could've been a random attack and Sarah Moss was just unlucky enough to be in the wrong place at the wrong time. Steve, would you update Chief Mendes when she's free?"

"Sure thing."

"Thanks." She steps forward. "Keep me posted, everyone."

The room empties except for Madison and Shelley. They watch Detective Adams walk to his new desk and switch his computer on. Chief Mendes would have provided him with passwords and an email address when he arrived this morning, along with his service weapon and detective shield. He pulls out a flash drive from his pants pocket and slides it into the tower. That must be the CCTV footage from the stores.

"What do you think of him?" asks Shelley.

"Well, he's been an asshole so far. I'm hoping it's just first-day nerves." Madison turns to her friend. "What's going on between you and Jake Rubio? I saw you both at the crime scene last night and it looked like you'd had an argument."

Shelley rolls her eyes. "The guy's a dick. Once a jock, always a jock, right?"

Madison wouldn't know; she's never dated one. But she does know Jake is notorious for being a player and has bedded half the town. He's only twenty-nine and it's not like he has a wife and kid at home, but it is time he grew up. He has a responsible job as an EMT, which she knows he takes seriously, but he also spends a lot of time in the bars downtown. "What did he do to piss you off? And what happened to you and Alex? I thought you two had gone on a couple of dates."

They both watch as Alex talks to Detective Adams. The forensic technician has a slim build and is around the same height as Shelley: five-seven. He couldn't be more different physically to tall, athletic Jake Rubio if he tried. "Alex is cute and all, and he's really sweet," says Shelley. "But I think that's the problem. He's too sweet. And reserved. He'll talk for hours instead of just kissing me, you know? I'm thirty-one already! I need someone to move quicker than that."

Madison laughs. "So you finally went out with Jake instead?" Shelley's had a crush on him for years, but had resisted his advances because of his reputation.

Shelley nods and her cheeks redden. "He took me to the drive-in movie theater, but all he wanted to do was get in my pants. It was like being back in high school." She looks exasperated as she says, "Seriously, Madison, what is wrong with guys? They either move too slow or too fast!"

"What did you do?"

"I left the car and took a cab home. He called me frigid as I walked away and then bombarded me with texts later on telling me he was sorry and he wanted to make it up to me."

It's Madison's turn to roll her eyes now. "What an asshole."

"I know, right? He can forget it. He had his chance and he blew it. I'm done with dating."

Shelley leads them out of the briefing room and Madison notices Alex glance over at her. "I better go," says Madison. "I want to pay Tracy Jones a visit. Hopefully she saw something in the parking lot last night."

"Okay, catch you later."

She leaves the station, zips up her jacket and heads to her car.

CHAPTER THIRTEEN

The small hair salon on Delta Lane looks the same as it did last time Madison visited two months ago, when she had to search one of the apartments above it for a missing waitress. It sits next to a tattoo parlor and a drugstore. As she gets out of her car, the icy cold slices through her. The snow is beginning to fall harder now, with a bitter wind forcing it into her eyes. Her shoulder-length blonde hair blows all over the place. She quickly pulls her gloves on and heads to the salon's entrance. One of the theories she's considering is whether a female could have killed Sarah Moss. Mainly because little Danny was left unharmed, but also because of what Alex said about the limited space available in the car to swing a weapon. A petite person would have more room.

It's noisy inside the salon. The customers are trying their hardest to hold conversations with their stylists over the sound of hairdryers. Madison doesn't spot Joely, the best friend of the waitress who went missing. Instead, a slim woman who looks to be in her fifties, with narrow shoulders and long dyed red hair, perfectly styled, greets her at the small reception area. "Hi. How are you?"

Madison has to speak up to be heard over the noise. "Hi. I'm Detective Harper. I'm looking for Tracy Jones."

The woman's smile falters. "I'm Tracy. What's happened?"

Madison smiles reassuringly. "I'm just here to ask some questions about the homicide that occurred last night. I understand you were shopping at the mall just before the victim was found."

The relief on Tracy's face is evident. "Holy crap, don't do that to me!" She laughs nervously. "I thought my husband had dropped dead at work or something."

Madison studies her face for signs of deception. Perhaps she was nervous for another reason. "Do you have a minute to answer some questions?"

The woman looks around to see if any customers are paying attention. Of course they are. Madison can see their eyes in the mirrors. They're all fixed on her. That's the problem with appearing on the news regularly; those who pay attention know you're a cop as soon as they see you. "Let's go to my office," says Tracy.

Madison follows her to a tiny room at the rear of the salon. The word *Manager* is stenciled on the door in flowery writing. Once they're seated, she asks, "Do you own the salon?"

"Sure do," Tracy says proudly. "For the last five years. Business is always steady and my customers are loyal. Can't ask for anything else."

Seeing as she's overdue a haircut, Madison says, "Maybe I should schedule an appointment soon."

Tracy assesses her messy hair. "That wouldn't be a bad idea. I think you'd look better as a brunette."

This kind of brutal honesty is why Madison doesn't visit hair salons very often. She pulls out her pocket notebook. "Did you know the victim: Sarah Moss?"

Tracy shakes her head. "I saw a picture of her on the news this morning. She definitely wasn't a client of mine or any of my stylists. It's all anyone can talk about in here. I've never met her or her husband, but Barbara has, that's one of my older clients. She said David Moss was very polite and held the door open for her one time. Barbara uses a wheelchair and most people can't be bothered to wait while she maneuvers through doors. How's he holding up? I bet he's devastated."

Madison thinks of how overwhelmed David was at the clinic earlier. He didn't have a clue how to break the news to his young sons. "He is. Which is why I need to find whoever killed his wife."

"How did you know I was at the mall last night?"

"We have a witness who saw your car leave the parking lot, and an employee of the discount store identified you."

Tracy nods. "Darlene, I'll bet. I had a few last-minute bits and pieces to buy—decorations and a couple of gifts. Oh, and chestnuts. I headed there sometime after six, once I'd finished up here. I can't have been there much more than an hour. I wanted to get home before I got snowed in."

Madison makes a note of the timings. "Did you see anyone hanging around the parking lot while you were there, or maybe as you were leaving? Or anyone in the far corner looking like they were getting into a black Lexus?"

Tracy is silent for a minute, frowning. "I can't say I was paying attention. It was bitterly cold and dark, I remember that, so I didn't hang around. The parking lot was busy when I arrived and I saw a couple of families come and go. But it was much quieter when I left, as it was near closing time. I can't say anything stood out as I drove away. Sorry."

That's disappointing. "Did you hear any screams while you were in the parking lot?"

"No. Nothing that made me stop and think someone was being hurt." She shakes her head. "You know, I've been wondering whether, if I'd arrived five minutes later or left the mall a little earlier, it could've been *me* who was killed rather than that woman with her poor child in the back of her car. He's going to be scarred for life."

As Tracy arrived at the mall before the murder and left afterward, she missed the whole thing. Madison takes a deep breath. At least she can eliminate Tracy as a witness. And as no one else has come forward with any information yet, she can only hope that Adams catches something on the surveillance footage. She stands. "Thanks for answering my questions. If you overhear anyone in the salon talking about seeing something useful, let me know."

Tracy takes the card she's offering. "Will do, Detective. Don't wait too long to schedule your haircut. I get busy."

Madison smiles. As she leaves the salon, her cell phone buzzes. It's Owen.

Don't forget I'll be at Grandpa's for dinner.

She loves how her father is trying to bond with his grandson. They only met for the first time last month and Owen has a lot of questions about law enforcement for him. She just has to hope her dad doesn't go into graphic detail about his time spent hunting serial killers. She types a quick response.

Have fun. I'll be at Nate's for dinner.

He replies with a thumbs-up. She slips her phone away and hurries to her car. She tries to start the engine, but nothing happens. "Dammit." It's time to trade this in for a better version, but that's not something she can afford right now. After several more attempts, it finally sputters into life and she heads back to the station.

In the police station's small communal kitchen, which is always messy with coffee-stained counters and unwashed dishes in the sink, Madison pours two hot coffees and grabs a large handful of chocolate candies from the sharing tub on the counter, one of the many treats brought in by Chief Mendes designed to keep everyone's energy and morale up over the coming days. Some staff see it as a cynical ploy, but Madison's always happy to accept sugary bribes.

She finds Detective Adams at his desk, still speeding through hours of surveillance footage. When she places a steaming cup of coffee and some candies in front of him, he looks up in surprise and mumbles a thank you.

"Pause that for a second." She doesn't want him missing anything. She pulls her chair over to sit next to him, unwraps a chocolate candy and pops it in her mouth. "Found anything?"

He sips the coffee and ignores the candy. Maybe he's a health nut. "This is the outside shot from the mall. Unfortunately, it's dark and the security camera has a low frame rate, which means it only captures a certain number of shots per second; it's not recording continuously. It makes the footage appear jumpy and it might miss crucial actions as they occurred." He turns to her. "I once worked a sexual assault case where the perp was caught on camera fleeing the area. He actually looked directly into the camera, but because it had a low frame rate, it captured the frame before and the frame after he looked, not the clear view of his face. It was infuriating and really bad timing on the camera's part." He shakes his head. "Asshole's still out there somewhere."

She suspects that will bother him for years to come. Looking at the screen, she has difficulty making anything out because of how dark it is, despite the few random street lights present. Plus, the snowflakes that fall nearest the camera appear huge, obscuring some of the activity.

"Don't get me wrong," says Adams. "Having this footage is still much better than none at all, but any fast movement probably won't be captured well. So far there have been several shoppers leaving the mall, but no lone dark figure who fits the ice cream parlor employee's statement. I'm up to six fifty p.m. If we're right about the time of the attack being around seven, we should see someone soon."

Madison hits play and they watch the screen. She can hear

Stella from here, fielding calls. There will be no reprieve for the dispatchers today, and anyone would think Stella was a social worker from the advice and numbers she's giving out. The suicide prevention hotlines, the hospital, and even the local churches feature heavily around this time of year. Madison tries to focus on Adams's computer screen, where a few juddery figures walk back and forth between the mall and the parked cars. Then a woman pushing a stroller appears from under the camera, where the mall's main exit is located. "That must be Sarah Moss with Danny."

They both watch as she walks across the lot and off screen. It's an eerie feeling knowing that the woman in this footage has no idea what's about to happen to her. Her time on screen is over in seconds, revealing nothing about what happened, and no one appears to follow her out of the mall. "Where's her car?" asks Madison.

Adams leans in and points off screen. "That would be over here, but the camera doesn't cover it. There are no other cameras in that corner, I checked with the mall's security guy."

"Typical." She sighs. "We just can't catch a break with this case."

"It's been less than twenty-four hours. Something will turn up."

As he's being cordial, Madison decides to ask him about his home life. "What does your wife do for a living?"

He turns to look at her, but she keeps her eyes on the screen as a new car has entered the lot. "She's a writer, a really good one, actually. So as you can imagine, we're always broke."

She snorts. Looks like he does have a sense of humor after all. "If you're broke, how come you can afford a Chevy Camaro?"

He shrugs. "You can always find money for what you really want."

If only that were true. "Was your wife okay with moving down here for your new job?"

"Not exactly." He leans back in his seat. "But she works from home and the kids will make new friends, so it's not the end of the world."

"Those newborns I saw on your phone are yours, I take it?"

"Yeah, but they're eight years old now. Twins."

"How do they fit in the back of your Camaro? I mean, the rear seats are so cramped, it's not exactly designed for kids."

He smiles. "My wife has a minivan." He glances at his screen and appears to relax for the first time since they met. "The girls are hard work most of the time, but I've got to admit I'm looking forward to getting home later so we can put out treats for Santa. Everyone keeps telling me that these years don't come back again, so I'm trying to make the most of them."

Madison knows how fast time flies when you have young kids. She'd give anything to experience one more Christmas with Owen as a child. Spending so many years in prison without him was unbearable. "You're Santa, I take it?" she asks with a smile.

"Of course. You have a teenage son, right?"

She tenses slightly. "You did do your homework."

"Not really." He reddens. "These days all it takes is a quick search online and you can learn anyone's life story in minutes. So was he an IVF baby? Ours were."

"What makes you think that?"

He shifts in his seat, looking a little uncomfortable. "I read that your ex was a woman. I just assumed you had to use IVF to have a baby." He stops himself from digging a bigger hole by holding up his hands and adding, "Sorry. None of my business."

Madison didn't use IVF and Owen wasn't planned, but he was conceived the regular way. Not that you can call sexual assault in any way regular. "I think that's enough of getting to know each other. Look." She nods to the screen, where the time in the bottom left corner reads 18:58. A woman appears.

She's wearing an apron over her clothes. She lights up a cigarette outside the mall just left of the camera's scope, and it's not long before the blue light of her cell phone screen appears.

"That's the ice cream parlor employee," says Adams. Just a minute later, a dark flash crosses the lot. "That's our guy," he says excitedly. "It has to be." He pauses the footage and then rewinds it frame by frame. The flash is nothing but a black blur, with legs and an arm visible, but no distinguishing features such as hair or skin color. It looks like he could be wearing a woolen hat or even a ski mask.

"Dammit," Madison says. "Maybe Alex could enhance the footage."

"I doubt it," says Adams. "It's too low-quality."

They watch some more of the footage in case the figure returns. Twenty-five minutes pass before Madison sees another woman leaving the mall with a baby in a stroller. "That's Julie Reid, the woman who discovered Sarah Moss's body."

They watch as she walks out of view of the camera. Then they see Tracy Jones from the hair salon get in her Nissan and drive away.

"The dark figure crossed the screen from the right-hand side of the mall," says Adams. "The fact that we haven't seen him again suggests he exited the parking lot in a different direction."

Madison nods. "See if you can pull footage from any cameras along Main Street. Whether he walked or drove away, he should be visible somewhere."

Adams stands up and pulls his jacket on. "I'll see what I can find."

She looks out of the window. It's dark outside, and snowing again.

"Are you working tomorrow?" asks Adams.

She sighs. "I wasn't until this happened."

"I'll be here too, but I was hoping to come in later, maybe nine thirty, ten? So that I can open presents with the kids first."

Madison realizes he's seeking her permission. "Of course. I would too if my son were still young. I can cover anything that needs doing first thing."

He smiles at her, and she notices he's more attractive when relaxed than when he's being an asshole. "If you're gone by the time I get back," he says, "I'll see you tomorrow."

She watches him leave the station. Maybe he'll work out after all.

CHAPTER FOURTEEN

Nate has the heat cranked up high at his place tonight. A church choir sings Christmas carols on the radio in the kitchen diner. He wasn't allowed a TV on death row, so his old radio kept him connected to the outside world. The calming sound of the choir is one of the many things he missed while incarcerated, and something he had loved listening to at his church when he was younger. It also makes it feel more like Christmas Eve, along with the snow accumulating outside his windows. He even bought a real tree earlier today, which he's hoping Madison will help him decorate. Although it was one of the last trees standing and had been slashed in price, so it's not doing so great. It doesn't help that Brody keeps drinking from the water bowl underneath it.

Nate worries that he should have cooked dinner, but he chose to order pizza instead. It feels mean forcing a delivery guy out in this weather, but they were still taking orders, so maybe they need the money. The doorbell rings. That's either the pizza guy or Madison. He glances at the oven's digital clock; it's just after eight.

Brody barks as he makes for the door, eager to see who has come to visit. Once there, he sits down and waits as Nate approaches, his tail swooshing back and forth on the wooden floorboards in anticipation. When Nate opens the door, Madison is standing there bundled up in a thick coat, a hat and gloves, and the snow quickly finds its way inside. He steps aside for her. "I gave you a key for a reason," he says with a smile.

She hugs him before slipping out of her wet jacket and hat. "What if you've got a woman in here? I don't want to walk in on *that*, thanks."

He laughs as he closes the door. "What are your dad and Owen doing tonight?"

"They're at Dad's apartment. Owen's teaching him how to play video games I've never heard of. They bought a bunch of junk food and my dad's reliving his youth."

Nate can't picture an ex-Fed like Bill playing video games. The doorbell rings again; this time it's the pizza guy, who is actually a teenage girl, probably no older than eighteen. She almost loses the pizzas to a gust of wind. Feeling bad, Nate tips her with his remaining cash: sixty dollars. Her eyes light up. "You want change?"

"No, that's okay. Merry Christmas."

"Wow, thanks. Merry Christmas!"

He watches to check she makes it off his icy driveway in her old Ford. When the car is a shadow in the distance, he goes back inside. Brody starts sniffing the air around the pizzas. "Don't worry. You'll get the leftovers."

Madison pours them each a glass of red wine. Nate grabs some plates and they sit at the breakfast bar while the choir on the radio sings softly in the background.

"Don't let me drink more than one glass," she says. "I know how you like to get me drunk, but I need to be able to drive home, as it'll be impossible to get a cab tonight."

"Hey, I don't get you drunk. It's the other way around." He spots a neatly wrapped gift next to his wineglass. "What's this?"

She reddens. "Remember, I'm broke, so it's not much. You, however, are rich, so I'm expecting something much better from you." She winks.

He picks it up and unwraps it, then opens the box inside. It's a rosary on top of a brand-new leather Bible.

"I know you still have Stacey's rosary," she says, "But I noticed you stopped wearing it after her killer was caught." Madison avoids saying the killer's name, and he's grateful. "So I thought you might want a new one that comes with no emotional baggage."

Nate had been on the path to becoming a priest before he met Stacey Connor, the niece of his mentor, Father Jack Connor. He hadn't intended to fall for her, but he did, and hard. They were only twenty, and she was the first woman he'd ever considered dating. After a lot of soul-searching, and upsetting a lot of people, he had given up on his dream of the priesthood and proposed to her. He just hadn't anticipated how quickly that decision would turn into a nightmare. He's definitely missed wearing a rosary, but Madison's right: it was Stacey's. She had left it at his apartment one day, and he wore it around his neck to remind him to give it back to her. He was wearing it on the night he found her dead in the garage. It's the only item of hers that he owns, but once her real killer was caught, he sensed he should take it off and finally lay her memory to rest. His hand still reaches for it instinctively every now and then. Usually when he's in trouble.

Whether he can ever turn to rosary beads or the Bible for comfort again, he doesn't know, but Madison's gift is thoughtful, and he's touched. He looks at her. "Thanks. I love them. And your gift will be ready for you within the next few days. You'll have to be patient."

"Wait a minute." She narrows her eyes. "You forgot to buy me something, didn't you? I'm a cop, remember. I can tell when people are lying."

He laughs. "I didn't forget. It's just not ready yet, that's all."

"That's okay. I guess I can settle for pizza and wine." She turns her attention to the pizza. "I'm starving. Apart from some candy, I haven't eaten since lunchtime." She grabs a slice of pepperoni and takes a massive bite.

"So how was your day? How is the homicide case going?" He takes a bite out of a slice of ham and mushroom.

"Busy, but I'm no closer to catching the guy who killed Sarah Moss. Oh, and my new partner threw my conviction in my face when we got into an argument earlier. Can you believe that?"

"He what?" He hates the guy already.

"I know, right? He said he googled me before joining the department, so now he thinks he knows everything about me and my family." She wipes her mouth with a napkin. "I can't tell yet if we're going to get along, but I'm trying my hardest. I just wish Mendes had given the job to Steve or Shelley."

Nate sips his wine. "Did Owen tell you he accepted an internship at Richie's?"

She raises her eyebrows. "No. That's great. How was Richie? Did you find out why his last office got firebombed?"

"Not really, but he said it wasn't anything to worry about. You know how he is."

She scoffs before starting on pizza slice number two.

"He offered me a job too." Nate has her attention now, so he adds, "As an investigator. He has a guy who already covers Prospect Springs, but now that he's moved his business down here, Richie wants me to be on call for anything that needs looking into for his local clients."

"And you said yes?" She seems surprised. Probably because she knows he doesn't need the money.

"It's hard to say no to Richie. And I figure it will give me something to do." He nudges her elbow playfully. "Because it's not like you need my help anymore."

She smiles as she drops the half-eaten slice and sips her wine. "Like I keep telling you: become a detective and we can work together again. Like Cagney and Lacey."

He laughs. "Monroe and Harper. It sounds good."

"Obviously I prefer Harper and Monroe."

He picks up his cell phone. "What's your new partner's name?"

"Marcus Adams. He's from Denver, or at least that's where he worked before moving here." When she realizes he's googling him, she says, "Wait, we shouldn't do that."

"Come on, where's the harm? Aren't you curious about who your new partner really is?"

She leans closer to him in order to see his screen. "Go on then. Just for a second."

Nate types Adams's name into the search bar and scours the results. There's surprisingly little about him. He probably uses a pseudonym on social media, like most cops. They find a few articles where he's given a quote to the press about one of his cases, and a couple of photos of him at crime scenes. Nate has a good look. "What's with the fake tan? And he dyes his hair, by the way."

Madison laughs and moves away. "You don't know that."

"Of course I do. He's probably the same age as me: forty, maybe a little older. So he must dye his hair; it's jet black in that photo!"

She looks at Nate's hair, which needs cutting, then runs her fingers over the back of it. It makes him shiver. "I never noticed you were going gray," she quips.

"Hey, it happens to the best of us." He purposefully stares at her hair for grays, and she pushes him away.

He puts his phone on the counter and they eat in silence. For the first time in a long while, Nate feels content. Brody is lying at their feet, waiting for spillages, Madison's in a great mood, and he's a free man. He looks at her and is overcome by a powerful wave of love. It scares him, but it's not new. He's been feeling this way about Madison for some time now. He's just been too afraid to do anything about it. That'll happen when you lose your fiancée to murder.

He thinks of Kristen Devereaux, the woman who helped free him from death row. As his only visitor inside, after his father passed away, he had eventually fallen for her. But she went missing before his release and is presumed dead. He often wonders if Stacey and Kristen would both be alive if they hadn't met him. He couldn't bear anything to happen to Madison. He can't imagine not having her in his life. But at what point does he start living again?

She notices that he's staring. "What? I've got pizza on my face, haven't I?" She stands up. "I need a mirror."

As she goes to pass him, Nate reaches for her hand and stops her. He gets off his stool. She appears confused, so he gently pulls her closer to him. His lips are on hers before he loses his nerve. He kisses her, gently, until he feels her kissing him back. No other thoughts go through his mind as he concentrates on Madison. He even ignores his phone when it buzzes with a notification. For a first kiss, it's pretty damn perfect. And intense. He's been so afraid of taking this step, which isn't just a step toward being with Madison, it's a step further away from his past. His hands are trembling by the time he pulls away.

Stroking her cheek, he fixes his blue eyes on hers. "Sorry. I couldn't resist."

She smiles at him, her own eyes sparkling. "Well, it's about time." This time she kisses him, and he wants to take her upstairs. He pulls away and takes a deep breath, running his hands down her body to her waist. "This could ruin everything."

"Well," she says playfully, "if it does, I get Brody. You can have Owen."

He laughs, feeling reassured. When his phone buzzes again on the breakfast bar, he glances at it, out of habit. Two

Facebook messages sit unread on the screen. As he reads them, his heart skips a beat and his blood runs cold.

This is Kristen Devereaux.

I'm looking for Nate Monroe.

He takes a step back from Madison, feeling like his knees are going to buckle. "You've got to be kidding me."

CHAPTER FIFTEEN

Madison can't understand the change in Nate's demeanor. His face has lost all color and he's shaking. "What's the matter?"

He points to his phone and she reads the messages. She's blindsided. Kristen Devereaux is the university law professor who used Nate's conviction as a case study for her class. They found discrepancies in the way his murder trial was conducted and eventually helped get it overturned. He's told Madison little about Kristen, but she knows he was in love with her. She was his only visitor toward the end of those seventeen years on death row, other than his attorneys, so it was inevitable that they'd develop a close bond. Unfortunately, she went missing just months before his release two years ago and he's never seen or heard from her since, not until a photo of her bruised and bloody face turned up at Madison's house recently as some kind of threat. A warning from the man who killed Nate's fiancée. Nate had assumed Kristen was killed for helping with his exoneration because it meant the real killer had to go on the run to avoid capture.

Nate's breathing has turned heavy. "Sit down." Madison leads him over to the dining table. Brody has picked up on the change of mood. He comes over and whines softly.

"Do you think it's really her?" asks Nate.

She takes the seat next to him. "We have to be cautious. It could be a hoax." On his phone she opens the Facebook account the message came to. It's a missing person account that he set up to get information about Kristen: sightings, tips, that kind of thing. It's only been open for a month and he's never mentioned getting any leads from it. "Is this the first time anyone's messaged this account?"

He shakes his head. "I get all kinds of crazy messages, but nothing about Kristen. Just kids wasting my time mostly. I should reply to this one, shouldn't I?"

Madison isn't so sure. If this is someone messing with him, it could send him on a downward spiral. He's been doing so well lately; no longer using cocaine as a way to cope with his past, and talking about getting his life back on track instead of talking about ending it. She can't watch him go back to that. It would be too painful, and he deserves so much more.

He grabs his phone and types quickly.

This is Nate. What's your cell number?

She's glad he's brief. It's all that's needed until he knows whether he's genuinely talking to Kristen. Madison can feel him trembling next to her.

He turns to her. "What if she really is alive? I was so sure she was dead. That photo made it look like her injuries were severe."

If she is alive, that complicates things for Madison. Having just experienced the most tender moment she's shared with anyone in a decade, she knows she'll have to step aside for Nate and Kristen to reunite. But it hurts to even think about it.

They both stare at the screen, but there are no dots indicating that anyone is replying. If it *is* a hoax, the person who messaged won't agree to speak to Nate on the phone. They'll want to carry on the charade anonymously for as long as possible. But if it *is* Kristen, there's no reason she wouldn't want to speak to him. Unless she's afraid the account he created wasn't set up by him.

A flurry of snow slams against the kitchen window. The wind is picking up out there as the storm sweeps in. She should get home before she's trapped here. Nate lives farther away from the police station than she does, and she needs to be available to get down there at a moment's notice. But she doesn't want to leave him. A minute ago, she was prepared to spend the night.

He stands, making the decision for her. "You should go. There's no guarantee she'll respond tonight and the weather's only going to get worse."

Her heart sinks. She wants to be here in case he does get a reply and it's not the one he's hoping for. "Are you sure?"

He rubs her shoulder. "I'll be fine. It's probably a random troll looking to upset me. I'll call you if anything happens."

She studies his face. His jaw is tight and he's clearly anxious. She just wants to protect him. "Has she replied?"

He glances at his phone. "No." He goes to the breakfast bar and boxes up the pizza she was eating. "Don't waste this."

She takes it off him. They just shared an amazing kiss and now she's leaving to go home to an empty house. But there's no denying the mood has changed drastically. After pulling on her coat and hat, she turns at the front door, not knowing whether to kiss him goodbye or not.

Nate's eyes are red. "I'm sorry," he says. "I hate how my past is affecting us."

She hugs him to her with her spare hand and says into his ear, "Don't shut me out. If this really is Kristen, we'll deal with it together."

He nods as she pulls away, then opens the door for her. The wind almost tears it from his grasp. The snow stings her face as she runs to her car. "Drive carefully," she hears him shout after her.

When she's alone in the car, she has to fight back tears.

Because she's realizing again that they're never going to be free of their pasts.

Sleep evades her. Madison lies in bed tossing and turning, wondering if "Kristen" has replied to Nate's message, and how he's coping with it all. Owen decided to stay at her father's apartment because it wasn't safe to drive home in the storm. She can hear the wind whistling through the trees outside and it wouldn't surprise her if there's a lot of damage and debris that needs clearing from the roads come morning.

Owen's cat came to cuddle up against her neck for warmth and listening to him purr feels nice. He normally sleeps in Owen's room, so he must be missing him. When her phone rings on the nightstand beside her, she jumps before exclaiming in surprise. Bandit vanishes off the bed in fear. He hates being startled. Her clock shows it's only 1.24 a.m., so she assumes it's Nate calling with an update. When she sees the screen, she realizes it's dispatch. Something bad must have happened if they're calling her at this hour. "Hello?"

"Hey, it's Dina. Sorry to wake you, but I had no choice. There's been another murder."

Madison switches on the light on her nightstand and blinks until she can see. "Where?"

"Outside St. Theresa's church. Female victim. I have Officer Vickers on her way as well as Alex Parker, and I'll let Chief Mendes know what's happened. I couldn't get hold of Detective Adams."

Madison can try calling him once she's at the scene. "I'll be there in ten minutes."

She leaps out of bed and changes into some clean jeans and a thick sweater. Once downstairs, she steps into a pair of boots and selects her thickest coat.

Outside, in the dead of night, her car fails to start three times and eventually a bedroom light comes on at her nearest neighbor's house. The noise of her engine failing is waking people up. Thankfully, on the fourth attempt it starts, and she carefully maneuvers out of her snow-covered driveway. She has to drive slowly because of the slippery conditions, so it takes her fifteen minutes to reach the church. Shelley is already there and an ambulance arrives behind Madison. Its lights are blazing but the siren is switched off, perhaps to avoid waking kids this early on Christmas morning. They shouldn't have to know that murder doesn't stop for Santa Claus.

The church's parking lot is full of cars. It must have been a busy midnight mass. Madison can see the headline now: *Midnight Mass Murder*. There's a crowd gathered around the center of the lot. Shelley is crouched next to the victim and Madison joins her.

The woman on the ground appears to be in her late twenties and she's dressed for the cold weather. She's lying twisted on her back with her arms outstretched in one direction and her hips in the other, as if she was attacked unexpectedly from behind. Madison leans in for a closer look at her head. It looks like she was hit with something, and more than once. Her eyes are open, snowflakes accumulating on her heavily mascaraed lashes. Her lips are fast turning blue, and the deep red blood spilling from her head injuries is in stark contrast to the blanket of white snow on the ground.

A large purse next to her has spilled its contents: a lipstick, some coins and a few small wrapped gifts, presumably for or from her churchgoing friends inside. A handful of flyers sit next to her left hand, but they blow away one by one until only a single one remains. Madison picks it up. It's advertising a yard sale in the new year, with the profits going to fund a new organ for the church.

A mound of snow next to the body catches Madison's attention. "What's that?"

Shelley looks over at her. "She had a child with her, a little boy. He was building a snowman when I got here."

Madison's mouth drops open. "Building a snowman?" She wonders if that was the child's way of coping after seeing his mother beaten to death. "Where is he now?"

"Some of the parishioners are taking care of him inside. He was found wearing a blue snowsuit and boots, but his little hands were freezing cold when I touched them. He wasn't complaining at all, though, so he must be in shock." Shelley shakes her head. "He's only three or four years old."

"Was the victim arriving or leaving when she was found?"

"According to the priest, they started the service without her because she hadn't arrived in time. They couldn't wait any longer because the kids were falling asleep. She was discovered as the congregation was leaving."

Madison shakes her head. The woman must have arrived late. The killer got to her before she reached the doors to the church, less than ten paces away. She was beaten to death while her friends sang hymns and said prayers. For this to happen on this day and in this way is especially depraved.

To Madison, it's immediately clear that this murder is linked to Sarah Moss's, because the circumstances are so similar: the victims were both hit on the head, attacked in a parking lot, their children left unharmed. "But why leave the child unharmed again?" she mutters, thinking out loud.

"Maybe it's a woman who did this," says Shelley, before shaking her head and instantly changing her mind. "No, this had to be a man. But what kind of creep kills someone outside a church on Christmas morning?"

It's a rhetorical question, so Madison doesn't answer. She leans in to look at the victim's hands, checking to see if the nails have been cut short like Sarah Moss's were. They haven't. They're nicely manicured and enviably long and shaped. It suggests that either Sarah's fingernails weren't cut by her killer, or that he didn't need to cut this victim's nails as she hadn't had a chance to fight back and unwittingly collect his DNA.

Rita, one of the EMTs, moves them out of her way. "Give me some space, ladies."

They both stand. Shelley pulls a roll of yellow tape from her pocket and begins taping off the crime scene and moving the onlookers away. "Please go and wait inside the church," she shouts. "We'll need to take your statements before you go home. If you need to leave immediately, come see me first so I can get your contact details."

An older woman is sobbing. "I can't believe this happened outside while we were just feet away, listening to that beautiful choir."

Someone puts an arm around her and Madison watches as everyone heads inside. She blows hot air into her gloved hands, as the cold is penetrating everything she's wearing. Snow is quickly building on top of the footprints around the victim. She gets the feeling she's going to be here for hours taking statements, so she considers calling Detective Adams in to help. But when she realizes it's not even 2 a.m. yet, she decides against it for now. If she lets him enjoy breakfast with his family, maybe she can get away later, in time for dinner with Owen and her father. Nate crosses her mind, and she's filled with dread. He's supposed to be coming to dinner later too, but she has no idea whether he'll turn up after what happened.

Another police cruiser arrives and Madison directs Officer Gloria Williams inside to help Shelley with the witnesses. Rita stands up and pulls her latex gloves off, shaking her head. "Jake's going to be shocked. I guess I better tell him before he hears it through the grapevine."

Madison looks at her. "Jake Rubio? He knows the victim?"

Rita nods. "Sure. This is Emily Cole. His girlfriend. Well, she was as close to a steady girlfriend as he's ever likely to get."

Madison looks down at the victim. "Is he the father of her child?"

Rita scoffs. "You never know with Jake, but if he is, it's not something he told me." Shelley appears from inside the church and Rita says, "Ask her. She'll know." She takes her bag of equipment back to the ambulance.

When Shelley reaches her, Madison asks, "Did you know that this is Jake's girlfriend, Emily Cole?"

Shelley looks down at the victim, surprised. "I didn't even know he had a girlfriend. Did Rita tell you that?"

Madison nods and Shelley goes over to talk to her. Alex Parker appears from behind the ambulance, protecting a camera around his neck from the snow and carrying an equipment case in his spare hand. He joins Madison. Before he can speak, his hat goes flying off his head, exposing his black hair. "I better get started before any evidence blows away," he says over the wind. "Is this how she was found?"

"Yes. With her son beside her. He's unharmed."

"Thank goodness for that." He starts snapping pictures of the body.

Madison wonders where Jake is tonight, as he's clearly not working. She approaches Shelley and Rita. "Could one of you give me Jake's address and cell number? I want to break the news to him. He might have an idea who could've done this."

Rita retrieves her phone and reads out his number. Shelley gives Madison his address and says, "Want me to come with you? He'll probably be devastated and might need a friendly face."

Madison shakes her head. "No, that's okay. I need you here. Get statements from as many witnesses as possible for me." She feels their eyes on her as she gets into her car. Thankfully, it starts first time.

CHAPTER SIXTEEN

Jake Rubio answers the door in nothing but his underwear. He's tall, with the physique of a football player; broad across the back and shoulders, with his six-pack on display and his hair thick and blond. Initially he appears confused at having someone wake him at two thirty on Christmas morning, but when he recognizes Madison, his expression changes to alarm. "What's happened?" he asks.

"There's been another murder. Can I come in?"

He steps aside, letting her enter his apartment. The decor is clean and modern, and other than his paramedic uniform hanging from a living room cabinet, the place is neat, which surprises her. She was expecting it to look like a frat house. With the confidence of a jock, he doesn't bother putting on any clothes. Instead, he heads to the kitchen and switches on the coffee machine. "Am I needed at the scene? It's meant to be my night off, but I guess if it's bad I can attend. I just need coffee first to clear my head." He grins slightly. "I had a few too many last night."

Madison approaches the breakfast bar and takes a deep breath. "Jake, I'm sorry, but the victim is someone you know. Emily Cole." She studies his face closely.

He frowns before shaking his head as if trying to wake up faster. "What do you mean?"

"She was attacked and beaten to death outside St. Theresa's Catholic church. Her little boy was with her, but he's unharmed and being checked over by Rita."

Jake stands motionless for a full minute. The only sound is the coffee machine gurgling. The smell of ground coffee makes Madison's stomach rumble. She'd give anything for some caffeine right now. Jake reaches for his head with both hands. "Are you serious?"

She nods. "I'm sorry. Rita told me Emily was your girlfriend."

He tilts his head. "She's not really my girlfriend, just someone I..." He has difficulty finding the right words, which tells Madison everything she needs to know.

"Were you with her today at any point?"

Jake heads for the couch and slips on a pair of gray sweatpants that were folded on the arm. "I need to sit down." He rubs his face with both hands. "I can't believe it. Is it the same guy who killed that woman the other night?"

Madison's surprised he doesn't remember the first victim's name. On the other hand, paramedics see a lot of different people every day, and he's just been given bad news. "It looks like it, but I can't say for sure." She takes a seat opposite him. "Did you see her today?" She checks her watch. "Or I guess I should say yesterday."

He nods. "I went to her apartment earlier, around four in the afternoon, I guess. The kid was at his dad's place, so me and Emily... fooled around."

"You had sex?"

"Right."

Madison makes a note. "I'm sorry to ask you this, but did you use protection?"

He glances up at her. "What?"

"If there's any stranger DNA on her body, we need to

figure out where it came from. It doesn't appear that she was raped, but it's something Lena will check during the autopsy."

Bewildered, he says, "I can't believe this is happening."

"Jake," she presses. "Did you wear a condom?"

"No, okay? We've known each other for years. We fool around every now and then. We're both single, so there's no harm in it."

Madison is taken aback by his defensiveness. Maybe it's embarrassment. "I'm not suggesting there is." She moves on. "What time did you leave her place?"

He exhales loudly. "About five, I guess. I went to a bar downtown: Joe's Saloon on Deacon Street." He suddenly looks up at her with suspicion in his eyes. "Wait. Are you trying to see whether I have an alibi?"

She doesn't reply.

"Come on, Detective. You *know* me."

She met Jake for the first time two months ago. It was at a crime scene where a baby girl had been found abandoned in the back of a car. The baby's mother was missing. Jake also saved Nate's life when Nate was intentionally mowed down by a hit-and-run driver last month. But she only knows him in a professional capacity, and this is the longest conversation they've ever had, so she can't vouch for his character outside of his job. And in *her* job, everyone is a potential suspect. "You know the drill, Jake. I'll be asking everyone who saw Emily yesterday what they were doing around the time of her death. It's the quickest way for me to rule you out and focus on finding her killer."

Beads of sweat line his forehead. "I got home sometime after eight. Then I watched TV and had some beers before I went to bed. It was just a normal evening."

She writes it all down. "What did Emily do for a living?"

"She was a manager at the Fresh Is Best grocery store. Someone needs to tell them what's happened."

"Do you know her parents? Where they live?" Madison will have to notify them next.

"No, I never met them. I think she said they live on the East Coast, but I can't remember where exactly. I don't think they got along real good."

It sounds to her as if Jake doesn't get to know any of his conquests very well. "Emily's boy, what's his name and who is his father?"

"He's called Zach Cole and he's four years old, I think. Maybe five now. He's not usually around when Emily invites me over, so I don't really know him."

"And his father?"

"Brian Slater. He's a cool guy from what I can tell. He wouldn't have done this, if that's what you're thinking." He runs a hand through his hair before adding, "But then what do I know? Maybe he did. I've only met him a couple of times."

Madison wonders if he's casually trying to point the finger of blame away from himself. "I'll need to notify him of what's happened so he can collect his son. Do you have his number?"

"Sure." He gets up to retrieve his cell phone from the bedroom.

She stands and watches him walk away, noticing that he doesn't have any bruising or scratches to his arms, neck or torso. She glances around again to try and get a glimpse into his personality. The apartment is actually more sterile than she first thought. It's tidy, sure, but it's more than that. There's no computer or tablet, no video games or books lying around. No framed photographs of family or any sign that he gets many visitors. In comparison, her own house is always messy, and she doesn't want to think about Owen's room. He may be a good twelve years younger than Jake Rubio, but there are plenty of signs of his personality in his room. So much so that she daren't go in there anymore.

When Jake returns, he reads Brian's number aloud.

"Thanks." She walks to the front door and turns. "I'm

sorry to be the bearer of bad news. Are you going to be okay? Do you have family nearby you can call on?"

"I'll be fine." He rubs his face again. "Just find the asshole who did this."

Madison nods. "I intend to."

CHAPTER SEVENTEEN

Madison spends the next few hours arranging for Brian Slater to collect his son and then tracking down Emily Cole's parents. She finally locates them in New Jersey and when she breaks the terrible news to Emily's mom, the woman is devastated, suggesting that Jake was wrong to claim she and Emily didn't get along. Her husband has to take the phone from her, and Madison can hear the emotion in his voice as he tries to keep it steady. This is without doubt the worst part of her job, and always leaves her wondering why she works in law enforcement.

It's 7 a.m. by the time she gets a minute to stop for her first coffee. The sun has yet to rise and the snow is still falling, although the high winds are starting to ease. As predicted, several trees and branches have succumbed to the storm, making a mess of the roads. When she reaches Ruby's Diner, she's relieved to see Vince has opened up today, despite it being Christmas. When she was a patrol officer, there was nowhere to go on Christmas Day to pick up coffee or food, and no restrooms open. It was depressing.

The diner is understandably quiet. Most people are home either still asleep or unwrapping gifts. She spots Gary Pelosi from the *Lost Creek Daily* sitting in a booth opposite another reporter she recognizes, though his name eludes her. There always seem to be so many of them buzzing around crime scenes, like hungry flies around human remains. They're both typing away on their laptops, proving the news doesn't stop for Christmas. Gary runs a hand through his graying hair and sighs as he reads back what he's written. Madison would age him at around fifty. He's wearing a wedding band and she wonders who his wife is. When he sees her looking, he nods with a smile before sipping his coffee. She's grateful he doesn't call her over to ask for the latest update on this morning's homicide. He and his pal probably spent all morning at the scene and know just as much as she does.

She heads to the counter and is surprised to find Owen and her father sitting there. The sight of them together makes her smile. She hugs Owen briefly. "What are you two doing here?"

Their attention had been on the TV above the counter. They're watching the news. "Merry Christmas, sweetheart." Her father hugs her. "We knew you'd be at work already because of that." He nods to the TV above the counter. "So we figured there was no rush to get to your place and open gifts. I thought I'd treat my grandson to breakfast instead." He opens his jacket to find his wallet and Madison catches a glimpse of the firearm attached to his belt. She's surprised he still carries a weapon now he's retired. Perhaps old habits die hard.

"What time's Nate getting to ours tonight?" asks Owen. "And do I seriously have to wait until then to open my presents?"

Her smile fades at the mention of Nate. She checks her phone. There are no messages from him, so she doesn't know if the person who contacted him on Facebook ever replied. She shoots off a quick text.

Merry Christmas.

Slipping her phone into her jacket pocket, she says, "I

don't know what time he's arriving or when I can get off work. I'll keep you posted. But I guess you can open your presents when you get home after breakfast." Though she'd rather he didn't. After all, she's had to wait a long time to see him open Christmas presents.

He must sense what she's thinking, as he says, "I'll do it tonight, when we're all together."

She smiles. "What have you got planned for today?" she asks her dad. "Are you hanging out at our place?"

Bill shakes his head. "No, I've got things to do. I'll drop Owen home after this and then return for dinner later."

A pang of guilt washes over her. Owen shouldn't have to be alone on Christmas Day because everyone in his family is too busy to spend time with him. She can't get off work right now, but her dad has no excuse to leave him. "What are you doing that's so pressing it can't wait until tomorrow?"

He glances at her and she can tell he doesn't want to say. "Just this and that."

They're interrupted by Carla, the head waitress. "Merry Christmas, Madison. I'll bet you're ready for some breakfast after dealing with that." She has one eye on the TV. "What'll it be?"

"Coffee, toast, bacon and eggs. Thanks." She's hungry.

Carla smiles. "Sure thing."

Before she goes, Madison says, "I didn't expect the place to be open at all, to be honest. Is Vince working too?"

"We open every Christmas. Vince didn't like spending the day alone after Ruby went missing, and he thinks opening up gives people a place to go if they don't have anywhere else to be. You'd be surprised just how many people that is. Anyway, he's taking the morning off to be with his son and grandson upstairs. You should see the amount of presents Oliver has to open." She smiles.

"And you don't mind working today?"

"Me and the other waitresses take it in turns, but I don't

mind really. He pays us well for it, but don't tell him I admitted that." She smiles again before turning toward the kitchen. "I'll get your order."

"Hey, Maddie," says her dad, pointing to the TV. "Didn't you go to high school with that woman? I remember her coming to our house."

Kate Flynn is doing a piece to camera. She's standing in the parking lot of St. Theresa's church. Her long brown hair is fighting a losing battle against the wind and her coat is zipped right up to her chin. She's probably been outside for hours as she pieces together what happened. They all listen in as Kate says, "She was found dead in the early hours of this morning, badly beaten and with her young child by her side." She shakes her head in disgust.

Madison frowns. That's not something a reporter does when they're live on TV.

"We need a nickname for him," says Kate. "Before someone else comes up with one." She's looking past the lens to Bob, her camera operator, and Madison realizes she doesn't know she's on air. They both think this is a rehearsal. "You know, I'm so sick of men," continues Kate as she jumps up and down on the spot to warm up. "Why can't they go to therapy like everyone else instead of taking their issues out on women? Why do *we* have to pay for these maniacs' mommy issues?" She stops jumping. "Hey, that's what I'll name him. The mommy maniac."

"Boss would never let you call him that," says Bob from behind the camera.

"Why not? It's true. We all know that whoever killed these women is just some impotent asshole with a small dick who probably wants to sleep with his mother and can't, so he's taking it out on anyone with a vagina."

"Holy crap," says Gary Pelosi over Madison's shoulder. "They've lost communication with the studio. No one can warn them they're on air. The producer needs to cut them off."

"I'm sick of turning up to crimes scenes involving dead women!" Kate shakes her head in anger. "Serial killers are so goddam clichéd. Why not try killing a guy for once? But of course, he won't. And do you know why that is, Bob?"

Bob doesn't offer a response and Madison wonders if he's started to realize they're on air.

"Because he's too chickenshit to try hurting a man," Kate continues. "He picks on women and children half his size because he's a loser. His sex life probably consists of watching porn on his mom's computer down in the basement while she's hard at work paying the bills he doesn't contribute to."

The live stream suddenly cuts to a break, and commercials take over. The whole rant probably lasted less than a minute, but it was a minute too long. Kate, Bob and the show's producer are going to regret it. Madison's mouth hangs wide open. She had absently started a text to Kate to let her know she was on air, but she stops now.

"Damn. Someone's losing their job today," says Bill.

Gary returns to his booth to gather his things, and he and his co-worker leave together. It's already shaping up to be a busy day for the press. Madison feels horrible for Kate. Instead of reporting about this tragic story, she's become a part of it.

"If you ask me," says Carla as she hands over a mug of coffee, "it's about time someone tells it how it is. She's only saying what people are thinking."

Owen looks as shocked as Madison is, but he's clearly amused. "She's in big trouble, but I bet she'll go viral. She's going to be famous."

Maybe that's why the producer didn't cut her off right away. It could be both good and bad for the station. Madison is lost for words. She knows Kate's been under enormous pressure with her marriage issues, but this is bad. Really bad. She turns to her dad. "She thinks the homicides are the work of a serial killer."

He considers it. "There's only been two so far, right?"

"Right."

"But they have similar characteristics?"

She nods.

He mulls it over for a minute. "Best not to jump to conclusions. Serial killers are relatively rare. Interview everyone in those women's lives. You never know, they could've both been screwing the same guy, or they could have another connection that you're unaware of: a crazy boss, or a jealous relative. But now that your friend's brought up the idea of a serial killer, you're about to get a lot more media picking up the case." He shakes his head. "And you don't want that, because they love serial killers. So do their readers. If I were you, I'd rule it out asap by finding the link between these two women. Find the link; find the killer."

Madison knows he's right, but it's not as easy as he makes it sound.

CHAPTER EIGHTEEN

OCTOBER 1996

Bill Harper looks through the notebook in front of him, but he doesn't need to. The contents are committed to memory. It contains the names of four female victims, along with their dates of birth, dates of death, causes of deaths and graphic crime-scene photographs. He sees those images when he closes his eyes at night. They're forever imprinted onto his eyelids.

It's been two years since he found the boy in the bloody bedroom. The body of his mother—Michelle—was quickly located once backup arrived. She was outside, in the backyard. She had been set alight in a poor attempt to destroy the evidence, but the fire had died out before it took away her features. She had been beautiful. With her high cheekbones and thick, naturally wavy hair, she could have been a movie star. Instead, she was only just getting by as a single mother in a small town.

With no one able to track down the boy's father—there was no name entered on his birth certificate, and the victim hadn't disclosed it to anyone who knew her—the child went into foster care and Bill lost track of him. The shame and guilt that comes from not solving a case never leaves you, and he's sad to admit he lost track of the boy intentionally. He wants to find his mother's killer before facing him again.

Although he can't talk to his wife and elder daughter about cases like this—Lynette can't stomach the details and Angie is ashamed that he's a cop because her asshole friends tease her about it—he *can* talk to his younger daughter. Madison's only fourteen, but she reads the newspapers. She stares at the victims' faces and imagines it happening to her or one of her friends. She asks Bill questions about the cases he works. He doesn't go into detail or she'd never sleep at night, like him, but he tells her enough to put her on her guard. Mainly so she can reduce the risk of becoming a grainy black-and-white image under a horrific headline.

Occasionally she'll ask him how this particular case is going and it increases his need to find the killer. He doesn't want to let the boy down, of course, but he also doesn't want to let Maddie down. He doesn't want her, Angie or his wife becoming the killer's next victim.

That's what today is all about. He's meeting Special Agent Pamela Rogers from the FBI. A knock at the door makes him stand in anticipation. An officer shows Pamela into the briefing room and then leaves them to it. The agent is dressed in black jeans and a crisp white shirt under a smart navy suit jacket. She smiles widely as she approaches. "Detective Harper. Pleasure to meet you at last."

"Please, call me Bill." He gestures to a seat at the meeting table. It's just the two of them, because no one else at Lost Creek PD believes they have a serial killer on their hands. The department's aging chief is happy to pretend that this was a one-off and the killer probably skipped town after. Bill thinks he's skipped town too, but he also thinks he's committed more homicides since then. "I hope your flight from Alaska wasn't too painful?"

Pamela waves a dismissive hand before removing her jacket. "Not at all. Finding Lost Creek, on the other hand..."

She raises her eyebrows. "That took me a while. I didn't realize just how remote this place was. And I thought the rickety old bridge into town was going to collapse under my rental car." She laughs. The One-Way Bridge acts as the only way in and out of Lost Creek by vehicle. It's an old wooden covered structure that has seen better days, but no one wants to pay to upgrade it until absolutely necessary. The town doesn't have money for luxuries like that. "The mountains are beautiful, though," she adds. "And the woods with the aspen trees are breathtaking."

He nods. "They sure are."

She slips into the seat. "I stopped by the hotel first to drop off my things, but I haven't had time for coffee yet, so I'm relieved you have some waiting for me."

He watches as she takes a long sip, ignoring the milk and sugar on the table. She looks to be slightly older than him, maybe around forty, with auburn hair and a fair complexion. Although he's spoken to her on the phone more than once, this is the first time they've met, and he expected more attitude. Feds are notorious for treating local cops as something foul they stepped in. "I'm conscious I only have you in town for twenty-four hours," he says. "So shall we get started?"

"Fine by me," she says. "Why don't you run me through which cases you believe are connected and I'll tell you what I think."

"Sure." He opens his notebook. Sliding the photographs across the table of that terrible crime scene he attended two years ago, he says, "This is the homicide that occurred in 1994." He's told her about it over the phone already but he reminds her of the details now. He knows they will be more meaningful once she sees the victims for herself. That's when they're no longer just names on a piece of paper. "The boy was four years old at the time and he was found in that bedroom, sitting in a pool of his mother's blood. He was completely unharmed."

"Where was the mother's body?" asks Pamela, studying the empty, blood-spattered bedroom in the photograph.

Bill passes her a photograph of the woman's remains. "She was found out back, badly burned but still identifiable. It's like the killer gave up halfway through, or maybe he left her burning to make his escape. He might've assumed the body would continue burning in his absence, but he didn't use an accelerant; no gasoline or lighter fluid. The fire chief believes he set fire to her skirt, and that the lack of accelerant suggests he was inexperienced. That tells me this murder was one of his first kills, if not *the* first."

She nods thoughtfully but remains silent.

Next he pulls out the photographs of two victims from Alaska; both women, both found dead next to their young children. Both boys under the age of five. Pamela would've studied these many times, as she's responsible for finding their killer. He looks at her. "Aside from the fact that the killer of your two victims didn't attempt to hide or destroy the bodies, I'd say these cases are in keeping with my killer's MO."

Her expression is hard to read, so he slides his final photograph across the table. It's taken from a newspaper article and shows a grainy image of the victim's high school yearbook photo. "This woman was found in exactly the same manner, but in Seattle, Washington, and just a month before your first victim was discovered."

She looks at him, eyebrows raised. "You think he's responsible for more than just our three murders?"

He leans in, determined to make her see what he sees. "I think the son of a bitch fled Colorado to avoid capture and on his way to the far ends of the United States he passed through Washington state and couldn't contain his desire to kill." He feels heat rising in his cheeks. The killer is under his skin and it pisses him off. "Pamela, this guy is a serial killer, and he started in my home town." He thinks of the boy from the bedroom and feels a lump in his throat. "I need to be the person who helps catch him."

Pamela spreads the photographs on the table and after a slight hesitation she appears to make a decision. She smiles. "I was hoping you'd say that. I can see how much this case means to you, Bill, and your persistent phone calls to my office together with the time you've spent tracing homicides outside your home town is commendable." She pauses. "I've told my boss all about you. He wants to offer you a job with the Bureau. Not just to solve this case, but to work on others like it."

Bill leans back in his seat, surprised. Did he hear that correct? "But I'm just a small-town detective. I don't know anything about working for the FBI."

She laughs. "Don't worry about that. We have an intensive training program; you'll know all about us by the time you've completed that. The downside is that you would be based in Alaska, like me. That would mean tearing you and your family away from this... interesting town."

Alaska? That's a million miles away. The kids are settled, with Madison in high school and Angie married to Wyatt McCoy. Lynette has a good job and would probably never agree to move away. But if truth be told, he and Lynette have grown apart. They married young and put on a united front for the sake of their girls over the years, but Lynette has made it clear she's unhappy in the marriage, and he's been planning to have a discussion about separating once Madison graduates. He considers whether it would be any worse for Madison if they broke up now instead.

He thinks about what's at stake if he says no to this opportunity. He could work for the FBI. He could hunt serial killers. He could make a real difference to people's lives. How often do these opportunities come along?

Sensing his hesitancy, Pamela says, "Being an FBI agent can take a toll on a person even more than being a cop can.

The kind of people we hunt... Bill, they're deviant in ways your average criminal could never dream up. They enjoy the cat-and-mouse aspect. They're predators hunting prey. And they'll get under your skin like no one else can." She sits forward in her chair. "They may even target your family and anyone else you love."

Dread builds in his chest. He wouldn't be able to cope if anything happened to one of his girls.

"I want to be honest with you." She leans back. "We have a high turnover of staff at our office. Some agents can't deal with the way this job impacts their home life. Some can't cope with living in Alaska. So if you have young children, or a partner who is co-dependent, or a parent who needs you as their carer, working for the Bureau is probably going to tear your family apart."

He appreciates her honesty, but he can read between the lines. She's telling him not to waste her time if he isn't serious about taking the job. She needs to work with people who are willing to go the distance.

"Having said all that," she continues, "this is a time-limited offer. I agree with everything you've said: the person who killed your victim is undoubtedly the same person who killed my victims, and perhaps the woman in Seattle too. And from what we know of serial killers, it's likely he won't stop until he's either caught or he dies. I'd like you to help me make one of those two things happen. But if you don't feel able to leave Colorado, I will need to find—"

"I'll do it." He blurts it out. "I'll make the move. I'll do whatever it takes." The feeling of dread intensifies, but he has to ignore it. He considers the risk to his family, but he already knows he has no intention of making them move all the way to Alaska. His marriage is practically over anyway and Madison's old enough to cope without him living at home. But more importantly, if Lynette and his girls stay behind in Lost Creek, they can't become targets. He can start a new life in Alaska, where no one even knows he has children. He can work as many hours in the day as he wants in order to put an end to this killer's crime spree. And one day he can tell that little boy from the bloody bedroom that he caught his mother's killer.

He looks Pamela in the eye. "Let's catch this son of a bitch."

CHAPTER NINETEEN

Detective Adams arrives at the station after what Madison can only assume was a long, lazy breakfast with his family, as it's mid morning now. She watches as he throws his wet jacket onto his desk. Outside, the snow has turned to icy rain, the kind that stings your face and leaves it red and raw. Adams looks like he needs a hot drink and a warm towel, but Madison hasn't got time to offer him either. She waits to be joined by the rest of her team outside the room they use for press conferences. The local media, and some not so local, are arriving thick and fast after Chief Mendes announced the briefing. The department needs the help of the media and the public if they're to catch this killer.

Madison shuts down any questions she's asked by the reporters who stop as they pass her, trying to be the first to get the inside intel. She peers into the room, looking for Kate Flynn. She's not here yet. Maybe she isn't coming. A quick check of her phone tells her Kate hasn't returned the call she made earlier, and Nate hasn't replied to her message either. She sighs.

Chief Mendes approaches. Aware of how serious the recent homicides are, she's come in on her day off. She's not wearing her customary pantsuit. Instead, she's in navy jeans and a baggy sweater. Dressing casual makes her appear younger than forty-five, but her usual serious expression hasn't changed. Once the rest of the team is huddled outside the conference room and all the reporters appear to be inside, she says quietly, "We need to manage this situation carefully."

Madison nods, then addresses the team. "I take it you've all seen Kate Flynn's outburst by now?" They nod. Not only are the TV channels playing it on repeat, it's found its way onto YouTube already.

"It was legendary," says Officer Sanchez, their newest recruit. He appears to find the situation amusing. "She's going viral for sure."

Chief Mendes gives him a stern look. "No matter whether we agree with what she said or not, she's going to have angered our killer. She embarrassed him on TV by talking about the size of his manhood and accusing him of wanting to sleep with his mother. There's only one way this can go. He'll be out for blood."

Madison agrees. "I'd be surprised if we don't have another victim by the end of the day. We need to advise everyone to say indoors until he's caught."

"I don't know," says Shelley doubtfully. "People won't like that. They'll say we're restricting their rights."

"They want the right to die?" says Alex, turning to her.

"No offense, Alex," she says defensively, "but you sit in an office for most of the day working with DNA and inanimate objects. You're not on the front line interacting with the community like the rest of us, so you don't know what people are like. The minute we advise them to do anything, they do the opposite in a bid to show it's a free country and they can do whatever the hell they want."

Alex shakes his head at the stupidity, but Madison suspects he's just annoyed at Shelley for blowing him off to date Jake Rubio instead.

"Officer Vickers is right," says Mendes. "We should advise people to only go out if necessary, but it's unlikely they'll resist visiting their families today. We need to step up patrol." She turns to Steve. "Call in all officers who aren't scheduled to work today, including Stella so she can help Dina out on dispatch. We need everyone on duty."

Steve nods. "Sure. What about the idea that this guy could be a serial killer?" he asks, keeping his voice low so that no one in the conference room can hear him. He needn't bother. The reporters are loudly swapping information and setting up their mics and cameras. "I know Dina's already fielding calls from the press about that, thanks to Kate's outburst."

"No way," says Detective Adams. "Two murders don't make a serial killer."

"But they do share the same MO," says Madison. "Both victims were mothers, their children were left unharmed, and both were attacked in a parking lot."

"Sure, but that's all easily explainable," says Adams. "Women are statistically more likely to be attacked, and they're also more likely to have a child with them than a guy is. Plus, it's easier to hurt someone as they go about their business than it is to break into their home." He shakes his head. "No. I'm not convinced we have a serial killer on our hands. Not yet. I think we should focus on how the two victims are linked and what the killer's motive is. Statistically it's more likely that they both know the guy than it is that we have a random serial killer sweeping through town."

Adams clearly likes his statistics, but that's more or less what Madison's dad advised too: focus on who or what the victims have in common.

He continues. "With both the victims' children being left unharmed, could our killer be female?"

Madison leans against the door frame and crosses her arms. "I considered that, but I don't see a woman being that savage. At least not to another woman. And in front of the kids?" She shakes her head. "But maybe the killer has a female accomplice, and they're making sure the children aren't hurt. Have you finished watching the CCTV from inside the mall yet?"

"Yeah," says Adams. "I watched Sarah Moss go in and out of every store and no one was following her or watching her closely. Whoever attacked her remained outside the building."

"That's annoying. This guy clearly knows what he's doing."

Alex says, "I have the snowsuit that Emily Cole's child was wearing, so I'll send that to the lab and hopefully it can be tested alongside the items from the first crime scene. Aside from that, there's nothing else at this scene that yields any clues. He didn't leave the murder weapon behind and the church doesn't have security cameras. The footsteps in the snow around the area were contaminated with those from the congregation and our team." He sighs. "Perhaps Lena will discover something during the autopsy, but it looks to me as if Emily Cole was attacked from behind with no warning, so she didn't even get the chance to defend herself."

"There you go," says Adams. "That's different than what happened to Sarah Moss. Sarah was attacked from the front as she sat in her vehicle, so she saw her attacker and had a chance to fight back."

"I think our best source of information right now is the children," says Chief Mendes. "We need to quiz them."

Madison isn't so sure. "Danny and Zach are so young. I don't see that working. Dr. Chalmers spent time with Danny but didn't glean anything useful. He advised Danny's father to take it easy with him. I got the feeling that trying to force information from a child that young isn't a good idea. Danny just wanted to chat about toys and Christmas."

Mendes relents. "I guess that's not an option right now then."

Detective Adams looks at Madison. "You know, I would

have liked a chance to visit the latest crime scene before you arranged this press conference. It would be nice to have more information than those guys in there. I literally found out about it by watching the news this morning."

Madison doesn't like his tone. "You're annoyed at me for giving you the opportunity to spend Christmas morning with your kids?"

"Damn right I'm annoyed. You're acting like you're in charge and you call the shots. I should've been there at the same time as you. Why didn't you or dispatch notify me?"

She shakes her head, disappointed. "Dispatch tried calling you. I don't know whether you didn't hear your phone or you'd switched it off overnight. I didn't try calling you when I arrived on the scene in the middle of the night because I thought I was doing you a favor. I won't make that mistake again."

Chief Mendes looks unimpressed. "You're here now, Detective Adams. If you don't want to be left behind, I suggest you hold the press conference. And I'd recommend you get up to speed asap, because it's starting in ten minutes."

Madison stares at her, mouth open. She's letting the *new guy* lead the press conference? Her cell phone rings. It's Kate. She needs to take the call. To Adams she says, "Fine. Steve will fill you in." She walks away from the team and answers her phone. "Kate, are you okay? I saw what happened."

"Madison, it's Patrick. I'm guessing you haven't heard from my wife since she made a fool of herself on air this morning?"

Her heart sinks. If Patrick has Kate's phone, then something is wrong. She's never without her phone. No decent reporter is. "I haven't. How did you get her phone?"

"It was on the couch at home. She must've come here straight after the disastrous broadcast. I guess she forgot to take it with her when she left."

"Maybe she's on her way to my press conference?"

Patrick sighs down the phone and it's clear he's angry with his wife for her outburst. Something else for them to argue about. It's a shame. With Ben and Sally to think of, Madison hopes they'll try harder to figure things out, but this latest situation is only going to add to their worries. Especially if Kate gets fired. And Madison doesn't see how she wouldn't be. "I have no idea," he says. "I got in the shower at around ten past eight and by the time I came downstairs twenty minutes later there was no sign of her or the kids. She left a note on the fridge to say she'd be back in an hour, so I'm assuming she was called in to see her boss. I don't know why she took the kids with her; maybe she's going to visit her folks on her way home. I'll try calling her mom next, because she's been gone longer than an hour now."

"Do that," she says. "And when you do see her, try to be understanding. I know you're both going through a lot right now, but put that to one side, because she's going to need a friend. Not a reminder that what she did this morning was... well, you know."

He sighs again. "I know. I can't believe she didn't realize she was on air. I called Bob and he said they lost their link with the studio because of the storm. They thought they had another five minutes before they went live, so they were just rehearsing."

Madison feels for her friend. "It's an honest mistake, and everyone will get over it eventually. But right now, she'll be mortified."

"Call me if you hear from her," he says. "I'll keep her phone on me."

"Of course. Drop me a text if you hear from her first."

"Sure." He ends the call and Madison is filled with dread. She's wondering whether Kate could be having some kind of breakdown. She's never done anything unprofessional before, and mocking a killer on live TV is a bad mistake. Who would want to hire a TV reporter who does that? Maybe she's devastated and can't face anyone right now. Or maybe there's more to it.

Dina interrupts her thoughts. "Madison? There's a caller on the line who says they saw a guy running away from St. Theresa's church early this morning."

She turns to Chief Mendes, who says, "Go. Detective Adams and I have got this." She nods to the conference room.

Madison quickly heads to her desk. "Dina? Put them through to my desk phone." When it rings, she answers immediately. "This is Detective Harper. Who am I talking to?"

"I don't want to give my name." It's a male voice. Madison doesn't recognize it, but he sounds younger than her.

"Okay, fine. What did you see this morning?"

He appears to hesitate before saying, "It was a guy dressed all in black. He was running from the direction of the church where that poor woman was murdered. He continued past my apartment and headed north on Pine Street."

She makes a note of the details. "What time?"

"Just before the ambulance turned up. I'd heard a cop car speed by and the sirens woke me, so I got up to see what had happened. Then I saw the guy running past, followed by the ambulance going in the opposite direction."

That would mean that the killer stuck around until the police showed up. That's risky, and suggests he's confident of evading capture. "Can you tell me anything about the male? Height, size, skin color?"

"He was tall and broad, and wearing either a black woolen hat or a ski mask. To tell you the truth, the snow together with the fact that I'd only just woken up and hadn't put my glasses on yet stopped me from seeing him clearly. At first I thought he was out for a jog, but then I realized, who jogs in a snow storm, right? Besides, he was running fast. I'm telling you, that guy did *not* want to get caught."

Her heart sinks at the vague description. "If you weren't wearing glasses, how do you know it was a male? Did you see his face?"

He hesitates, before saying, "No. But I could just tell, you know? From his demeanor."

"And there was no one else with him?"

"No, ma'am. I watched the road for a good ten minutes after, and not one person walked or ran by my place after him."

She nods. This information is actually great, because at least now she knows they're looking for a lone male who is tall and broad. It has to be their guy. No one else would be out at one thirty on Christmas morning in a storm. Unless it was a member of the congregation leaving midnight mass. But it's unlikely he would have run home when Shelley had ordered them all to stay put so they could be questioned. "Are you sure you don't want to leave your name and number?" she asks. "It would remain confidential. We wouldn't give it to the press."

He's adamant. "No. Sorry, Detective. I don't trust that it wouldn't get out somehow and I don't want to be this guy's next victim."

It's disappointing but understandable. "Thanks for calling in. You've been very helpful."

"No problem. Good luck catching the SOB."

Madison puts the phone down and turns to Dina with a smile. "We have our first break."

CHAPTER TWENTY

Nate and Owen have been called to Richie Hope's office. Nate's driving. Apparently the building lost half its roof in the storm overnight and Richie can't entice any construction workers away from their families in order to fix the roof and help him move boxes of paperwork out of the way of the rainwater. Janine refused to come in too, so Richie tried calling Nate, Owen and Frank. Nate doesn't think Frank will travel down from Prospect Springs in this weather and he doesn't blame him. He's not in the mood to help anyone right now either. He still hasn't heard back from the person claiming to be Kristen Devereaux on Facebook. And that's precisely why he needs to get out of his house.

The longer he dwells on the thought that Kristen might be alive, the worse he feels. It would be amazing if it really was her, but he suspects someone's playing games with him. Internet trolls think it's amusing to contact the accounts for missing persons and raise the hopes of the victims' loved ones. Sometimes they do it for more sinister reasons—what's known as the second wave of predators—and try to extort money from families in return for false information about where their loved ones are. Until he gets a response, Nate won't know one way or the other whether it's a hoax, so he needs to distract himself.

"Do you think he'll pay us double?" asks Owen from the passenger seat.

"Maybe." Madison wasn't at the house when Nate swung by to collect Owen, and he was relieved, which makes him feel like an asshole. Their kiss last night should be something positive, the start of something new. But the Facebook message has left him confused and drawn to his past. What happens if Kristen is alive and she shows up one day? So much has happened since she and Nate last saw each other. Since they fell in love.

"Are you okay?" asks Owen. "You seem distracted."

Nate pulls into the parking lot outside Richie's building. If Owen's picked up on his darkening mood, he needs to pull himself together. He doesn't want to ruin anyone's Christmas. "I'm fine." He forces a smile. "Let's see what Richie's got for us."

Inside is a mess. All the boxes Janine was sorting during their first visit are soaked through and Richie is desperately trying to push them into a dry corner. When he spots Nate and Owen, he walks over with open arms. "Merry Christmas, and thank you so much for coming to help!" He hugs them both. "Where's Brody?"

"I left him at home," says Nate. "Thought he might get in the way. So what can we do?"

The door behind them opens and Frank and Janine appear. "You better be paying us triple the going rate," says Janine. She's wearing a sweater with Rudolph the reindeer on the front. His nose is flashing red. In her hands is a tin of what looks like home-made cake.

"I thought you would only work today over my dead body?" says Richie, hands on hips.

Janine gives herself away by glancing at Frank. Maybe once she heard he was coming, she changed her mind. Like

Frank, Janine lives in Prospect Springs, so he must have offered her a ride down here. "I'll make coffee," she says, leaving the room.

Frank nods at Nate before saying to Owen, "Shouldn't you be spending Christmas with your folks?"

"My mom's a cop, so she's working on the homicide investigation." Owen appears proud as he says it, maintaining eye contact with Frank and lifting his chin as if daring anyone to have an opinion on that. He doesn't mention his deceased father.

"Must be tough, having a cop for a mother," says Frank.

"Why?" asks Owen defensively.

"Sorry, kid. I'm not trying to offend you. If it were me, I'd be worried about her, that's all. But I'm sure she can take care of herself." Frank looks up at the damage to the ceiling. "I can patch that up on the inside, Richie, but you'll need a professional to get on the roof. I'm not going up there."

"My contractors won't work today," says Richie with a sigh. "Janine!" he shouts. "Work your magic. You must know someone who can repair a roof." Under his breath he adds, "God knows you've slept with half the construction workers in Prospect Springs."

She returns, slipping her coat off. "I heard that. I could sue you for slander, you know."

Richie smiles. "I suggest you look up what slander means. You wouldn't have a case, since you enjoy telling me all about your many conquests."

"Damn right I tell you," she says, crossing her arms. "I'm not ashamed of it. I spent twenty years with an abusive alcoholic for a husband. Now I'm free of him, you better believe I'm going to sow my wild oats before I lose my figure."

Richie goes over and squeezes her shoulders affectionately. "I wouldn't want you any other way. I'm just hoping you can use your feminine wiles to get my roof fixed, that's all."

Janine sighs. "I'll see what I can do, but you're going to

have to make it worth their time. With money, I mean. How much can I offer?"

A loud gust of wind rattles the remaining loose roof tiles, sending more rainwater into the reception. "Oh Jeez," says Richie. "I'll pay whatever it takes. Just get someone here pronto."

Frank goes out to his pickup truck and Nate watches through the window as he opens a large toolbox and selects what he needs for the job.

"Would you and Owen mind moving these boxes to the back office?" asks Richie. "We need to get them dried out so that you," he nods to Owen, "can eventually enter the paperwork onto the computer. It's time my office turned paperless so nothing like this can happen again. Plus, it'll save me paying for storage."

"Sure," says Owen.

Nate notices that some of the boxes are charred black. They must be the survivors from the firebombing of Richie's last office. This guy has bad luck.

"My storage unit is up in Prospect Springs," says Richie. "There's plenty more boxes of this stuff there to keep you busy."

Owen gives Nate a look that suggests he might regret agreeing to intern for Richie. Nate can't help but laugh. He realizes that being here is better than being alone today, and he suspects Owen feels the same way.

"Are you open?" says someone behind them.

Nate turns around and sees Jake Rubio standing in the doorway. Jake's medical training saved Nate's life last month, but he was unconscious at the time so they've never actually spoken. "Hi," he says. "Remember me? I'm the guy who owes you a beer."

Frank glances down from the ladder he's now standing on, to see who's arrived, then returns to hammering nails into the ceiling.

"Sure I remember you," says Jake. "You looked like roadkill by the time I got to you." He smiles. "I'm glad to see you're good now. Although I bet your ribs haven't healed yet, have they?"

Nate instinctively reaches for them. "No, they're still giving me some trouble."

"They'll be right soon enough." Jake turns to Richie. "Are you a lawyer?"

"I am indeed."

"I saw the lights on, so I thought I'd take a shot and see if you're open for new business."

Richie steps forward with his hand outstretched and a wide smile on his face. "Here at Hope & Associates, we're always open for business. I'm Richie Hope." Jake shakes his hand and takes a wide-eyed look around the messy office. "Don't you worry about any of this," says Richie. "We're in the middle of a renovation. How can I help you, son?"

Jake appears uneasy at discussing his business in front of everyone, so Richie leads him into his office. Not that they'll get any privacy in there. Nate overhears Jake say, "I'm in trouble."

Richie pulls out a legal pad and Nate tries not to watch them as he helps Owen move boxes, but he's intrigued. "Then you've come to the right place," says Richie. "Take a seat. What kind of trouble are you in?"

Jake clears his throat. "I think I'm about to be arrested for murder."

Frank whistles and looks down at Nate with raised eyebrows. "Never a dull moment in this place."

Nate can't tell whether he's talking about Richie's office or Lost Creek.

CHAPTER TWENTY-ONE

Madison stands at the door to the conference room, watching Marcus Adams give reporters an update on the two homicides. He looks smart in his crisp navy suit. She wonders how long it will take before he switches to jeans and a shirt like the rest of them. Clothes have a way of getting ruined in this job, whether from a victim's bodily fluids or the smell of crime scenes and people's homes. It's not worth wearing your finest suits to work.

Adams speaks confidently into the cameras, but she can tell he's nervous. He keeps sipping the water in front of him. She feels for him. He doesn't know any of these reporters yet, so it must feel like swimming with sharks.

"No," he says in response to someone's question. "The murders were not sexually motivated."

"In your opinion," says Gary Pelosi, "do we have a serial killer in Lost Creek?"

Adams scoffs. "Not at all. Obviously we've all seen the footage of Kate Flynn's outburst this morning, where she raised the prospect. But that was purely speculation. There's no evidence at all to suggest that this is a serial killer, and it's not a theory we're working on. What we *are* focusing on is finding a motive. If anyone has any information at all, call us immediately."

Madison joins him at the front of the room. Leaning in to the mics, she says, "Before you all disappear, I want to add some new information we just received. A lone male figure dressed all in black was seen running away from St. Theresa's church at around one thirty this morning, shortly after Emily Cole's body was found. He was heading north along Pine Street. If anyone else saw this person, please call us urgently. Alternatively, if you have a partner who told you he was going out for a run in the early hours because he couldn't sleep, we want to be able to rule him out. Anything you disclose will be treated in confidence, and you can remain anonymous if you wish." She pauses, before adding, "If you're watching this and it was *you* who went for a run, or you left the midnight mass service without speaking to the police, let us know so we can eliminate you from our investigation. Thank you." She steps away from Adams.

The reporters start throwing more questions at him, so he says, "That's it for now. I'm sure you all appreciate we have a killer to catch. The best thing the community can do today and tomorrow is to stay indoors wherever possible. If you need to go out, don't go alone. We have stepped up patrol around town, but you should still report any suspicious activity to LCPD. Thank you."

Madison leaves the conference room. Detective Adams and Chief Mendes follow her. They stop outside Mendes's office, and the chief tells Adams he did a good job. "What's your next move?" she asks.

Adams looks at Madison. "I want to speak to the victims' partners. I know you already have, but I want to see what these two women have in common."

"Fine," says Madison. "You know about David Moss, but I'll text you the number for Brian Slater. He's the father of Emily Cole's boy, Zach, although he and Emily broke up a while ago. He was shocked when I told him what had happened and came straight to collect his son. He says he was home with his girlfriend and her family at the time of the murder, so interview them all, but it's a pretty solid alibi."

"Sure." Adams waits as she forwards him the details. "Was Emily in a relationship with anyone?" he asks.

"Kind of. Jake Rubio, a local EMT, was the closest thing she had to a partner, and he saw her earlier in the day. He says he left her place at around five p.m. and was home alone at the time of her murder, but he doesn't have any way of proving that." She thinks of the description given of the lone figure. "On the one hand, he's tall and broad, like the man seen by our witness, but on the other hand, he saves lives for a living. He doesn't exactly fit the description of a violent killer."

"Well," says Adams, "I don't know the guy, so I'm not biased. I'll see if he's willing to talk to me."

"And you?" asks Mendes, looking at Madison.

"I need to check in with a friend, and then I'll go through any tips coming in to dispatch."

Mendes nods. "Would this friend be Kate Flynn?"

"Right. I'm worried about her. She left home with the kids earlier and didn't take her cell phone. She's probably been fired, and she's under considerable strain in her private life too, so I'm concerned she isn't thinking straight."

Adams says, "She's made our job a lot harder by suggesting a serial killer is responsible for our homicides. I hope you'll tell her that."

Madison glares at him. "You have no idea what she's going through right now, so keep your opinion to yourself." She grabs her coat from her chair and leaves the station.

The rain has stopped, but it's too cold for the ground coverage to melt away and it's slippery underfoot. Once seated in her car, Madison calls Owen. It's lunchtime already and she feels guilty for not being around today. He answers the phone on the third ring. "Hey, Mom. How's it going?"

She sighs. "Busy. How are you? Not eating everything in the house, I hope."

"No, I'm at Richie's office. His roof is leaking, so me and Nate are helping him move some stuff while Frank and the contractor fix it."

She frowns. She doesn't know who Frank is, but she's surprised that Owen is with Nate. Nate never responded to her earlier text. "How long will you be there?"

"I'm not sure. We'll be back in time for dinner, though. What time will you be home?"

She checks her watch and sighs. "I have no idea. I'm sorry Christmas isn't working out the way we planned."

"That's okay. Richie implied he'd pay me well for coming in today, so it doesn't matter to me."

She smiles. "How's Nate?"

"He's right here. Want to talk to him?" She tenses, but before she can answer, Owen says, "Oh, wait. He's disappeared. Want me to get him to call you?"

Disappointment sweeps over her. Nate must be avoiding her. "No, that's okay. I guess I'll leave you to help Richie."

"Wait, I have some gossip." She hears shuffling sounds and a door closing before he lowers his voice and says, "You know Jake Rubio, right?"

Madison watches out of her windshield as Officer Sanchez passes in front of her car. He gets into a cruiser and pulls out of the parking lot. "Sure, I know Jake. Why?"

"He came by the office earlier and told Richie he was in trouble and needed a lawyer."

She tenses. "Did he say what kind of trouble?"

"Yeah," he whispers. "He said he might be arrested for murder."

Her mouth drops open. Owen probably shouldn't be telling her this considering he works for an attorney now, but she's glad he did. Why would Jake Rubio feel he needed a lawyer? She wasn't particularly hard on him with questions when she notified him of Emily's death in the early hours of this morning. So why would he assume she was going to come back and arrest him?

"Mom?"

"Sorry. Thanks for telling me." She takes a deep breath. "I'll aim to get home by five, but I can't promise anything with the way things are going."

"Sure. I'll let Nate and Grandpa know. Where is Grandpa anyway?"

Madison has no clue. "He said he had things to do, but I don't know. He's probably with Vince at the diner. Anyway, I better go. I'll see you tonight." Then she adds, "Maybe stay away from Jake Rubio."

Owen laughs. "I knew you'd say that. Bye, Mom."

She thinks about it. Is Jake only hiring a lawyer because she asked him about his alibi earlier and he wants to get some advice, or does he know she could uncover something unsavory about him? She texts Adams, who is still inside the station.

Just heard Jake Rubio has lawyered up. Ask David Moss whether his wife knew him.

If both victims knew Jake, that could confirm he's a good person of interest.

She eventually gets a thumbs-up emoji in response. While Adams checks that, she needs to look for Kate. The detective part of her considers Kate and the kids missing until they show up, but she's hoping she's overreacting. She starts the car and drives over to Kate's house.

Patrick's car is the only vehicle on the driveway. He's already at the front door when she approaches. "Have you found them?" he asks, looking frantic.

Her heart sinks. She was hoping they'd be home by now and no one thought to tell her. It's past noon already and Patrick said they'd left the house at eight thirty. "I'm sorry. I haven't heard from her at all." She follows him inside. The living room floor is covered in torn gift wrap. It looks like Ben and Sally opened some of their presents while Kate was reporting from this morning's crime scene. She must have been upset when she came home to this, knowing she'd missed seeing her children's faces light up.

The Christmas tree lights are off and the house is dark because of the gray sky outside. Madison switches on a table lamp. "Did you turn them off?" She nods to the tree.

He looks up. "Yeah. I'm not in the mood. I'm worried, Madison. Where has she taken the kids?"

A creeping sensation of fear sweeps through her as she starts considering whether the person who killed Sarah and Emily might have done something to Kate in retaliation for what she said about him. Madison doesn't let her concern show. Instead, she asks, "Who have you tried calling?"

"Her boss at the TV station said he texted her right after her meltdown on air and told her to go see him, but she never showed up. Bob, her camera guy, said she was upset when she left the church's parking lot. Embarrassed mainly, but she knew she'd lose her job over it and maybe Bob would too, so she was feeling guilty. Before she got into her car, she told him she was going home."

"And you didn't see or hear her when she got here because you were in the shower?"

"Right. The kids were playing downstairs. I'd told them to wait for their mom to get home before they opened their gifts, but when I got down here, the living room was like this, Kate's phone was on the couch and her note was on the fridge." He shows her the note.

Back in an hour.

It's definitely in Kate's writing, which reassures Madison that she hasn't been snatched. It's more likely she's beating herself up over what happened and needs some time out. "Do you know if she dressed the kids warmly?"

He nods. "Their winter coats and snow boots are gone, along with their hats, scarves and gloves."

That's something. Madison thinks it's strange that Patrick didn't hear his wife come and go. And why was he showering instead of watching the kids and waiting for Kate to get home? Surely he was anxious about how she'd cope with what she'd said live on air? Her gut tells her something is wrong, but she can't work out if it's just because she knows the couple has been going through a hard time. She's witnessed them argue and knows how unintentionally aggressive Patrick can appear when he's angry. But Kate's never disclosed any physical violence in their relationship. "Did her parents call after seeing her on the news?"

He nods. "Her mom called her cell phone, so I answered and told her Kate had probably gone to work. I didn't want to worry her. They're both coming here for dinner later. What happens if she hasn't returned by then?"

Madison doesn't know. "Did Kate ever mention Jake Rubio to you?"

He frowns, confused by the change in direction. "The paramedic? No, she didn't. Why? What are you saying?"

"Nothing. It's not important. Have you checked with the neighbors to see if anyone saw which direction she drove away in?"

"Yeah, no one saw her leave, and our doorbell camera is deactivated since Kate heard they were being used for burglaries."

Madison doesn't like that. She wonders if Patrick could be lying. Maybe he deactivated it to cover his tracks. She tries to think where else Kate could be. "If she's not at work or with her parents, where should I look? Does she have any other close friends? Or what about *your* parents?"

He stands up, angry. "Look, I've tried everyone I can think

of. It's your turn now. I need you guys looking for her. Because if anything happens to my children..." His voice cracks.

She gives him some space and looks around the room. "Is anything missing? Any of their toys?" She thinks of Ben and his selective mutism. About how he's been using his iPad to communicate for the last few months. He has an app where he can press a button and it will speak his chosen word for him. "Where's Ben's iPad?"

Patrick looks for it under the discarded gift wrap and on the couch. He checks the kitchen too. "It's not here. He was using it when I went upstairs to shower."

"That's a good sign. It means Kate was thinking straight when she left the house." She was worried when she heard Kate had left her phone behind, but the fact that she thought to take Ben's iPad with her means she's rational and hopefully not intending to harm herself or her kids.

Madison's cell phone buzzes in her pocket. She pulls it out. It's Steve. She looks at Patrick. "Sorry. I have to take this." Turning around, she raises the phone to her ear. "Hi, Steve."

"Have you seen the news?" he asks.

She takes a few steps away from Patrick. She has a horrible feeling Steve's going to tell her Kate's been found dead. "No, what it is?"

"Someone posted a flash drive to David Moss's home. It contains a video showing Danny in the back seat of the Lexus, watching his mom get beaten to death."

Madison gasps. "Oh my God."

Patrick spins her around forcefully by her shoulder. "What's happened? Is it Kate?"

She pulls herself out of his grasp, shocked by his aggression. Her shoulder hurts where he grabbed her. She's never seen him like this before. "No. It's nothing to do with Kate." Turning away from him again, she takes a few steps toward the front door. "Is it definitely Danny?" she asks Steve.

"Afraid so. His dad confirmed it. And unfortunately he

gave the flash drive to an online reporter before informing us about it, which means any prints that were on it are now contaminated. The video has already been uploaded to their website, although hopefully not for long. We've asked them to take it down."

Madison shakes her head. "Why would he give it to the media?" She considers whether David Moss could be Sarah's killer, and it was him who filmed it. Handing the flash drive to a reporter could be his way of trying to cover up his involvement.

Sighing, Steve says, "I have no idea. Alex is going to see whether he can identify any sounds or see any reflections in the video that might give us a lead. I'll send you a link to it. I'll warn you, though, it's horrific."

She swallows. "Okay." After ending the call, she turns back to Patrick. "I'll make all officers aware we're looking for Kate and the kids. If you're intending to go out and search for her, be careful on the roads. They're icy, and the last thing your family needs is you getting into an accident."

He nods, and Madison leaves the house, dreading what she has to do next.

CHAPTER TWENTY-TWO

Nate stares out at the snow-topped mountains as they speed by his window. He and Frank Brookes are on their way back to Lost Creek in Frank's pickup truck after visiting Richie's storage locker in Prospect Springs. The roads are quiet, but the country music playing on the stereo is not. Frank's erratic driving as he tries to avoid ice patches at speeds he has no business doing in this weather causes the boxes they collected to slide around in the back seat. Nate drowns it all out as he's stuck in his head, thinking about Madison and Kristen.

"Woman trouble?" asks Frank, keeping his eyes on the road.

"What?" asks Nate.

Frank turns the music down. "Well, you've barely said a word all the way there and back. Either you can't stand me or you've got woman trouble."

"No." Nate sighs. "Life's just decided to get a little complicated, that's all."

Frank glances at him with curiosity. "I'll level with you, Monroe. I know who you are. Once Richie introduced us, I recognized your name, so of course I looked you up. I'm sorry if that offends you, but I like to know who I'm working with."

Nate shakes his head in annoyance. "It doesn't offend me; it pisses me off."

Frank nods. "Yep. Thought it would. Well, at least I'm being honest with you. Now that I know who you are and what you've been through, I find myself wondering what in the world could be complicated about your life since you became a free man with the financial means to never work another day."

Nate looks at the aging cowboy and senses he isn't trying to cause offense. He surprises himself by opening up. "Someone I care about has been missing for almost three years. I don't know if she's dead or alive, and until I do, I feel like I'm stuck in the past, unable to move forward."

Frank's silent for a minute. "Have you tried looking for her?"

Nate's too ashamed to tell him no, not properly at least. He hasn't had the emotional strength to do that yet, because since getting off of death row, all his energy has gone into surviving.

Understanding the meaning of his silence, Frank asks, "Want me to look for her?"

"You look for missing people?" Nate's surprised. "What's your background, law enforcement?" All he knows is that Frank investigates for Richie and hates Lost Creek. He hasn't asked anything else about him yet, and realizes he's been living in his own head for too long and neglecting to focus on anyone else.

"You don't need to have been *in* law enforcement to *know* law enforcement," says Frank. "I grew up around it. And just as your young friend Owen has probably absorbed a lot from being around his detective mother, I did the same, whether I liked it or not. It's probably why I'm an investigator. I can't look at anyone and see a purely innocent person. I'm always wondering what they're hiding."

Nate tenses at the flippant way Frank talks about Owen. "If you googled me, I expect you googled Owen too?"

"Well, he and his mom were mentioned in the articles about you, on account of Detective Harper bringing you to Lost Creek with her earlier this summer." He glances at Nate. "Seems like you two are forever linked online."

Nate looks away. Forever linked to Madison. *That doesn't sound so bad.*

"Sounds like she's had it almost as rough as you. And as for young Owen..." Frank shakes his head. "I'm willing to bet he's the one who suffered most. The kids always are. And to think he lost his mom for, what, six or seven *years*, over a stupid family grudge? What a waste. Excuse me for being frank, no pun intended, but in my opinion a boy needs his mother during those crucial years. The fact that he didn't have her around is bound to have repercussions down the line."

Nate resists the urge to defend Madison. Because her incarceration wasn't down to a *stupid family grudge*. It was down to greed and deception, and none of it was her fault. He knows there's no use explaining that to Frank. Once your life has become tabloid fodder, people make up their own minds about you and there's no changing it. Nate knows that better than anyone.

"I apologize if I've upset you," says Frank. "It's a long journey and I'm just trying to pass the time. Ignore me. I mean, what do I know, right? The offer still stands, though. I can help you find your missing person. I'd actually be glad to. It's something I'm good at."

Nate considers whether he wants someone else to do his job. On the one hand, he feels like he should be the person to find Kristen, but on the other, he keeps putting it off. Maybe having Frank look into it will be better for his mental health. But then he doesn't know anything about the guy. All he knows is that nothing comes for free in this world. Perhaps Frank's looking to earn some extra money. Maybe he's planning to fleece him by taking the money and not doing the work. Or maybe it's time Nate started trusting people. "I don't know. Why would you do that for a stranger?"

Frank keeps his eyes on the road. "I understand your hesitancy. And you're right not to trust strangers. I mean, we only just met. For all you know, I'm an asshole." He pauses for a long minute. "Maybe I shouldn't have offered. I just can't help myself. I hate to see people in turmoil, that's all."

They fall silent as Frank drives across the One-Way Bridge. Nate can see the top of the water tower from here, with the Ferris wheel at Fantasy World behind it. After a while, he asks, "Why didn't you want to move down here to be closer to Richie's office? Because a long commute to work seems like a waste of time to me, not to mention the cost of gas."

Frank takes a deep breath. "Everything I know about Lost Creek I learned on the news. Child abductions, homicides, crime writers getting killed, vigilantism, women beaten to death in front of their kids... No, sir. It doesn't sound like the kind of town I want to live in."

Nate can't fault his logic. But he thinks of Madison and Owen, and how there are good people like them living here too. People who are trying to make a difference. Guilt sweeps over him again. He never responded to Madison's text this morning and then he deliberately avoided talking to her when she was on the phone with Owen. He's being an asshole. The only way to stop that is to get closure with Kristen, one way or another. After another long silence, he says, "Her name's Kristen Devereaux. If you've read up on me, you'll know who she is."

Frank glances at him. "The law professor who got you out of prison."

Nate swallows. "See what you can find."

CHAPTER TWENTY-THREE

Madison has watched the video four times. She watches it again now at her desk, with Steve and Detective Adams standing behind her chair. They seem shell-shocked by it too, unable to believe someone could stoop so low. The sun has set outside and it's eerily quiet in the office. Everyone would rather be home with their families. Especially after watching this horrific footage.

Madison concentrates on her computer screen, trying hard not to look away. She's muted it this time, unable to bear to listen to the screams of the victim over the child's own cries. The camera is focused on Danny. He's positioned behind the front passenger seat, staring at his mother in the driver's seat. The footage and car rock with the impact of the blows to Sarah Moss. It looks as though the killer positioned the camera— possibly a GoPro—on some kind of mount that he's attached to the outside of the window directly behind the driver's seat, because there's no way he could have held the camera during his attack. The driver's door is open, and the internal lights illuminate the scene. At several points Danny looks away, glancing out of his window as if searching for help. Seconds later, tears roll down his face and he tries to reach for his mother. The toy car he was clutching drops onto the seat, instantly forgotten. When the rocking stops, it's clear the attack is over. Sarah Moss is dead and Danny stares at the killer while sucking his thumb. The footage ends.

It's the thumb-sucking that does it for Madison. "He's self-soothing," she says. Her voice cracks and she's helpless against the tears that fall. She feels a hand gently rub her back, probably Steve's.

"We don't need to watch this again," he says. "Leave it for Alex to analyze. That's his job."

Detective Adams exhales loudly and returns to the desk opposite hers. Their computer monitors sit back to back as their desks touch. "Well, that answers the question as to whether Danny was in the car while the attack happened. He saw the whole goddam thing."

Steve crouches next to Madison. "Are you okay?"

She grabs the tissue Stella has brought over and wipes her eyes. "It's not just the video. I'm exhausted. I didn't get any sleep last night, and was called to the second crime scene at one thirty this morning. Normally I can keep it together, but..."

"Shit, that's my fault," says Steve. "I should've made you leave before now." He stands. "Go home. I'm serious. It's four o'clock already, and you've worked straight through. You need some downtime. Open presents, have dinner with your family, get some sleep and then come back tomorrow morning. Between us we can cover the rest of the day. Right, Adams?"

Adams nods. "Sure. I mean, I can't be too late because of the kids, but I'll stay as long as I can."

Madison hates that the new guy is seeing her like this. Steve has seen her emotional many times before, but she knows he won't judge her for it. He's a close and trusted member of the team who always has her back. But Adams is new, and she doesn't want him to think she breaks down every time the going gets tough. With her eyes heavy and feeling shaky with hunger, she has to admit defeat. When

Steve stands, she switches her computer off and grabs her jacket and scarf. "I'll be here early tomorrow. But let me know if you need me overnight. And if anyone finds Kate Flynn."

"Of course," says Steve. With no partner or children, he doesn't have anyone waiting for him at home. He's a workaholic by choice, so she doesn't feel too bad about leaving him in charge.

Stella hugs her. "Try to have a good evening with your boy."

"Are you sure you don't want to join us for dinner?" asks Madison. "I can't promise the food will be great, but I have lots of wine."

Smiling, Stella shakes her head. "I'm sure. I'd rather be here to help Dina field calls. Besides, Chief Mendes says we can order takeout on her credit card. If I'd known that sooner, I would've worn my stretchy pants to work."

Madison attempts a smile before exiting the station. As she walks through the dark parking lot to get to her car, she has to admit she's looking forward to getting home. Steve is right, she needs a break from the depravity of the case. She checks her cell phone. No messages or missed calls. She's starting to feel like Nate and Owen don't need her anymore, as they rarely contact her. Once Owen leaves for college next year, all she'll have to occupy her time is this job. What a terrible thought.

She sighs and surveys the poorly lit lot. Is someone hiding out there, just waiting for an unsuspecting victim to cross his path? She has to dismiss the thought or she'll never get any rest.

Before she can slip into her car, Steve runs out of the station. When he reaches her, he touches her arm. "I just wanted to check you're okay. I have a feeling you wouldn't admit anything else in front of the new guy."

She smiles. "Thanks. I'll be okay by tomorrow morning. It's just... this case feels like the most disturbing one we've ever had, don't you think? I mean, there seems to be no reason for it, and anyone could be the next victim."

He leans against her car, slipping his hands into his pockets to keep them warm as he's not wearing a jacket. "I think we're dealing with someone who doesn't care about consequences. Being locked up won't bother him as long as he gets to hurt as many people as possible before he's caught."

"That's a terrifying thought."

He looks at her. "Don't carry the burden on your own. That'll send you crazy. Use all of us. We're a team, remember?"

She finds herself wondering why Steve is single and spends all his time at work. He's a lot like Nate in some ways; looking out for everyone else at the expense of his own life. "What about you?" she asks softly. "When do you relax, because we've all noticed you never go home."

He deliberates for a few seconds, as if weighing up how to answer. Eventually he stands straight and smiles. "Call me crazy, but maybe I enjoy spending time with you guys. That's not a crime, is it?"

She laughs. "No, but it should be."

He turns and heads back toward the station, just stopping long enough to say, "Merry Christmas, Madison."

She watches him go, feeling like he was almost going to open up for the first time. She wishes he had done, as she senses he's lonely, but she can't make him reveal anything he doesn't want to. She tries the handle of her car, but it's frosted over and requires some force to open it. After scraping ice off the windshield, she slips into the freezing driver's seat and starts the engine, marveling how it always starts first time when she's not in a rush.

The roads aren't as treacherous as earlier, as the snow-plows have been out, so it doesn't take long to reach her house. As she pulls onto the driveway, she sees her dad's SUV and a black rental car next to it. She frowns, wondering who that belongs to. Nate's car isn't here yet and she doubts he'll come.

Her legs are heavy as she walks up the porch steps and unlocks the front door. Inside smells of cigars, and she gets her first craving for a cigarette in a while. She takes her jacket off, hangs it by the front door and enters the living room. Her dad is sitting on the couch next to a man she's never met. He's younger than her father and he's the one who's smoking. Bandit is curled up on his lap, too trusting of a stranger. The guy must've fed him a treat.

"Maddie, you're home!" says her dad. He switches the TV off and stands up before coming over for a hug. "This is Mike Spence, an old friend of mine. He had nowhere to go today so I suggested he join us for dinner."

Her heart sinks. She wanted some quality time with her dad and Owen, and she wanted to take a bath before dinner and change into something more casual. Mike must sense her disappointment, because he tries to stand, but Bandit protests so he sits back down. "If it's a problem," he says, "I'm happy to leave. I don't want to intrude on precious family time."

"No," she says. "That's okay. We have plenty of food to go around. But I'll need some help in the kitchen." She looks at her dad as she speaks, hoping he'll realize she's exhausted and can't do it all herself.

"Say no more." He turns to his friend. "Find something to watch on TV, Mike. I'll be back with a drink once I've helped my daughter get started."

Mike does as he's told, and Bill follows Madison to the kitchen. "Sorry, honey. I had no idea he was coming into town and I couldn't exactly turn him away given the weather and all."

She sighs as she washes her hands. "That's okay. But I'm exhausted. I might not be good company. Have you seen the latest news? Our killer filmed the victim's son while he beat the boy's mother to death."

He nods gravely. "It's despicable. The guy needs a fast track to death row once he's caught."

She turns to him as she dries her hands. "What would you do next if you were investigating this case?"

He leans against the counter and crosses his arms. "Like I said before, find the link between the two victims, because this isn't random. The guy who did this wants the victims' families to hurt. He must do if he's sent that video to one of them. He probably has a video of the other murder ready to send to that woman's partner too."

"Emily Cole wasn't in a relationship."

"Then he'll probably send it to her mother. He's angry and he wants people to know it." He considers another possibility before saying, "Maybe he's angry with David Moss, and he killed his wife out of revenge for something Moss did to him. Look into what he's hiding."

"That wouldn't explain why the killer went on to kill Emily Cole this morning, though."

Bill shrugs. "You're not always dealing with sane, rational people, honey." He takes a deep breath. "Try not to think about any of that tonight. If I learned anything during my career, it's that everyone needs downtime. You can't work a case twenty-four seven, or you'll burn out and miss vital links. The investigation will still be waiting for you to solve it tomorrow."

She takes a deep breath. He's right. She has a partner now, someone to share the workload. It's Detective Adams's turn to be in charge.

She gives her dad the potatoes and vegetables to peel while she gets changed upstairs and then fixes them all a drink. She learns that Mike doesn't drink alcohol, so he's sipping a soda. Her dad has a bottle of beer, but it sits forgotten as he helps her chop vegetables.

The turkey is starting to brown in the oven by the time she hears Owen's key in the front door. "Hi, Mom," he shouts from the hallway. As she goes to greet him, Brody runs past her, toward the smell of meat. "Sorry we're late," he says. "We had to collect Brody on our way back."

Madison looks up hopefully and sees that Nate is behind Owen. He clearly hasn't shaved today and he looks as tired as she feels. He smiles sheepishly as he greets her, but his eyes are serious. Sad, even.

She turns away and clears the lump in her throat. "Someone needs to set the table and feed the cat. Brody can have our leftovers after dinner."

Nate runs his hand down her back as he passes her to enter the kitchen. It makes her shiver. Maybe he's sorry for the way he's been acting, but any conversation will have to wait until they're alone.

CHAPTER TWENTY-FOUR

The dining table is covered with dishes of vegetables, potatoes and turkey, along with small candles glowing softly and various half-empty wineglasses dotted around. Christmas carols play quietly in the background. Somehow Madison manages to feel festive at last, despite everything that's occupying her thoughts.

Over dinner, Owen tries to keep the cat off the table while telling them all about his new job at Richie's law firm. He talks about Janine, who runs the office, and how she has the hots for Frank, the other investigator. "She was telling me how she met Frank in a bar up in Prospect Springs," he says. "When she heard he was looking for work, she told him that Richie was looking for an investigator. That's how he got the job. I think she was hoping he'd ask her on a date, but Frank told me he doesn't get mixed up with women because they're all trouble and after a man's money. He prefers to live alone and enjoy the quiet life."

Madison tries to concentrate, but Nate is positioned opposite her and she feels his eyes on her a lot of the time. It makes her self-conscious.

"Richie told him he must be going to the wrong places if

that's the kind of women he's attracting." Owen laughs. "Richie's funny."

"I'm not a fan of lawyers," says Bill. "They'd sell their soul for a quick buck."

"Maybe, but Richie's different," says Owen. "He's not pretentious."

Nate glances at Bill and Mike. "How do you two know each other?" he asks.

The pair exchange a look before Mike answers. "We met up in Alaska, through a friend of a friend. When Bill told me he was moving all the way down here, I had to visit to see what the appeal was. I just didn't expect it to be as cold as Alaska, or I'd have stayed home." He smiles.

"Did you hunt serial killers too?" asks Owen.

"Wait a minute, are you saying I look like a Fed?" Mike quips. "No, I'm not a Fed. I'm just a high school teacher."

Madison wonders if Mike is related to her father's second wife, and if that's why the two men seem a little awkward talking about how they know each other. When her dad first came back into her life last month, she had asked where his wife was. He's never confirmed that he remarried when he moved up north, probably because of some long-held guilt for leaving them all behind, but he did confirm he'd been in a relationship, admitting that it hadn't worked out. Madison didn't press the issue, as it was clear he didn't want to talk about it, but they need to discuss the past eventually. She wants to get to know her father properly.

"At least the storm's passed," Bill says. "Now we just need the snow to clear from the roads."

"The plows have been out this afternoon." Madison suddenly remembers what Owen told her about Jake Rubio. She turns to him and, careful not to let Mike overhear information about an ongoing investigation, she whispers, "Did you hear anything else Jake said to Richie earlier?"

Nate drops his fork and looks at Owen. "You told her Jake stopped by the office? Did you tell her why?"

Mike and Bill stop talking among themselves.

Owen stops chewing and raises his eyebrows. "Yeah. Why? Is that bad?"

"Think about it," says Nate. "What would Richie say if he knew? You work for an attorney now, Owen. We both do, which means everything that happens in that office or with Richie's clients is confidential."

Madison knows he's right, but she's annoyed that he would chastise her son. "He did the right thing in this scenario. That particular person is a potential suspect for the two homicides."

Nate shakes his head, clearly disappointed. "It doesn't matter. It's not right for one of Richie's employees to disclose to the police, or anyone else for that matter, what he overhears while at work. And you and I both know that just because someone hires a lawyer, it doesn't mean they're guilty. It's what I would do if I were in his position seeing as most cops can't be trusted."

This is how he was when they first met; his hatred of anyone in law enforcement clouded his judgement. His feelings were understandable back then, with a crooked detective being partially responsible for landing him on death row, but he's since seen for himself that not all cops are like that. It's frustrating that he's feeling this way again. And Madison knows Richie won't be happy if he finds out Owen told her about Jake seeking representation, but he's just an intern. She looks at her son. "Have you signed a contract for your internship yet?"

Owen looks like a rabbit caught in the headlights, and she can tell that Mike and her dad are feeling awkward, as their eyes are focused on their plates. "No, not yet," he says. "I was only helping him move boxes. It's early days."

She turns back to Nate. "There you go; he's not officially employed yet, which means he didn't do anything wrong."

Nate looks at her. "I just think he needs to learn to pick a side in these situations. You might be his mother, but you're a cop, and he's working for the guy's lawyer. It doesn't feel right to me."

Madison feels like he's betraying her. If it was anyone else, she wouldn't care so much, but it's Nate. She leans in, her face warming with frustration. "If you'd had to watch the video that was sent to one of the victims' husbands today, you'd know that Owen did the right thing. The guy who murdered those women is a violent, dangerous person who needs to be caught before he kills again, and my son telling me about a particular person acquiring a lawyer means I now know he probably has something to hide." She gets up and leaves the room.

Once she's upstairs and in her bedroom, she leans against the closed door and lets the tears fall, already regretting the scene she's caused and the way she handled it. What must Mike think of her? And as for Nate, it's clear that he regrets their kiss. Is this his way of telling her it was a mistake? She hates being this emotional, it's not like her. She's normally better at bottling things up. But Danny Moss's distraught face won't stop playing on repeat in her head. And the one person she thought she could rely on to always have her back appears to be turning against her.

A soft knock at the door makes her step away. The door opens and her dad cautiously enters. "You okay, honey?" She moves to sit on the edge of her bed and nods. He sits next to her. "Being a cop is hard," he says. "What your friend might not understand is that we have to get information any way we can in order to keep our communities safe."

"He should know that by now," she says.

Bill pats her hand. "Don't be too tough on him. Your mom and I used to fight all the time about my investigations, do you remember?"

She smiles faintly. "Mom hated it when you brought the crime-scene photos home."

He laughs. "Only because you were sneaking a look at them. She wouldn't have known otherwise!"

It's true. Madison was fascinated by her dad's job, and terrified by the photos she'd go hunting for, even though he tried to hide them on top of the kitchen cabinets. He didn't have a home office or a safe; their house was too small for those kinds of luxuries. When her mom found her poring over the photos one day, she went crazy. Back then Madison was too young to appreciate why she was so upset. Now she realizes her mom must have feared her younger daughter would follow in her husband's footsteps and join the force. That she'd be putting herself in danger every day.

Although Madison had to suffer through her time in prison with no family support, she'll be forever grateful that her mother wasn't alive to see her locked up. Lynette Harper wasn't like Madison and Bill. She had what back then was referred to as a nervous disposition—what doctors would now recognize as generalized anxiety disorder.

"Who was the woman you left us for?" she asks. "You never talked about her during our phone calls."

Bill stares hard, as if he's trying to gauge whether she can take what he has to say. Then he takes her hands in his. "I didn't leave your mom for another woman."

She frowns. "That's not what Mom told us."

"We were protecting you from the truth. There *was* a female agent I was working in collaboration with, Pamela Rogers, but we weren't having an affair." He pauses. "I left town because I was chasing a serial killer and I didn't want any of you becoming a target. Those SOBs play dirty, Madison." He slowly shakes his head. "I pray you never come across one while you're a detective."

She wishes she'd known the real reason when she was younger. It might have been easier to understand his decision to move so far away from them. "That's why you lost contact with us too. So that he wouldn't know we existed and we'd be safe from him?"

He nods and she realizes how much he sacrificed for his job, and to protect the public and his family in the process. Pride swells in her chest. But it's quickly followed by hurt. Maybe she's being selfish, but she wishes he'd stayed with them instead and let someone else find the bad guys. Angie might not have turned out the way she did, saving them both from prison time and years of upset.

"Working for the FBI was a privilege," he says. "I couldn't turn it down, and I couldn't do it from here. It's also the kind of job where you always need to leave a packed suitcase in your trunk, because it's twenty-four seven. Vacations were impossible; we were all on a short leash when it came to responding to new developments. If a lead came in, we'd be expected to drop everything and chase it, no matter what we were doing or where we were." He looks at her. "I know I missed out on being a part of your life, and it's a regret that I'll carry to the end, but there was no physical way for me to be present for you. Not while I worked for the FBI."

She feels tears building. "Was it worth it, prioritizing work over family? Did you at least enjoy your job?"

He looks away. "Getting a serial killer locked up for life is a reward no family memories can match." His words sting her. "My team and I caught seven killers during my time there. Probably doesn't sound like a lot to you, but between them that's *hundreds* of victims over their lifetime if they're not caught." He looks her in the eye. "That's men, women and children who are needlessly slaughtered by some asshole with a God complex."

She looks down at her hands. "So you're saying it *was* worth it."

"Listen, honey, what I really wish is that I could've experienced both. But life doesn't work that way." He tries to meet her eyes. "Did it really make much difference not having me around? We made some great memories when you were a little girl, and you were a teenager when I left. Not far off moving out and starting your own life. You didn't need me anymore. Not really. And look how you've turned out. I couldn't be prouder of you."

She's surprised he's unable to put himself in her shoes, to understand what it was like being left behind by her father. With no extended family nearby, that left just Madison and her mom. She doesn't count her older sister, as she and Angie were never close. Angie never liked her. That resentment eventually grew thanks to the actions of Angie's husband. If their dad had been around, Wyatt McCoy would never have dared to prey on Madison, a horrific catalyst for what happened next. Madison would never have spent six years in prison for someone else's crimes.

But when she looks at her dad to say these things, she sees a white-haired, weary man who has had to live a lifetime of lonely regret. A lifetime of keeping his distance from people in case they became targets of the predators he was chasing. If she tells him all that happened, he might not be able to live with himself, and she doesn't want to hurt him.

"I'm sorry," he says. "I'm sorry I wasn't here for you. I'm glad you've accepted me back into your life, because I have nothing else. I'm a washed-up Fed destined to spend the rest of his bone-weary days either playing bridge with his elderly neighbors or hitting balls at the golf club, no real use to anybody." He scoffs. "At one time I was being pulled in all directions, but now..." he shakes his head, "no one needs me anymore."

She swallows a lump in her throat. "I thought you were writing a book? Something to highlight the unsolved cases you worked on."

He smiles. "We'll see." He leans in and kisses her on the forehead before standing. "We have a lot to talk about, but not tonight. It's Christmas, and you're exhausted. Get some sleep, honey. The guys and I will tidy up. I'll make sure there are some leftovers in the fridge for you."

She watches him leave before lying on the bed. Her thoughts turn to how different her life has been from what she expected as a teenager. She's glad she ended up in law enforcement and can understand that side of her dad's life; the urge to find those who hurt people for their own enjoyment. She considers what her dad said about how many victims each serial killer takes from the world. It makes her think of the two recent homicides and whether their killer will strike again. If he does, it could mean Lost Creek does have a serial killer in their midst. The town will be relying on her to find him. But is she up to it?

Before long, her muscles begin to relax and she falls asleep.

CHAPTER TWENTY-FIVE

SEPTEMBER 1998

Special Agent Bill Harper sips a cold beer in the D&G Tavern, located on the quiet outskirts of Anchorage, Alaska. He's alone. Pamela is at home, taking a rare personal day to try to decompress from the recent stress they've been through with their investigation. He spoke to her an hour ago and she told him she was planning to take a long, hot bath and she doesn't want him home for at least a couple of hours. He smiles at the thought of her relaxing naked in the tub, no doubt with a glass of white wine in her hand, her body covered in bubbles.

Their courthouse marriage was a cheap and cheerful five-minute exchange of declarations. They almost didn't go through with it, not wanting the predators they hunt to know they were romantically involved, but after moving in together the year before, it was already obvious to anyone who was watching their movements that they were a couple. Lynette, his ex-wife, hadn't contested the divorce when he left Colorado at the end of '96, so he was free to remarry. Leaving his daughters behind wasn't so easy. When he visited Angie, she screamed at him for cheating on their mom, even though he hadn't done, but she wouldn't listen and her asshole husband told him to leave their house and never return.

Bill may not have been cheating on their mom, but the working relationship between him and Pamela had gradually grown into something else after he accepted the FBI role and moved here. They spent almost every hour of the day together, working under stressful circumstances, so perhaps it was bound to happen. Madison took the news that he was leaving with quiet dignity. But he knows she spent months crying in her room after he left, because Lynette would tell him whenever he called the house.

He takes another sip of beer. It's Madison's sixteenth birthday today. How did *that* happen? It seems like just yesterday when he brought her home from the hospital, swaddled in a soft blanket. His watch tells him it's almost eight o'clock in Colorado, so he gets up and leaves the bar, heading to the pay phone outside. He could use his cell phone, but when he calls Lost Creek, he'd rather it was untraceable. It's been raining for three days straight, and the gray clouds overhead make it darker than it should be at this time of year.

Madison answers the phone right away, expecting his call. "Hey, Dad. Thanks for the card and money."

"My pleasure, honey." He can feel the smile on his face. Nothing beats talking to his daughters. Although Angie no longer takes his calls and he suspects he won't hear from her until she has children of her own and realizes how difficult it is to be a parent. "How's school?"

"Boring. We had career day today, but the career counselor believes all us girls should go to college to learn secretarial skills before we even consider doing anything else. You remember my friend Kate Flynn, right?"

"Sure."

"Well, she wants to be a journalist so she told the counselor that and he laughed in her face before saying, 'Who do you think you are, Lois Lane?' She was so pissed she wanted to slash his tires. I mean, come on, it's 1998! Mom said it sounds like the same crap she was told when she was in high school."

He smiles, because that's the first time he's heard her curse. He should probably chastise her for it, but he finds it cute. His smile falters as he realizes she's growing up fast and he's missing every second of it.

"Seriously, Dad, he was so sexist. I almost told him that, but I didn't want to get into trouble. The teachers already assume I'm a troublemaker thanks to having Angie as a sister."

He feels for her. Angie went through a rebellious phase in high school and put them through some tough times. Bill wishes he could fly down to visit them, but that would put them in danger. It's best that no one knows he has an ex-wife and two daughters in Colorado. When he first met Pamela, she told him it was advisable not to have any connections in this job. It means there are fewer people to get hurt. It didn't stop them falling for each other, but it did make them cautious. Until the wedding, at least. That was one risk worth taking, in his opinion.

"How is your sister?" he asks. "I don't hear from her anymore."

Madison groans. "I don't know. She doesn't tell me or Mom anything. We barely see her. And her husband's a creep who looks at me like I'm an animal he wants to hunt." Bill's jaw clenches. Wyatt McCoy better stay away from Madison. He's already ruined Angie's chances of a good life, and if Bill were still a cop in Lost Creek, he'd have the guy behind bars by now for whatever charge he could make stick.

At the other end of the phone he hears a woman's muffled voice in the background—Lynette's—before Madison says, "I've got to go, Dad. Mom's taking me out for dinner to celebrate my birthday and we're already running late."

"Okay, honey. Sorry I can't be there. Take care."

"You too. Bye."

When he hangs up, he's filled with a deep longing to flee Alaska and go see his girls. But it's impossible. He's in the middle of hunting the Snow Storm Killer, named as such by the media because he almost always strikes in a blizzard. He's the guy Bill suspects killed the women in Lost Creek, Seattle and Anchorage. And it feels like he's getting close. He just has to catch him before he flees Alaska and strikes elsewhere.

He re-enters the bar and removes his jacket, then stops when he sees a fresh beer waiting for him at his table. Next to it is a note, folded in half. He looks up to see who left it, but no one is paying him any attention. Slipping his jacket onto the back of the chair, he takes his seat and picks up the note. As he reads it, his blood runs cold.

> *In many ways, you and I are similar. More than you'd like to admit.*
>
> *For instance, like me, you have no family. Not as of five o'clock tonight, anyway.*
>
> *I'll be your family, Special Agent Bill Harper. And you can be mine.*
>
> *See you at Christmas.*
>
> *SSK*

The room feels airless as a shudder runs through Bill's body. He jumps up and yells to the bartender, "Who left this? Did you see anyone near my table?"

The bartender looks shocked at the sudden outburst. "No. Sorry, man. I was busy."

Bill swings around to ask the other customers if they saw anyone, but no one else is paying him any attention. It's busy tonight, easy for someone to slip in and out unnoticed. His back was to the entrance while he used the pay phone outside. If he had turned at any time, he would've seen the son of a bitch with his own eyes! He looks up at the ceiling, searching for surveillance cameras, but there are none. He knows there are none outside either, one of the reasons why he favors this bar. You can be anonymous in here. No one can track you.

"Dammit!" He glances at his watch. It's six o'clock. A vast and heavy dread swells in his chest as the implications of the note hit him.

You have no family... Not as of five o'clock tonight.

His mouth is bone dry and his heart pounds against his chest. The killer can't be referring to Lynette or Madison as he's only just spoken to Madison. And Angie's always with Wyatt, who would see off any stranger daring to set foot on his property with a bullet through the chest. Which means the killer is talking about Pamela.

On shaky legs Bill grabs his jacket and runs out of the tavern. He looks around the parking lot but doesn't see anyone waiting to ambush him. He almost wishes they were, because that would mean that what was written in the note was merely a trap to get him alone outside. He'd be glad to face this guy one on one. But that's not how killers of this nature work.

He tries to block out images of Pamela in the bath, surrounded by her own blood, as he pulls out his cell phone and calls his home number. He waits as it rings, over and over, without being answered. "Shit!" He tries her cell phone, but there's no answer there either.

He runs to his car and frantically forces the key into the ignition, dialing 911 as he goes. When dispatch answers, he tells the guy to send officers to his house immediately. As he races out of the parking lot, he narrowly avoids a collision with a lumber truck. Trees and buildings are a blur as he speeds by them. All he can think about is protecting his wife.

By the time he gets home, his legs are trembling. He runs up the damp porch steps and instantly sees the front door is ajar. "No." His heart pounds in his chest as blood roars in his ears.

He draws his weapon and slowly enters the house. "Pam!" he shouts as loud as he can. There's no reply. He slowly and cautiously searches the downstairs with his gun outstretched, expecting the Snow Storm Killer to round a corner and take him by surprise. He tries to keep in mind that Pamela is trained to shoot. Trained to kill. She can defend herself. But still his heart wants to burst.

A search of the downstairs is clear. He walks back through the kitchen on his way to the staircase, but before he gets there, a drop of water splashes his face. He stops and wipes it away. Looking up, he sees a patch of liquid spreading across the ceiling and seeping through the cracks. His legs give out from under him as he realizes he's standing under the bathroom, and the patch of slowly spreading liquid is crimson red.

CHAPTER TWENTY-SIX

Madison is jolted awake by someone shaking her shoulder. It takes her eyes some time to adjust to the soft glow of her bedside lamp, and when they do, she realizes it's Nate. She looks at the clock; it's 6.12 a.m. She's still dressed in yesterday's clothes, which means she must have fallen asleep after dinner and slept right through. Nate is sitting on the bed, leaning over her slightly. She can feel his warm arm across her chest as he gently holds her shoulder.

"Hey. Sorry to wake you." His voice is low, presumably so as not to wake Owen. His hair is messy on one side and he's even more in need of a shave now. "Owen asked me to stay over. I was sleeping on the couch when your cell phone went off." He hands it to her. "After the third consecutive call I thought it was worth waking you."

She hadn't realized she'd left the phone downstairs. She looks at the screen. "It's the station. Something must have happened." She sits up and makes a self-conscious attempt to smooth her hair into place.

Nate says, "Jump in the shower. I'll get breakfast started."

As he goes to stand, Madison reaches for his hand and stops him. "Nate. Are we okay?"

He offers a forced smile. "Sure."

"What happened with the person who messaged you on Facebook?"

He looks away. "Must've been a hoax. They didn't reply to my message." He goes to the door and then hesitates. "I'm sorry about what I said at dinner. Your dad told me I was being a jerk, and he was right."

Relief washes over her. She just wants to hug him. "I'm sorry too. Everything you said was right. I was just being defensive." She stands up, but her phone rings again, just as Brody enters the room, tail wagging. As she answers the call, Nate leaves, taking the dog with him. "Hey, Steve. Sorry, I was asleep. I just need a shower and I'll be in."

"No problem," says Steve. "Have you seen the news?"

Her stomach flips. She hates it when someone asks her that. "No. Why, what's happened now?"

"We've located Kate Flynn's daughter."

Madison frowns at the way he words it, because it wasn't just Sally missing, it was all three of them. "Is she okay? What about Kate and Ben?"

"Sally was found shortly after you headed home yesterday, and aside from being half frozen, she's going to be fine. Unfortunately, Kate and Ben are still missing." He pauses, before adding, "It looks like our killer has them."

Her mouth drops open and she sinks to the bed in shock. "What? Why do you think that?"

"Because Sally was left behind. This guy clearly has a thing about mothers and sons. Meet Adams at Kate's house, he'll fill you in. Patrick Flynn's waiting for you; he's the one who found Sally. She was too tired to talk to anyone once her dad got her home, so he let her sleep all night. She's feeling better now."

Shocked, she mutters, "Sure. I'll be there in twenty minutes."

Madison has the quickest shower of her life, pulls on the

first warm clothes she can find and then heads downstairs to slip on her jacket, gloves and boots. She doesn't even have time to dry her hair. She briefly wonders what time Mike and her dad left last night and would bet it wasn't long after she fell asleep.

She finds Nate in the living room, where Bandit is snuggled up against Brody on the rug in front of the fire. The Christmas lights are still twinkling and the presents under the tree are untouched. They must have decided to wait for her before opening them. Unfortunately they'll have to wait a little longer.

Nate stands before handing over a warm travel mug and a slice of buttered toast. "I'll keep an eye on Owen as much as I can today. You do what you've got to do."

She meets his eyes. "Thank you. Tell him that once I've caught this killer, you, me, Owen and Dad can sit down and do Christmas properly."

"Sure, but don't worry about him. He understands." He hesitates before asking, "Are you arresting Jake Rubio this morning?"

"Not as far as I know. Steve was calling to tell me Kate's little girl has been found alive and well, thank God, but Kate and Ben are still missing. He thinks our killer has them." She swallows the lump in her throat and heads to the front door. Nate follows her. When she opens the door, a cold blast of air makes her want to climb back into bed.

"Be careful," he says. "This guy you're chasing is dangerous. Worse than anyone we've dealt with together."

She nods and then walks out into the darkness, with no attempt at a hug by either of them. She can feel him pulling away from her emotionally. Maybe he's planning to leave town soon to find Kristen. Maybe she'll never see him again. She has to push the thought away to concentrate on getting to work.

It's bitterly cold again this morning and it looks like it snowed overnight, but only a couple of inches. She gets in her car and notices that Nate's already scraped the ice and snow off the windshield for her. As she goes to put her travel mug in the cup holder, she sees a square gift box on the passenger seat. It must be the present Nate said he'd got her. He's still watching her from the house, so she smiles at him through the windshield and puts the gift in the glovebox for later. She doesn't want to open it in front of him. It feels weird. Instead she takes a bite of the toast he made her and drives as fast as she can to Kate's house.

The first thing she sees is an ambulance parked outside. It looks like Rita and Jake are packing up their things and getting ready to leave. She gets out of her car. "Jake!"

He turns around, and his shoulders slump when he sees her. Turning away, he says, "What?"

She's taken aback by his attitude. "Is Sally Flynn okay?" She can see the little girl isn't in the ambulance.

"She'll be fine. She's woken up with a bad cough and a fever, so her dad just wanted her checked out." He slams the ambulance door shut. "Is that everything?"

"Have I done something to upset you?" she asks. Jake isn't aware that she knows he hired an attorney. He also hasn't been formally questioned about the murder of his on-off girlfriend. So she can't understand why he's being an asshole.

"Not yet," he says. "But I suspect it's just a matter of time. Which is why I hired a lawyer."

She feigns surprise. "You think I'm going to arrest you for Emily's murder?"

He shrugs. "I'm not stupid. I spent time with her before she died and I have no one to corroborate my alibi, which means I'm probably your primary suspect."

She crosses her arms, mainly because she's cold. "The guy spotted running away from the church that morning was tall and broad, like you. And he was seen running in the direction of your street."

He rolls his eyes. "Listen, I see where this is going. If you want to talk to me about Emily's murder, call my lawyer, Richie Hope." He moves to the front of the ambulance and gets in. Within seconds, Rita has driven them away.

Madison watches after them before walking up the driveway. When she enters Kate's house, the living room is empty and she hears voices from upstairs. Detective Adams calls down to her. "We're up here."

She finds them in Sally's bedroom. It's decorated with white walls and pink trim and is full of stuffed animals and ballerina tutus. Detective Adams has forgone his suit jacket in favor of a smart navy sweater over his shirt. Sally is sitting in bed in her pajamas, with Patrick on top of the covers next to her.

"Hey, Sally," she says, kneeling next to the bed. "How are you feeling?"

The little girl's cheeks are pink with fever, but overall she looks fine. "Hungry. Daddy says I can have pizza for breakfast."

Adams laughs. "I'm jealous."

Madison smiles and looks across at Patrick. His face is expressionless. "Can we talk?" she says.

Patrick gets off the bed and leaves the room behind her. Adams stays with Sally. Madison's hoping he'll gently question the little girl while her dad is out of earshot. Downstairs, she and Patrick sit opposite each other in the living room. "What happened?" she asks.

He runs a hand through his hair. "I was out all yesterday afternoon looking for them. Just before five o'clock I spotted something at the old gas station over on Layton Road. You know the one I mean?"

She nods. That place has been boarded up since she returned to Lost Creek, ready for demolition.

"I saw the back end of a car poking out from behind the building, so I went over to check if it was Kate's. It was too dark to know for sure from the road. All the doors were closed but the car wasn't locked. Kate's purse was on the passenger seat, and her thick winter coat was in the back, but all three of them were gone." He shakes his head. "I figured she must've run out of gas and decided to walk to get help because she didn't have her cell phone with her, but I couldn't understand why she'd leave her coat behind. I got back in my car and headed downtown. That's when I spotted Sally." He chokes up.

"Where was she?" she asks gently.

"She was walking along the side of the road all by herself. She's five years old, Madison. She could've been hit by a car or taken by a sex offender!"

She sits next to him and rubs his back. "But she wasn't. She's here and she's fine."

"But where are my wife and son? It doesn't make any sense."

"What did Sally tell you when you pulled over?"

"She didn't speak at first and wouldn't answer any of my questions; she was too cold, I think. She seemed a little pissed off, too." He scoffs. "As if she was mad at me for making her walk in the snow. Anyway, she let me pick her up. I got her in the car, turned the heat up and drove her home. When we walked into the house, she asked if she could open the rest of her Christmas presents." He smiles sadly. "Of course I said yes, but she didn't seem enthusiastic and she was reluctant to tell me anything. I made her a hot chocolate and then she just wanted to go to bed. She didn't even want to eat anything. She slept almost twelve hours."

"She must've been scared and emotionally drained by the time you found her," Madison says.

He looks at her reproachfully. "I called your station once she'd fallen asleep and they said you'd gone home for the day. Sergeant Tanner questioned me about what had happened and said he'd attend the scene as soon as he got off the phone.

He told me to let him know the minute Sally woke up so that she could be questioned, which I did."

Madison feels guilty for leaving work early yesterday, but there's nothing she could have done if Sally needed to sleep off her ordeal. She runs a hand through her damp hair. "So she hasn't mentioned what happened to her mom or Ben, and she hasn't cried?"

"Right."

Sally might be traumatized, but she's slightly older than Danny Moss and Zach Cole, which means she could be the department's best witness. "Do you mind if I ask her some questions now? I'll stop if she gets upset."

Patrick nods, and when she heads upstairs, he stays where he is. In Sally's room, she pulls Detective Adams to one side. "Has she said anything?"

Adams sighs. "Only that she wishes she'd waited for her mom and brother to come home before she opened her gifts."

Madison's shoulders sag. What if she can't find them? The killer didn't abduct the other two boys, so she can't understand why he took Ben. Unless it's revenge for what Kate said about him on TV yesterday.

Adams leans in and says quietly, "You realize that if our killer's got them, they're probably dead already, right?"

She leans back and looks him in the eye. "Don't do that. Don't give up on finding them alive just twenty-four hours into their disappearance. It's our *job* to find them in time." She just lost all respect for the guy, and she didn't have much to begin with. Any detective who jumps to conclusions ends up on a slippery slope of ignoring vital, and sometimes subtle, evidence that suggests otherwise. They slow the pace of the investigation by looking for dead bodies instead of live victims who could still be saved if everyone acts fast enough.

Adams backs away, holding his hands up. "Fine. We'll find them alive."

Madison turns to the little girl snuggled under the covers.

Sally looks like she could fall back to sleep any minute. Sitting on her bed, Madison says, "Hey, sweetie. How are you feeling?"

"Okay." She coughs loudly.

"That's good. We're all glad you're home and safe." She smiles. "Do you know where Ben and your mom went?"

Sally nods. "I waited for them to come back because Mommy told me to. But I got too cold in the car so I went to find Daddy."

"Your mom told you to wait in the car?"

Sally nods again.

"Where was she going?"

"A man wanted to talk to her and Ben."

Madison tries to ignore the creeping feeling of dread spreading through her chest. "Did you see or hear the man your mom was talking to?"

Sally shakes her head. "No. But I heard his car stop just behind the wall. Then I saw a hand holding a gun."

"Did he point the gun at your mom?" Detective Adams moves closer to Madison and she knows he'll be as alarmed as she is right now.

"Uh-huh. But I wasn't scared, because when Mommy came back to get Ben, she said it was a pretend one that he got for Christmas from Santy Claus and he just wanted to show it to her." She coughs again.

Madison tries to smile, but she's even more afraid for Kate and Ben now. "Did your mom and Ben get in his car?"

"I think so."

She shudders. Like most women, Kate knows how to try to protect herself from predators. She carries pepper spray in her purse, she has a doorbell camera, she's taken self-defense classes and she's always aware of who is around her when she's out alone. In her job—reporting on violent crime every day, and more often than not against women—she would be even more cautious than the average woman. So Madison can only imagine how hopeless she must have felt agreeing to leave her daughter behind and go off with a predator.

He must have threatened to kill her or her children if she didn't obey him. She must have had no viable way out of the situation. Because all the safety precautions in the world are no match for a violent assailant pointing a gun at you. And who knows, maybe Kate thought it was better to be able to save one of her children than neither of them.

"Mommy gave me her coat and started the car. She said it would keep me warm until she came back, but the snow got in her window."

Madison thinks that means Kate cracked the window slightly so that Sally wouldn't succumb to carbon monoxide poisoning. The chances of that would be slim outdoors and in such a new car, but she clearly wasn't taking any chances.

"Mommy was gone ages and I fell asleep, but when the noise stopped, I woke up and started getting cold. And scared."

The noise must be the engine that was running to keep the car warm. It must've run out of gas. "Is that when you decided to get out and walk home?"

"Uh-huh. But it was even colder outside, until I started running. I didn't know how to get home, so I went to the road. It was dark and I was scared."

Madison strokes her hand. "You were brave, sweetie. I bet you'd like to have some breakfast soon, huh?"

"Pizza?"

She laughs. "You bet. Why don't you take a little nap until it's ready, okay?"

Even though she just slept for twelve hours, Sally's eyes close, and within minutes she's breathing heavily. Madison stands and motions for Adams to follow her downstairs.

Patrick is making them drinks in the kitchen. The overhead light highlights the dark circles under his eyes. He looks exhausted. "What did she tell you?" he asks.

Adams repeats what Sally said as Madison watches

Patrick's reaction. She's wondering how come he was the person to find his daughter when there were cops out looking for all three of them. Something about it has her questioning how well she knows him, especially as he fits the description of the guy spotted running away from the second crime scene. She thinks of the night before Christmas Eve, when she had come by the house to have coffee with Kate. Patrick hadn't been home yet, despite it being close to eleven o'clock. Where would a bank manager be at that time? Washing off the blood from killing Sarah Moss? It seems unlikely, but it's her job to consider all the options.

"Did you know Emily Cole?" she asks. "The woman killed outside St. Theresa's on Christmas morning?"

Patrick frowns. "Only from the news stories."

"What about Sarah Moss?"

He stiffens slightly. "She was a customer at the bank, so I knew *of* her. I think I helped her and David with a home loan a few years ago."

"David? You're on first-name terms with her husband?"

"Not really. That's his name."

Madison studies his face. "You'll have to forgive me for asking this, Patrick, but I hope you'll understand why I have to. Are you cheating on Kate?"

His mouth opens and he glances at Detective Adams in disbelief before looking back at her. "What kind of question is that?"

"Is that a no?" Adams presses.

Patrick places his cup on the kitchen counter. "I have never cheated on my wife. We have kids, for God's sake." His eyes show disappointment and Madison thinks it's aimed at her. "I think it's time you left. I need to be with Sally and you guys should be out there looking for my wife and son."

Their drinks remain untouched as they turn and head for the front door. Madison glances back over her shoulder before leaving. "We'll be in touch."

CHAPTER TWENTY-SEVEN

It's not yet 8 a.m. when Madison arrives at the station, closely followed by Detective Adams. The office is as busy as always, with patrol officers coming and going and the constant sound of at least one desk phone ringing non-stop. Alex Parker is already in, helping Stella remove the frankly lousy display of Christmas decorations scattered around the place. When he notices them, he stops what he's doing. "Ah, Detectives. I have an update for you. Care to follow me to my office?"

"Hold that thought," says Adams. "I need coffee first." He disappears in the direction of the kitchen.

Madison switches her computer on and takes a seat at her desk, next to a window. Rain pelts hard against the glass, and as it's still dark out, she can see her tired reflection. She's always surprised by the woman staring back at her, as she looks more like her mother than she expects to. Her lungs constrict as a heavy sense of dread washes over her. She has to get Kate and Ben home unharmed. She doesn't know if she could bear to be responsible for letting something bad happen to them.

When Alex appears behind her reflection, she spins around and fixes a smile on her face. "How are you, Alex? I imagine living in the US is tough at this time of year without your family around."

"Not really," he says, leaning against her desk and smiling. "My family still manages to annoy me, even from thousands of miles away."

"Did you spend the evening alone?"

He nods. "Yes, but you needn't feel sorry for me, Detective. I have plenty of things to keep me occupied. I know a lot of people find this time of year difficult, but living alone really doesn't bother me. After spending most of my time at work, it's actually a relief to go home to an empty house."

She's not sure she believes him. "Call me a romantic, but I thought I saw a spark between you and Shelley recently and kind of hoped you two would be dating by now."

He reddens slightly. "It's become evident I'm not her type. I believe she's more into former high school football stars like *Jock* Rubio." He takes a deep breath. "Sorry, I'm being vindictive."

"No, she isn't," says Madison. "She went on one date with him before realizing he's an asshole who, when it comes to his treatment of women, never mentally graduated from high school. I'm pretty sure she's available and I know she likes you."

A hint of a smile appears on his face, before he straightens up. "Probably best not to mix business and pleasure, especially as we work different hours a lot of the time. Imagine how awkward things would get around here if we broke up."

Madison thinks he's looking for excuses when actually he just lacks confidence, which is a shame. Detective Adams rejoins them. He has a coffee for her, but it's black like his. If he had bothered to ask, he'd know she likes milk or cream in hers. As she takes it from him, she realizes the mug hasn't been washed since the last person used it. She grimaces.

Adams looks at Alex. "I'd offer you coffee, but I assume you don't drink it, what with you being British and all."

Alex offers a patient smile. "Speaking on behalf of the entire British population, I can dispel that myth once and for all and confirm that we are in fact capable of enjoying both tea and coffee."

Madison laughs. Adams misses the sarcasm.

With coffees in hand, they follow Alex to his office. It's small, cramped and messy, although Alex would say it's an organized mess. He moves some boxes to make room for Madison to sit down, and for Adams to lean against the cluttered desk. "So how long have you lived over here?" asks Adams.

"Four years now," says Alex as he sits in front of his computer. "I came to study a specialist forensics qualification in Denver and never left. Something about the Colorado landscape drew me in. I'd wanted to visit ever since I watched *The Shining* as a teenager."

Adams scoffs. "You watch that kind of crap?"

"Horror's my favorite genre."

That doesn't surprise Madison, but Adams says, "I thought it would be sci-fi, what with you being a geek. I bet you loved that *Game of Thrones* shit, am I right?"

Alex smiles faintly and Madison can tell he thinks this guy is a moron. "*Game of Thrones* is actually fantasy, not science fiction."

"If you say so. Hey, I hear it never stops raining in the UK and you all live off fish and chips." Adams winks. "That right, Parker?"

This time Alex glances at Madison, and she has to stifle a laugh. He says, "You don't travel much, do you, Detective Adams?"

Adams frowns before shuddering. "Why's it so goddam cold in here?"

He's right. This side of the building has always been cold, and as this room used to house evidence before Alex joined the department, no one ever thought to make it more comfortable to work in. Alex turns on the small electric heater that lives under his desk.

"Can we get back to business?" says Madison. She doesn't want to waste any more time.

"Of course," says Alex. "I recreated Sarah Moss's crime scene yesterday, by trying to attack someone in the driver's seat of her car." He smiles. "Officer Sanchez played an enthusiastic victim. I discovered that I may have been wrong about the killer not having much space in which to wield a weapon. I've since learned that there was no car parked next to Sarah Moss's door, so he could have opened it wide and easily attacked her with a weapon in his right hand. I didn't manage much success with my left hand because of the angle of the victim and her injuries. I still don't believe he used anything long, and after discussing the injuries on both victims with Dr. Scott, we believe it's likely the weapon was some kind of tool. A hammer would be my best guess, the kind anyone would keep in their toolbox at home."

Madison makes a note. "Good to know. That means the tall, broad guy seen running away from the second crime scene could have been responsible for both murders. And that our perp is likely right-handed." She thinks. "Have you had any lab results from the items you sent for testing?"

He shakes his head. "Not yet. Officer Vickers—"

Adams interjects. "Which cop is that?"

"Shelley," says Alex. "The officer with long brown hair and perfectly matching eyes."

Madison raises her eyebrows and tries to hide her smile. He's clearly smitten.

"Oh yeah," says Adams with a grin. "I know who you mean."

Alex glares at him before continuing. "Officer Vickers has been studying surveillance footage from around the mall's parking lot and St. Theresa's church, but she hasn't had any luck finding anything useful. Our suspect must have used back roads to get around, suggesting he checked the area for cameras before the attacks. I enhanced the footage taken from the mall of the black blur from around the time of Sarah Moss's murder, but it has no detail to it unfortunately, which renders it useless."

With a sigh, Madison asks, "What about the video the killer sent David Moss; does that offer any clues?"

"No, and I'd rather not watch it again unless absolutely necessary." Alex's expression is somber. "The killer didn't speak and there was no reflection of him anywhere, but the footage does explain the circle of clean glass on the rear passenger window that confused me at the crime scene. The killer used a suction-cup mount for his camera. I'd say it was a GoPro, as you can buy all kinds of mounts for those and they're nice and compact."

"Wouldn't attaching that to the window slow him down?" she asks.

"No," says Alex. "They're incredibly simple to operate and it would take just a few seconds to stick it on the glass and then remove it after."

Approaching footsteps halt the conversation. Steve appears at the door. "Morning, guys. I hope you're all ready for another long day."

Madison cautiously takes a sip from the grimy coffee mug. "Morning. Did you know Jake Rubio has lawyered up?"

Steve raises his eyebrows. "Interesting. He's got a bad reputation at my gym."

"You go to a *gym*?"

He crosses his arms. "Is that so hard to believe?"

"Sorry." She smiles. "It wasn't meant to come out that way. I mean, it's obvious you go, of course. I've just never heard you talk about it." Quickly moving on, she asks, "What's his reputation?"

"He's known for hitting on women while they're trying to

work out," says Steve. "The manager told me they've had two women cancel their memberships because of him."

She hadn't realized he was that bad. "He's starting to sound like a sex pest."

"How'd it go at Kate's house?" Steve asks. "Is her daughter okay?"

"It was odd," says Detective Adams. "I find it weird that Patrick Flynn was the one to find her, don't you?" He looks at Madison.

She nods. "A little. But that doesn't mean he was involved in his wife's abduction." Although she can't help feeling that that would explain why Kate went willingly with her abductor, because deep down she knew he wouldn't hurt her or their kids, despite pointing a gun at her. "Has Kate's car been processed yet?"

"It's next on my list," says Alex.

Madison leans back in her seat. "I'm not expecting anything to be found, because Sally said the man who took her mom kept out of view and didn't approach the car."

Steve hands the keys to Alex. "It's parked out back. Let me know when you're done."

"Will do."

He motions for Madison and Adams to follow him back to the main office. Once seated at her desk, Madison says, "According to Sally, Kate pulled over at the deserted gas station and then a guy pulled in behind them, his car hidden by the store. He pulled a gun on Kate and told her to go with him. She made sure Sally would be warm first, but for some reason she took Ben with her."

"The guy must have a thing about little boys," says Steve.

"But he doesn't harm them," she says. "It's bizarre."

After a slight hesitation, Steve says, "I know we don't even want to entertain the idea, but could he be sexually assaulting the boys before leaving them next to their dead mothers? Have they been checked out?"

It's an unbearable thought that makes Madison wish she were in a different job. "Danny Moss and Zach Cole were both checked by the ambulance crew at the scene and given the all-clear." Dread suddenly fills her stomach. "Although it was Jake Rubio who checked Danny."

"Would an EMT be able to tell if a boy was assaulted without taking him to the hospital?" says Steve. Then, catching up with her thoughts, he asks, "Could he have lied about the kid being okay so that he wasn't thoroughly checked at the hospital?"

She seriously hopes not. "I mean, if he's our perp, then sure, it's possible he lied. But he wasn't at the second crime scene; Rita was in charge of Zach." She turns to Adams, knowing they need to check this out. "Would you go speak to Jake's boss and also his co-worker, Rita Mellor? We need to ask them their opinion of Jake. Maybe Rita's seen his behavior around women, or she's had to listen to stories about his conquests. Ask for a copy of Jake's report on Danny Moss, too."

He nods. "Sure." He slips his jacket on. "You know, my gut tells me he's our guy."

"Why so certain?" asks Steve.

"Think about it: our victims are Sarah Moss, Emily Cole and Kate Flynn. That gives us three credible suspects in their partners: David Moss, Jake Rubio and Patrick Flynn. Out of those three, from everything I've heard so far, Rubio would be my bet. I paid him a visit yesterday, after checking out Brian Slater's alibi, and he said he was too busy to talk. Who does that when someone they know has just died?"

"He thinks I'm going to arrest him any minute," says Madison. "So he's being cautious with what he says. His lawyer probably advised him to keep quiet."

Adams appears unconvinced. "I know guys like that, men who value women based on what they can get from them, and it never ends well." He zips his jacket up. "I'll let you know what I find out."

When Steve and Madison are alone, she asks, "Have we had any sightings of Kate and Ben yet?"

"Nothing."

"I don't get it. Someone must've seen what happened at that gas station."

Steve shrugs. "It was Christmas Day and we'd told everyone to stay home. Chief Mendes has notified the media that they're missing, presumed abducted, so the networks are going crazy with it. The story is on almost every channel because it's one of their own. It should help that Kate's well known in the community; she's more likely to be spotted."

That's something at least. "Was there anything at the scene that could help us?"

He shakes his head. "Apart from her car, nothing. Officer Sanchez and I had a thorough search of the area. We have Kate's purse, but there's nothing useful in it. She left a can of pepper spray behind, so she didn't even want to risk getting caught with that up her sleeve."

Madison's heart sinks. Kate must have been terrified she'd get her or the kids shot if she tried anything. "I don't yet know where Jake Rubio was when Kate and Ben were abducted. I visited him at two thirty yesterday morning to tell him Emily Cole had been murdered, and Kate went missing sometime after eight thirty that same morning. In between, he had time to watch her outburst on TV and fly into a fit of rage." She's considering whether it's time to bring him in for questioning. "His alibi for the time Emily Cole was attacked is weak too. He was home alone, apparently."

Steve crosses his arms. "Aside from Jake, who else are you liking for the murders?"

She leans back in her seat. "No one seriously yet. But Adams is right; with three victims now, we have to consider each of their partners. David Moss isn't tall and broad, and he's got two kids to look after so presumably he wouldn't have the opportunity to just go out whenever he gets the urge to kill someone, certainly not without some careful planning. The same could be said for Patrick." She sighs. "It will be telling if no one else gets killed now he's solely responsible for caring for Sally while Kate's missing."

Steve approaches her computer and brings up the criminal database. He types Patrick Flynn's name in. Nothing comes up. "He has no criminal record."

"Neither does Jake Rubio or David Moss," she says. "I've checked. But Jake's the only one out of those three who has lawyered up." She chews her lip as she thinks. "I guess there's always the possibility that Kate was right during her little outburst yesterday and we're dealing with a serial killer. Someone unrelated to any of the women."

He nods. "True. But let's rule out Jake Rubio before we go down that road."

"Detective?" says Dina behind them. Madison turns to look at her. "Gary Pelosi has called in to say he wants you to stop by the newsroom as soon as you're free. He thinks he has something that could help you locate Kate Flynn."

Madison turns back to Steve, eyebrows raised. "I better go see him."

"Sure. Let me know what he says and whether I need to get a warrant for Jake Rubio's arrest."

She grabs her damp jacket and quickly heads out of the station and back into the rain.

CHAPTER TWENTY-EIGHT

Nate watches as an ambulance pulls into the parking lot of the fast-food restaurant where he's arranged to meet Jake Rubio. Richie has tasked him with delving into Jake's life in order to find a way to keep him out of jail should LCPD attempt to arrest him. Brody is in the back seat, watching people come and go from the restaurant, his nose sniffing the air for the scent of greasy food.

It's not long before both paramedics get out of the ambulance. Jake's male co-worker heads inside the restaurant, so Nate gets out of his car and waves Jake over. "Get in," he says.

Jake slips into the passenger seat and is immediately sniffed all over by Brody, who leans in from the back seat. "Does he bite?"

"Only perps."

Jake laughs nervously, and it's obvious he's not a dog person. Brody immediately becomes agitated, his demeanor changing from pet to K9. He sniffs Jake's uniform, focusing on a spot near the left cuff, then pulls back, looks at Nate and barks so loudly that passers-by glance over at them.

Nate knows what this means. Brody can smell blood. His police training has kicked in. He opens his glovebox and pulls out a tennis ball. It's the only thing that will stop the dog from barking now. His reward for a job well done.

"What's going on?" asks Jake as he watches Brody settle down on the back seat, chewing his ball. His hands are shaking.

Nate takes a deep breath. "How long have you been on duty?"

Jake looks puzzled. "About two hours. Why?"

Nate has to be careful, because if Jake has blood on him for the wrong reason, he's going to need to tell Richie that their guy could be guilty. But Jake's a paramedic, and it's plausible he has blood on him from his last patient. "What call-outs have you attended so far this morning?" He eyes the patch of uniform Brody honed in on. There's no visible blood, not even a speck.

Running a hand through his hair, Jake says, "We just took a woman to the hospital. She'd cut her finger off while making breakfast. It was messy, but she'll live."

Nate nods. That could explain it. "It looks like Brody can smell her blood. He'll be fine now he has that thing."

Jake glances over his shoulder at the dog before saying, "I don't get a long break, so can we get this over with? Richie told me I've got to be honest with you from the get-go."

"How about we start with your alibi for the night Sarah Moss was murdered."

Without hesitation, Jake says, "That's easy. I was working. I was called to the crime scene at the same time as the cops. And immediately before that, my partner and I had a call-out to a heart attack. Some old guy was at home and took ill. We saved his life and took him to the hospital. Went straight from there to the victim at the mall."

"Good." Nate writes it all down. "And what about your alibi for the time Emily Cole was killed."

Jake's eyes drift away and he stares out of the windshield.

"Emily was a friend. I'd seen her that afternoon, between four and five."

"Were you alone together or out somewhere?"

"We had sex at her place. She was fine when I left, about to take a shower. Then I went to Joe's Saloon. I'll be on CCTV there until I left at around eight. I ate dinner there and nursed the same drink all evening. I knew it would be impossible to get a cab because of the storm, so I made sure I could drive myself home."

Nate's making notes. "Then you were home alone, is that right?"

Jake nods. "Right. Maybe my neighbor heard me come back, but there's no way of proving I was there. I got a little drunk before going to bed and then slept until Detective Harper woke me with the news about Emily."

Nate nods. Jake sounds like he's telling the truth, but that doesn't mean anything. "Your cell phone won't show you anywhere else?"

Jake looks at him. "No."

"Good. So, is there anything I need to know now that the cops could find out later?"

With a blank expression, Jake asks, "Like what?"

Nate studies him closely. "Prior arrests or convictions. Any arguments with Emily that could've been overheard by someone. Any history of domestic complaints made against you."

A flash of disgust passes over Jake's face. "No. I'm not an asshole."

"What about the first victim, Sarah Moss. Did you know her?"

Jake's phone buzzes but he ignores it. "I've lived in Lost Creek my entire life. In my job, you get to meet lots of people. It's possible I may have spoken to her before."

Nate thinks he's choosing his words carefully. "Okay, let's try that again. If you were on trial for murder and the prosecutor asked you the same question, how would you answer?"

Beads of sweat appear on Jake's forehead. "You seriously think they're going to arrest me for this?"

Nate's not trying to scare the guy, but he has to prepare him for the worst. Because most people can't appreciate how difficult it is to try to defend themselves in court. They won't fully understand how determined prosecutors are to go for the jugular in order to win a case. It's a lesson that most people—like Nate himself—learn too late. "I don't know," he says. "But you need to have your story straight, just in case. And the best story—the one that *should* keep you out of any trouble—is the truth, no matter how bad it makes you sound. Because if the cops, the DA's office or the media find out whatever you're trying to hide, they'll make it sound ten times worse." He pauses. "Now, Sarah Moss. Did you know her or not?"

Jake licks his lips. He's looking a lot less carefree now than before he got in the car. "I'd seen her around town a few times. She always smiled like it was a come-on, you know? She seemed interested."

"You didn't know she was married and had two young boys?"

"No! I'm not responsible for what's going on in someone's private life. If a woman flirts and I'm single, why wouldn't I flirt back?"

"Did you ever go on a date or sleep with her?"

Jake swallows. "No. I bumped into her in the grocery store a week before Christmas. I was in uniform, so she asked me about my job, I found out her name. She didn't have kids with her."

Nate feels sorry for the guy. Just because he flirted with a married woman doesn't make him a killer, but that's not how it will look in court. "But you never took it any further?"

"No. She was a maybe."

He raises an eyebrow. "A potential date for another time."

"Right. Women love the uniform, man. They can't help themselves. And I like to flirt, so what? That doesn't make me an asshole. I don't have a wife and kids at home, and hopefully I never will. That life isn't for me. I like dating different women. It's not a crime."

Nate rubs his freshly shaven face as he thinks. This guy is a prosecutor's dream suspect, and a jury of mostly women would hate his attitude. But the truth is, he's young, free and single. He can do what he wants, as long as it's consensual. His gut tells him Jake isn't the guy Madison is looking for.

"Holy crap." Jake's checking his phone.

"What is it?"

"Rita, my co-worker, has messaged to say she's been questioned by Detective Adams this morning. He was asking her and our boss all about me." He looks at Nate. "They're going to arrest me, aren't they?"

Nate looks him square in the eye. "Not if I can help it."

CHAPTER TWENTY-NINE

The newsroom at the *Lost Creek Daily* is quieter than Madison expected. It's only small, and has a staff to match, and it looks as if most of them are out chasing the news. At the front desk she asks for Gary Pelosi and while she waits for him to appear, she texts Owen to see what he's doing. He responds fast.

On my way to Prospect Springs with Frank from the office.

She frowns. She doesn't know this Frank guy. What if he's a bad driver and her son gets in an accident?

What for?

She watches the dots on screen until his reply comes through.

Richie needs some stuff from his storage unit. I'll be back in time for dinner and presents.

She smiles. He tries to act like he's an independent adult, but every now and then the little boy who loves Christmas comes out. Part of her worries she won't make it home in time for dinner, and that unwrapping Christmas presents will have to wait even longer. She remembers the gift in her glovebox from Nate. At some point she should open it.

"Thanks for coming, Detective." Gary appears, so she slips

her phone away. His shirt is crumpled and he looks stressed, but Madison's never seen him look any different. "I'm covering Kate Flynn's disappearance for the paper." He runs a hand through his thick brown hair, which is graying in places. "I think I've found something that's... disturbing. Can we talk in private?"

Madison's stomach lurches with dread. "Sure. Lead the way."

They pass a kitchen and Gary offers her coffee with cream, which she accepts gratefully. He then leads her through the newsroom and on to the editor's office, which is empty apart from old newspapers and paperwork covering every surface, even the two chairs. "Sorry for the mess. Jackie's a hoarder."

"Jackie's the editor, I take it?" She moves some papers before sitting down.

"Right. She's working from home today. Her arthritis is bad."

Madison's never met Jackie and she's never been in the newsroom. But she has been in the newspaper many times, thanks to her wrongful conviction. "So, what have you got?" she asks.

Gary pulls the chair out from behind the desk to sit next to her. He has a folder and a legal pad on his lap. "As far as I'm aware, there are three victims of the perpetrator you're looking for: Sarah Moss, Emily Cole and now Kate Flynn. Have there been any other murders or abductions that you're linking to this guy?"

She bristles slightly. It feels like he's brought her here under a false pretext and is actually fishing for information. "No."

"Good." He takes a deep breath. "We both know Kate's an excellent reporter. She was the only one who would share information with me when I first arrived in this town, back when I was a parachute journalist."

She tilts her head. "A what?"

"Oh, you've never heard that term? A parachute journalist kind of describes what we do: drop in wherever the story is, report on it for whichever news publication pays the most and then move on to the next town-in-terror. I managed to get a freelance position here at the paper just before the diner waitress went missing back in October. That was an exciting case and didn't turn out how I expected. Do you ever visit her in prison?"

"No. I've been to see her baby, though. She's doing well."

He nods. "Good. After that, I decided to stay." He smiles wryly. "Let's face it, living somewhere like this means I'll never be short of something to write about, which in turn means my income will be reliable."

She knows he's joking, but she wishes her home town had a lower crime rate. "I assume you haven't heard from Kate since she vanished?"

"No. Like I said, we have a good working relationship, where we sometimes swap information, and buy each other coffee when we've been standing out in the rain for hours, but we don't socialize or anything. I have a lot of respect for her and I know I'm not alone among other members of the media in wanting to see her returned safely."

Madison takes a deep breath. "Part of me thinks if anyone could get away from a madman, it's Kate. She's seen all sorts of nutjobs in her line of work and she knows what these guys are capable of. She's smart and I'd like to think she'll outwit the asshole."

"Wouldn't that be great?" he says. "Okay, so I brought you here because I was looking into Jake Rubio's background. You know who he is, right?"

She raises her eyebrows. "Why Jake specifically?"

"He has a weak alibi for the night Emily Cole was murdered, and Kate mentioned more than once that she thought he was a creep for the way he treated women." Gary sips his coffee before adding, "So of course I did some digging.

I didn't find much about his family, so I dug a little deeper. I wanted to know who his parents are. I managed to obtain a copy of his birth certificate. It only lists his mother's name."

Madison doesn't see how Jake's parents are relevant to any involvement he might have had in his girlfriend's murder, but Gary is clearly excited by what he's found, so she says, "And?"

"Do you know about his mother?" he asks.

She frowns. "What do you mean?"

He opens the folder on his lap and pulls out a newspaper clipping with a black-and-white crime-scene photograph. She takes it from him. It shows a small bedroom, empty of people, and at first she doesn't realize the carpet is covered in blood. "What am I looking at?"

"In 1994, Jake Rubio's mother, Michelle, was murdered in this room when he was just four years old."

Her mouth drops open and she looks at him. "You're kidding?"

"No. Read the article. It says the police found young Jake sitting in his mother's blood. Her body was eventually discovered in the yard, badly burned. The killer was never caught."

Madison's mind is whirring. Jake lost his mother so young, and he must have witnessed her murder if he was found at the crime scene. What does that do to a child?

"There was no father in his life," says Gary. "So in the immediate aftermath of the murder, he was cared for by an aunt who is long since deceased. I haven't been able to find out anything else beyond that. I assume he was taken into care until he was old enough to live independently."

She looks at him. "As tragic as this is, what makes you think it's relevant to the recent homicides?"

He fixes his eyes on hers. "Don't you think this explains why he treats women so poorly? Losing his mom at such a young age could have caused some deep-seated resentment toward the whole female population. Maybe he has mommy issues. Maybe he has abandonment issues. Or maybe the murders of Sarah Moss and Emily Cole was Jake Rubio re-enacting his mother's murder."

Madison looks at the crime-scene photo again. It's true that witnessing his mother's murder could have had a negative impact on him that has spilled over into his treatment of women, but he's never been accused of assaulting anyone. He's almost thirty years old. If he had a real problem with women, it would have manifested long before now, and she'd like to assume someone would have come forward to report it. Besides, he has a responsible job that involves saving people's lives, not taking them.

She's reminded of what Shelley told her about their date. Jake had just been fixated on getting in her pants. But isn't that true of most guys his age? Madison doesn't know; it's been a while since anyone came on to her. Anyone other than Nate, who's a decade older than Jake and far more mature in every other way too. "His mother's crime scene is different to that of Sarah Moss and Emily Cole. They were both killed in parking lots."

"True. But wasn't he dating Emily?" Gary leans in. "As clichéd as it sounds, you and I both know that it's usually someone close to the victim who is responsible for their death."

She resists the urge to roll her eyes. She's known plenty of homicide victims who weren't related to their killer. "Thanks for telling me about this. I appreciate it."

"You're welcome. I want a happy ending to an abduction story for once," says Gary. "Because in my job, as in yours, it gets pretty damn depressing otherwise. Besides, imagine the story Kate would have to tell. She could make a fortune giving an exclusive interview, or maybe she'd even get offered a book deal if she wrote about her ordeal."

Madison raises her eyebrows at the thought.

"What's wrong with making a little money from your trauma?" he says. "It could pay for any therapy she might need."

He nods to the newspaper clipping. "You can take that copy. I have others."

Madison needs some time to think about what all this means. Her mind is whirring with possible scenarios. All of them bad. She downs the coffee he made her and stands, glancing at the article. Something jumps out at her, and she gasps. "Oh my God."

"What is it?" Gary peers over her shoulder.

"Jake's mom was discovered by Detective Bill Harper." She looks at him. "That's my dad."

He looks confused. "I didn't know your father was a cop too."

"He moved to Alaska years ago and only just came back." She feels blindsided, but she's not sure why. A closer read of the article tells her that Bill Harper was the first person from law enforcement to arrive at the crime scene. He carried Jake out of the house while he waited for backup to arrive. She considers whether this has implications.

She's only had a few interactions with Jake since she returned to Lost Creek this summer, so they certainly don't know each other well. But was he aware that it was her father who helped him that day? If so, why didn't he say anything? It's possible he was too young to ever know the name of the man who found him, which suggests her father didn't stay in touch with him over the years.

"Is everything okay, Detective?" asks Gary. There's concern in his eyes.

She takes a deep breath. "Sure, sorry. I was just surprised for a minute. I guess I can ask my dad what he remembers from that day, and what happened to Jake next. Just do me a favor, would you? Don't subject Jake to trial by media. I have no reason to believe he's a killer, and he's been through the worst experience imaginable losing his mother in that way. Don't publish all that for no reason. Imagine how gut-wrenching it would be for him to read about."

Gary doesn't make any promises. "It's up to my editor what gets published. But I understand your concerns. I suggest you find Kate as fast as possible before anyone else figures out Jake Rubio makes a good suspect. I mean, my first thought was that he was a copycat killer, imitating the person who killed his mom. So if my mind went there, so will other people's."

She tries not to react, because she's thinking the same. As she works her way out of the building, she tries to contain her horror at what Jake's past means. She didn't want Gary Pelosi to pick up on her true feelings, but her instinct tells her that Jake is caught up in this somehow. He was already her best suspect for the two homicides because of a weak alibi and the way he treats women in general. But she needs to speak to her father. She needs to hear what he knows about Jake and his mother's killer.

Once she's exited the building, she pulls her cell phone out and selects her dad's number. The rain has turned to sleet and her hands soon get cold. Bill doesn't answer the first time, so she immediately tries again. There's still no answer, so she runs to her car and, once inside, shoots him a text.

Call me asap.

Feeling like she has to act fast to prevent another murder, Madison starts her car and races out of the parking lot. Speaking to her dad will just have to wait until Jake Rubio is in police custody.

CHAPTER THIRTY

Nate has brought Jake to Richie's office. It's still messy inside, but the leaking roof has been fixed so it's drier than it was yesterday. Janine's eyes light up when she sees them both enter the reception area. "Morning, boys."

Nate smiles at her and turns to make sure Brody has followed them inside. "Janine, would you mind watching Brody for a few minutes? Jake and I need to speak to Richie."

Her expression softens when she looks at the dog. "Sure, why not?" Brody parks himself in front of the window to keep an eye on what's happening outside.

"Where's Owen?" asks Nate.

"Frank took him to the storage locker," says Janine. "They'll be back in a couple of hours."

Nate checks his phone for messages. None. Not even from Facebook.

"Good morning, Mr. Rubio." Richie appears from another room. He looks at Nate quizzically. "Everything okay?"

"The cops are questioning Jake's boss and co-workers."

Before Richie can respond, Jake's cell phone rings. He answers it. "Hello?" As he listens, the blood drains from the young man's face. "I'm at my lawyer's office."

Nate and Richie exchange a look. It's clear who he's speaking to.

"I mean, I guess. But you're wasting your time," says Jake into the phone. "I had nothing to do with any of it." After a few seconds he says, "Fine." He puts his phone in his pocket and says to Richie, "Detective Harper's coming here. She wants to speak to me. Should I be worried?"

Nate feels sorry for the guy, but Madison's instincts are rarely off. Maybe she knows something he doesn't.

"I'll make some drinks," says Janine.

Richie leads them into his office. He slips his glasses on and listens carefully as Nate and Jake update him on Jake's alibis for the times of Sarah Moss and Emily Cole's murders. Richie considers the information carefully. "What about when Kate Flynn was abducted? Where were you then?"

Janine enters to hand out hot drinks and Jake takes his with shaky hands. He puts it on top of a stack of paperwork on Richie's desk. "When was she abducted? All I know is what I saw on the news; that she didn't come home after her screwup on TV yesterday."

"Do we know the precise details of the reporter's disappearance?" Richie asks Nate.

"No, but I can find out. As he stands, intending to look into it, Madison appears in reception. She's come alone, which is something. It means she isn't about to haul Jake off in the back of a squad car. Her hair is wet and tangled and she looks stressed. He wonders why her new partner isn't with her.

Janine greets her. "Hey. I'm Janine, Richie's admin support. You must be Owen's mom."

Madison smiles as Janine shakes her hand. "I am. I hope he's pulling his weight around here."

"Oh, sure. Unlike my boss, he says yes to whatever I need him to do. He's currently on his way to Prospect Springs with Frank."

Richie stands. "I've got this, Janine." He exits his office and approaches Madison.

Nate watches as she smiles widely at her former attorney. This is the first time she's seen Richie since he sprung her from jail this past summer for a charge that didn't stick. "Long time no see," she says.

Richie goes in for a hug. Madison has to stoop a little, as he's shorter than her. "Well, if we don't see each other much, it means you're staying out of trouble," he chuckles.

Nate notices that Jake is watching his lawyer with interest. Then he stands abruptly. "You know, I'm not sure I've hired the right lawyer. No offense, Mr. Hope, but you're clearly buddies with the cop who wants to arrest me, and on top of that, you employ her son *and* her boyfriend." He glances at Nate. "I'd consider that a conflict of interest."

Nate watches as Madison's face flushes red with embarrassment.

Richie leads Madison into the office. "Don't be stupid, son. I'm your best hope of staying off death row. Now, I'm sure we can all solve this little problem by having an amicable discussion. Take a seat, everyone." Nate heads to the door to leave them to it, but Richie stops him. "I may need you, Nate."

He sits back down, in between Jake and Madison. There's an awkwardness about it, and Nate thinks Jake could be right. This feels wrong. Mainly because he and Madison are working against each other for the first time. He's here to help Jake Rubio, and she's here to arrest him.

"Now, what can we do for you, Detective?" says Richie.

Madison takes a deep breath. "I'd like to question Jake in more detail about his location during the two recent homicides and the abduction of Kate Flynn."

Richie nods. "Go right ahead."

Jake answers her questions carefully and doesn't deviate from what he told Nate, except this time he's honest right away when asked whether he knew Sarah Moss. He explains how they flirted in the grocery store a week before Christmas but says he hasn't seen her since then.

Madison is studying his face closely. "Where were you on Christmas morning between seven and ten a.m.?"

"That's easy, I was sleeping. You'd woken me up early to tell me about Emily's murder. I was tired and upset, so I slept late."

Nate turns to Madison to see what she'll ask next. "You didn't visit your family on Christmas morning?" she says.

Jake's face clouds over. "I don't have any family. My mom died when I was a kid and I don't know who my dad is."

Nate makes a note of that. It might be useful.

"I'm sorry for your loss," says Richie.

Jake shakes his head a little. "It's fine. That was years ago. I don't even remember her."

"She was murdered, right?" says Madison.

Nate's eyebrows shoot up, and both he and Richie turn to look at Jake. A flash of anger passes over Jake's face. "How do you know that?"

"I came across an article about the homicide," she says softly. "It was awful, and I'm sorry your mother suffered. That *you* suffered. No one should grow up without their mother. Not you, or Danny Moss, or Zach Cole."

Jake fidgets in his seat. "My memories of that day are hazy to say the least, but I remember that the paramedics who took care of me after the cop removed me from the house were good to me. I remember riding to the hospital in the ambulance. They let me switch the sirens on and try some of their equipment." He swallows. "They stopped me from bawling."

Madison looks solemn as she says, "I learned something today that I think you should know. The detective who found you that night was my father."

Jake's expression is hard to read. "I should've guessed, what with your last name being the same as his, but I try not to think of the guy. I never saw him in person again after that night. He never once checked on me." Jake's face clouds over. "These crime movies you see on TV, they make out cops are so worried about the kids they save and that they visit them all the time, but not your dad." He looks her in the eye. "He didn't give a shit about me."

Madison looks like she wants to defend her father, but for some reason she doesn't. Maybe she doesn't know the facts herself yet. Nate turns to Jake. "He was probably distracted with finding your mom's killer."

"That's a joke. The piece of shit didn't even manage that."

Madison remains calm and focused. "Do you know your biological father's name?"

"No. My mom didn't tell anyone who got her pregnant. What's my mom's murder got to do with any of this anyway? I've told you where I was when those women were killed or abducted or whatever. So are you going to arrest me or not?"

Nate's taken aback by his attitude. He's not doing himself any favors.

"Let's calm down, shall we?" says Richie, trying his best to be diplomatic. "Is it your intention to arrest my client. Detective? Because I have to warn you, unless you've found something to suggest he's lying about his alibis, or you have some physical evidence linking him to any of the three crime scenes, then I can't understand why you would."

Madison appears to be weighing it up. Her cell phone rings, and when she pulls it out, Nate sees her dad's name flash up. Madison silences it before standing. "I need to look into some things, but I suggest you don't leave town for the foreseeable, Jake. I might have more questions for you by the end of the day."

Jake shakes his head in annoyance, but Richie assures her, "He won't skip town, Detective. Innocent men rarely do."

Madison looks like she doesn't believe him, but she lets it go. "Nice to see you again, Richie." She leaves the office, but

Brody stops her before she reaches the exit. He wants some attention, so she leans down to stroke him.

Nate looks at Richie. "I'll just be a minute." He follows her out. "Can we talk?"

"Sure."

They both go outside, into the blustery snow that has appeared out of nowhere. The sky has turned a light gray color and it feels as if a blizzard is sweeping in. Brody goes to sniff a nearby lamp post as they talk. "You think he's murdering women because his mom was murdered, don't you?" says Nate. "Like some kind of copycat killer."

She sighs as she pulls her gloves on. "It's not that simple. Anyway, I can't talk to you about this case, because we're on opposite sides."

He's disappointed that she won't make eye contact with him. He feels like she's distancing herself and he only has himself to blame because of the way he treated her after their kiss. "I trust your instincts, Madison, but think about it. Richie would be able to find a hundred patients who could testify about Jake's kind and caring nature. Because Jake *saves* lives for a living."

She finally looks at him. "Exactly. It's the perfect cover."

He shakes his head. "Not necessarily."

"Come on, Nate. How many killers and predators do we know of who managed to get away with their crimes because they lived in plain sight or had a respectable job? Jake's job has him attending crime scenes. He knows what kind of things Alex looks for, and he'll know what to destroy. On top of that, his attitude toward women is abysmal. He acts like he's still in high school. One of my officers can attest to that." She pushes her hair, wild from the wind, out of her eyes. "Nate, his mother was murdered in front of him. That's got to mess someone up."

He knows it looks bad, but Jake's bravado left him the minute he thought he was going to be arrested. There was no cockiness anymore; he was terrified. But Nate suspects that if he pushes this with Madison, it will harm their friendship even more. All he can do is his job. And the best way to clear Jake as a suspect is to find the real killer.

"I'm just trying to find Kate alive," she adds. "I can't let my friend die." The pressure she's under is written all over her face.

He reaches out and takes her gloved hand, but she looks back toward the office and pulls it away, aware Jake could be watching. She takes a step away from him. "I'm a little annoyed that Owen has gone all the way to Prospect Springs with a complete stranger, especially with the weather turning bad. How well do you even know this Frank guy?"

Nate slips his hands into his pockets in an attempt to warm them. "Frank's okay. I went there with him myself. He's a good driver; Owen will be fine."

"He better be." She starts to walk away, clearly annoyed.

"Madison, wait." Nate reaches for her hand to stop her because he doesn't want them to part like this.

She stops and looks back at him. There's wariness in her eyes, as if she expects him to hurt her. As he's about to speak, his phone buzzes with a notification. He changed the notification tones last night so he knows this one is from Facebook. He drops her hand and reaches for his pocket.

Madison walks away. He barely notices as she gets in her car and disappears, because his new message is from Kristen.

CHAPTER THIRTY-ONE

It's been a long time since Madison has felt this dejected. She feels like Nate's working against her, Owen doesn't need her and her dad is hiding things from her. On top of that, one of her closest friends is still missing, and if it isn't Jake who has Kate and Ben locked up somewhere, then Madison has no leads whatsoever.

Her phone buzzes with a message. It's her dad.

Sorry I missed your call. I'm at the diner now. Call me back.

She drives straight to Ruby's Diner to see him. She needs to know about Jake Rubio's mother and what happened the day of her murder. Slipping her car into a free space next to her father's SUV, she gets out and heads inside.

The diner is warm and inviting, and busy as people place their lunch orders. The aroma of salty fries hits her, making her stomach rumble. She spots her father seated in a booth at the far end. She smiles at Vince Rader as she passes the counter, and he gives her a nod. When she reaches her father, she says, "Hi, Dad."

Bill's face lights up as she removes her jacket and slips into the seat opposite him. "You didn't have to come all the way here," he says.

"I was in the area when I saw your text."

Carla quickly appears, ready to take their orders. "What can I get you two?"

Madison feels like she's on a deadly countdown to find Kate and Ben before they're killed, but she also knows this might be the last chance she gets to eat for a while. She chooses something that's fast to both cook and eat so she can be out of here as quickly as possible. "Soup of the day is fine, thanks."

"I'll have an all-day breakfast, sweetheart," says her dad.

Madison cringes. She hates it when men call her sweetheart or honey, but Carla doesn't appear to mind. She must get that a lot in here, as the diner's usually full of old-timers seated at the counter. Carla pours coffee for Madison and tops up her dad's mug before disappearing.

"How's the case going?" Bill asks her.

Madison looks him square in the eye. "I almost arrested Jake Rubio for murder this morning." She watches for any flicker of recognition at the name.

Bill's eyes widen slightly before he slowly nods. "How's he doing?"

Madison senses he's disappointed in her, but she doesn't know why. "You were the cop who found him at the crime scene, weren't you?"

His eyes, normally bright with joviality, turn serious. "That was a God-awful case. We found his mother's body in the backyard. She was burned."

"Did you catch her killer?" Jake said he hadn't.

Her dad looks away. "Not yet."

She frowns as she watches him. *Not yet.* That's a strange way to phrase it. He's retired, so it's not like he's going to catch him now. "Why not?"

Carla appears with their food. "Here you go." She slides Bill's plate in front of him, but he looks like he's lost his appetite. Madison's soup is cream of tomato, with a generous slice of white crusty bread next to it.

She glances up at Carla. "Thank you."

"No problem. Let me know if I can get you folks anything else." The waitress returns to the counter to chat with customers.

Madison is so hungry she dips the bread into the soup and takes a bite while her father thinks of how to respond. Finally he says, "I don't know why. Some you catch, some you don't. It's the nature of the business, Madison. You should know that."

She's surprised by his attitude. He's defensive. "Jake tells me you never saw him again after that day. That can't be right." Most cops worry about what happens to newly orphaned children they find at horrific crime scenes. They make sure child protective services does its job properly, and they visit the kids to provide regular updates on what they're doing to catch the person who killed their loved ones. Granted, Jake was only four when his mom was murdered, so she wouldn't expect her dad to be giving him updates at that age, but she'd be surprised if he didn't stay in touch during those first few years.

He slices into a sausage. "All my time was taken up looking for the killer."

Jake was right, then: he didn't visit. Madison's disappointed. Maybe her father wasn't the detective she thought he was. They eat in silence for a few minutes until she speaks. "Did you have a suspect for it?"

He drops his knife and fork and leans back against the booth. "What's with all the questions, Madison? This case is twenty-five years old. I don't know what you want me to say. Policing was different back then. We didn't have the same resources as you guys have now."

She pushes her bowl away. "Why are you being so defensive? I'm just curious. Jake seems mad at you, that's all."

His eyes glisten with disappointment. "He's mad at me?"

"He feels like you didn't care enough to stay in touch. To check in on him every now and then."

He shakes his head. "It was too hard. I mean, how could I face him?" He raises his voice. "How could I go there to watch the disappointment in his eyes when I told him his mother's killer was still out there? That the son of a bitch had got away with it and in the meantime he'd have to grow up in foster homes?"

Madison glances over her shoulder and sees a couple at the nearby table staring at them. She leans in to her dad. "Listen, I get it. Of course I do. You tried your hardest to find the killer and guilt kept you away from Jake. That's fine. But now you're back in town, you're bound to bump into him some day and he might recognize you. Jake's an EMT now, which means I have to work with him, and I never even knew about your link to the guy." She takes a deep breath. "The least you can do is go see him sometime. He must have so many questions about what happened to his mom." Madison knows that some cops keep the worst details away from the victims' families. They mean well, but it can leave unresolved feelings for those who are left behind. They live with questions they never get the answers to. That's probably why Jake is angry at her father. As a four-year-old kid, he wouldn't have been told anything.

"I'll face him when I catch his mother's killer."

Madison rolls her eyes. "Well that's not going to happen any time soon, is it? You're retired." As soon as the words leave her mouth, she experiences a sudden sinking feeling. "Oh my God."

He leans forward. "What? What's the matter?"

She fixes her eyes on his. "I can't believe how stupid I've been."

He frowns. "What are you talking about?"

She feels sick. She wishes she'd never eaten anything. "You didn't come back to Lost Creek to reunite with me."

He swallows, then tries to laugh it off. "Of course I did. What else would drag me back to this godforsaken place?"

Not wanting to believe what has suddenly become so obvious, she says, "When you came back unannounced last month, you told me there was one serial killer who got away. One predator you never managed to catch." She shakes her head. "You were talking about the person who killed Jake Rubio's mom."

Her father lowers his eyes.

"And I'm willing to bet he's the one who murdered Sarah Moss and Emily Cole. The one who has Kate and her son." Her hands have gone stone cold. "You didn't come home for me. You came home to find *him*."

Her father's face is pale, but he doesn't deny it. "Honey, you don't understand what this guy—the Snow Storm Killer— has done. It started here in Lost Creek with Michelle Rubio, then I followed him to Alaska—"

She stands abruptly, wanting to get away from him.

"No, wait!" He stands too and blocks her from leaving. "Maddie? I followed him to Alaska and never caught him. *Twenty-five years* and I never caught him. I got so close so many times..." His expression is pained. "You have to understand. He'll keep killing. He needs to be stopped, and only I can do that."

She remembers how her dad wasn't around on Christmas Day because he had things to do. She thinks of the guy who turned up at her house for dinner. "Your friend Mike is a Fed too, isn't he? Even though he said he wasn't. He's here investigating with you, right?"

Bill nods. "He's the guy who's taken over the case from me. The FBI, they make you retire at fifty-seven, you have no choice. But for the past few years they let me stay on as a consultant on this case, assisting Mike. They know that only *I* have insight into this sick bastard's mind."

She can feel her face reddening with anger. "If you

knew my victims had been killed by him, why didn't you tell me so I could stop wasting my time on other suspects?" she yells. "I mean, I almost arrested one of his victims' kids today!" The thought is horrifying. Jake Rubio has been through enough. "You've wasted so much time, Dad! I could've found this guy before he abducted Kate." Her voice hitches at the end.

He shakes his head and looks desperate as he tries to explain. "No, honey. I need to be the one to find him. It has to be me."

She can't believe what she's hearing. Her father is obsessed with this guy. To the point where he's put other people's lives at risk in order to settle a score.

"I thought if I could entice him back here to a small town and where it all started, he'd be easier to catch," says her father. "I thought he'd stand out like a sore thumb here. And I knew he'd follow me if I pretended to retire for good and move away from Alaska." He places a hand on her arm. "He lives for the cat-and-mouse aspect of our relationship."

"Your *relationship*?" She shakes his hand off. She can't believe what she's hearing. He pretended he came back to reunite with *her*. He pretended he missed *her*. She feels like she might vomit. Then something else dawns on her. She looks at him.

"My God, Dad. You enticed a serial killer to the town where your daughter is the lead detective. And I bet you made sure he'd hear about where you were retiring to, and how you were hoping to reunite with your long-lost family." She shakes her head in frustration. "You've told me countless times how serial killers go after the families of those chasing them. You've knowingly placed me and Owen in danger by using us as bait!" Her heart aches as she realizes how little he must care about them.

When Vince approaches, Madison notices everyone is watching them. Listening in to all the gory details of her humiliation. He appears uncomfortable as he says, "How about we take this upstairs?"

"No." She pulls her jacket on, barely holding back the tears that threaten to fall. She glares at her dad. "As far as I'm concerned, my father died when he moved to Alaska, because I don't recognize you at all. And I never want to see you again."

CHAPTER THIRTY-TWO

Bill's showdown with his daughter leaves him feeling miserable and he declines Vince's invitation to go upstairs to his apartment over the diner. Instead, he heads home to his own apartment. He needs to speak to Mike. Mike may be lead agent on this case since Bill's enforced retirement, but they both know that Bill is in charge. It was his idea to entice the killer home by pretending to move back here, and Mike had eventually given the green light. He visited the crime scenes with Bill on Christmas Day and has been working out of the motel room he's staying in. Bill texts him now and tells him to come over so they can discuss their next move.

A glance out the window has him wondering whether the storm is going to disrupt their plans and play into the killer's hands. Because the SSK lives for weather like this. In the early days, he didn't always kill during snowfall, which suggests his crimes were more opportunistic back then and less methodical. But his MO has evolved over the years, meaning he's honed his craft, and his last thirteen murders were all committed during snow storms, and always around Christmas. Now, with the weather and timing perfect for him, and with Bill in town to witness him getting away with his crimes, it's only a matter of time before he goes after his next victim.

Bill shrugs off his wet jacket and goes to his bedroom to retrieve a large box. It's full of case files: every single victim of the Snow Storm Killer. From Jake Rubio's mother, Michelle, in 1994 to the last kill in Alaska two years ago. The killer moved and worked across several states in between, but he came back to Alaska after a break. Bill assumed the guy had spent some time in prison for a misdemeanor, and that's what put him out of action for a while, but he doesn't know for sure. He only knows he came back, which gave him an odd sense of relief, because it meant he hadn't died and therefore got away with his crimes.

He opens the box and his heart skips a beat as he pulls out the only wedding photo he owns. It shows him and Pamela dressed smartly and standing in front of the judge in the small courthouse room as they made their brief vows to each other. An American flag stands proudly behind them and the judge is smiling down on them.

He strokes his wife's face. Even all these years later, burying Pamela is the hardest thing he has ever had to do. Even harder than leaving his daughters to move to Alaska. It was the guilt that made it so difficult to bear. He should never have left his wife alone, ever. They got sloppy. They were happy and thought no one could touch them, despite all the evidence to the contrary. He discovered most of her body in the bath, as he feared he would after reading the letter the SSK left for him in the bar. To this day her head has never been found. He still has nightmares over that, and can't even bring himself to speculate on what the son of a bitch did to her beautiful face.

He slips the photo into his shirt pocket and digs deeper into the box for the letters. The first one he received was the night of Pamela's murder in '98. They've continued since then, the ramblings of a guy so screwed up that he appears to believe he and Bill are brothers or something. He pulls one out at random and sees it's ten years old and sent from Chicago. The killer always favored the colder states.

Agent Harper, or should I call you Bill now? Maybe. Or maybe not until you catch me and we can look each other in the eye, which is something I'm starting to fear will never happen.

Have you remarried yet? A man shouldn't live alone. He needs a partner, and children. I do wish you'd had children. I would love to have met them. Although I suspect your line of work makes that difficult, as you're never home long enough to impregnate anyone and your wives tend to get themselves killed.

I'm writing because I'm a little bored. You aren't getting close enough, so the fun is fading from our relationship. With all the advancements in technology since my first kill, I would have thought you'd have found me by now. Maybe you're not going to be the one. Not to worry; our game can be distracting from my real purpose.

Have you figured it out yet, Agent Harper? Have you figured out why these women are dying? Why their children are left unharmed? It's so obvious to me, but I have more pieces of the puzzle than you do. Perhaps I should give you a clue...

I loved my mother very dearly.

There. Take it and run with it. Run with it in my direction, because I fear it's all been for nothing anyway. I fear I'll never get the answers I seek. Just like you.

As always, merry Christmas, Agent Harper. Give my best to the department.

SSK

Bill screws the letter up in his hand like he has a hundred

times before. It's a copy of the original, which is secured back at the office in Anchorage. The letters have all been tested a million different ways, but they yield no clues as to the identity or exact location of the killer.

The line offered by the SSK about loving his mother dearly confused Bill and his team no end. Mothers often get the blame for a killer's actions: they were too overbearing, they weren't protective enough, they ridiculed their son's lack of a love life, yada, yada, yada. So he considered the idea that the killer was throwing him a red herring rather than a clue, something designed to steer him in the wrong direction. Still, he looked at it from all angles, even taking a course in psychology in order to gain a deeper understanding of child development and the effects of the mother-child bond.

Maybe this guy's mother *had* screwed him over, and he had loved her more than she loved him, but that was a poor excuse to murder fifteen women—sixteen if Kate Flynn turns up dead. His team worked on the theory that the victims' children—always boys—represented the killer as a child. That he felt neglected by his mother somehow, perhaps unseen by her. But delving into his psyche hadn't brought anything new to the table. Bill always believed that good old-fashioned police work was what would catch this guy, not acting like a psychotherapist.

He selects the Last letter he received. It's dated December 14th, almost two weeks ago, shortly after he moved back to Lost Creek. It confirmed that his plan to entice the SSK home had worked, which filled him with equal measures of dread, regret and excitement.

You did a good job of keeping your family a secret all these years, Agent Harper. I thought the only person you loved was Pamela. I didn't know about Lynette and the girls back in our home town, somewhere I haven't been since I left shortly after killing Michelle Rubio.

So imagine my surprise when I found articles dated last year about a woman called Detective Madison Harper who was sensationally released from prison after having her conviction for manslaughter overturned. Imagine my excitement at thinking Special Agent Bill Harper has a daughter who killed someone! A killer in the family! It took me a while to realize you couldn't have known about her arrest seven years ago, because if you had, you would have returned home sooner. Unless you're as cold-hearted as the killers you seek.

I've learned your elder daughter is in prison—that must surely hurt your ego—and that Madison is now back on the force. Back working for the same police department you were at when I made my first kill. I bet you're proud. She must be a real chip off the old block.

Tell me, Bill, does she have any experience hunting serial killers? Perhaps she can do what you couldn't. Wouldn't that be fun...

And congratulations on becoming a grandfather to young Owen! He's had a tough upbringing, hasn't he? Let's hope it's made him resilient, and aware of the dangers in this world. Your family fascinates me. It appears they've had as much tragedy as I have, and you weren't there to protect them because of me. I only wish I could share Christmas dinner with you all. Because it will be your last.

Come get me, Bill. Or send your daughter if you think she can do a better job.

Merry Christmas.

SSK

His hands are clenched with anger. The way this piece of shit mocks him is infuriating. Bill always believed he could catch him, or he would've left the job years ago, and the fact that he still hasn't is professionally embarrassing. It's made him question his skills as a detective and a special agent. Should he have said no to Pamela all those years ago when she made a special trip down here to offer him the job? Was he too cocky? He doesn't want to believe that, which is probably why he kept it all from Madison. Why he didn't tell her the real reason he'd returned.

He screws the letter up and drops it back into the box. He loves his daughters, both of them, but he doesn't know them as adults. Angie is in prison awaiting a murder trial, and Madison is turning into a better cop than he ever was. If she catches the SSK before him, he'll be humiliated, sure, but not only that. It means he would have dedicated his life to something he will never achieve. It would mean all the personal sacrifices were for nothing. That Pam's death was for nothing.

He can't let that happen. He retrieves some paperwork from his coat pocket, printouts taken from the internet. More SSK victims: Sarah Moss, Emily Cole and Kate Flynn. He shakes his head sadly as he struggles to let go of Kate's photograph. This one hurts more than the others, because she's the only one of the three he knew personally. Madison had just become friends with Kate before Bill moved away. Kate had spent time at their house, joining them for dinner. She was a bubbly teenager with the gift of the gab. She always had a witty comeback and would pretend to be reporting from their dinner table.

He smiles as he recalls her holding her fork as if it were a mic, and narrating as Lynnette brought dinner over to the table. "I'm Kate Flynn reporting live from the Harper household. I have some breaking news for you now, folks. Tonight's dinner is roast chicken with a side of mashed potatoes. I don't yet know which vegetables will be served, but I'll keep you abreast of the situation as soon as I have more news. Now back to the studio."

Madison found her friend's antics hilarious. He swallows the lump in his throat. Could he still save Kate Flynn and her boy? Or is it too late for them? His thoughts turn to Madison. He hasn't yet let his mind go there, but if the SSK's final act is to kill his daughter, Bill won't be able to live with himself.

A knock at the door rouses him. He gets up and opens it. Mike is standing there, with snow melting on his shoulders. "What's the plan?" he asks.

Bill looks him dead in the eye. "The plan is to catch this son of a bitch before he kills what's left of my family."

CHAPTER THIRTY-THREE

Madison tries to drive back to the station, but she's hampered by heavy snow. Forced to pull over, she waits in the parking lot of a liquor store and wipes the tears from her face. She's in shock about her father's deceit, unable to believe what he's done. Using her and Owen as bait for a dangerous predator is unforgivable. He fed her so many lies. She feels stupid for believing he came back to spend his retirement being a father and grandfather at last.

Her first instinct after hearing the revelations was to call Nate, to hear his reassuring voice, but she didn't. She glances at her cell phone on the passenger seat, still tempted. But no, he isn't reliable right now. She doesn't know if he ever will be again. Maybe she's being too hard on him, but she doesn't want to be anyone's runner-up prize. He can chase after Kristen Devereaux if he thinks it will make him happy. Madison survived before meeting Nate Monroe, and she'll be just fine without him going forward.

She angrily switches the car's wiper blades off; they're helpless against the snow. It quickly covers the windows as she thinks of her son. Her heart aches for him, because when he finds out his grandfather lied to them, that he doesn't care about them, he'll be devastated. She picks up her phone to call him. Not with the intention of telling him what happened, but to see whether he's headed back into town before the blizzard gets worse. Her hands are like ice, so she turns the heat up in the car as she waits for him to answer. The ancient engine can't cope with the demand and switches itself off. "Shit." It's going to get cold fast.

Her call eventually goes to voicemail, which worries her, so she leaves him a message. "Owen, call me when you get this. The snow's pretty bad here now, so I want to know where-abouts you are. I hope Frank's driving carefully." She hesitates before adding, "Do me a favor and stay away from Grandpa today. I'll explain later." She drops the phone in her lap and frowns. Owen rarely misses a call or a text; he's obsessed with his phone. With a long sigh, she leans back against the headrest.

A figure appears in her rear-view mirror, obscured by the snow. It walks slowly from the trunk to the driver's side. The hairs on Madison's neck stand on end and she touches the butt of her firearm. The tall figure rounds the front of the car before reaching for the passenger door. She sits up straight as the door opens, spilling in snow and a gust of bitter wind. When she realizes it's Detective Adams, she rolls her eyes.

He slips into the car with three takeout coffee cups in a cardboard cupholder in his spare hand. "Hey," he says, closing the door behind him. "I spotted your car from the road. I've just been to fetch these from Ruby's Diner. Now *that* is what I call a small-town diner." He smiles. "Makes me feel like I'm living in some kind of low-budget crime movie."

She's glad to see a friendly face, even if it belongs to Adams. "Who are they for?"

He hands her a cup. "Us now. We can't drive in this, it's too heavy. Hopefully it'll pass in a few minutes."

She takes it from him and the heat feels wonderful in her

hands. She takes the lid off and sees it's a cappuccino with plenty of chocolate sprinkled on top. It tastes good.

"Where have you been?" he asks, before noticing her red eyes. "Hey, what's wrong?"

Unfortunately, Madison's not one of those women who look dignified after crying. Her eyelids swell up, there's a steady stream of snot to contend with and she gets red dots under her eyes if she's been sobbing really hard. She pulls down the overhead mirror and takes a look at her reflection. "Oh God." Her under-eye concealer is worn away, revealing dark circles. Her nose is bright pink and she looks like she needs a week's worth of sleep. She snaps the mirror closed, and because she'd rather focus on finding Kate and Ben than talk about her father, she says, "I'm fine."

"You're obviously not. What's happened?" When she's reluctant to open up, he adds, "We could be here a while, and if *we* can't move, neither can the killer. So consider this a timeout in the investigation and tell me what's upset you."

She looks at him and sees genuine concern on his face. Everything comes spilling out of her: her father's deception, the loneliness she's feeling now she can't rely on her dad or Nate, and her worries for Kate and Ben. When she's done crying, Adams pats her arm. The gesture is so unbearably awkward that it makes her snort with laughter.

"What?" he says, with evident relief that she's stopped crying at least. "I'm trying to be nice!" As she wipes her eyes with an old tissue, he adds, "You can't catch a break, can you? In fact, you might be the unluckiest person I've ever met."

She scoffs. "Aren't you glad you moved all the way down here to partner with someone like me?"

He waves a dismissive hand. "Oh please. I thrive on drama. I have two daughters, remember."

She's glad he's revealing his lighter side at last. "In all seriousness, we now know that we're looking for a serial killer. And a seasoned one at that. I mean, if the FBI couldn't catch this guy after twenty-five years of searching, then how are we going to?"

He drinks the rest of his coffee as he considers a response. "Treat him the same as any other killer, I guess. Find his mistakes. Because there will be some. A piece of DNA left behind, or a witness who was never taken seriously by the cops."

She sips her drink, disappointed. Adams should know that serial killers are different; that they don't commit random crimes in the heat of the moment. They're methodical. They plan their crimes in advance and they're good at keeping their true personalities secret from those around them. Which makes them harder to catch. She sighs. "You realize this means we're not just working to solve the two recent homicides and Kate Flynn's abduction anymore?"

He frowns. "What do you mean?"

"We need to solve the killer's cold cases too if we're to find clues as to his motivation, and as of right now, we don't know how many other victims there are."

He looks away as it dawns on him how much work they need to do. "We could bring in the Feds to help."

Madison's not against working with the FBI, but they're just going to put her father in charge, and she knows now that he's not reliable. He's already deceived her about who was responsible for these homicides. "If they were going to be any help at all, don't you think they would've caught him by now?"

Eventually, he nods. "We don't get paid nearly enough to catch serial killers."

His attitude is disappointing. "I hate to break it to you, Adams, but if you're in law enforcement for the money, you're in the wrong job."

He glances at her. "I'm just saying. I mean, how much do you think your dad was paid to try to catch this guy? It's got to be a hell of a lot more than what we're on."

Madison's more worried about the fact that this investigation will result in a huge increase in workload for their small department. It would be helpful if she could bring another investigator on board to lend a hand. Nate, for instance. But he's busy working against her, and even if Jake no longer needs a lawyer, Nate's distracted with other things. "Did you learn anything about Jake Rubio from his boss and co-worker?"

"They both spoke highly of him. Said he's never done anything wrong while at work, and there haven't been any complaints made about him by patients or co-workers."

Jake's far too young to be the serial killer, considering he was just four when his mother was murdered, so she'll need to apologize to him at some point, both for considering him a suspect *and* for her father's failings. Although, it would mean more if she could catch his mother's killer. Madison knows where she needs to start with that; researching the Snow Storm Killer and his crimes. She needs to get inside this guy's head.

After checking her phone and finding no reply from Owen, she turns her key in the ignition with her fingers crossed. Luckily, the car starts. She looks at Adams. "We need to get back to the station and update the team. Kate and her son are relying on us to find them."

He smiles. "Beat you there." He takes the empty coffee cups with him as he climbs out of her car.

Madison gets out too and clears her windshield of snow. There's a break in the flurry, so she quickly gets back in and backs out of the parking lot ahead of Adams.

CHAPTER THIRTY-FOUR

Some of the team is assembled in the briefing room awaiting an update. Most of the officers are out on patrol and actively searching for Kate and Ben, but Shelley Vickers, Gloria Williams and Luis Sanchez are huddled together chatting. Alex Parker and Sergeant Tanner are waiting silently. Everyone knows they need to disseminate whatever they learn in the next ten minutes to the rest of the team. Chief Mendes is the last person to enter, and she closes the door behind her.

Madison approaches the uniforms. "Any sightings, leads or information yet?"

"No," says Shelley. "We've canvassed what feels like the whole town and I've watched a lot of surveillance footage, but no one spotted Kate in her own car that morning, let alone in someone else's."

"Because it was Christmas morning," says Gloria. "Most people were at home. The streets were pretty empty."

Madison chews her lip as she tries to think. "Someone must've seen something. I'd like you to visit all the gas stations in the area and any other stores that were open. The abductor could've stopped somewhere to pick up supplies first. And check out any condemned or abandoned buildings you know of. He's holding them somewhere and it's probably not in his own home."

"There's plenty of abandoned buildings around these days," says Sanchez. "It feels like half the town is boarded up. Gold Rock is even worse."

Gold Rock is a small mining town nearby; it's where Madison's older sister lived until her arrest. "You're in charge of checking Gold Rock," she says to Sanchez. "It would be a good place to hide someone."

He nods.

"Just remind me how old Kate's little boy is," says Shelley.

"Ben's four years old. He's adopted and he's going through a phase of not talking. It's called selective mutism. Just be aware of that if you find him. He's extra shy around strangers."

"Sure."

Detective Adams joins Madison as she heads to the front of the room. He offers a quick reassuring nod as she takes a deep breath. "Okay, everyone," she says. "We've had a break-through in the case and it means our jobs just got a lot harder." After a pause, she says somewhat hesitantly, "Some of you may not know this, but my father was a special agent for the FBI."

Officer Sanchez grins. "Cool."

Chief Mendes looks like she's wondering where this is going. She was on the phone when Madison arrived at the station, so Madison couldn't give her a heads-up about what she'd learned.

"He was tasked with catching serial killers," she continues. "One of those killers has evaded capture for twenty-five years so far."

"Oh my God," says Shelley, catching on quick.

"He's known as the Snow Storm Killer..." Madison glances out of the window. "And it seems we have the perfect conditions for him here in Lost Creek, which unfortunately is his home town, so he knows the place well." She looks Chief Mendes in the eye. "I have reason to believe this guy is responsible for the murders of Sarah Moss and Emily Cole. And I believe he's holding Kate Flynn and her son captive."

Gloria turns to Shelley and says under her breath, "God help us."

Mendes turns pale. She'll be considering how much attention this will bring to their town. "Why exactly do you believe this? Did your father tell you he sees similarities between our homicides and his?"

"Not exactly." Madison tries to think of a way of explaining just how badly her dad has betrayed her without being dramatic.

Adams steps forward. "It seems that Madison's father didn't want to end his career until he found this sorry son of a bitch. For some reason he thought that a good way to corner him would be to lure him to Lost Creek using Madison and her son as bait."

Shelley and Gloria gasp. Chief Mendes shakes her head in disgust and Steve looks at Madison like he wants to come over and hug her.

From the corner of the room, Alex Parker says, "I'm sorry to hear that, Detective. There's no betrayal quite like family betrayal."

Madison glances at him and wonders if that's why he moved here from the UK. She clears her throat. "It's fine, my life is already like a soap opera, right? I should be expecting these plot twists by now." She attempts a laugh, but it doesn't sound convincing. "He could've told me sooner that this guy was responsible, but as Detective Adams says, he wanted to catch him himself, which means we're behind in our investigation. I suggest we all get up to speed on the history of the Snow Storm Killer, because I don't know anything about him. Alex, would you look into his previous crime scenes and figure out what forensics we should be focusing on."

Alex nods. "Consider it done."

Steve clears his throat. "I'll find a record of his previous victims and liaise with the other states and the FBI to see what information they can give us."

"Great, thanks." She looks at the patrol officers. "There isn't much reason for people to be out in these conditions today unless they really have to work. So if you see any males on their own, driving aimlessly or pulled over talking to women, stop and question them. And if you see any women who seem like easy targets, make them aware they're in danger."

Chief Mendes says, "I'll notify dispatch of the situation and ask them to relay it to all units. Do we currently have any other description for this man, other than the fact that he's tall and broad?"

Madison shakes her head, but then thinks of something as she recalls the heated discussion with her dad in the diner. "From what I can tell, this guy's first kill was Jake Rubio's mother, twenty-five years ago."

The blood vanishes from Shelley's face. "Jake's mother was *murdered*? He never told me that."

"I don't think he tells anyone. He was just four at the time. He was found sitting in his mother's blood."

"Damn," says Officer Sanchez. "That's got to mess a guy up, right?"

After a pause, Madison says. "It was my father who found Jake that day. Detective Bill Harper."

"Your father worked here before he joined the Bureau?" says Steve, his eyebrows raised.

She nods. There's so much they don't know, but she doesn't have time to fill them in on everything. "Jake was my original person of interest for the two recent murders, but if the SSK is responsible for our homicides, I was obviously wrong about that. Michelle Rubio was killed in 1994, so in all likelihood we're looking for someone who's at least forty years old now. I'd say we should be considering someone aged between forty and sixty, given that they'd need to be old enough to kill in '94, but not so old they can't still beat someone to death and run away from the scene."

"Your father is the best and fastest source of information about our assailant," says Chief Mendes. "Are you bringing him on board?"

There's an awkward silence as everyone looks at Madison. Despite everything her father has done, she would work with him in a heartbeat if it meant getting Kate and Ben back alive. But from what he told her, she knows he won't work with them to find this killer. "As far as he's concerned, this is his case. He wants to be the person to make the catch, and he won't be interested in our help."

Mendes raises her eyebrows. "Wow. I'm sorry to say this, Madison, but your dad's obsessed. I've seen it happen before; an agent putting their own ego before the investigation."

Madison inwardly cringes, because she's right. "Alex? Did you find anything useful in or on Kate's car?"

"Nothing at all. The abductor was careful not to touch it, as we suspected. I've also been through Kate's cell phone, which her husband dropped in for me. There's nothing of interest on there. She hadn't made any calls that morning or given any clues as to where she was going with her children."

"Nothing from Patrick that could cause concern?"

He shakes his head. "No. If they were arguing, they were doing it face to face."

"Or Patrick deleted the exchanges before handing the phone over."

Madison tries to think. David Moss is too young to have killed Michelle Rubio, but Patrick is almost forty. He would have been around fifteen when Michelle was murdered. Is that too young to be a killer? Maybe not, if it was his first kill. She knows he left Lost Creek after graduating, but she doesn't know where he lived before returning home and marrying Kate. She sighs, frustrated. She worries she's clutching at straws. But Patrick's alibis are weak. He got home late the night Sarah was murdered, and he was home alone with the kids when Kate supposedly left with them, missing the whole thing because he was taking a shower. She hasn't asked him where he was when Emily Cole was attacked.

Would a fifteen-year-old be capable of bludgeoning a woman to death? Probably, although it doesn't bear thinking about. Maybe because she knows Patrick. She's seen him with Kate. They may be going through problems at the moment, but it hasn't always been that way. "What's confusing is that the killer doesn't appear to have just one MO," she says. "Michelle Rubio was killed inside her home and then dragged outside to be burned; our two recent victims were killed outside in parking lots, and Kate's abduction doesn't fit at all. It's almost like he snapped when he heard what she said about him on TV, and reacted out of rage or humiliation. But I thought serial killers were more controlled than that."

Alex agrees. "As we don't have Kate's and Ben's bodies, he must be holding them captive. That's a completely different situation than he'll be used to. It's much harder to hide people than it is to kill them."

"Perhaps serial killers evolve over time," she suggests.

"And let's face it," says Steve, "it's a lot harder to break into people's homes these days than it was in the early nineties. It's easier to kill out in the open by taking people unaware. That's how he managed to abduct Kate. But having said that, I think the differing MO suggests we should consider whether we have a copycat killer." He pauses when Madison raises an eyebrow. "Maybe there are two assailants," he says. "The guy who killed Michelle Rubio and any other victims back then, and the guy who killed Sarah and Emily. In which case, our guy could be younger."

"Yeah," says Sanchez. "Which means it could still be Jake Rubio. Or any of the partners really."

Shelley lowers her eyes and crosses her arms. It can't be

nice considering the possibility that the guy you recently went on a date with could be capable of murder.

"Anything's possible," says Madison. "And I do think we should be open-minded, which would mean David Moss and Patrick Flynn also make good suspects for a copycat killer. I need to research the SSK's previous kills, to see if he's deviated from his MO before. Alex, would you call the crime lab and try to get the items you sent them tested today? I have a feeling DNA might be our best shot at catching this guy."

"Of course." Alex leaves the room right away.

Chief Mendes looks around at the rest of the team. "As we'll have no FBI assistance in this case, we need to get to work. Let's aim to get Kate Flynn and her son home by the end of the day."

Madison lowers her eyes. She's ashamed of her father. She always believed he was a hero, but now he's harming their investigation and putting more lives at risk. Which is the very thing he's supposed to stop from happening.

CHAPTER THIRTY-FIVE

Brody is panting heavily. He's agitated because Nate is pacing up and down the kitchen. "It's okay, boy. Everything's okay."

Except the truth is, everything's not okay. Nate's hands are sweating so badly he's at risk of dropping his cell phone. His heart is drumming against his chest and he's filled with dread. He hasn't had anxiety this bad for a long time. When his phone buzzes, he jumps. He checks who it is and is disappointed to see Richie's name.

Just had word that Jake Rubio won't be arrested today.

That's something, at least. Part of him wonders whether Madison's found a better suspect, but he's distracted by the Facebook message he received when he was with her outside Richie's office earlier. The person claiming to be Kristen Devereaux asked for his cell phone number, which he sent straight away. Since then, he's ignored two calls; from Vince Rader and from Owen. Owen's call stopped before he could answer it. Nate didn't call him straight back because he didn't want to be on the line when Kristen calls, but he intends to check in on him later.

Nate doesn't really believe it's Kristen messaging him, because of how badly beaten she was in the photograph Father

Connor left for him to find at Madison's house in October. The priest wanted Nate to know she'd suffered because she had helped to secure his release from prison, but it wasn't possible to tell whether she was dead. There was still some color in her lips, but her eyes were closed and bloody. It was a close-up shot of her face that gave little away, and that's why a tiny part of Nate—the part that should probably know better by now—wants to believe she's still alive. At this stage, over two years since her disappearance, he just needs to know either way.

His phone rings and he drops it in surprise. Brody barks, probably his way of telling Nate to calm down. Nate leans over to retrieve it and is relieved to see it's unbroken. He feels dizzy as he stands. The caller's number is withheld. He's so afraid that this is some kind of scam that he can't even take a breath. He accepts the call, but is unable to speak.

After a few seconds a woman's voice says, "Nate? Is that you?"

A chill goes down his spine as he recognizes Kristen's voice. He slides onto a chair at the dining table. Brody sits at his feet, staring at him intently. "It's really you," he whispers.

He hears her weeping on the other end of the phone. "It's really you, too," she says. "I thought the Facebook page was some kind of hoax." After a long pause, she adds, "I wish we could meet in person, but I can't, Nate. I can't meet with you or let you know where I am and put myself in a vulnerable position for you again. I almost died last time."

Her accent, a combination of French and American, brings back a lot of painful prison memories for Nate, and he has to wipe his eyes. "I'm sorry. I'm sorry for everything. You should never have been caught up in that mess. If I could go back in time..."

"I know," she says softly. "It wasn't your fault. That man was fixated on you. He was possessed." The last word is said with venom.

She doesn't need to name him. He knows she means Father Connor, the person who killed Nate's fiancée and framed him for it twenty years ago next month.

"I found a clip from a news report on YouTube of you walking out of prison," says Kristen. "I was overwhelmed with relief when I saw that Rex was there to greet you. I didn't want you to go through that alone."

Rex Hartley was Nate's other savior. His involvement in freeing Nate got him killed. At least Kristen is still alive. It's a miracle. And Nate had all but given up on miracles. "I wish you had been there. If it wasn't for you, I'd be dead by now."

She sighs heavily. "It seems our fortunes were reversed. I may not be on death row, but until that man is convicted, I'm not able to live freely."

Her words hurt him more than she can know. The knowledge that she's going through all this because of him is torturous. "I intended to look for you once I got out, but I..." How does he finish that thought? He had to take care of himself, because he was in no fit state to help anyone back then. Without Rex's hospitality and guidance, he would have given up on himself. And when Rex died, it was Madison who became his rock. He finds himself wondering if he can ever find the strength to stop being a burden to others.

"He abducted me," she says, her voice thick with emotion.

Nate's jaw clenches. Father Connor has a lot to answer for.

"He was waiting at my apartment and pulled a gun, forcing me into his car," she continues. "I tried to fight, but he'd handcuffed me. I knew what he'd done to your fiancée; I'd obviously seen the crime-scene photos and knew your case inside out. I... I didn't want to end up that way, so I went with him to avoid being killed on the spot. I thought I could outsmart him. Somehow talk him into letting me go eventually. He kept me locked up in an outbuilding in New Mexico for months. He beat me whenever he was frustrated at you." Nate winces. "He took photographs of me like that. Then one day he vanished, and left me behind with no food or water. I broke out of the building, but I didn't trust that it wasn't a trick, so I daren't go to anyone I passed. Instead, I found a women's refuge and pretended I'd left a violent partner. The scars and bruises worked in my favor. They took care of me for a long time. Eventually I was able to trust them and disclose what had really happened. I didn't mention names, but I did make it clear that my life was in danger and going to the police wasn't an option."

She takes a deep breath. "When the time came to leave, I was too afraid to go back to Texas or to try to contact you or Rex. I just knew Father Connor would come after me if he realized I'd escaped. Someone at the refuge eventually agreed to get me a fake ID. I've used that ever since and will continue to use it until he's either convicted or dead. Then I'll be free."

Nate couldn't feel any worse. It's clear that Kristen's life has been ruined because of helping him. Brody whines softly as he watches Nate clench his spare fist. He considers telling her that she would be free sooner if he killed Father Connor for her. He almost did it the night the priest was caught, but Madison managed to talk him out of it. Sometimes, like now, he regrets listening to her. Perhaps he could visit the priest in prison and somehow do it there. Would it be worth going back to death row for killing the man who ruined their lives? Nate thinks it would but he knows he can't go back there. "Then we can meet in person," he says hopefully.

She sighs down the phone. "That would be nice. But it's not possible, Nate. I'm leaving the States."

He closes his eyes. "Because of him?"

Silence as she gulps back tears. "I'm not made for this. I don't feel able to give testimony, to be in the same room with that man. I don't feel able to be in the same *country* as that man. I need a fresh start. I've been in touch with my parents, and they've agreed to move back to France with me."

He realizes she's afraid. Because if Father Connor is acquitted, he'll come after her again, just as he will undoubtedly come after Nate again. He strokes Brody's soft head. "I bet they were overjoyed to hear from you."

She sobs loudly for a whole minute. "The police had told them I was likely dead, but my parents never stopped looking for me. My mom said she just knew I was alive, that she could sense it. I haven't seen them yet. We're being cautious, because I don't want the police or the FBI to know where I am. They'll want me to testify, and as I said, that's not something I can do." She laughs bitterly. "I'm a former law professor who spent years helping to get innocent people acquitted and released from prison, and now I can't even bear the thought of testifying against a known murderer. That's what he's done to me." She composes herself before adding, "I'm moving to France shortly, and my parents will follow in a month or two."

He knows it's the right thing for her. Some people aren't cut out for facing their abusers in court, and he fully understands that because he doesn't know if he's cut out for it. He's just hoping that by the time Father Connor's trial starts next year, he'll have found some inner strength from somewhere.

"Nate, I need you to know that what I felt for you while you were in prison was real. I wasn't pretending to make you feel better about your life. I know you were worried about that back then; that I was just trying to give you false hope to keep you from hurting yourself." She pauses. "But that being said… things are different now."

He lowers his eyes and drops his hand from Brody's head. He's under no illusion that their feelings for each other back then were the result of circumstance. He had a need for human contact on death row, while for Kristen it was about saving a soul, and pity probably also played a part. But now that he's out and she's gone through hell because of him, he's not surprised she no longer has any romantic feelings for him. Their experiences at the hands of Father Connor are the result of the man's hatred for him. Part of her must blame him for that, no matter what she says. "I know," he tells her. "It's fine."

She sighs with relief. "Have you acclimatized to life on the outside?" Almost shyly, she adds, "I've read about your work with Madison Harper. You seem to be a good team."

Nate closes his eyes and is overwhelmed by his emotions for Madison. He smiles at last. "I've found someone almost as messed up as me. At least, she was when I first met her. Since then, she's proven herself to be more resilient than I am."

"Nate," says Kristen, "don't do that. Don't judge yourself for adjusting at a different pace to her. From what I read, it sounds like you had different experiences. Besides, maybe she's more resilient because she's had you by her side. Did you ever think about that?"

He doesn't know what to think. Listening to Kristen's voice is hard. He feels like he could be back in that tiny inter-view room in Texas, where his hands would be shackled to the table and Kristen would be feeding him hope in snippets of legal loopholes she'd found that he didn't really understand.

"I have to go," she says.

"Already?"

"I'm sorry. I need to be cautious." She takes a deep breath. "Please don't tell anyone I'm alive."

"I understand. Madison knows you messaged me, though, so I'll have to tell her you're safe."

"She'll want you to talk me into coming forward to testify." There's concern in her voice.

"No. She knows what I've been through with the guy. She'll understand."

"Nate, she's a cop. We don't trust cops, remember? That's what you always said in prison, and I've studied enough wrongful convictions to believe that more of them are dirty than not."

He nods. "I know. But Madison's different." He can't even begin to explain how, but she is.

Kristen sighs. "I guess it's up to you. I just don't want to go through any of this again. I'm overjoyed that you're free now, but I'm not. Not yet."

The truth stings, and he wonders how he's supposed to bear the guilt he feels for getting her involved in all this. "If I can do anything to help you, call me. I'm serious. Any time, day or night. I have money. I can wire you any amount you need."

"Thank you. Knowing you're at the end of the phone makes me feel better. I have your number saved." Silence, then, "Take care of yourself, Nate. Because if you don't, all of this—getting you off death row, my abduction, Rex's murder— will have been for nothing. I can bear it if I know you're living your life now and moving on, but I can't bear it if I think you're going to do something stupid, like putting an end to *that man*, or worse, to yourself. You understand?"

He nods as he wipes his eyes again. "I'm so sorry, Kristen."

"I know you are, but you've said it enough, and none of this is your fault. I'll be okay eventually. Especially once I see my parents." She takes a deep breath and her voice becomes thick with emotion. "You've physically left death row, Nate. Now leave it mentally. Live your life. Live it for me and for Rex. Make us proud."

He's too choked up to reply, and Kristen eventually ends the call.

CHAPTER THIRTY-SIX

Madison's eyes begin to blur as she reads page after page of documents and articles about the Snow Storm Killer and his crimes. Detective Adams is doing the same at his desk and every now and then she hears him whistle in disbelief at what he's reading. She knows how he feels. This predator is sick. It will take hours to read up on all his victims, but from what she's read so far it appears that most of them were beaten with a hammer during a snowstorm, and usually around Christmas time. Plus, all the victims had a young boy with them who remained unharmed.

It's not difficult to understand that the serial killer has issues with his own mom, and the child left behind is meant to represent him. But Madison can't figure out why the guy is mad at his mother. Or at least why he *thinks* he's mad at his mother. She's not expecting the logic of a psychopath to make sense. The fact that his crimes aren't sexually motivated is unusual too. She doesn't believe he took the time to abuse the boys before fleeing the scene, because that would take time and increase his chances of getting caught in the act.

She sighs as she checks her cell phone. She hasn't heard from Owen yet. He and Frank must be pulled over somewhere, waiting out the storm. She's heard it's worse up north, so if they didn't leave Prospect Springs soon enough, they could be stuck for hours. Worried, she reluctantly texts Nate.

Have you heard from Frank or Owen? I'm scared they've had an accident.

Chief Mendes approaches her and Adams. She's holding a sheet of paper. Madison slips her phone away. "I've been speaking to a former co-worker at the CBI," says Mendes. She worked at the Colorado Bureau of Investigation before she joined LCPD. She's given little away about her time there, and no one knows why she left. "He's worked on a serial killer case before, so I wanted his thoughts on what we need to be aware of."

"Great," says Madison. "What did he say?"

"A lot we already know: serial killers usually stick to their preferred MO, meaning that whatever worked for them the first time they killed, they'll repeat so they don't get caught. That's not to say they don't evolve or mix things up every now and then, to throw law enforcement off the scent, but they are generally creatures of habit, and for good reason."

Adams leans forward. "Our guy must've seen red after watching Kate Flynn's outburst. He took her because he was mad at her. Which gives us our best chance of finding him, because for the first time, he wasn't thinking straight. He could've got sloppy with her abduction on account of his rage."

"If he was so mad at her, why hasn't he killed her yet?" asks Madison.

"Maybe he has," says Mendes. "Maybe he's keeping her body to exact further revenge. He could be mutilating it." Madison closes her eyes against the thought. Chief Mendes looks back at her notes. "We also need to find out if he's taken trophies or keepsakes from the victims. Steve now has a full list of the other victims accredited to the SSK and is going to try and track down the detectives in charge from other states. I've asked him to check whether taking trophies is something the SSK liked to do."

Madison pulls out the crime-scene photos from the two recent murders. The interior of the Lexus in which Sarah Moss was killed is much tidier than Madison's car. There are no junk-food wrappers or grocery bags shoved down crevices. A couple of Danny's toys sit on the back seat, along with a small gift-wrapped box and a bag containing other newly bought gifts from the mall. She turns to Emily Cole's photos. Next to Emily's body is her purse, spilling its contents. That also contains a few gifts, and some flyers. "If something was taken as a trophy, it's not obvious."

Adams says, "Don't they normally take creepy shit like the victim's eyelids, or teeth? I saw that in a movie once."

Chief Mendes glares at him. "We're not solving this case using bad movies, Detective."

He leans back and shuts up.

Stella from dispatch approaches them. "Er, Chief?" She's gone pale. "I've just had a caller ask whether we've seen the latest video yet."

Madison's stomach fills with dread. "Do you mean from the killer?"

"The caller, a woman I know named Barbara, said it's on YouTube. She's emailed me a link." Stella indicates her computer.

Madison, Mendes and Adams all approach the computer and watch the screen as Stella clicks on the link. Within seconds, a video appears. The camera is focused on Zach Cole this time. He's sitting on the snow-covered ground outside St. Theresa's church. His mother's feet are visible at his side. It's clear she's already dead. Zach has tears on his face, but he isn't crying. He's watching whoever is holding the camera. Madison hears a groan off screen and the camera shakes as the killer hits Emily Cole again, perhaps delivering the fatal blow. Zach turns to his mother for a second and then starts grabbing handfuls of snow. It reminds Madison there was a small mound found next to the body, as if he was trying to build a snowman.

She feels tears prick her eyes. The boy reminds her of Owen at that age; so innocent and unaware of how awful life can be. She thinks of Kate and experiences a sudden sinking feeling. If she doesn't catch the killer soon, she has no doubt that she'll be forced to watch her friend in the next video that appears.

"He's a psycho," says Adams.

Madison leans in to see what name the account is in. SSK. The video's description consists of two short sentences.

It's not over because you retired, Bill. It's over when I say it's over.

"It's a message to your father," says Chief Mendes.

Madison nods. "I can guarantee you he's already aware of this." She scrolls down. Although the video was only uploaded an hour ago, there are over a hundred comments already.

Sick asshole.

Agent Harper needs to come out of retirement and finish his goddam job!

That kid built a snowman lmfao.

I can't believe no one has caught this guy yet.

Madison feels her phone vibrate in her pocket. It's a text from Nate.

Not heard from either of them since this morning.

Her stomach flips. Why has no one heard from Frank and Owen? And Nate sounds like he doesn't even care. He hasn't offered to look for them.

"Problem, Madison?" asks Mendes.

Madison looks up from her phone. "My son. I don't know where he is." She becomes aware of her heartbeat speeding up as dark thoughts occur to her. She looks at Adams. "I was supposed to be bait for the Snow Storm Killer, right? My dad thought that if the killer knew he had family here, he might come back to get me, giving my dad the opportunity to catch him."

"What are you saying?" Adams asks. "You think this SSK guy has your son?"

It sounds ridiculous when she hears it out loud, but she hasn't heard from Owen for a while now, and she has to be sure he's safe. "Probably not. It's just that I don't know this Frank guy, the person Owen's working with today. I need to call their boss to see if he's heard from them."

Chief Mendes nods. "Fine. But be quick." She disappears into her office.

Madison lifts her desk phone and realizes she doesn't have the number for Richie's office. She googles it with shaking hands, and although the number given is for a Prospect Springs address, he must've arranged for the line to be transferred to his new premises, because Janine picks up. "Hope & Associates. How may I help?"

"Janine? It's Madison. Owen's mom."

"Oh, hey. How are ya?" It sounds like she's chewing gum.

"I'm looking for Owen. Is he back yet?"

"You know, I was just saying to Richie that they've been gone a long time."

Madison's stomach lurches with dread. "Have you tried calling Frank?"

"Sure. It goes straight to voicemail, but then he rarely answers my calls, so don't let that worry you."

Madison hears a male voice in the background, and Richie comes on the line. "Don't you worry about Owen. He's in good hands with Frank Brookes. I have no doubt he can drive safely even in this weather."

"I'm more concerned that I don't know Frank or his intentions." She's frustrated that she can't tell him why, but she can't let anyone know the SSK is in town, because it will bring unwanted attention and possibly hinder her investigation. "How well do *you* know him?"

"I know him well enough to trust he'd take care of Owen." Richie's voice turns suspicious. "What's the problem here? Is everything okay?"

Janine comes back on the line. "There's nothing wrong with Frank, Detective. When I first met him, I could tell right away that he was a good guy. That's why I talked him into applying for the investigator role. And I have to say, he's been nothing but the perfect gentleman. He's not a criminal, if that's what you're worried about." She's obviously cottoned on quicker than Richie. "If he was the man who killed those two ladies, I'd be dead by now too, right? Because he's given me more rides than I can count." Richie says something that Madison doesn't catch, and Janine exclaims, "Richie! I meant rides to work, you idiot."

Despite her worry, Madison relaxes a little. She's relived that Janine and Richie can vouch for Frank. It means her fears are probably unfounded. But experience has taught her that she needs to be sure. "What's his date of birth?" She wants to run a background check.

"He's a Gemini, like me," says Janine. "Born June fourth. I think he's around fifty-eight, fifty-nine, but he could easily pass for early fifties if you ask me."

"Okay, thanks." Madison writes it down. "Well, keep trying to get in touch with Frank, and I'll keep trying Owen. In fact, I'll send a patrol officer toward Prospect Springs to see if they're stuck in the snow somewhere."

"Good idea. Don't worry, they'll be back soon. I'm sure of it."

Madison thanks her and puts the phone down, then immediately runs a criminal background check using Frank's full name and approximate date of birth. Nothing comes back, which is good. But she'll be glad when she hears from Owen all the same. This job can make you paranoid. She clings onto the hope that the SSK would come for her rather than Owen, because that would hurt her father more.

She turns to Stella and arranges for Officer Sanchez to head a little farther than Gold Rock to check if there's anyone stranded in the snow awaiting recovery. Next she fires off a text to Owen.

Call me asap. I have an officer out looking for you.

Detective Adams leans over from his desk. "I can't tell from the crime-scene photos whether the killer took any mementos. Maybe he's too lazy for that kind of thing."

Madison stands up. "Google it. There could be one detail that jumps out at you from all the articles online. Or maybe there's a true-crime podcast that has noticed something."

"Sure. Where are you going?"

"I'm going to the evidence room. I want to check the victim's belongings." She grabs her phone and walks away.

CHAPTER THIRTY-SEVEN

Nate has been unable to peel himself away from the dining room table, and with Brody asleep at his feet, he suspects he'll be here a while. Even though he finally knows that Kristen is alive, he fears he's spiraling downhill because of where his thoughts are. He's fantasizing about putting an end to Father Connor. He's wishing he'd never set foot inside that priest's church as a naïve college student all those years ago. The Bible Madison gave him as a Christmas present sits on the table in front of him, the rosary in his hands. It feels comforting to hold, but he's still craving something to blur the memories for him. Something that won't make him care anymore. If he had a way to score some coke right now, he'd take it.

A knock at the door makes him jump. He turns to look at it, but he doesn't get up. Brody rushes straight over and barks.

"Nate? You home?"

He recognizes Vince Rader's voice. He distractedly slips the rosary around his neck and under his T-shirt, then gets to his feet and joins Brody at the front door. When he opens it, a cold gust of wind hits him.

Vince is wrapped up warm and smiling. He's holding a bag of takeout food from the diner in one hand. His smile vanishes when he realizes Nate isn't pleased to see him. "What's wrong?"

Nate turns, letting Vince enter the house. Brody is all over the bag of food. "Hey, boy. There's a sausage in there for you. But the rest is for your dad."

"Put it on the side," says Nate. "We'll eat later." He has no appetite.

Vince does as he's told, and then stands awkwardly next to the dining table. He doesn't take his snow-covered jacket off. "What's going on?"

Nate takes a deep breath. "I've just spoken to Kristen Devereaux."

Vince's eyes widen. The diner owner knows all about Nate's past. He has a special interest in true crime due to the disappearance of his wife and grandson six years ago. When Nate moved to town with Madison earlier this year, Vince tried to get them on his podcast to talk about their shocking experiences with the criminal justice system, but they both declined. Nate considers Vince a friend now, and the older man is always finding reasons to come by and visit him. Normally he brings a six-pack of beer. "If she's alive, why aren't you happier?"

Nate doesn't know how to answer that. "You can't tell anyone I've spoken to her. I shouldn't have told you really. She's disappearing for her own safety."

"Of course. I understand," says Vince, taking a seat next to him. "Seems to me that talking to her has brought back some bad memories for you. Would that be a correct assumption?" When Nate nods, Vince places a hand on his back briefly. "That's fine and all, but how about you come back to the present for a little while. Because your friend needs you."

Nate looks at him. "What do you mean?"

Vince takes a deep breath. "I witnessed Madison and Bill having a heated argument in the diner earlier."

"Really? About what?"

"Well, I tried not to listen in, but it was pretty hard not to hear what they were saying. It sounds to me like Bill didn't come home to be reunited with her and Owen." He shakes his head. "Nope. He came home to lure a serial killer to town."

Nate frowns. "But he's retired. Why would he do that?"

"He's still consulting on the case, apparently. The Snow Storm Killer. Heard of him?"

Nate shakes his head.

"Turns out Bill's been trying to catch the guy for twenty-five years. Can you even imagine what that does to a person? I did a little research once he left the diner, and if you ask me, the SSK could easily be responsible for the town's recent murders. I wouldn't be surprised if he's the sick bastard who took Kate Flynn too."

Nate swallows. "How was Madison?" She must be going out of her mind.

"She stormed out after telling her dad she never wanted to see him again. She was pretty upset." Vince glances at him. "I reckon she could do with a friend right about now."

Nate doesn't think she'll want to see him after the way he's treated her lately. "She texted me to ask if I knew where Owen is. Do you have any idea?"

Vince shakes his head. "Haven't seen him."

Nate stands, which makes Brody rush to the front door. It can't be a coincidence that Madison's looking for Owen after hearing that her father has brought a dangerous killer to town. He knows exactly what she'll be thinking right now. "Could Owen and Madison be targets for the SSK?"

Vince gets up too. "From what I know of serial killers, it appears they sometimes target family members of the cops in charge of finding them. It's a way of showing they're in control of the game."

Nate grabs his phone from the breakfast bar before slipping his jacket on. "If you see Owen, get him to call me or Madison right away."

Vince looks alarmed. "Of course."

Nate locks the front door after them before racing to his car with Brody. The dog jumps into the back. Vince lets him get away first, and the ice on his driveway has his car slipping all over the place.

"Slow down," shouts Vince from behind. "You're no good to anyone dead."

Nate doesn't listen. He needs to get to Richie Hope's office to see if Frank and Owen are back. As he drives, he tries to think whether Frank Brookes could be the Snow Storm Killer. He knows from the news that Madison's victims were beaten to death with some kind of tool. Frank had a toolbox in the back of his truck. "Shit."

He told Madison he'd keep an eye on Owen while she was busy investigating. He should never have let Owen go to Prospect Springs. Frank's a stranger to them and could be anyone. He could be living under a fake ID. Although surely Richie asked for references before employing him? Snippets of their conversation in Frank's truck on Christmas Day spring to mind. Frank offered to look for Kristen for him, and when Nate questioned whether he had a law enforcement background, he replied, *You don't need to have been* in *law enforcement to* know *law enforcement.*

Did he know it because of his experience of being chased by the FBI for decades? Frank already knew about Madison's past too. He'd googled her along with Nate. *Sounds like she's had it almost as rough as you,* he'd said. *And as for young Owen... I'm willing to bet he's the one who suffered most. The kids always are.*

Was that a nod to something he'd experienced as a child? Something that caused him to become a killer and a reason as to why he leaves the children behind unharmed?

Brody barks from the back seat, anxious to be put to work, but there's nothing he can do. There's nothing either of them can do for Owen until they track down Frank Brookes.

CHAPTER THIRTY-EIGHT

Madison unlocks the door to the evidence storage room. It's next door to Alex's dark and dingy office on the other side of the station. The large room has no window, and when she manages to find the light switch, a single bulb flickers to life. The room is scheduled to be decorated and modernized, and the contents properly archived, so hopefully soon it will look less like a torture room from a horror movie. In the meantime, it's freezing cold and smells musty. Boxes are getting damp with age, and the coppery smell from old bloodstained clothes lingers, despite the best attempts of what looks like an ancient air freshener plugged into the electrical outlet.

She slips on a pair of latex gloves and locates the two boxes of evidence taken from the recent crime scenes. The one marked *Sarah Moss* is bigger. Alex has sent anything with blood spatter on it to the crime lab, so what she pulls out is mostly Sarah's and Danny's personal belongings. Sarah's purse still has its contents inside: makeup, tissues, a wallet, various small toys, a child's spare T-shirt and a pack of mints. Her cell phone is in a plastic bag, already processed by Alex. Madison looks at the items Sarah purchased from the mall that night, toys mostly. She smiles sadly. Poor

Danny and Scotty Moss will never get to play with these. But then they'll never get to play with their mom again either.

One of the presents is gift-wrapped, but there's no name card on it. She doesn't want to open it; it feels intrusive. Maybe it was for Sarah's husband, David.

She opens the box of Emily Cole's belongings next. Her purse is bigger and full of flyers for the yard sale, along with the usual items Madison would expect to find in any woman's purse. There are several gift-wrapped presents, and she remembers thinking Emily must have been taking them to midnight mass to hand them out to her friends.

"Detective?" She spins around to find Alex standing in the doorway. "I've spoken to the crime lab. They've now tested everything I sent them: the boys' clothes, the victims' clothes and the trace evidence I took from the crime scenes."

"And?"

"The blood at Sarah Moss's crime scene was all hers. The only DNA found there matched either hers, her two sons' or her husband's."

That's disappointing. It doesn't rule out David Moss as her killer, but on the other hand, his DNA could be there simply because he would have been in close contact with Sarah before her murder and it's highly likely he'd been in her car on numerous occasions. "And Emily's evidence?"

"There was nothing of interest found at all. I'm sorry, I know you were hoping we'd solve these cases using DNA evidence."

She takes a deep breath. "I guess that would be too easy. Did Lena find anything during Emily's autopsy?"

"Only that she believes the same weapon was used for both murders. There were no other injuries aside from those to her head, and she said Sarah Moss's toxicology results show she didn't have anything questionable in her system at the time of her death."

Madison didn't really suspect Sarah had been drugged or poisoned, but it's always best to check.

"Lena also mentioned that she'd spoken to David Moss about whether Sarah was a habitual nail-biter, because of her nails being cut so short."

"And?"

"She was. So they weren't cut by the killer in an attempt to remove any DNA she scratched off him."

"Unless David is lying because he killed her," she says.

"Always a possibility, of course. Which would make him a copycat killer, as he's too young to have killed Michelle Rubio." Alex takes a deep breath. "Maybe we're overcomplicating things and the answer to all this is simpler than we think."

Madison nods. "It's a difficult case because of how many murders we're dealing with now. Which means we have to consider every possible line of investigation." She turns back to the contents of Emily Cole's purse and looks carefully at everything laid out together. It's not long before something stands out that she didn't notice before. "Wait a minute."

Alex steps forward to see what she's looking at. "Everything okay?"

She swallows as the implications hit her, and wishes she'd noticed before now. She holds up two identical gift boxes. "This one was found in Sarah Moss's car. And this one was in Emily Cole's purse." Both are wrapped in exactly the same paper; red with small gold stars. And both have silver ribbon tied around them.

Alex raises his eyebrows in surprise. "Playing devil's advocate; could our victims have bought them from the same place?"

"I mean, maybe that would explain the gift wrap, but the same-sized box? And what are the chances of two murder victims having identical items on them?" She shakes her head and her adrenaline kicks in. "I don't like coincidences, Alex. Do you know what this could mean? The SSK doesn't take trophies from his victims, he leaves something behind instead. Calling cards." It occurs to her that this must be why, when Dr. Chalmers was trying to speak to Danny in the clinic after his mother's murder, all the boy wanted to talk about was toys. He could've been trying to explain that the killer gave him a Christmas present.

Alex is normally unshockable, but he's turned pale. With trepidation he asks, "Are you going to open them?"

She looks at the two boxes in her hands. They could contain anything: some kind of detonation device, a note, a body part. "Dust them for prints, then we'll carefully open them outside, just in case we're in for an unwelcome surprise."

"I don't think they contain explosives, Detective. They're too small, and it's likely the killer wants you to see what's inside them; that's why he went to the effort of leaving them behind. It could be some kind of clue." He looks at her. "Maybe after all these years on the run, he wants to be caught."

She wishes she could ask her father for his opinion. Maybe he already knows that the SSK leaves a calling card... "Oh my God." Her blood runs cold.

"What?"

She hands him the two gifts. "Check these for prints. I need to fetch something."

She races through the station, past the offices and out past the front desk. Once outside, she stops running and slowly approaches her car. It's late afternoon and dark now. The snow is still falling and she shivers without a coat to shield her from the blustery wind. When she left home early this morning, there was a small gift in her car. She thought it was from Nate and felt too awkward to open it with him watching her from her front door, so she stuffed it into her glovebox.

It was too dark earlier to know what kind of gift wrap was used, but her gut is telling her it's the same as the two gifts she just saw.

Before she opens her car, she hesitates and considers whether the box contains a bomb, designed to detonate when the killer is close by and watching her. She turns around and peers into the darkness, but the shadows are too big to spot anyone lurking. She shakes her head. No, he would've detonated it already if that were the case, as he's had ample opportunity since this morning. As she hesitates, she hears someone racing toward her. It's Detective Adams and Chief Mendes. They must've seen her run out of the station.

"What's going on?" asks Adams as he comes to a stop next to her. Mendes crosses her arms against the bitter cold.

"I think the killer leaves calling cards with our victims," says Madison. "Small gift-wrapped boxes. I found one in my car this morning, but I thought it was from a friend. It's not."

"How do you know?" asks Mendes.

Madison unlocks her car and with a deep breath pulls the door handle. She exhales with relief when the vehicle doesn't explode. Leaning in, she opens the glovebox and retrieves the gift, holding it up to Adams and Mendes. "Because it's wrapped in the same paper as those left with our victims." It's red with small gold stars on it. A silver ribbon secures the box.

Adams's mouth drops open in horror. "You've got to be kidding me? He was in your *car*? This is messed up." He puts his hands to his head. "You mean to tell me this guy is targeting cops now?"

"I told you I was bait," says Madison.

"But where's the line?" he says, clearly afraid. "What if he comes after me now that I'm working the case? I've got two young daughters and a wife at home. I don't need this shit!"

Madison can't believe his outburst. It's fine to be afraid, she's gets it, but to act like a child about it is unprofessional. Luckily, Chief Mendes voices her thoughts. "Detective Adams, you must have been aware when you joined law enforcement that you could be subjected to targeted threats. I mean, we're in the business of hunting hardened criminals. We're not selling candy to school kids."

He glares at her. "I don't need a lecture, thanks, Chief." Madison raises her eyebrows, and Mendes gives Adams a cold stare, but before she can say anything, he continues, "I've been a cop for nine years. I know the risks. But nothing like this ever happened in my old department." He shakes his head in frustration. "The guys there thought I was insane to move down here. They said small towns attract a whole new level of crazy. Turns out they were right." He turns and strides back toward the station.

Chief Mendes turns to Madison and sighs. "I should've picked Steve or Shelley for the job."

Madison agrees. "Too late now." She shivers again. "Let's get this to Alex. We need to see what's inside."

CHAPTER THIRTY-NINE

Bill holds his cell phone up for Mike to get a clear view of the latest video from the Snow Storm Killer. They're sitting in Bill's SUV at the abandoned gas station where Kate Flynn and her son were abducted. The windshield is thick with snow because they've been here so long trying to figure out how the killer got Kate into his car and whether he left any evidence behind. They hadn't found anything after scouring the area, and had to conclude that Madison's team would have taken everything away for processing. Now their focus is on the small screen, where the child of the SSK's fifteenth victim is attempting to build a snowman next to his mother's lifeless body.

Mike shakes his head before running a hand down his face in frustration. "Wait until the media get a load of that."

"He didn't always record his crime scenes, not in the early days. Now it's every single goddam time." Bill drops his phone into his lap. Every horrific video he has to watch, every letter he receives and every news article he reads about the SSK is a sucker punch to the gut. He feels them all as a personal attack. The killer is always one step out of his grasp, and he worries he's reached the end of the road. That his investigation will never successfully conclude. "No one else knows about the other videos but us. He sent the last one to the victim's husband and uploaded this one online himself for the whole world to see."

"But why?" asks Mike.

"Because he wants more attention. He wants to become a household name. That's why I never told the media about the other videos. I didn't want to make him famous."

Mike sighs. "So what now? Is it time to bring your daughter on board?"

Bill glares at him.

"Come on, Bill. She's in charge of the investigation down here. If we combine what we know with what happened here, we have more chance of catching him. You know that."

"She works for a small PD. There's no way they have the resources to find this guy or tell us anything we can't learn for ourselves. We can find him."

Mike shakes his head. "He's making a fool out of us."

"Give it a break, would you? I'm trying to think." Bill has a sequence of events he runs through in his mind every time he tries to figure out the missing pieces of this case. The sixteen victims—if he includes Kate Flynn—flash before him: names, ages, their deathly stares, their children, their method of death, the states they were killed in, and always ending with Pamela's headless body in the bloody bath. He closes his eyes against that one.

This time, images of Madison and his grandson also flash up. Bill has grown close to Owen since he moved back to Colorado. He didn't even know Madison had a kid until he arrived. The boy has been through so much, spending six years without his mother while she was locked up for someone else's crime. Then he lost his girlfriend to murder. Bill would've thought that would make Owen bitter and cynical, but some-how, he's not.

It's admirable that he wants to become a lawyer so he can

help others fight injustices like the one his mother experienced, but Bill suspects he's in for a shock once he graduates and starts practicing law. The justice system in this country isn't fair, and most newly qualified lawyers soon find the job is nothing like they were told it would be in law school. Most attorneys burn out young, fed up and disappointed with the system they're trying to defend. With dirty DAs, cops and judges all pulling the invisible strings, there's little a kind, warmhearted person like Owen can do for his clients. Bill worries that the system will break his grandson, and wishes he'd choose a different career path. It's bad enough that Madison became a cop. Especially as it was her job that landed her in prison.

He feels a stab to the heart. A mixture of guilt for not being around when she needed him, and shame at the danger he's placed them both in by coming back here. He swallows the lump in his throat as he considers how close the SSK is to his family. "Why did you let me bring him here?" he says softly.

Mike leans in to see his face. "What?"

Bill looks at him. "It was stupid. I should've kept well away from Lost Creek."

"You were insistent," says Mike. "You assured me he would stick out like a sore thumb somewhere like this."

Bill nods. "I know. But I didn't appreciate how long I'd been away. How much the town would've changed in my absence. It's evolved. The residents are different. I don't know anyone anymore. I thought only the killer would be a stranger, but it turns out everyone is. Even my own daughter."

Mike inhales deeply next to him. "Jesus Christ, Bill. You've brought us on a wild goose chase. I could've spent Christmas with my family."

Bill glances at him. He knows how much the guy hates being away from his wife and kids. Mike's flirted with the idea of early retirement several times. Unlike Bill, he never put work before his home life and somehow managed to attend most of his kids' important events over the years. He never let the job consume him. Bill used to think that was a weakness. That any agent who didn't spend ninety-nine percent of their time at work wasn't dedicated and had no hope of catching America's worst criminals. But now he feels like they must all be laughing at him for wasting his life on something that was never achievable.

He clears his throat. "You should travel home to Alaska. Take a proper break with Anne and the kids. Maybe think about that early retirement. Because in my experience, all this," he gestures to the freezing-cold car they're sitting in, "isn't worth it. We can't catch this guy. If we could, we would've done it already. *I* would've done it already. We may even be fueling his need to kill by chasing him." He lowers his eyes. "Maybe if we back off, he will too. Because he'll have no one to play his games with."

Mike looks as if he's seriously considering the advice. Eventually he says, "That sounds mighty tempting, Bill. Mighty tempting."

They sit in silence for a few minutes, lost in their own thoughts. So it comes as a terrible shock when Mike's door is suddenly pulled wide open from the outside and they see a man dressed all in black, with a ski mask over his face, standing there aiming a gun at them. Bill doesn't even have time to draw his own weapon before a round goes off. The sound pierces his ears, disorientating him for a few seconds and leaving his eardrums throbbing, during which time the assailant vanishes.

He looks down at his own body, fully expecting to see a bloody hole in his chest. There's plenty of blood spatter, but it doesn't take him long to realize it's not from him. "What the hell?" He looks across at Mike. "Oh Jesus. No. Mike!" He shakes him by his shoulders, but it's pointless. His partner is already dead.

Seething with anger, Bill gets out of the car and pulls his

weapon. He frantically spins around in all directions, but sees nothing but a few passing cars on the road. He looks at the footprints in the snow. It's impossible to make out which direction the killer went, as his indentations are mixed with Mike's and his own from when they searched the area.

He releases his frustration by yelling expletives into the air. It doesn't make him feel any better, because now he has another death on his conscience. He forces himself to walk to the passenger side of the car. Mike's right eye is staring at the ceiling. His left eye has been pushed to the back of his head with the force of the bullet, which is lodged in the headrest behind him.

The Snow Storm Killer has come closer to him than ever before. And Bill intends to make him pay.

CHAPTER FORTY

Nate has given up trying to reach Owen by phone, because his calls are diverted straight to voicemail, indicating that the phone battery has either died or been removed. He curses himself for not asking Frank where in Prospect Springs he lives, and as he races toward Richie Hope's office, he considers whether to alert Madison that he's worried Frank has done something to her son. If he's wrong, he'll upset her for no reason. But if he's right, she can get the whole station looking for them. He decides to check in with Richie and Janine first to see if they know anything. At least he can get Frank's address from them.

Skidding to a stop outside the office, he and Brody get out of the car. The dog runs ahead of him and almost slips on the ice. As Nate follows him into the building, Janine isn't her usual welcoming self. Her smile has been replaced with a frown. "What's wrong?" he asks, fearing the worst.

Before she can speak, Richie appears. "Boy, am I glad to see you. It appears we have a problem."

Nate has never seen Richie this serious before and it makes him tense. "It's Owen, isn't it?" He runs a hand through his hair. If anything's happened to him, Madison will never forgive him. He'll never forgive himself.

"Let's not panic," says Richie. "It's just that Madison called us to see if we'd heard from Frank or Owen, and we told her everything was fine and they're bound to be back shortly, but it's been a while now and we can't seem to locate them."

Nate's blood runs cold. "I need Frank's address. I'm going up there. We need to tell Madison so she can get officers looking for them."

Richie sighs. "I'm afraid it appears he's given us a false address."

"What?"

Janine speaks up. "I asked my neighbor to go knock on Frank's door to see if he was there and she said an old couple answered. Frank doesn't live there. He never has." Her face is lined with worry. "This is all my fault. If I hadn't got talking to him in that bar, he would never have worked for us. I was so sure he was a good guy. I should've known otherwise the minute he told me he was a Gemini."

Nate feels panic building in his chest. He has to keep it in check. "What time did they leave to go to the storage locker?"

She looks flustered. "I don't know for sure, just that it was this morning."

He checks his watch. It's just after four now. "And do we know if they made it there?"

"I'll call the manager and check." Janine goes to her desk and picks up the phone.

Richie removes his glasses and rubs his eyes. "I'm ashamed to admit I never checked Frank's references. The firebombing incident followed by the office move and then the storm... it all distracted me from running a background check." He looks like he's welling up.

Nate rests a hand on his shoulder. "We all could have done things differently. Let's just focus on finding them. I'm going to call Madison."

Brody is at his feet, alert and waiting for instructions. "I wish I had a job for you, boy." The dog is best at locating dead bodies, and Nate can only hope he won't be needed. He pulls his cell phone out.

The rumble of an engine outside the building makes everyone stop. It sounds like it's coming from something big, like a pickup truck. Brody barks loudly and races outside, and before Nate reaches the front window he races back in, tail wagging furiously and looking back over his shoulder at who is following him inside.

Nate's mouth drops open when Owen appears. He's laughing at something Frank has said behind him. Richie raises his eyes to the ceiling, whispers something and then goes over to hug the boy.

Janine slams the phone down, cutting off the person on the other end of the line. "You're a sight for sore eyes!"

Owen looks puzzled. "What's going on?"

Frank is bewildered by their reaction too. "What did we miss?"

Nate feels his heart beating out of his chest, but he couldn't be more relieved. "Where have you been? Why didn't you answer your goddam phones?"

He rarely curses, so he has Owen's attention. "We went to the storage locker. What's wrong?"

Nate goes to the boy and pulls him in for a hug. "We thought you were dead."

Frank says, "Sorry, folks. That'll be my fault."

Nate steps back and crosses his arms as he waits for an explanation.

"I took the kid for a slap-up meal at my favorite restaurant after we'd finished loading the boxes. The storm set us back too, and once we got on the road, I guess I got a little carried away with the country music. I turned it up so loud it probably stopped us hearing our phones ringing."

"My battery died an hour ago," says Owen. "And thanks to

Frank, I know almost every Dolly Parton song by heart now. I'm never getting '9 to 5' out of my head."

Nate doesn't smile. Owen will never know how glad he is that he's safe. He may not be the boy's father, but Owen is as close to a son as he's ever likely to get.

Richie slips his glasses back on. "Well, Frank. I'm sorry to do this to you, but I have some awkward questions that need answering."

Frank removes his aviator shades and turns serious. "Oh yeah? What would they be?" He stands tall and looks like he's ready to defend himself, so perhaps he knows what's coming.

"I've discovered you gave me a fake home address. And I imagine your references are baloney too. Would that be a fair assumption, or should I try calling one of the previous employers you listed?"

Frank's eyes don't leave Richie's, but there is some hesitation before he responds. "I'm a good employee, aren't I?"

"Oh sure," says Richie, clearly not intimidated by the taller man. "Your investigation skills are second to none. But none of that means diddly-squat if I can't trust you."

Janine attempts to break the awkwardness by laughing. "Now come on, Richie. He brought the kid back, didn't he? And he's always been good to me. I'm sure he just has something in his past that he'd rather we didn't know about, that's all. I mean, don't we all hide certain things? I know I sure do."

Richie turns to her with raised eyebrows. "Janine, you haven't stopped talking since the day I met you, so I can guarantee there's nothing you haven't told me about yourself."

Owen stifles a laugh.

Richie looks back at Frank. "What are you hiding, Frank? Let's hear it, so we can all get back to work."

The investigator takes a deep breath and crosses his arms, appearing to assess whether it's worth being honest at last. Then he looks at Nate. "I'm surprised you didn't guess."

Nate doesn't know what he means, but he's fearing the worst because the guy volunteered to search for Kristen.

"I'm a Fed." says Frank, his eyes fixed on Nate.

Nate's mouth instantly goes dry, and his heart rate quickens. The last involvement he had with the Feds was when they turned up to take Father Connor away two months ago. He was forced to give a statement about what had happened in their final showdown, and the Feds said they'd be in touch again once they'd investigated the priest's crimes. Nate wonders whether Father Connor might have somehow managed to persuade law enforcement that he's innocent. They could be taking a bribe. It wouldn't be the first time. That must be why Frank offered to look for Kristen. He's searching for evidence to put Nate away instead of the priest. His legs go weak and his craving for cocaine is the strongest it's been in a long time. "You're working undercover, aren't you?"

Frank nods.

"Is that why you offered to locate Kristen Devereaux? Because you think I killed her and you're trying to pin her murder on me? Has Father Connor offered to pay you for framing me?"

Frank looks puzzled. "What are you talking about?" His expression suddenly softens. "Oh, right. You're paranoid about going back inside, huh? I guess that's what serving someone else's sentence does to a person." He takes a deep breath. "Look, I offered to help because I thought I could find her, that's all. Like Bill Harper, I'm not getting any younger, and the FBI has chewed me up and spit me out. Officially, I'm a retired Fed, but if I can keep my mind active in my retirement, I will. Same as you taking on cases when you don't even need to work." He turns to Owen. "I worked with your grandpa for fifteen years."

Owen looks confused. "What's Grandpa got to do with anything?"

Suddenly it all makes sense to Nate. "You're in town to

help him catch the Snow Storm Killer. You're working as a consultant on the case, same as Bill."

Frank nods.

The relief that washes over him is immense. He thought he was about to be arrested again. His hands are visibly trembling.

"Wait a minute," says Richie, who has turned pale. He looks at Frank. "You're a *Fed*?" He gulps. "Er, that box of undeclared earnings in my office? I'm going to see to it that Janine submits them to the IRS immediately." He laughs nervously. "I don't know why she hasn't done it already, to tell you the truth."

Janine puts her hands on her hips. "Hey! You told me not—"

"That's enough, Janine!" Richie cuts her off before she can finish. "I'll give you a handsome Christmas bonus if you go make coffee for everyone. I'm parched. Anyone else?"

She marches out of the room, muttering obscenities as she goes.

"You can relax, Richie," says Frank. "As long as you're not killing anyone, I'm not interested."

"Why are you working for Richie if you already have a job?" asks Nate.

"I needed a cover. I'm trying to fly under the radar so that I don't stand out, while keeping my eyes and ears peeled for the SSK." He turns to Owen. "When Richie offered you a job here, Bill told me I was to keep eyes on you so nothing bad could happen to you."

"That's why we've been in Prospect Springs all day?" asks Owen.

"Right. Bill's convinced the SSK will come after you or your mom."

Owen takes a seat, and Nate watches the disappointment sink in as he realizes his grandfather put them in danger. "Is that why he came back here? To catch a serial killer?"

Frank nods. "Right, but it's complicated. It doesn't mean he doesn't love you, kid. He's been hunting the guy for twenty-five years and he's desperate. Doesn't want to die without seeing the asshole behind bars."

Owen looks up at Nate. "Do you think Mom knows?"

Nate goes over and takes a seat next to him. "Apparently she does. Vince told me she and Bill had a huge fight about it in the diner. She was pretty upset."

"We need to see her." Owen stands. His concern for his mom is touching.

Frank's phone rings. When he answers it, Nate hears a man's voice shouting down the line. "Whoa! Calm down, Bill," Frank says. "What's going on?"

They all hear what Bill says next. "It's Mike! The son of a bitch killed Mike!"

Frank's mouth drops open. He listens for a few minutes and then ends the call with "Roger that." Hs hands are trembling as he lowers the phone from his ear. "It seems things have taken an unexpected turn. The SSK must have a death wish, because he just killed a federal agent."

"Oh dear God," says Richie.

"I need to get you somewhere safe," Frank tells Owen. "There's no telling what he'll do next."

Nate's heart rate speeds up. "You go and help Bill. I'll take care of Owen."

Frank hesitates. "You carry a weapon, Monroe?"

Nate shakes his head. He's not a fan of anything that might get him put back inside.

Frank pulls a gun out of a holster under his shirt and holds it out, butt first. When Nate doesn't take it, he says, "You stand a better chance of protecting young Owen with this than without."

Nate still hesitates. "What if it goes off by mistake? What if I shoot the wrong person? In fact, what if I shoot the right person? I'm not a cop or an agent; if I kill someone, I could be arrested and charged with murder."

"Well, knowing the judicial system, I can't promise that's not a possibility, but I would say it's unlikely given the circumstances." Frank takes a deep breath. "I guess you need to ask yourself whether it's a risk worth taking in order to save Owen's life."

A few seconds go by. Nate glances at Owen, but the boy won't make eye contact with him. Eventually he grabs the gun, checks the safety is on and then slips it into his waistband, under his jacket.

Satisfied, Frank turns and heads out of the building.

Owen looks up at last. His expression is that of a scared child. "What about Mom?" he asks. "We can't be with her while she investigates, so who's going to protect her?"

Nate swallows. "I'll call her. I can give her the heads-up about Mike's death and tell her you're safe at the same time." He thinks of Madison's new partner, Detective Adams, whom he's yet to meet. Madison said he wasn't all that. What if he isn't good enough to have her back when she needs help? He could get her killed. "I'm sure she has a good team around her," he lies.

CHAPTER FORTY-ONE

The Mountain View Senior Care Home is quiet this afternoon, allowing him to slip in undetected. It probably won't get much busier later on either. The residents' families did their festive duty yesterday by visiting their ailing relatives. They won't be back for weeks or perhaps months, smug in the knowledge that they are good people for devoting a whole hour on their busy Christmas Day to performing this much-dreaded chore.

It makes his blood boil. None of them have any respect for their parents and grandparents. None of them realize how lucky they are to still have them in their lives. He lost his own mother at a young age, and now his father, Larry, sits in this awful room of fake brightness that carries an aroma of urine mixed with bleach, staring at the walls and unable to trust his own memories. Although when it comes to Larry, this is all he deserves, along with his diagnosis of dementia.

"Were you happy when you married Mom?" he asks the old man.

Larry looks at him, suddenly conscious that he's not alone in the room. He was enjoying an afternoon nap until being rudely awakened by his son. "Of course. We had some great times. She was so young and sweet." His eyes sparkle only when he talks about his wife. No one else. "And she just loved to cook! She was happy to stay home and raise you; she didn't need a fancy job, not like women these days. You don't find women like her anymore, that's for sure."

He nods. His memories of his mother are all good too. She never raised her voice or told him off. She'd dance around the living room with him to the voices of aging crooners on the record player. And she made Christmas so special, with her hand-made decorations and gingerbread houses.

"My wife was an angel."

He frowns. "Then why'd you kill her?"

Fear, followed by annoyance, appears in Larry's watery pale blue eyes. "How do you know about that? Are you a cop?"

He shakes his head sadly. "No, Dad. I'm not a cop. I'm your son. I watched you beat my mother to death while I played with the train set you bought me for Christmas all those years ago."

"I thought I wore a ski mask."

"You did. But over time, it became clear to me."

His father finally looks at him. "So why didn't you tell the cops?"

Anger builds inside his chest. His dad is voicing his own long-held concern. "I have a feeling I'll never know the answer to that question."

"Where's my wife? I want to see her."

"You killed her for the insurance money, didn't you?" His father inherited a tow truck business at a young age, and he was about to go bankrupt at the time of her murder. On that fateful Christmas Day, he had been called out to help the police retrieve a car stuck in the snow after it had gone off the road. But later it became obvious that he'd had enough time before leaving home to kill his wife. The life insurance eventually paid out, setting Larry on the path to a successful auto repair business. How the police didn't put two and two together remains a mystery, but it could be because good old Larry had a lot of friends on the force.

Tears roll down the man's wrinkled face. "I only married her because she got pregnant. She wasn't my first choice. Stupid woman refused to take care of the problem, and her father threatened to kill me if I didn't marry her. I believed he'd do it too."

He's noticed his father contradicts himself a lot. One minute he says he was madly in love with his wife, the next he says she was nothing more than an inconvenience. He doesn't know which is true, as his own memories don't stretch to his parents' interactions; he was too young. He has only stored the memories of his own time with his mother. However, given the fact that his father eventually killed her, it suggests the marriage wasn't as perfect as he sometimes makes out.

Larry turns to face him and there's a viciousness in his expression. "I know what you are. I knew the minute I saw what happened to that poor woman on the news in '94. Michelle something. I knew you'd dated her, and then she turned up dead. Half burned in her own backyard." He shakes his head in disgust, which is ironic considering what he'd done to his wife years earlier. "No one could figure out who that little boy's dad was. But I knew. I should've come forward. I should've told the cops."

He inhales deeply. "It's true. And being my first kill, I didn't know what I was doing, so she probably suffered the most. I think she was still breathing when I set fire to her skirt. I was an amateur back then, but with each kill, you learn, like in all good experiments. You would know that if you'd gone on to kill again."

"I only killed your mother," Larry spits. "That was for a reason. Not like what you do. You're sick in the head."

I only killed your mother. "Only? You took away my chance of a normal life."

Larry scoffs. "I should've killed you too. It would have saved a lot of lives."

Taking his father's hand in his, he squeezes. "You did kill me, Dad. You killed my innocence, and left behind..." He gestures to himself. "This." He kisses the thin, drooping skin on his father's cheek before standing. "I have things to do. See you tomorrow."

Tomorrow they will repeat this conversation again. Like they've done almost every day since he returned home to Lost Creek. Because he likes to remind his father of the chain reaction he started. He never wants him to forget what he did to his only child. He wants the old man to suffer the consequences of his actions for the rest of his life, just as he is doomed to.

CHAPTER FORTY-TWO

An impressive crowd builds around Madison's desk. Detective Adams is watching from a distance, probably wishing he could afford to quit his job and skip town now he knows the SSK isn't afraid of breaking into a detective's car and leaving a threatening calling card.

Alex Parker has all three gift-wrapped boxes lined up on the desk in front of him. He's dusted them for prints and found none, and now he's volunteered to open them. He seems positively excited about it, which has Madison a little worried. He's definitely a strange one. With gloved hands, he uses a scalpel to snip through the silver ribbon. Madison watches with bated breath as he carefully takes the lid off the first box. There's no smoke and no bang, which is a relief. Inside is a small wooden passenger car taken from a child's train set.

She frowns. Turning around to Steve and Chief Mendes she says, "I don't get it."

"Let's see what else there is," says Mendes.

Alex opens the lid of the next box and finds an almost identical passenger car; the color is the only difference, as this one is green instead of blue. The third box, taken from Madison's car, contains a small wooden locomotive engine. They all fit together.

"Huh." Madison's confused.

Alex sighs. "Well, that's disappointing."

"Maybe his mom died on a train?" says Adams, making his way toward them for a look.

Madison tries to think. "There has to be a reason he left these behind. They have to be linked to his motive somehow." She turns to Steve again. "How many other PDs have you managed to speak to about the SSK's previous victims?"

"Only two so far; in Seattle and Chicago. They weren't keen on sharing any details with me."

"So you don't know if they had similar calling cards at their crime scenes?"

"No. They said they only interact with the FBI about their SSK victims."

"Typical," says Chief Mendes. "See if any of his victims were from small towns; you might have better luck with those PDs. They'll probably be grateful for any collaboration, same as us."

"Sure." He heads straight to his desk.

Madison's cell phone buzzes in her pocket and she retrieves it immediately, hoping it's Owen. Nate's number is on the screen. A nervous chill goes through her as she walks away from her desk for privacy. "Hi, Nate. Everything okay?"

"Hey, Mom. It's me."

She closes her eyes. "Thank God. I didn't know where you were. Are you safe?"

"Yeah. I'm at Richie's office with Nate. My phone battery died and I was busy all day. Sorry for not calling you back sooner." He sounds upset.

"Are you okay?"

There are a few seconds of silence before he says, "I know about Grandpa. Why he really came back here."

She leans her head against the wall and takes a deep

breath. "I'm sorry. It sucks, doesn't it?" He doesn't respond, suggesting he's disappointed. "Listen, Owen, he may have come back for the wrong reasons, but I know he loves spending time with you. He's just obsessed with the killer and won't relax until he's caught the guy."

Owen obviously doesn't want to discuss it right now, because he says, "Nate wants to speak with you."

"Okay. I'll see you soon." She has to swallow the lump in her throat. Her heart aches for him.

Nate comes on the line. "Madison?"

"Owen's upset, isn't he?"

"Yeah, but he'll be okay. I'm sorry about your dad. How are you holding up?"

"Luckily I'm too busy to dwell on it. I still haven't found Kate and Ben. I feel like time's running out." She stops herself from opening up about everything that's going on. She doesn't have time for that and he's probably not interested anyway.

"Need my help? Or Brody's?"

She chews her lip. Of course she wants his help. But there's an awkwardness between them now so she doesn't know if he really means it. Besides, Chief Mendes says she has to stop relying on Nate and use Adams instead. Not that he's turned out to be much use.

When she doesn't reply, Nate says, "There have been a couple of developments you should know about. For starters, Frank Brookes, who Owen was with all day, is actually an undercover Fed. He's working with your dad to find this serial killer."

"You're kidding, right? I thought he was the killer when I couldn't get hold of Owen."

Nate scoffs. "Tell me about it. I was about to drive all the way up to his house and kick his door down." Madison smiles, because she knows he'd do it. "Your dad instructed him to look out for Owen. That's why they disappeared all day."

At least that shows her father is capable of thinking of his grandson. "Has Frank told you anything about the SSK that I can use?"

"No, because your dad called him shortly after we found out he was a Fed, so we haven't discussed it." His voice turns serious. "Madison, that guy Mike who came to your house for Christmas dinner—"

"I know. He's a Fed too. It sounds like Lost Creek is crawling with them. Not that they're making themselves useful. If my dad is too stubborn to work with me, you'd think Mike would. Isn't he Dad's boss or something? He should be overruling him."

Nate clears his throat. "Mike's dead."

She gasps. "What? You've got to be kidding me?"

"No. The SSK ambushed him and Bill while they were in your dad's car. Bill seems fine from what I could hear of his phone conversation with Frank."

Madison's spare hand goes to her mouth. "Oh my God. He could've been shot too." Then she realizes he hasn't phoned her to tell her any of this. He hasn't even phoned the station to notify them of Mike's murder. Her concern turns to anger. "Where is he now?"

"I don't know. Frank's gone to meet with him. I guess they're going to throw everything at finding this guy now he's killed an agent. I'd be surprised if they don't send for backup from the Bureau. I'm going to keep Owen with me, just in case..." He trails off, not wanting to say it.

She can tell he's worried that Owen will be the SSK's next target. She shudders. "Don't go to my house. Take him somewhere he won't be found, and keep in touch so I know you're both safe."

"Of course, but you need to make sure your team has your back, because this guy could come for you too. How's the new guy?"

Madison glances over at Detective Adams. He's sitting at

his desk, leaning back in his chair and gazing out of the dark window at his own reflection. "He's a disaster."

"Then don't take him with you if you get a lead. He could get you killed." Nate pauses, before adding, "Maybe I should come to the station. I could leave Owen with Vince."

She smiles. "As if Chief Mendes would let us work together. She already thinks we're joined at the hip." He doesn't reply, and there's an awkward silence. The smile fades from her face. "I'll be fine," she says. "The rest of my team is more than competent. Just keep Owen safe and away from my dad. Because I have a feeling there's a showdown coming between him and this serial killer, and I don't know which one of them will make it out alive."

"That's what I'm worried about too. Do you have any leads on this guy?"

She sighs. "He's left calling cards with his victims. Parts of a toy train." She doesn't tell him she had one herself.

"Interesting," he says. "I wonder if a train signifies the moment he lost his innocence and became a killer."

She considers it. "Why do you think that?"

"I used to read a lot of true-crime books in prison. Serial killers follow similar patterns of behavior. If he's left something behind, it's important to him. It's something he wants Bill, or whoever's chasing him, to understand about him. So the toy train must be significant somehow."

She slowly nods. "Good to know. I'll keep that in mind." Chief Mendes is looking over at her. "I better go."

"Sure. Keep me updated so we're not worrying about you."

"I'll try." She ends the call, feeling like she wants to go and protect Nate and Owen more than she wants to protect the public. But this is her job. She has no choice.

To Chief Mendes she says, "The SSK killed a federal agent this afternoon. One working with my father."

Mendes's mouth drops open. "Where's the body?"

"I don't know. We need to get patrol to step things up a gear, because he seems to be on some kind of final hurrah. His latest killing spree isn't going to end until he's caught. Which means Kate and Ben might already be dead." She swallows.

The chief nods gravely. "I'm calling the FBI. It's time they took responsibility for this mess." She heads to her office.

Madison approaches Detective Adams. "Okay, I need you to find any link between our serial killer and that toy train." Her mind is buzzing with possibilities. "Maybe his parents died in a train crash when he was a kid, or he works with trains, or maybe he was abused on a train." Adams raises his eyebrows, so she adds, "I don't know. I just know he left those toys behind for a reason, and I need your help finding out what that reason is. Steve's going to check if he left anything similar at his older crime scenes."

Adams slowly leans forward and wakes up his computer. With little enthusiasm, he says, "I'll see what I can find."

Madison shakes her head at his attitude. She should probably bite her tongue, but instead she says, "Listen, Marcus. I get it. You're questioning your decision to work here because you're worried about your family's safety. That's how we're *all* feeling right now. But doesn't it make you want to catch the asshole who's making you feel this way? Can't you channel that fear and anger into finding Kate and her son so that there are two fewer victims at the end of all this?"

He looks up at her for a second. "Do you really believe we can get him?"

"I have to, or what else are we doing here? Why wear the badge and carry the weapon if you're not going to do the job?" She softens her tone. "Imagine how it would feel to go home to your wife and kids tonight and tell them you helped catch the person who's been terrorizing our town. Wouldn't that feel good? You'd be their hero."

He rolls his eyes, but there's a smile forming. "You're

laying it on a little thick there, aren't you, Harper? Using my first name is a nice touch, I always fall for that, but you sound like a used-car salesman desperate for a sale."

She smiles. "Find the link and maybe I'll do you a great deal on my crappy Honda."

CHAPTER FORTY-THREE

The Feds are on their way. According to Chief Mendes, Madison's father and Special Agent Mike Spence were acting without permission when they lured the SSK back to Lost Creek. Madison can't absorb everything Mendes tells her. She just wants to find her friend as fast as possible. She's looking into the other murders, starting with Michelle Rubio. According to her father's investigation notes, there was no toy train found at the scene, but she thinks it could've been missed. Or another possibility is that since Michelle was the killer's first victim, he hadn't yet refined his act. She leans back in her seat as she tries to think.

"Detective?" says Stella behind her. "I have Gary Pelosi on the phone for you. He's not the only reporter who's been calling. They must know something's up."

Madison rolls her eyes. Somehow, the media always know. "Put him through." She wonders if he's discovered something else while researching Jake Rubio's parents. When her desk phone rings, she answers right away. "Gary?"

"Hi, Detective. A few of us have been wondering if you're holding a press conference about the latest murder."

She stops what she's doing. "What murder would that be?"

He hesitates, as if confused. "At the old gas station on Layton Road. Your officers are there now, surrounding a black SUV. There's a dead guy in the passenger seat."

Madison breathes a sigh of relief. She thought for a second that another body she wasn't aware of had turned up. At least patrol has found Mike. The SUV is her father's. She wonders where he's gone now that he's carless. Maybe he's driving Mike's vehicle. "We're focused on finding the serial killer right now, Gary."

"Serial killer?"

Madison cringes. She didn't mean to say that. The media don't yet know the SSK is in town.

"Detective? Are you saying the recent homicides are the work of a serial killer?"

She sighs. Maybe it will help find the guy faster if the media are aware. Could it really do any harm? Sure, it will attract more reporters and news stations to Lost Creek, but along with a greater FBI presence maybe that'll make it harder for the killer to strike again. She decides to tell him, knowing he can disseminate the information faster than any press conference she holds. "Listen to me carefully, as I don't have time to repeat myself. I'm about to give you the inside scoop. Got a pen?"

"Hold on." She hears a beep before he says, "I'm recording our conversation now, so anything you say from this point forward is on the record. That okay?"

It's too late to back out now. "Sure. So, I have reason to believe that the person who killed Sarah Moss and Emily Cole, and who abducted Kate Flynn and her son, Ben, is the serial killer referred to as the Snow Storm Killer." She waits for a reaction, but for once, Gary is lost for words. "Today he killed a federal agent, so the public need to be aware that he's extremely dangerous. If they see anyone acting suspiciously, they should get away from him and call the police *immediately*."

Gary says, "Do you have a description of him?"

"Unfortunately, we don't. All we know is that the person seen running away from Emily Cole's crime scene was a tall, broad male. I can't tell you his ethnicity or how old he is, but we're working on the assumption that he's between forty and sixty, give or take a few years."

"Got it. So you're ruling out Jake Rubio for the more recent homicides? You don't think he's acting like some kind of copycat killer, offing women the same way his mother was killed?"

She takes a deep breath as she considers it again. "I don't think so. Jake saves lives for a living, and he's never been accused of assaulting anyone. Like I said to you at the newsroom, I think it would be a mistake to drag him through the mud. He's suffered enough."

"Sure. How about Patrick Flynn; is he a person of interest? Because he fits the description and he's married to one of the victims."

She might need to reconsider Patrick as a suspect, because she hasn't yet asked him for his alibi for the time Emily Cole was killed. She was too fixated on Jake. Not that she intends to tell the press that. "He's not a person of interest right now, no."

"And do you have any leads on where Kate and her son are?"

"None at this time." She sits up straight. "Which means I need to get back to work. Will you share these details with other news agencies?"

"I'll do it right away." Before he goes, he says, "The federal agent who was shot, that wasn't your father, was it?"

She hesitates, because it could so easily have been him. "No. His boss."

"So did your father come here specifically to work the case?"

He's caught on too quickly, and she doesn't want to get into that. "I have to go."

"Sure. Thanks for the information."

She puts the phone down and looks over at Adams. "That was a local newspaper reporter. He's going to spread word about the SSK being in town."

He nods. "I guess the media have their uses. Let's hope someone helps us find this guy." Leaning back in his chair he says, "So, I have a question." She raises her eyebrows. "You think Michelle Rubio was this guy's first victim, right?"

"Right."

"Well, it occurs to me that most domestic homicides are the result of the husband or wife killing their partner. So did your dad ever arrest her boyfriend or husband?"

Madison thinks back to what she read of her father's case notes. "Michelle didn't have a partner at the time of her murder."

"Okay," says Adams. "So who was her kid's father?"

"Jake doesn't know his name and Gary Pelosi found out it's not listed on his birth certificate." She scans the case notes again. "Says here Michelle never revealed to anyone who Jake's father was. Even her friends didn't know, which means it could've been a one-night stand, or perhaps a sexual assault."

"Sounds to me like the father didn't want anyone to know he was screwing this woman and had a kid. Someone who thinks like that could be cold-hearted, wouldn't you say?"

She nods slowly. "Cold-hearted enough to kill a woman he knew and leave his child an orphan. And he might've enjoyed it so much he kept on killing." Adrenaline floods her body as she realizes the implications. "If we can find out who Jake's father is, we could have the identity of the SSK." Her cell phone buzzes. "Hello?"

"It's Patrick. I'm going crazy here, Madison. Are you any closer to finding them?"

She wonders why he's keeping his voice low, but then she hears little Sally singing along to a TV show in the background. Her heart sinks. "We're working on it, I promise you.

The whole team is out searching the town and talking to the community to find witnesses. We're watching surveillance footage and we're following every lead that comes in." She's going to have to tell him about the SSK before he hears it on the news.

"Then why haven't they been found?" he asks, exasperated. "There must be a trail or some piece of evidence that can lead you to them. You can't have nothing at all to go on, right?"

"Nothing was found in or on Kate's car because her abductor didn't go near it." She thinks of the gifts left at the other scenes and realizes there wasn't one in Kate's car. "Wait a minute. Where's Ben's iPad?"

"What? Why do you want that?"

"Do you have it?" Patrick told her Kate had remembered to take Ben's iPad with her when she took the kids on Christmas morning. But it wasn't in the car when they checked it.

"I haven't seen it around the house. Sally brought her backpack with her when she left the car to walk home. Maybe she put the iPad in it so she could give it back to Ben. Let me just check." Madison hears him say, "Sweetie? Where's your pink backpack?"

"Oh, I forgot about that," says Sally.

Patrick says down the line, "She's gone to fetch it. I forgot she even had it with her because I was so relieved to get her home. She must've dumped it in her closet. If the iPad isn't in the backpack, Ben must have it with him."

Madison crosses her fingers. She knows how much Ben liked to record videos on that thing. If he was recording at the time of the abduction, they could have footage of the killer.

"Here you go, Daddy."

Madison listens as Patrick unzips the bag. "It's in here. Want me to bring it to you?"

"No!" she almost screams. "Don't touch it at all! Leave it where it is. I'll come and collect it right away."

"Okay," says Patrick. He sounds confused, but Madison doesn't have time to explain. She grabs her coat.

"Where are you going?" asks Adams.

"You mean where are *we* going. Bring your jacket. I think I just found a lead." She races out of the station.

CHAPTER FORTY-FOUR

Bill Harper stands outside what used to be Michelle Rubio's house. A layer of snow builds on his shoulders, but he isn't cold. A raging fire within keeps him warm. He stares at the narrow two-story building. This is where it all started. Where he carried a little boy to safety, not knowing it would trigger a chain reaction that took him away from his family and on a journey to hell.

He can almost see himself entering the house, his arm outstretched, clutching his service weapon. He wishes he could go over and pull himself away from that door. If he could, he would get into his car, drive to LCPD to quit his job, and then go home to be with his family. But it's impossible, of course. No one gets a second chance at life. No one gets to erase their mistakes and try again.

He shakes his head sadly, tempted to bust down the door and storm the house, because it would be satisfying if the SSK were inside waiting for him. But this isn't a movie, and life rarely has satisfying endings.

A shadow approaches the window of the bedroom where Michelle Rubio was brutally beaten to death. He briefly wonders if he's watching her ghost, but then a hand pulls back the blinds and a woman's face peers out at him. The woman drops the blinds and backs away, as if she's scared he's come to hurt her. Bill realizes it's time to go. But where? He's all out of leads and his boss has been murdered. Once the FBI hears what's happened down here, he'll be in huge trouble. Possibly even charged with involuntary manslaughter for endangering Mike's life.

He hears a buzzing in the distance, overhead, and within seconds it gets louder. The unmistakable sound of a helicopter. He looks up. Some way off, two choppers are shining lights down on nearby Gold Rock. Backup has arrived. News has reached the FBI. They'll be here in no time. He swallows, transfixed by the lights in the darkness.

The whirring of the helicopter's blades almost blocks out the approaching footsteps, but the crunch of the snow gives them away. Before Bill can turn, he feels cold metal pressed against the back of his head.

"Evening, Bill," says a male voice. He cringes as warm breath touches his bare neck. "It looks like we've caused quite a stir."

He keeps his eyes fixed on the helicopters. Maybe they'll reach him in time to take out the killer. All he knows is that he doesn't have time to draw his weapon.

"I knew you'd come here eventually." The killer sighs. "You know, Jakey—my son—bawled his little eyes out while I attacked his mother in that bedroom. I was convinced he'd be scarred for life and would end up on a psych ward, or maybe killing himself. So imagine my surprise when I found out he saves lives for a living. Isn't that ironic?"

Bill daren't speak. There have been so many times he's thought about what he would say to this asshole when they finally met, but all words seem meaningless now.

"You've been the one constant in my life, Bill, so it's reassuring to finally meet you in person. I've only ever watched you from afar before killing your boss earlier today. That doesn't mean we haven't come close. I've walked past you on the sidewalk up in Anchorage more than once. I even sat next to you and Pamela in a coffee house one time. I enjoyed watching you interact. I could tell you genuinely loved each other, because neither of you noticed anyone around you. You had a chemistry that was obvious to outsiders." He laughs as if he's just heard a joke. "You know, even though there's only twelve years between us, I feel like you and Pamela are my parents. I enjoyed following you around and watching your relationship progress. I would've loved to have attended your wedding."

Bill feels hot, angry tears build behind his eyes at the mention of Pamela, but he refuses to show any emotion in front of this monster. "Where's the rest of my wife?"

"You don't need to worry about Pamela. Your beloved wife's skull is safely tucked away in my fish tank. I take it with me wherever I move, and even run things by her every now and then. She's a good listener."

Bill squeezes his eyes shut against his rage. His fists clench and he decides there and then that it would be worth dying right now if he could only see who his tormenter is. Before he can overthink it, he takes the risk and spins around.

The SSK grins at him, bare-faced. He's not hiding behind a ski mask and he doesn't look like a monster. He's just your average middle-aged guy off the street. Bill's disappointed that he doesn't recognize him. It means the man has never been a suspect, and Bill has never once been close to catching him.

"You look as if you expect me to kill you!" says the SSK with a laugh.

"Just do it already, you sick pile of shit."

The killer relieves him of his weapon while holding his own to Bill's forehead. "I can't kill you yet. It's time you understood me. I have something I want you to see." He leads Bill past Mike's car and on toward an old gray Ford. Gesturing to the driver's side with his gun, he says, "You're coming home with me. Because for our game to finally end, you have to see where it all began."

CHAPTER FORTY-FIVE

Madison's car fails her. It won't start, despite several attempts, so she has to ride with Detective Adams to Kate and Patrick's house. The red leather seats are unbelievably comfortable and the interior is a million times more modern than her car. It's pleasantly warm in here too. But Adams drives frustratingly slowly, and she's tempted to ask him why he even has a powerful car like this if he's scared of crashing it, but she bites her tongue. By the time they pull up outside Kate's house, she's itching to get out. She runs up the driveway and bangs on the door.

Patrick opens it. "Do you really think there could be something on there?" His face is full of hope.

Madison tries to manage his expectations. "Probably not, but it's worth checking."

He moves aside, letting them into the living room. Sally is sitting on the couch in her lilac-colored ballerina pajamas. She looks at Madison. "Is Mommy with you?"

Madison glances at Patrick. How is she supposed to answer that? She takes a seat next to the little girl. "I'm afraid not, honey. I've come to look at your brother's iPad. I hear you brought it home for him?"

Sally nods emphatically. "He'll want it when him and Mommy get home."

"I'm sure he will. Was he playing on it in the car before they left?"

"No, he wasn't playing games. He was recording Mommy. She was whispering bad words and she thought we couldn't hear her so we were laughing."

Madison forces a smile. Kate must've been worrying about how her outburst would go down with her boss. It's promising that Ben was recording in the car, though. It means he could've captured footage of the abduction.

"Here." Patrick holds out the bag containing the iPad. She snaps a pair of latex gloves on before taking it from him. Then he hands her a charger. "The battery has died. Maybe because it was in the cold car for so long, or maybe because Ben didn't switch it off."

Adams plugs the charger into a socket for her and she connects it to the tablet. It comes to life and requests a passcode.

Sally is watching. "It's one, two, three, four."

Madison smiles as she enters it, and the iPad lets her in. She finds the video folder and opens it. It's filled with hundreds of video clips.

"Start with the latest one," says Adams, rather obviously. She gets off the couch so that Sally can't see the screen. She doesn't want to upset her with anything that's on here. She stands between the two men and hits play.

They watch Kate from behind as she drives. She's clearly agitated, leaning forward and gripping the steering wheel. "If I have you guys with me," she mutters quietly, "Tom will have to go easy on me, right? I mean, he wouldn't want to ruin your Christmas."

Madison understands now. Tom is Kate's boss. This explains where she was headed and why she took the kids with her. She was desperate to try to keep her job.

"What the hell?" says Kate, looking in her rear-view mirror. The camera turns to Sally, who is giggling behind her hand and looking over the iPad at Ben.

The car takes a sharp turn off the road and the camera catches a glimpse of the gas station where it was eventually found. Kate can be heard saying, "Why's he waving me over?" She stops the car and undoes her seatbelt. "Like I don't have enough to worry about. Wait here, you two."

Ben turns the camera to watch his mom leave. She walks around to the back of the car, pulling her coat closed against the cold. Then a loud voice says directly into the iPad's mic, "I spy with my little eye, something beginning with S."

Sally lights up on the couch. "That's me!"

Adams smiles at her. "It sure is. Were you trying to deafen your brother or something?"

She giggles.

Ben is silent throughout the video, but he points at items beginning with S. After a minute or two, raised voices can be heard outside the car, but despite holding the iPad to her ear, Madison can't make out what they're saying. Not until Kate says, "Oh my God, okay, okay. Fine. I'll come with you."

Her abductor must say something they can't hear, because Kate sounds shocked when she next speaks. "Please, no. Leave them here. Please don't hurt them."

Ben turns the camera to his window and they're able to see the very front of a car parked behind the gas station building. It's gray, but it's impossible to identify a make or model, or the license plate, from this angle.

"What's Mommy doing?" Sally asks her brother.

The front passenger door opens and Ben films his mom's face as she leans inside, looking pale and afraid.

Patrick glances at Madison. "If Kate noticed that Ben was recording, she might have named who she was talking to, to leave a trail for you guys."

Ben drops the iPad lens-down in his lap and that ends

their visuals, but he leaves it recording, so there's still hope. "Is that a real gun, Mommy?" asks Sally.

"No, honey, don't worry. It's just a toy gun from Santa." Kate's voice is strained. "Now I need you to listen carefully, okay? Your brother and I are going to go with—"

The video ends.

"Dammit!" shouts Madison, her frustration getting the better of her. "We were so close!"

"The goddam battery died," says Patrick. He rubs his face and lets out a long, agonized groan.

"We don't know that she was going to name him," says Adams, trying to make them feel better. "There's a good chance she didn't know him and she was just going to say 'that man' or something."

Madison looks at Sally. "You didn't see the man your mom was talking to, did you, honey?"

"No. And I wasn't allowed to go with them. But I didn't want to anyway, because he told Mommy he was going to show Ben a train set. Trains are BOR-ing."

Madison glances at Adams. "Trains again. They mean something to him." She spots Sally's backpack next to the couch and peers inside. There's a coloring book and a doll, but no toy train or gift-wrapped box. "I suspect he has a train set in his home and that's where he's taken them." Her mind is in overdrive now. "People usually get obsessed with things like trains as a child, right? Maybe he received a train set for Christmas one year and that's when it all started."

Patrick looks confused, so Madison leaves Adams to explain the calling cards and the SSK to him while she steps away to make a call. When Steve answers, she says, "I have a theory and I need you to check something for me."

"Go ahead." The station sounds busy behind him. Phones are ringing off the hook and she can hear the staff talking over each other.

"Our killer is obsessed with trains," she says. "And I'm

willing to bet it's because something happened to him as a kid when he was playing with a train set. It could be that one or both of his parents were killed. He could've been given a train set the same day and that's what he's doing to the kids he's leaving behind; he's gifting them the same toy he got. Maybe he's trying to console them, because having a train set comforted him." A shudder goes through her.

Steve seems unconvinced. "How about don't kill their moms in the first place so they don't need consoling?"

She sighs. "I know, right? It's just a hunch that probably won't go anywhere, but could you check the system for any homicides that happened around Christmas that match the suspected age of our killer; between forty and sixty."

Steve is typing as she speaks. "Okay, that's twenty years, so we have a lot of results. Let me filter out any that don't sound relevant."

While she waits, she watches Patrick's reaction to Adams telling him that they suspect the SSK has his wife. Whether Patrick has heard of the killer or not, the implications are clear; the odds of getting Kate and Ben back alive are slim. That doesn't mean it's impossible, though, and that's what she has to hold on to.

"Okay, I'm down to three," says Steve.

"Tell me about them."

"Janet Purdue was murdered in her home on Christmas Eve. She left behind five children and her husband was convicted of her murder."

"Did he serve time?"

"Just checking... Yeah, he's serving life without parole, so that's him out. Okay, the next one is a Jodie Allen, who... Oh, wait, no, she wasn't the victim. She killed her boyfriend. And it looks like they had no kids, so scratch that. Okay, that leaves us with Maureen Anderson. Murdered in her home on Christmas Day 1975. She was found by her husband and the case has never been solved." He pauses as he reads.

"Anything else?"

"They had one child; a boy named Dale. He was four years old at the time of the murder. Holy shit."

"What?" Her adrenaline is starting to kick in now. Could they really be about to unearth the identity of the Snow Storm Killer?

"It says here that when officers attended the scene, he was playing with a train set next to the body of his dead mother. Apparently he bawled his eyes out when they tried to remove him from his toys. One officer wrote that the kid seemed more bothered about his train than his mother."

Madison looks up at the ceiling and says a silent prayer. To Steve she says, "We've got him. The SSK must be Dale Anderson." But it's a name she's never heard of. "Was the husband questioned for Maureen's murder?"

"Looks like it. Several times, but nothing stuck. He passed a polygraph too. But hang on... Ah. It looks like he was a friend of the police department back then. He had a tow truck company and a repair shop. He used to help them clean up road traffic accidents and he had a contract to service the squad cars."

"What are you saying: that maybe they didn't try too hard to nail the guy?"

"It's a possibility."

"What's his name?" she asks. "And how old is he now? Maybe *he's* the SSK."

"Larry Anderson. He's sixty-eight years old."

That seems a little older than Madison would expect their killer to be. Their guy was spotted running away from St. Theresa's church like a bat out of hell. "Run a check on him and his son. I want to know their current addresses."

"On it."

Larry and Maureen Anderson's son would be in his late forties now, so he's a better suspect. Adams approaches her while Patrick takes Sally upstairs to bed. "We've got a name," says Madison. "Dale Anderson. His mom was killed by his father on Christmas Day in 1975 when he was four years old. He was found next to her body, playing with a train set."

"Jesus Christ," says Adams. "You can't make this shit up."

"You ready?" says Steve down the line.

"Go ahead."

"I can't find any known address for Dale Anderson. Maybe he moved away at some point, which I guess would fit, seeing as our killer went on a cross-county crime spree. Larry Anderson, however, is a resident of the Mountain View Senior Care Home."

"Then the SSK must be his son." Madison runs to the front door, phone in hand. "We're on our way there now." She ends the call and leads Adams out to his car. "Give me the keys."

He stops dead on the driveway. "What?"

"Give me the keys!" she repeats. "You drive like an old woman and we don't have time for that."

He hesitates, but to his credit, he eventually throws her his keys. The Camaro's engine revs nicely on the first try as she waits for Adams to jump in. Within seconds, they're on their way to question the SSK's father.

CHAPTER FORTY-SIX

The Mountain View Senior Care Home sits in the shadow of Grave Mountain, so-called because of the number of climbers and prospectors—and more recently, overconfident hikers—who have died on its slopes over the years. At this time in the evening, the mountain isn't clearly visible because the sky is gray with snow clouds. Madison skids to a halt right outside the ramp leading up to the care home's entrance and runs inside, not waiting for Adams.

She isn't a stranger to this establishment. Just last month, one of the care workers was murdered, and Madison came here to speak to the staff about her. The staff members she encountered then were much more welcoming than the dragon covering the reception desk now. The woman stares at her with beady eyes and an air of hostility. She looks like the kind of person who enjoys saying no to everything, so Madison pulls out her badge and flashes it. "I'm Detective Harper from LCPD, and my partner and I need to speak to one of your residents as a matter of urgency."

The woman doesn't even glance at the badge. "It's six o'clock. Evening visiting hours are between seven and nine."

Madison stands her ground. "I'm not visiting. I'm here to question a potential murderer."

The nurse doesn't register shock. Instead, she tilts her head to one side and says, "You know you're in a care home for senior citizens, right?"

Madison crosses her arms. "Do you want to be responsible for the death of a mother and child? Because that's what will happen if you don't let me speak to someone in authority right this second."

The nurse has the audacity to roll her eyes. She slowly picks up the desk phone. "I'll need to call the manager."

Madison turns to Adams and shakes her head. They're wasting precious time.

The nurse turns away to have a quiet conversation into the phone. When she finally turns back to them, she puts the phone down. "He'll be out in just a second."

It actually takes five long minutes for the manager to appear. He introduces himself as Mr. Kane and shakes their hands. "I must say, this is very worrying. I can't imagine that any of our residents are criminals, let alone murderers. They're just older folk living out their twilight years."

Madison raises an eyebrow. It's tempting to tell him that even killers and sex offenders age eventually, but she knows that society sees all older people as frail, decent people who should be treated with kid gloves. The truth is, there are far more criminals out there who haven't been caught than have been, and they can end up in care homes just like this one, same as everybody else. "We're following a lead and we'd appreciate your full cooperation," she says.

"Who are you here to question?"

As there are staff and residents passing by, Madison leads him away from the desk. "Larry Anderson."

Mr. Kane frowns. "Larry suffers with dementia. He's been with us for three years now. Even if he committed a homicide in his younger years, I don't see that questioning him will help your case."

"Well, we still need to try," says Adams.

"We're not here to arrest him," says Madison when she sees doubt on the manager's face. "We think he can help us find the missing reporter Kate Flynn. You've heard about how she and her son were abducted, I take it?"

"Of course. It's all over the news."

"Then you'll understand how important it is that we speak to Mr. Anderson."

He studies her face before coming to a decision. "Fine. Follow me."

Madison shoots Adams a look of relief, and they follow the manager down a long corridor, stopping outside the last room on the right. Beyond is a stairway with an exit sign. Mr. Kane knocks before entering, but he doesn't wait for an answer. The detectives follow him inside.

The room smells medicinal. A white-haired man sits in an armchair by the window, watching some kind of game show on TV.

"Sorry to bother you like this, Larry," says the manager. "I have two police officers here who would like a few words. Is that okay?"

When Larry looks over at them, Madison sees clarity in his eyes, followed by alarm. But almost as quickly it's replaced with indifference. He's dressed in blue jeans and a plaid shirt over a clean white T-shirt. There are well-worn slippers on his feet. Madison tries to picture him killing his wife as a younger man. Maybe he didn't have anything to do with that, but his wife's murder almost certainly turned his son into a killer. She just needs to prove it.

"Hi, Mr. Anderson." She takes a seat on the bed next to his armchair. Adams is peering at photographs and belongings without touching anything. "We just have a few questions and then we'll be on our way."

Larry's eyes stay on the TV. "Took you long enough," he says.

She raises her eyebrows. "I'm sorry?"

He looks at her. "Who are you here for, me or my boy?"

She resists the urge to look at Adams, but the hairs on the back of her neck stand up. "Which one of you should we be questioning?"

He looks away. "Both of us, I guess." With a long sigh, he adds, "I should've killed Dale as well as my wife."

Her heart sinks. So he did kill the mother of his child, setting in motion a terrible chain of events. A quick glance at Mr. Kane tells her he's stunned. He and his team have been taking good care of a murderer for the last three years, and now he knows that, he'll be wondering what happens next. What his responsibilities are toward this resident.

"I tried to get child protective services to take him off me after her death," continues Larry. "They did an evaluation and I overheard them talking. One of the social workers said he was odd. They watched him at school and said he pretended to be like the other kids. He'd laugh after seeing them laugh at a joke, and he'd copy what they said in response to questions from teachers. It was like he didn't know how to be himself and was looking for guidance. On more than one occasion he even tried to go home with one of the other kids' moms."

It's clear to Madison that Dale struggled with witnessing what happened to his mother. Part of her feels bad for the young boy, but plenty of kids lose their parents to murder and don't go on to hurt others. "Did he grow up in care?" she asks.

"No. I couldn't do it in the end. Because it was my fault he turned out that way. Besides, I couldn't trust that he wouldn't tell a foster family about what he witnessed that Christmas." Larry looks at her with watery eyes. "How come I only remember the bad stuff? I want to remember my wife alive and happy, when we first met. But all I see is her dead body next to my son."

"Why did you kill her?" Madison asks softly.

He scoffs. "My business was on the brink. We would've lost everything. I needed the life insurance payout."

"So you chose your business over your wife," says Adams, clearly disgusted.

He's right to feel that way. The way that taking a woman's life is viewed as such an easy solution to a man's financial problems is truly disturbing, and Madison doesn't see a time when a woman's life isn't considered so worthless, but she wishes he would tone it down, because she's trying to get answers.

"Who are you?" says Larry, noticing him for the first time. His concentration has been broken by the comment.

"I'm a cop," says Adams.

Larry tries to get up. "I'm not talking to cops. You'll frame me for something I didn't do."

Madison gently pushes him back into his seat. It's clear he's become confused. "That's okay. We're not here about you, Mr. Anderson." Not today, anyway. "We've come to talk to you about your son."

"I don't have a son," he says convincingly.

"You remember Dale?" she asks.

His face clouds over and he gulps. "He's worse than I ever was. I only killed one person, which was bad enough and something I've regretted my entire life. But that boy killed many women. And now he's back here torturing me.

"If you tell me where he is, I'll stop him."

"I don't know where he is and I don't want to know. I just want to be left alone to die in here. I'd do it myself if I could. Just so I don't have to speak to him ever again."

He's clearly upset. Madison doesn't know how the law works with arresting dementia sufferers; she'll have to ask Chief Mendes. For now, all she can do is station someone outside his door. She stands. "Thanks for your time. We'll leave you alone now."

"I'd rather it was you visiting me than that devil. Make him go. I don't want him here anymore. It's torture."

Larry makes it sound like his son is here with them. Alarmed, she checks the small closet, and Adams looks under the bed. Nothing. He must be confused. "Your son isn't here, Mr. Anderson."

"He was. He never misses an opportunity to remind me of what I did to his mother. That kid was unnaturally attached to her. Never stopped talking about her after she died. He figured out I'd killed her and he wanted to make me pay."

Madison looks at him. "Are you saying Dale comes here to visit you?"

Larry looks up at her, and his expression suggests she's the one who's confused. "He was here right before you."

She looks at Mr. Kane. "You've met Dale Anderson?"

He looks aghast. "No, I haven't. As far as I'm aware, Larry has never had any visitors."

Madison remembers the stairway next door to the room. "He must be sneaking in and out. Do you have CCTV?"

"We used to, but the staff said they felt it was invasive. They thought management was watching them work, so they insisted we remove it or they'd strike."

She shakes her head in frustration. "Dammit."

Looking back at Larry she says, "Do you have any idea where Dale might be staying? Has he mentioned a partner he lives with? Or a friend?"

Larry scoffs. "He never wanted friends. He pretends. Uses people until he gets what he wants. And the only girlfriend he ever had before fleeing town was Michelle. She was beautiful. Until he killed her."

Madison swallows. "Michelle Rubio?"

He nods.

She looks at Adams. "Dale could be Jake Rubio's father." She does the sums in her head. "He would've been twenty-three when Michelle was killed."

"That was his name: Jake," says Larry. "My grandson. He was a cute kid. Blond hair like his mom. I never got to meet him. I just saw pictures of him on TV."

Adams approaches Madison and says quietly, "If Michelle Rubio was Dale's first kill, maybe he has Kate and Ben at the house where it happened? Maybe he wants to end this where it all started."

She thinks about it. She knows the address already, from reading her father's case notes. "It's worth a try. Let's go."

CHAPTER FORTY-SEVEN

Adams lets Madison drive again, but only because she still has the keys and she beats him to the car. She speeds out of the care home's parking lot, wiper blades whooshing back and forth in an attempt to keep the windshield clear of snow. Adams turns the heat on, and she's astounded at how quick it works compared to her car, but it doesn't stop her body from trembling with adrenaline.

When her cell phone buzzes, she hands it to Adams so she can focus on the road. "Answer that."

He takes it from her. "Hello?"

Madison listens and thinks she hears Nate's voice. Adams says, "She's driving. We're a little busy, buddy. Maybe you can call back later." He doesn't know Nate. He probably thinks he's no one important. After listening to him for a few seconds, he says, "Listen, pal, I don't know who you think you are, but I suggest you don't speak to me that way. I'm a detective, and if you keep that up, I'll arrest your sorry ass."

Madison rolls her eyes. That's all she needs, Nate and Adams going at it. "Put him on speakerphone and let him speak," she says.

Adams looks at her. "He called me an asshole!"

She tries not to smile. "He's a friend who's keeping an eye on my son. Let him speak."

"Fine." He switches the speakerphone on.

"Nate?" she says. "I think we know where the killer's hiding. What do you want? Is Owen okay?"

"He's fine," says Nate. He sounds serious. "Madison, Frank Brookes just called me. He said your dad's gone missing and the car he was using—Mike's—was found abandoned outside Michelle Rubio's old house."

"Oh shit." She checks the rear-view mirror, and when she sees there are no cars behind her, she slams on the brakes, intending to pull over. But the car skids on some ice and slams into a parked truck by the side of the road. The impact isn't too bad, but the sound of metal on metal makes her cringe as she thinks of the inevitable damage to the Camaro's bodywork.

"What are you doing?" yells Adams. "You've wrecked my car!"

"I'm sorry, but didn't you hear that? My dad's missing!" She takes the phone off him, and he gets out to survey the damage, letting in the snow and cold.

Nate says, "Frank spoke to the current resident to check whether the SSK could be hiding inside. She said she saw an older guy standing outside earlier on, just staring at the house. He fits your dad's description."

Her stomach flips with dread.

"When she looked again, your dad was driving away in a different car and there was a passenger next to him." He pauses. "She said it looked like the passenger was holding something to Bill's head, but she couldn't be sure."

Adams gets back into the car and looks like he's about to launch into a tirade of abuse, but when he sees Madison's expression, he thinks better of it. Madison shudders and grips the phone tighter. "Oh my God, Nate. The killer's got my dad, hasn't he?"

"It sounds like it. Frank says some Feds have arrived to

work with your department, and he's headed to the station now to tell Chief Mendes everything he knows about the SSK. He said the only real clue the killer volunteered to your dad over the years was something about how much he loved his mother."

She hears a helicopter somewhere nearby. That must be the Feds, which is fine by her. She's willing to take all the help she can get. "I need to go to the station and speak with Frank."

"Sure. Just keep in mind that your dad knows how to take care of himself. He won't do anything that gets him killed, and he's probably armed."

She swallows. "I hope so."

Ending the call, she drops her phone into her lap and starts the engine.

Adams looks at her. "I'm sorry, Harper, but I have to insist on driving us to the station. You're obviously upset. I don't want you causing an accident and getting us killed before we can save your father."

She ignores him, because she knows he's just worried about his precious car. As she pulls back onto the road and revs the engine to pick up speed, something occurs to her about the clue Frank gave Nate. It's obvious that Dale Anderson was negatively impacted by witnessing his mother's brutal death when he was a child. And it's obvious that the women he's killing represent her. Maybe it's his way of taking his anger out on her because she allowed herself to be killed, in his mind at least. "Oh my God." She slams on the brakes again and jerks the steering wheel full circle so she can turn the car around. The tires skid and slide underneath them.

"Whoa, whoa, whoa! What are you doing?" yells Adams. "You've already ruined the bodywork, and now you want to wreck my car completely?"

When the vehicle has turned one-eighty, she hits the gas and speeds off in the opposite direction to the station. It's satisfying to have a car that's so responsive to her touch, and fast with it. She glances over at Adams, who looks positively stressed. "The son of a bitch does want to end it where it all started, but it didn't start with Michelle Rubio." She focuses her eyes back on the road. "It started with his mother. We need to go to his childhood home. That's where he'll be holding Kate, Ben and my father."

She just has to hope they get there in time to stop whatever the killer has planned.

CHAPTER FORTY-EIGHT

Bill's eyes take a moment to adjust to the bright lights. When they do, the first thing he sees is a Christmas tree in front of a roaring fire. A rancid smell hits the back of his throat, one that he's been around many times before, making it unmistakable. He's slouched to one side on a couch, and as he tries to sit straight, pain sears through his head where the SSK hit him with the gun after opening the door to this house. He tries to move his hands, but they're tied together at the wrists in front of his stomach. When his vision focuses, he notices a fish tank on top of a sideboard in the corner of the living room. "Oh God. No."

His wife's skull stares back at him as several tiny fish swim through the gaps in her jaw. He retches in shock, but nothing comes up. His anguish has him torn between wanting to fish it out of the murky water so she can finally be laid to rest all in one piece, and finding something sharp that he can use on himself to stop this never-ending nightmare.

A woman's voice forces him to focus. She's pleading with someone in a room behind him. He turns his head to look, but the pain makes him grimace. It's then that he realizes there is a large wooden train set in front of the Christmas tree. Next to that, a little boy is sitting on the floor. He's ignoring the train set and watching Bill with an expression of fear on his face.

"Are you okay, kid?" Bill whispers.

The boy shakes his head, and Bill's heart sinks as he watches a tear slide down his cheek. He turns away and sees a small video camera on top of a tripod next to the couch. It's aimed at the boy. Bill realizes that the SSK is about to record something happening. Alarmed, he tugs at the rope binding his wrists. His ankles are free, so he considers jumping up, grabbing the boy and getting out of here. The front door isn't far away.

"You're meant to be singing along," says a male voice. "Or it won't be authentic." The voice is coming from what looks to be the kitchen.

"You're a psycho," says the woman. "I'm sick of playing along with your messed-up games. What's the point? You're just going to kill us anyway. I've reported on a hundred freaks like you, and you're all the same. You're so goddam clichéd."

Bill's heart sinks. It's Madison's friend, and she's just going to anger the killer if she keeps talking to him like that. Maybe she's had enough of being tied up and terrified. She must believe there's no hope of her and her son getting out of here alive if she's refusing to do what her abductor says.

He hears a loud slap. After a pause, it sounds like Kate spits in her abductor's face. "You're going to pay for that," the man says. Then footsteps come into the living room. "Stand up, Bill. You're about to get a starring role in the story of my life."

Bill looks at the guy. His eyes are wild as he distractedly wipes his face with his sleeve. He's acting like a director on the set of a big Hollywood movie. "How long have you been back in town?" Bill asks.

"Put it this way, I arrived some time before your naïve plan to lure me back." The SSK laughs. "Did you really think you could fool me into believing you'd come here to reunite with your family? I know you don't care about your daughters, otherwise you would've returned a long time ago."

It's difficult to listen to someone like this mocking him for his weaknesses. Bill thought he was one step ahead of the killer this time, but the asshole was already in Lost Creek. "So why haven't you killed Madison or Owen already?" he asks.

The killer rolls his eyes. "You have such a low opinion of me."

"Well, sure. You slaughtered my wife, didn't you?"

"Yes, because she was investigating me, and she was far more likely to catch me than you were. But your daughter didn't even know about me, so I didn't need to harm her. Besides, I was intrigued to see whether she'd do what you couldn't. But now that she's telling reporters I'm in town, she'll have to die, of course."

Bill's jaw tenses. He doesn't want to listen to this psycho talking about hurting Madison. "So what's going on? Why are we here?"

The killer scoffs. "Come on. Haven't you figured it out by now? Are you really that stupid? Look at the camera. Doesn't that give you any clues?"

Bill glances around him. It's as if this lunatic is recreating a Christmas from his childhood. He turns and manages to catch a glimpse of Kate in the kitchen. Even in her anguish, she has a defiant expression on her face. His heart jumps into his mouth as he notices the killer has her dressed in an apron. Her hands are bound, like his. The oven is humming. There are potatoes waiting to be peeled on the kitchen counter, but there are no knives within reach. He looks back at the boy, and it suddenly dawns on him. He turns to the SSK. "Your mother was murdered when you were a kid. On Christmas Day." He pauses. "Oh dear God. You're recreating the crime scene."

The killer beams at him, and there's no sanity behind those eyes. "You finally get it!"

"Not really." Bill swallows back his fear. "What have you

got to gain from recreating it with strangers? Why go to all this effort? You want to be famous, is that it? You want to be the most fucked-up and famous serial killer out there?"

The guy shakes his head. "I'm not a serial killer, Bill. I'm not bloodthirsty or sadistic, or some kind of monster who gets his thrills from hurting people. Killing these women is time-consuming, messy, and a chore I could do without. Don't you *see*?" He sighs. "I'm conducting an *experiment*. These people aren't victims, they're *variables*. I'm testing the children for their reactions."

Bill closes his eyes as he realizes for the first time that none of this was about the women. It was all about the children. How did he not see it sooner? He's gone about his investigation completely the wrong way, wasting so many years. So many *lives*. His shoulders sag as he finally admits defeat.

"I'm trying to understand why I carried on playing with my train set the day my mother was brutally beaten to death in front of me," the killer continues. "Because over the years afterward, I heard the social workers and my father's cop buddies say that my reaction wasn't normal. That there must be something wrong with me. It confused me. Was I supposed to do something? I was only four years old! What in God's name was I supposed to do?" It's clear from the earnest look in his eyes and his rising voice that he desperately wants Bill to understand his logic. "I'm trying to figure out whether I was supposed to react differently. So I've subjected other young boys to similar circumstances to see how *they* react."

Kate groans from the kitchen and Bill knows how she feels. This guy killed all those women just to see how their children react to witnessing their mothers' deaths. All because he wants to know whether he's *abnormal*? "You're like a kid holding a magnifying glass over a bug on a sunny day. Except worse, because kids don't know any better."

The killer's face reddens. "It's not my fault I have to do this. Blame the person who bludgeoned my mother to death in front of me. These women should be grateful my mother wasn't raped first."

His words are chilling, and Bill shakes his head in disgust. This psycho has no remorse at all. He's unable to feel empathy for his victims, their children or the rest of their families. It's all about him and how useful they can be to his deluded experiment. Forcing himself to speak, in order to buy time for the Feds to find them, he says, "Were your experiments worth it?"

"Not so far, no. Every single child cried for his mother or tried to get away, and not one of them opened the gift I left for them. The only one who did anything different was Zach Cole, at the church. Sure, he cried at first, but then he began building a snowman. I'm telling you, Bill, that kid needs watching as he reaches puberty."

Bill can't believe what he's hearing. "And all this." He gestures to the Christmas tree, the boy and the train set. "What's all this about?"

A grin breaks out across the killer's face. "This is my childhood home, where my beautiful mother was killed. I wanted to lease it, but the current tenants wouldn't sublet it to me, not even for a month. They regretted that decision when I came back to take it from them yesterday."

Bill closes his eyes. That's what he can smell. More victims. They must be dumped upstairs, or maybe in the basement.

"For the first time ever, I have an extra person to help me, and I have almost all the correct variables: the same house, a similar train set, a boy of my age. Sure, it's not Christmas morning, but it *is* snowing outside. The conditions are almost perfect for the first time, so the results will be more meaningful. I can watch it all play out as you enter through the back door and chase my mother through the kitchen and into the living room."

Bill steps back in horror. "No. I'm not doing that."

"You'll strike her over the head three times in all, with

this." The killer takes a hammer from the dining table. It looks well worn, and Bill would guess it's the same one that killed this guy's mother.

Kate has clearly heard enough. She starts yelling for help, hoping a neighbor will come to their aid. She picks up a large pan and tries to smash the kitchen window. The killer runs over to her and stuffs a dishcloth in her mouth so forcefully that Bill shouts for him to stop. The killer slaps her hard across the face. He turns to Bill, his eyes dark with rage. "If you don't do it, I'll hack her limbs off one by one."

With no hope left, Bill drops onto the couch. He can't think of a single way to get out of this, or to help Kate and her son. He's consumed with guilt for not catching this guy years ago.

When a car approaches outside, all of them look toward the front window. Bill thinks it might be Frank or the local cops. He swallows. It could be Madison. His heart pounds hard against his chest as blood roars in his ears. If that's his daughter outside, she could die here tonight.

CHAPTER FORTY-NINE

Madison and Adams cautiously get out of the car and look at the neat row of small and medium-sized two-story homes. The house the SSK grew up in has a driveway, but there's no car on it. The street is deadly silent. The residents must be heeding the warnings to stay at home. A curtain twitches opposite.

"You stay out here in case anyone exits through the front door," Madison says. "I'll go around the back."

"I think we should wait for the Feds."

She wants to yell at him. Can't he see how urgent this is? "If you want people to die here tonight because you were too chickenshit to do your job, then that's on you. I'm going in." She doesn't wait for his reaction. She heads around the side of the house, her gun drawn. A wooden gate stops her from gaining access to the backyard. As she reaches over the top to see if there's a bolt she can slide open, she hears a male voice behind her whisper, "Detective Harper?"

She slowly turns, raising her weapon at the same time, frustrated that Adams let someone creep up on her. Nate would never have let that happen. Luckily, it's only Gary Pelosi from the newspaper, walking from the direction of the driveway. She lowers her gun. "Jesus Christ, Pelosi. What are you doing here? You're going to get yourself killed." If he's here, it's just a matter of time before more press turn up.

"I had a hunch, and it looks like the same one as you." He keeps his voice low. "Do you think Kate is in there?" He tries to look over her shoulder into the yard. "You have backup on the way, right?"

"Gary? Get out of here right this minute or I'll shoot you myself," she hisses. "You're putting my investigation and Kate's life in jeopardy. Now piss off!"

He holds his hands up. "Okay, okay!"

The lengths reporters will go to in order to get a scoop never cease to amaze her. She watches as he runs back down the driveway, clearly freaked out by her reaction.

Madison forces the gate open with her shoulder, then approaches the large kitchen window. There are no blinds, so she peers cautiously inside. The light is on but there's no one in the room, so she goes to the back door and tries the handle. It's unlocked. She quietly turns it all the way and winces as the door creaks when she opens it. She stops and listens. It sounds like someone is sobbing inside. With a deep breath, she raises her gun and enters the kitchen.

The sobs are louder now, and chills run through her entire body when she recognizes her friend's voice. Kate's alive. She's whispering reassurances to someone, and Madison can only hope that it's Ben. She has to blink back tears of relief as she moves through the kitchen to the doorway beyond. A terrible smell reaches her, but she doesn't react. She peers around the corner of the doorway, into the living room.

Kate is sitting on the floor clutching her son. Blood runs down her arm, onto the carpet. Madison can't see anyone else in the room, but it could be a trap. Ben locks his eyes on her and raises his arm to point. Madison shakes her head to say no. She doesn't want the killer to know she's here. "Madison," he says.

Her mouth drops open. That's the first word he's spoken in months.

Kate looks up and sees her standing in the doorway. "Oh, thank God!" With some effort she gets to her feet. Madison goes to her and hugs them both, trying to keep one eye on the rest of the downstairs. She assumes her dad has gone to chase the killer, and just the thought makes her feel sick. Because she knows he'll see this through to the bitter end. As she pulls back, Kate stumbles over her words. "He's gone. He's not here anymore." She swallows before adding, "Madison, it's Gary Pelosi!"

"What?" Madison's shocked. She takes a step back. She's looking for someone called Dale Anderson. How could it be Gary Pelosi? How could he have fooled her? She remembers he told her he only arrived in town two months ago. He fed her a line about moving here because of getting divorced. He must have assumed a false identity and been lying in wait. She suddenly realizes that while her father believes he lured the killer to Lost Creek, in reality it's the other way around.

"He just crept up behind me at the side of the house," she says. A shudder runs through her as she realizes he could've killed her there and then. "He pretended to be here on a hunch. I told him to leave."

Kate says, "Yesterday morning he flagged me down at the old gas station. I thought something was wrong with my car, and I knew him, so I didn't for one second think he'd try to hurt us. He pulled a gun on me and made me and Ben get into his car." She visibly shudders. "Where's Sally? Is she okay?"

"Sally's absolutely fine. She's at home with Patrick."

Kate starts sobbing. "I had no choice but to leave her behind. He said he'd kill her if I didn't."

Madison tries to reassure her. "You don't need to explain any of your decisions to me." Seeing the blood that's now all over her own shirt, she says, "What happened to your arm?"

Kate's clutching it now and she looks like she could pass

out. There's no blood left in her face. "The asshole shot me as he left, but I think I'm just clipped."

Madison's mouth goes dry. "I didn't hear a gunshot."

"He has a silencer on it."

The front door opens behind her and she swings around, raising her weapon again. It's just Detective Adams.

"What's going on?" he asks, gun in hand.

"The killer is going by the name of Gary Pelosi, and he just escaped." Madison rushes to the front door and orders Adams to get Kate and Ben out of here and to the hospital. "And call for backup. I'm going after him."

"Wait! Madison?" says Kate.

She turns around. "What?"

"He took your dad with him. He forced him out the back door at gunpoint when he heard your car arrive. There's an alleyway beyond the yard that leads to a dirt road. He was parked out there. He said..." She hesitates.

"What?"

"He said they were going to die together tonight."

Madison swallows. When Gary crept up on her, he must have already locked her dad in his car and then walked around to the front of the street to make it appear he'd only just arrived. Her heart skips a beat. "No chance."

CHAPTER FIFTY

Madison races out of the house and slips into the Camaro, having no choice but to take the car and leave Adams to call for a ride from patrol. She drives down the street, looking for the alleyway behind the row of houses. When she locates it, she enters and speeds up. It doesn't take her long to reach the dirt road. There are no street lights here, and with a heavily wooded area on one side, and rocks and potholes in the road, it's a dangerous place to drive in the dark.

The car's tires handle the dirt and ice well. She can see the Ferris wheel at Fantasy World looming out of the darkness some distance ahead of her. The wheel's neon lights are out and it's not moving. The park is closed. The perfect place to hide, perhaps? Speeding up, she hits a huge pothole and winces as the car lurches to one side. Adams might need a new tire as well as some bodywork repair by the time she's through.

She looks up and spots a helicopter nearing her location. Its spotlight bounces off a car not too far ahead. The other vehicle is slower than the Camaro and she's able to catch up to it. When she finally gets close enough, her headlights illuminate two people in the front seats. It looks like her father's driving. She daren't breathe. The thought of her dad sitting next to that sadistic killer leaves her cold.

The car in front zigzags as it avoids fallen branches and potholes, and she sees the passenger raise a weapon to her father's head. They appear to be arguing. Madison grips the steering wheel tighter as she prays that her father doesn't get himself killed. His driving remains erratic and she wonders what he's planning. If she could just get ahead of them and stop the vehicle, she might have a chance to shoot Gary.

Just as Madison speeds up, the car in front suddenly veers off to the right and hits a large rock. "Oh shit!" It flips onto its side before going all the way onto its roof and then over again, eventually coming to a stop. Her heart is in her mouth as she watches. Her father is in there! She slams on the brakes to try to avoid hitting it, but the front of the Camaro crashes directly into the back of the overturned car before finally coming to a stop.

She feels the impact in her neck and sees stars for a few seconds. The airbag impacted her face and she can feel her nose swelling already. She's forced to take a minute to deal with the pain while keeping an eye on the overturned Ford. She has no doubt her father deliberately crashed to try to kill his nemesis. But in doing so, he may have killed himself. She fights back tears and undoes her seatbelt before climbing out of the car. She needs to check her father's okay. Her neck feels stiff and painful as she stands, but she has to ignore that for now.

She cautiously approaches the upside-down vehicle, listening for any movement inside. The wheels are still spinning and steam is coming from somewhere.

She stops, and watches in disbelief as Gary Pelosi pulls himself free and stands, blood running down his face and into his mouth. She notices his teeth are stained red as he says, "At last. I finally have you both together. If Owen were here, we would be like one big happy family." He immediately makes a beeline for her, pulling something from his waistband as he speeds up. He's fast. He fires his weapon as she draws hers and the bullet only just misses her right shoulder. She turns and runs, trying to lead him away from the overturned car so her father can escape.

"Don't run from me," says Gary. "I just want to talk."

"Then why are you shooting at me?" she shouts over her shoulder.

He stops advancing and lowers his weapon, so she stops too. Her hand hovers over her holster as she turns to face him, trying to catch her breath. Her nose is throbbing now.

"I'm not a serial killer," he says. "You have me all wrong."

Madison is incredulous. How can he be so deluded? "Try telling that to the women you murdered." She tries to peer behind him. She can't hear her dad at all, and she could really do with his help. "I spoke to your father about you. Visited him at the care home before coming here."

Gary's face contorts with anger. "He's a monster. He killed my mother. None of this would've been necessary if he hadn't done that."

Madison shakes her head in disgust. "So, what, *you're* the victim in all this? I don't think so, asshole. You chose to react to your loss this way. I'd say you enjoyed it too."

Red in the face, he suddenly lurches forward, raising his weapon. Without hesitation, Madison pulls her gun and shoots him in the chest. He goes flying backward and hits the ground, where he eventually lies still.

Madison hears coughing coming from the driver's side of the wrecked vehicle. She hurries forward to see her father trying to crawl out. He doesn't get far, as he's unable to free his legs. In the sky above, the helicopter hovers over them, lighting up the scene. It's then that she sees her father's head is bleeding heavily and he's gasping for air. There's a bone sticking out of his thigh, through his pants, and he's deathly pale. Her whole body starts trembling with dread. This doesn't look good.

Above them, a voice speaks through a loudspeaker. "This is the FBI. Federal agents and paramedics are on their way." The helicopter remains close as it scours the area with its spotlight for anyone who might be running away from the crash. They don't know what's happened yet.

"Dad?" Madison says through her fear. "You hear that? The ambulance guys will fix you up."

He doesn't speak. She holds his hand and watches as he tries to regulate his breathing. She can't lose him. It wouldn't be fair to have been reunited for just one lousy month after twenty-three years apart. But then nothing about her life has been fair. The faint sound of ambulance and police sirens reach her as they make the long drive down the dirt road toward her location. She tries to cling to the hope that they'll get here in time.

Her father rouses. He clutches her hand and says, "Did I kill him? Is he dead?"

Her heart sinks. That's all he cares about. He was willing to kill himself if it meant taking the Snow Storm Killer with him. "You don't have to worry. I shot him."

His eyes are panicked. "Have you checked his pulse?"

She frowns. "No. But he took a bullet to the chest. You don't have to worry about him anymore, Dad."

He tries to sit up to get a look at the body. Defeated by the pain in his ribcage, he fixes his panicked eyes on hers and speaks with a quiet intensity. "Maddie, listen to me. You need to shoot him in the head. He won't die otherwise, and he needs to die. You understand me? Don't arrest him and let him stand trial and live out his days behind bars. That's too good for him. He needs to die or it was all for nothing!" He bursts into a coughing fit, and blood spatters her jacket. She's truly afraid now. Afraid her father won't make it.

She's about to turn around when she hears a sound from

behind her. It can only be Gary. She can't understand how he survived a bullet to the chest, and her confusion temporarily distracts her. He hits her over the head with the butt of his gun and a searing pain shoots through her skull. Before she can get up, he yanks her backward by the arm, dragging her away from her father.

"Get away from her, you son of a bitch!" yells Bill. The effort has him coughing and clutching his chest.

Gary drops her on the cold ground and comes around to look at her face. He aims his gun at her chest and grins like he's enjoying it. "You know, your father's been the one constant in my life," he says. "Someone I look up to and crave attention from. He's practically my surrogate father, which means you and I are like siblings."

She tries to catch her breath as she plans how to take him down. If she reaches for her gun, he'll shoot her, so instead she slowly stands, hands raised, her head throbbing. "Why did you do it? Why did you kill all those women?"

Gary glances over at Bill. "*He* knows why. That's all that matters."

Madison wants to distract him enough for him to lose his focus. She points up at the helicopter, which is shining its powerful light in the wrong direction, looking for escapees who don't exist. "They'll gun you down at the first opportunity. There's no getting out of this alive unless you give yourself up."

"They won't dare shoot if I have you with me." He glances at the wrecked Camaro. "Get in the car."

"Don't go with him, Maddie." says her dad. His voice is weaker now. "Do *not* get in that car!"

Madison could cry. Her father might not make it, and instead of spending their last few moments together, she's being forced to listen to the ramblings of a madman. Anger builds in her chest. She needs to finish this once and for all.

Gary angrily approaches Bill, shifting the aim of his

weapon as he walks. Madison takes the opportunity to act. She draws her own gun and this time points it at his head. "Gary?"

He glances back at her, and she sees what he's thinking as he notices her weapon is aimed at him. He's let his hatred of her father distract him.

"He's not your father, asshole. He's mine." She shoots him through the forehead just as he goes to fire at her.

Gary hits the ground hard and she exhales in relief. Her head and nose are throbbing, but she steps forward to check that this time Gary Pelosi—Dale Anderson—is dead. There's no need to check his pulse, because the ground around him is covered in blood. She pulls up his shirt and finds a bulletproof vest underneath. He was prepared.

"Is he dead?"

She turns to her father. "Yes, Dad. He's dead."

He lies flat and weeps. "I can finally rest."

Madison holds back tears as she crouches next to her father and gently strokes his bloody forehead. "The ambulance is almost here."

He coughs again, and they're both silent for a minute. Eventually, with damp eyes, he says, "I'm sorry I'm not who you want me to be, Maddie. Who you needed me to be."

"I don't care about any of that." Her voice is full of emotion. "Just don't leave me again."

He looks like he wants to say more but doesn't have the energy. Several seconds pass and Madison realizes what's happening. Her father is slipping away. She leans down and gently hugs him to her. As her tears fall, she whispers into his ear, "I love you, Dad. Owen loves you too."

After a couple more seconds, he goes limp in her arms. All she can do is sob at everything she's lost. He wasn't perfect by any means, and they were near strangers at the end, but that's not what she's thinking about. She's remembering how strong, funny and caring he was toward her and Angie when they were kids. She remembers him reading her bedtime stories and overacting his part. Driving her to school and singing along to her favorite music on the stereo even though he thought it was awful. It felt like he always put her and Angie first back then. So she can't help but feel bitter that the Snow Storm Killer took him away from her a long time before tonight.

CHAPTER FIFTY-ONE

Several vehicles screech to a halt behind her and she hears Shelley and Officer Sanchez assessing the scene and talking into their radios. She feels a hand squeeze her shoulder and suspects it's Shelley, but she remains crouched next to her father, unable to walk away just yet. Before long, a pair of cowboy boots appears next to her. She looks up at a tall man she doesn't recognize. He takes his hat off and shakes his head as he gazes down at Bill's lifeless body. "I told him this investigation would kill him one day."

She assumes this is Frank. She looks back down at her father. "Did he ever talk about me?"

He doesn't reply right away. He must be weighing up whether to lie for his old friend. "I wish I could say he did, but the fact is, I didn't even know he had kids until he told me he was moving back down here."

She closes her eyes and nods slowly. "Do I need to notify his ex-wife, or whatever she was, of his death?"

He hesitates again. "She was his wife. Unfortunately, that evil son of a bitch behind us killed Pamela back in '98. Revenge for trying to catch him. Ever since then, your dad's been a broken man. I believe that's what drove him to take so many risks." He sighs. "I'd say I'm surprised he never told you about that, but he was evidently a man of many secrets."

Madison has so many questions, probably none of which she'll ever get the answers to. The fact that the SSK killed her father's second wife is devastating, and she wishes he had given up the chase and come home then. Things might be very different tonight. She notices something poking out of her father's shirt pocket and pulls it out. It's a photograph of a couple getting married. Her father is beaming with joy at his bride.

"That's her," says Frank. "They were good together and Pam was an excellent agent. She didn't deserve to go out the way she did."

Madison's tempted to ask how she was killed, but decides it doesn't matter. Losing her obviously had a devastating impact on her father and stopped him from getting close to anyone else.

"Madison!" Nate runs up beside her and Frank walks away. She pockets the photograph. "Are you okay?" When Nate realizes Bill is dead, he kneels down and embraces her. Instead of relaxing into it, she tenses, unable to forgive him for his recent behavior. It's then that she knows things will never be the same between them.

Eventually he gently pulls her up. "Are Kate and her son okay?" he asks.

"Yeah. They're with Adams."

He takes a deep breath. "I'm sorry about your dad. I wish I could've helped somehow. I should've talked him into laying low with me and Owen."

She scoffs. "Dad would never have done that." An awkward silence settles over them. Eventually she looks up at him. "I feel like I don't know you anymore, Nate."

He winces as if he's been slapped. He hesitates, then says, "Owen's with me, but I made him wait in the car. We should get out of here so he doesn't see his grandfather this way. I'll drive us to my place. We can talk things through."

Madison shakes her head. "No. I want to be alone with my son. We can't trust anyone else."

As she goes to pull away, he steps in front of her and places a warm hand on her cold, wet face. She flinches in case he touches her throbbing nose, and it makes him remove his hand, disappointed. "Don't freeze me out, Madison. I was wrong to focus on Kristen, and to work against you with the Jake Rubio case. I'm sorry. Just don't push me away. I couldn't bear it."

She gazes into his dark blue eyes. She wants to forgive him. She wants to trust he'll always be there for her, but he's clearly not healed yet. And it's her and Owen who will suffer. "What about Kristen?"

"She's alive. I've spoken to her. She won't testify against Father Connor. She's too afraid, so she's leaving the country. I'll never see her again."

She's happy that Kristen is alive, but if it's not her holding Nate back, it will be something else. Father Connor's murder trial is sure to affect him badly. He may even turn to drugs again to get him through it. She can't have that around Owen. She turns away from him as the ambulance crew arrive.

Jake Rubio approaches her father's body. He hesitates for a second as he recognizes the older man on the ground as the cop who found him at his mother's crime scene all those years ago. Bill's name and image will be forever linked to the case, and it's highly likely that Jake would have searched online at some point over the years in a bid to answer his own lingering questions about what happened to his mother. Despite his residual anger toward Bill, Jake drops to his knees and begins chest compressions. "Rita?" he yells over his shoulder. "I need the defibrillator!"

Madison walks away. She knows there's no bringing her father back. He died the night he left Lost Creek for Alaska. Right now, she needs to focus on Owen.

As she walks to Nate's car, she wonders whether she would ever let a case get to her in that way; whether she'd prioritize catching a killer over her own son. She'd like to think not, but she's smart enough to know that policing gets to you in ways that other careers might not. It's all-consuming, and sometimes keeping strangers safe takes precedence over the safety of your loved ones.

Owen gets out of Nate's car and meets her halfway. Nate gives them some space. He looks dejected. She hugs Owen to her and says into his ear, "I'm sorry, honey. Grandpa's gone." He tries to put on a brave face, but it's not long before he starts sobbing. She struggles to remain composed herself. "I'm sorry. I know he loved you. But this has taught me that all we have is us. You understand? We can't trust anyone else."

He pulls aways and wipes his devastated face with his sleeve. When he's more composed, he says, "Surely you don't believe that? What about Nate?"

She swallows the lump in her throat. "Nate isn't always capable of taking care of himself. We can't rely on him to be around when we need him. He still has stuff to figure out."

"Well, he better figure it out before I leave for college next year, or I'm not going."

"What? Owen, you're going to college no matter what happens."

He shakes his head. "No. I can't leave you completely alone in this shitty town feeling like you can't trust anyone." He crosses his arms. "So you better fix things with Nate, or I'll be working at a fast-food joint my whole life."

Madison smiles through the tears that run down her cheeks, but Owen is serious.

"Just because Nate has issues doesn't mean he isn't worth trusting. You're being too hard on him."

She wishes he was right, but it was Nate who pulled back after they kissed. Nate who avoided her calls and became distant. Before that, she had been ready to take a chance on him. "When did you get to be so grown up?" she says.

"After Nikki died." Owen's teenage girlfriend was murdered at Fantasy World this past summer. "She always felt worthless, no matter how much I told her she wasn't. But the time we spent together made her happy, I know it did. So I figured it's better to have some happy moments than none at all. If Nate takes off one day, then that's on him. But he's here now, isn't he? I think you should enjoy the time you have together and see what happens. I mean, he bought you a car for Christmas. Doesn't that show you how he feels about you?"

She raises her eyebrows, surprised. "He did?"

"Sure. A brand-new Toyota Sienna. It's being delivered tomorrow."

She feels guilty that Nate went to all that trouble for her, but buying someone an expensive gift isn't the same as being emotionally reliable.

"Come on, Mom. Who made you so perfect?"

"I've never claimed to be perfect, Owen."

"So if you can make mistakes, why can't Nate? Why can't Grandpa?"

She can see he's desperate for her to be happy, and he thinks that means being with Nate. Maybe it does. She's not sure of anything anymore. They both turn to look at their friend, who is leaning against his car, his arms crossed and his gaze fixed on the ground. Even with Brody by his side, he looks lonely, and like he has the weight of the world on his shoulders. Madison feels sorry for him. Maybe she's allowed herself to lose sight of his internal battles and the guilt he carries not just for his fiancée's murder twenty years ago but for what happened to Kristen Devereaux and his friend Rex Hartley. And on top of that, for everything that happens to her and Owen.

She takes a long, deep breath and looks at Owen. He nods toward Nate. She rolls her eyes playfully before heading over there. Nate looks up. She can see the pain behind his eyes. She leans against the car next to him and says, "I sometimes imagine what life would be like if we hadn't met."

He looks thoughtful. "I'd probably be dead by now."

She winces at the thought. "No. You'd still be working as a PI, helping other people solve their problems."

"And you?" he says. "Where would you be?"

She considers how she only found Owen and got her job back because Nate took on her case and came all the way here from California to help her. "I'd still be living in a halfway house, working at the burger joint and screwing up the orders."

"I don't think so," he says. "You would've convinced some other schmuck to help you by now." A smile plays at his lips.

She attempts a laugh. "God, we're pathetic, aren't we?"

He acts offended. "Hey, speak for yourself."

She leans in to him and he embraces her. She feels something around his neck and realizes he's wearing a rosary under his shirt. She daren't check whether it's the one she bought him or his dead fiancée's. She takes a deep breath and stays where she is. She doesn't know what the future holds for them, but maybe that's okay. "Did you really buy me a car for Christmas?"

"I did. A navy Toyota. That okay?"

She pulls away and shrugs. "I mean, sure, a Toyota's okay, I guess. Although to tell you the truth, I'd prefer something like that." She smiles sheepishly as she points to what's left of Adams's Camaro.

Nate laughs. "I should've known you're a woman with expensive taste. How about I see what I can do?"

She leans back against his car. Owen approaches them and kneels down next to Brody. He's quiet and reflective, and she knows he'll need time to mourn his grandfather. They watch in silence as the ambulance crew covers Bill's body and prepares to take him away.

Jake Rubio approaches Madison. "I'm sorry for your loss."

She swallows. "And I'm sorry for yours."

He shrugs. "It's not the same. I never knew my mom. I was so young when she died."

She hesitates to tell him what she means, but it's her job and she has to do it before he finds out on the news, so she takes a deep breath and says, "I meant your dad." She nods toward Gary's body. "I'm sorry to have to tell you that he's your biological father."

His mouth drops open. "Gary Pelosi's my dad?"

"Afraid so. His real name is Dale Anderson."

Jake's jaw tenses as the realization of what his father has done dawns on him. She doesn't tell him how Gary tried to frame him for the recent murders by calling her to the newsroom and making her aware of Michelle Rubio's death. He implied Jake must've been messed up by witnessing it so that she'd make him her number one suspect. He doesn't need to know that. Sometimes it's better not to know what your parents are capable of.

He takes a deep breath. "He's the one who killed Emily and Sarah?"

She nods.

"And my mom?"

"Yes. I'm sorry." She doesn't know if he's heard of the SSK and she doesn't want to go into all that here. "You'll have a lot of questions over the coming days. I'll be ready when you want to know the answers."

He looks her in the eye before nodding. Then, with his head lowered, he walks to one of the ambulances and climbs inside. Her heart goes out to him. They both lost their fathers here tonight. But the truth is, they lost them years ago.

Owen stands up beside her and Nate squeezes her shoulders as they silently watch the ambulance drive away.

A LETTER FROM WENDY

Thank you for reading *Catch Her Death,* book 5 in the Detective Madison Harper series. Book 5! How did we get here so soon?

You can keep in touch with me and get updates about the series by signing up to my newsletter here, and by following me on social media.

www.bookouture.com/wendy-dranfield

Well, I tried to get Madison and Nate together for you, but they're a stubborn pair! Despite things not working out as we might like this time, it's reassuring to know there is still hope, and they still have each other's backs. I can't imagine Madison without Nate in her life and who knows what's in store for them next? Certainly not me! I guess we'll just have to wait and see. After all, that's half the fun, isn't it?

I'm still blown away by all the love for the series. You've really taken these characters into your hearts, which makes it more fun for me to write about them. You'd think I would know what's coming next, but they have a way of surprising me! Right now, I'm wondering whether Detective Adams will keep his job after his less than impressive attempt at being Madison's partner. If he gets fired, how will he afford his car repairs?!

If you enjoyed this book, please do leave a rating or review (no matter how brief) on Amazon or wherever you bought it, as this helps it to stand out among the thousands of books that are published each day, thereby allowing it to reach more readers and ensuring the series continues.

Thanks for coming on this journey with me.

Wendy

www.wendydranfield.co.uk

facebook.com/WendyDranfield1
twitter.com/WendyDranfield
instagram.com/wendy_dranfield

ACKNOWLEDGMENTS

Thank you to the readers for trying my books. Hopefully I've made you forget about your problems for a while as you get lost in Madison's and Nate's lives. For those who interact with me on social media; it's lovely reading your supportive and sometimes hilarious messages. It makes me feel like I'm not alone as I write and that I'm not crazy for caring about the characters as much as you do.

Thank you to the advance readers and book bloggers who share reviews of my books online. Your enthusiasm is contagious!

As always, thank you to everyone at Bookouture who has worked on this latest book in the series.

Special thanks to the reader of all my first drafts; my husband.

And the final mention goes to my beloved cat, Sookie, who sadly passed away when I was halfway through writing this book. She was one week shy of her eleventh birthday when kidney disease took her from us. Sookie spent most of her time asleep in her little round bed on my desk and slept through the writing of all my novels. Even though I still have two boy cats, they spend most of their time lounging in the garden, so my office feels far too empty without Sookie's gentle snores. Animals are amazing, aren't they?

CPSIA information can be obtained
at www.ICGtesting.com
Printed in the USA
LVHW031520060922
727695LV00004B/618

9 781803 146553